D1366587

ECLIPSE

ECLIPSE

A NOVEL BY RENÉ BELLETTO

Translated by Jeremy Leggatt

Mercury House, Incorporated
San Francisco

English translation copyright © 1990 by Mercury House, Incorporated. All rights reserved under International and Pan-American Copyright Conventions. Originally published in France under the title *L'Enfer,* © P.O.L. éditeur, 1986. This work is published with the assistance of the French Ministry of Culture and Communication.

Published in the United States by
Mercury House
San Francisco, California

Distributed to the trade by
Consortium Book Sales & Distribution, Inc.
St. Paul, Minnesota

Manufactured in the United States of America

Library of Congress Cataloging-in-Publication Data

Belletto, René
  [Enfer. English]
  Eclipse : a novel / by René Belletto : translated from the French by Jeremy Leggatt.
      p. cm.
  Translation of: L'enfer.
  ISBN 0-916515-64-8 : $20.95
  I. Title.
PQ2662.E4537E613   1990
843'.914 – dc20
                                                            89-32148
                                                                CIP

ONE

I undertook to write a letter intended for my adoptive mother, a suicide letter, a letter I would send her shortly before doing away with myself in a few days' time, or in a week, or a month, I really was not sure, but in any case it would already be over and done with, I mean writing this letter.

Explanations, thanks, forgiveness sought, I embrace you and love you, Michel.

Two and a quarter pages of discourse and writing from beyond the grave, but sustained, buoyant, compact pages, almost lighthearted in their way, at first I wanted to weep a little, in the middle a lot, in fact I very nearly buried my head in my folded arms and surrendered to sobbing, the kind of sobbing that wrenches your abdomen. By the end, relieved perhaps, and absorbed by my efforts at written expression, no urge to weep at all, I even spat through the open window with a certain relish after licking stamp and envelope, licking glue has always disgusted me.

I was sure I had no stamp. Yet I went on looking for a long long time, too long, almost forgetting what I was looking for, and wonder of wonders, I finally discovered one, dirty, rumpled, cowering at the bottom of the left rear pocket of one of my pants, a place where I never put stamps and where it must have been languishing for weeks if not months.

Mrs. Liliane Tormes, 21 Chemin du Regard, 69100 Villeurbanne. I tried to spit again, but there was no hint of saliva, just the noise and the face I made. It was too hot, too dry.

I was thirsty.

I slid the envelope across until it lay dead in the center of the table, central to the last millimeter. I took all the time I needed. Then I gripped the edges of the table, left and right, my arms taut, and remained thus for a few seconds looking like a master of the universe.

Abruptly I straightened. A drop of sweat flew. The chair skidded, tottered, almost fell, did not fall.

I went over and leaned out of the back window. It was virtually walled in. You could have touched the blank, crumbling wall opposite with the tip of an unsharpened pencil. No coolness at all. The air motionless, even stiller than elsewhere. It was suffocating.

In the kitchen I drank water. In the bathroom I splashed my face. In the toilet I urinated noisily. The flush mechanism was scarcely noisier. Of course it didn't work too well. Once again I noticed that my whole body hurt. When I urinated noisily, or blinked too hard, or bumped my shoulder or any other part of me against anything else, or if I pinched myself, for instance, on my forearm or the skin of my belly, I could feel my body burning and vulnerable as if I had a raging fever. Could I have a fever? No, I didn't think so. The endless summer heat, my relentless insomnia, my chaotic diet, and the sad state of my soul were reason enough for this impression of raging fever.

I came back to get the letter, caught my feet in the telephone cord, crossed the hallway into the front room, again caught my feet in the telephone cord, for there were two phones in the apartment, a relic of the time when two people who were strangers to one another had lived here, one in the front room, the other in the back room, and I suppose one day decided to enhance their independence through this arrangement. I almost fell and had to fight off the impulse to rip out the telephone cord in response to a sudden surge of anger. It was as if I were cocked to go off. Then quite suddenly I reverted to my sleepwalker mode. The only purpose those two instruments served was to irritate me. They rang simultaneously. A double noise, in other words. And I caught my feet in the cords.

True, they never rang. Unless my mother called, except that it was generally I who called her. And her phone was out of order. Impossible to get through to her.

I put the sealed and stamped letter (I had found a stamp! I couldn't get over it) in the bottom drawer of a chest once stained walnut by the one who had been my companion within these confines and who, weary of my person and my ways, which would have driven a stone statue mad, had fled to other pastures one fine day. One fine afternoon, to be exact. Around four o'clock. In winter.

I tucked the letter away among various articles, a plastic pencil case with a defective zipper (you could no longer either close or open it), a tube of dried, hardened glue, a slingshot I had made in the days of my youth, a deck of marked cards, a cap pistol, a ton of letters, personal and official, whose senders had been awaiting my response for thousands of days, a two-pronged tuning fork (laaaa), the packaging and instructions for my digital alarm (it had neither gained nor lost a second in a year), my ancient malfunctioning typewriter, a roll of pink caps, four key chains, a handful of those little felt pads you stick under chair legs so as not to disturb half the city when you scrape chairs across the tiled floors of kitchens in a rage for some reason or other, a copy of Liliane's poor last will and testament, an aluminum ashtray weighing about a tenth of an ounce, a yellowing edition of my book *On Bach's Fugues,* and a bottle of Alymil 1000, Dioblaníz Pharmaceutical Laboratories, DPL, five tablets ingested at one-minute intervals would put a man out for eternity if my information was reliable. And it was indeed reliable.

It was indeed.

I opened the french window. August 1. Rue de la République was deserted. Not a soul. I might have been alone in the world.

I took a step out onto the balcony. I could hardly have taken more than one. Could you even rightly call it a balcony? An insignificant jutting outward, a semblance of a balcony. On my left was a tiny patch of soil; God knew how it had got here. Three blades of grass, now burned brown, had managed to take root in this soil. No resemblance at all to vast natural expanses like plains or plateaus. And yet, on this small cement surface, up against those rusty railings, you got a better view of the world (if by some chance the urge to view it took hold of you) than a mere window would ever give you.

I remained for twenty seconds or so on this semblance of a balcony, turning my head in every direction and rolling my eyes like a naughty dog. Not a human presence all along the sidewalk as far as the Opera House. Nor on the nearby Place de la République.

Give or take a few yards in any direction I probably lived right in the center of Lyon, in the neighborhood around the Hôtel-Dieu, the hospital where I first saw the light of day thirty-six years ago.

The splashing of the fountain in the square reawakened dreams of coolness and lightness. But alas, the heat, the appalling, insalubrious, murderous heat of a city in a continental climate (heat that shattered all records in Lyon that summer), merely seemed the more oppressive, a heat to expire in, 160 degrees in the shade at the very least. Out in the sun, impossible to gauge, there was no one foolhardy enough to venture out and set up a thermometer in direct sunlight, certainly not with any hope of coming back in. The thermometers themselves ran screaming back into the shade.

The sky blinded you, wherever you looked at it.

And the sun! God deliver us from the sun, I told myself as I went back in, closing the french window, drawing shut the thick curtains of dark velvet, God deliver us from the sun! Already drenched, my white shirt had soaked itself anew. As a result, certain of my movements made slapping sticky sounds, faint perhaps, but slapping and sticky all the same.

I removed the garment and soaked it in a basin in the bathroom, using far too much detergent, I had trouble controlling the flow of bluish powder from the packet my febrile fingers had ripped open clumsily and too far.

Back to the front room. A large part of my life was made up of these small journeys within the apartment. There was always a reason for going from one room to another. I was not really bored. This was not really boredom.

To be more comfortable I also removed my white denims and collapsed onto the couch where I remained, I believe, for several hours without moving a muscle, the books lining the wall in front of me were black with dust, I studied them for a long time, and for a long time too the portrait of Johann Sebastian Bach blown up to poster size and held in place on the left of the connecting door by a multitude of little strips of yellowed Scotch tape, every now and then a piece would come unstuck with an explosive plop, faint but explosive all the same, tsplokh! An orderly person, a person sure of living, would have replaced the strip each time with a fresh strip of tape and would thus rapidly have renewed them all, or might even have replaced them all at once, the dryness of one strip arguing more or less persuasively for the dryness of all the others, but not me, when too many rebellious strips of Scotch tape rustled as I passed by I would tame them with a firm pressure of the thumb, and that was that, they would hold for another few hours!

And hold they did. That was the main thing. The poster stayed in place.

The portrait was of Bach as painted by Haussmann in 1746. The face bore the marks of struggle. Especially the eyes, but the lines around the mouth as well. The whole face. For Bach could hardly see anymore. Perhaps no more than the painter who was recording the anguished sensuality of his features that year, for posterity, I almost felt like listening to a little music, it was five days since I had listened to a little music, a real exploit, but getting up, going over to the chest, sticking a tape into the little Saba tape player, twiddling the knobs, no, not now, later, in my increasingly slack posture the sweat was collecting on my bare belly, now and then I laid my hand on it, palm flat, fingers spread, and pushed in, sliding down as far as my hipbone with no trouble at all despite the inward pressure of my hand, then started over again, all that vaguely mucky wetness was unintentionally disturbing, so much so that at one point I felt a tremor in my virile member, a faint stiffening and stretching, a pricking at the tip, a tip that even managed to negotiate the elastic barrier of my underpants and make a discreet appearance, but an appearance so little noted that it did not insist and within seconds had withdrawn into its gloomy, moist, tufted den, and I returned to the contemplation of other things, that is to say of nothing and of everything.

•

I rubbed my shirt at the armpits, or went through the motions of rubbing, wrung it brutally, and spread it out. It looked spotless. Hardly surprising. The amount of detergent I had poured into the basin would have whitened a wagon of coal. And I don't get clothes very dirty. For a long time I believed that I didn't get clothes dirty. Quite late in my life people pointed out to me, sometimes with irritation, that I did get things just as dirty as everyone else. Possibly. Undoubtedly. And yet. I have trouble believing it. I still sometimes think of my dirty clothes as clean.

In a quarter-hour, a half-hour at most, it would be dry.

I tugged at the door of my dilapidated refrigerator. A ruin. Miraculously it opened. The entire contents of the refrigerator was two beers. I took one. The motor that operated the device, defeated like myself by the heat, breathed with a heavy, uneven, irregular breath that boded no good.

The impotent rage of impending death.

I took a swing, a full-armed swing, to slam the door shut, as violently as if I were trying to send the whole heap of antiquated junk hurtling far beyond the confines of the city. It shut, and stayed shut, amazing. Shutting it was simple. Depending on the door's temperament and on your mood of the moment you adopted either an angelic delicacy — floooop, closed — or else a seismic brutality, any intermediary approach being quite hope-less. You just had to know. Opening it on the other hand was an operation that made nonsense of rational planning. No rules. Anything was possible. A normal tug, or an abnormally light or abnormally violent tug, might or might not prove effective: total refusal was always in the cards. That was the worst. In such a case you dragged the refrigerator across the apartment by its handle like a recalcitrant beast, ripping out the electricity behind it as well as part of the wall from around the socket, but to no avail, the door remained obdurately welded to the body of the apparatus. Yet ten minutes later the lightest of touches would swing it wide open, generously open, with a deep sigh as if the machine itself was relieved, or else (and this too was possible) with intense reluctance, emitting an unbearable high-pitched, sneering, grinding noise, seemingly ready to close again with a hateful slam.

It sometimes even opened all by itself, for no reason, out of bravado. Then I would shut it again with a slam whose already considerable power was multiplied a hundredfold by incontrovertible vengefulness.

The bottle of beer felt barely cool against my palm.

I listened at last to a little music. I listened to Bach's Cantata no. 82, for the Feast of the Purification, gulping down the beer that felt barely cool against my palm before it could become too burning hot for my throat. Once upon a time this cantata had moved me because the bass voice said things like: slumber now, weary eyes, close in sweet bliss, I rejoice in my death, ah! if the Lord would deliver me from the chains of my body! and often I myself longed to close my weary eyes, I listened and I was moved all over again, some of the emotion of long ago managing to reach and trouble me.

The poster was at eye level. Unthinkingly I took a step to put myself in Bach's field of vision, I was looking at him but he was not looking at me and would never look at me. Four years later, in the last days of March 1750, an itinerant oculist, John Taylor, had attempted two operations on Bach. Bach died as a result of them four months afterward (and not six, as Forkel, who repeats many mistakes from the 1754 Necrology, has claimed). Indeed Bach was by no means the only patient dispatched to an early grave by Taylor's arts. An ophthalmological operation in 1750! At one time I was not even aware such a thing could have happened. I had thought all they could do in the way of ophthalmological surgery in 1750 was gouge out the infected eye with a knife and

disinfect the wound with a red-hot iron. No. Taylor for example
treated cataracts, in consequence of which his patients, now truly
blinded, died after a few days of inhuman suffering, but anyway
this kind of operation was at least attempted.

Slumber now, weary eyes!

I began to sweat like an animal. The beer. And I was seized
with a powerful urge to piss. I went to relieve myself. I flushed
the toilet. Alas, the results would not have disturbed a sick ant
crawling at the bottom of the bowl. Worse and worse. Another
few weeks and the conveniences would start to feed excrement
back into the house where it would ripple out lethargically and
capriciously instead of being sucked straight down into the
bowels of the earth.

It would be loathsome.

My rent was paid until the end of August.

The next piece on the cassette was the Prelude and Fugue in
B Minor from *The Well-Tempered Clavier*, the last from the first
book, played on the piano by Rainer von Gottardt. Of course I
was not crying, still not crying. But I felt the urge. An urge,
curiously enough, that seemed disembodied, what I mean is: no
constriction of the throat, no gulping for breath, no stinging of
the eyes, on the one hand the urge to cry and on the other me,
yes, most curious, Rainer von Gottardt in his inspired fashion
was playing fast, but with a reflectiveness generally possible only
when playing slowly, despite his speed you waited for each note
as if its predecessor had been played yesterday, yet the notes
followed closely on one another's heels, very closely, relentlessly,
it was sharp and slow, frenzied and intense, on the surface all
boiling eddies and below them three thousand fathoms of peaceful deeps, you were caught up in a slowly heaving maelstrom,
you lived out your whole existence with each note, yet you didn't
have the time to catch your breath.

I listened until the end. Six minutes fifty-three seconds. I
rose. I turned off the little Saba. Silence returned, made itself at
home. Then the telephone rang in my absent neighbors'. It
happened a lot. I jumped, my heart leaped in panic, I caught my
breath, and in this catching of my breath the urge to weep,

hitherto fugitive, took root and flesh, but rage drove it away, five, seven, twelve times the phone jangled, I dreamed of smashing through the partition, of picking up the phone and of giving vent to such words that the person at the other end of the line would resolve never to dial the number again, or even any number remotely resembling it, and would even prudently give up using the telephone altogether and cross the street whenever he saw a phone booth.

Terribly telling words.

·

The sun had dropped, the sky was turning pale, night threatened. But the heat remained glued to men, miring them, oppressing them. And yet the notion of coolness, best kept at bay during the day, opened a tentative path into the minds of these same men, and in order to help it open, this path, a little less tentatively I shaved and took a shower, and even tweaked out two rather long whiskers waxing unrestrainedly on my left earlobe. There was no personal vanity in this act of tweaking. Through these days of crazed heat and solitude, personal aesthetic concerns did not obsess me, and if forty feet of thick monkey fur had sprouted from my ears only the resulting severe discomfort would have bothered me.

I tweaked.

Pleek! Pleek! It gave me goose bumps over my whole body.

I pulled on shirt and pants. No noticeable difference in whiteness. An internationally recognized expert on comparative whiteness might perhaps have detected one, but not me.

I opened the windows wide.

Out of habit, I slung my wool and silk navy blue coat over my arm, it was a little shiny at the elbows and shoulder blades, very shiny in fact, you could see yourself in it, but still very wearable, the only coat or garment of this kind I boasted, and descended the five floors to the street, letting myself drift pliantly and effortlessly, using gravity to conserve what energy I still had, merely taking care not to develop too rapid a momentum, which might prove perilous when I reached my destination, and all the while savoring the bearable temperature of the staircase.

In the street it was thirty times hotter, but still forty times less than during the heat of the afternoon.

I walked toward the Place de la République. After a dozen steps I turned around, believing myself observed. I was. My upstairs neighbor was taking the air on his balcony. He was not leaving Lyon till the fourth. He was a former firefighter, very tall, very heavy, very ugly, a man of Norwegian origin who had won thirty thousand dollars in a promotional competition in the year of his retirement and had purchased that upstairs apartment at a price much lower than its true value from a supermarket owner whose daughter he had rescued from the flames or from drowning, I no longer recalled which. A giant. His balcony, as cramped as my own, reached to his knees. He looked as if he was standing upright in a swallow's nest.

We greeted one another with simultaneous waves, his was expansive, very expansive, expansive enough to sweep away the clouds had there been any clouds, since he had learned I was alone in the apartment his outward signs of friendship had become more marked and his speech less terse, and his long-distance greetings more expansive.

I made my slow way to Rue Stella, where my Dauphine was parked just short of the Hôtel des Étrangers.

Silence. The key scrabbling in the lock made the complex din of an airplane accident.

I started up. It was the time of day when you could contemplate setting your hands on the steering wheel without having to dash screaming for the Rhône a second later in order to plunge them, scarlet and smoking, into the water. I took the waterfront route, turned right onto the Lafayette Bridge, then the Cours Lafayette and its continuation, the Rue Tolstoï, several miles in a few minutes, everything swam by leaving no trace on the retina or the cerebrum, the city was dead, it had given up the ghost during the night of July 31 and August 1, I had to drive all the way to the light on Place Grandclément before I encountered a living soul, and even then to be candid not much soul and not much living, two old folks prevented by the severity of their infirmities from fleeing the summer, who crossed the street in front of me, bent double, the whites of their eyes protruding, shod in heavy winter footwear, chewing grimly on their gums.

I continued to push on into deserted Villeurbanne along the Rue Léon Blum. As I crossed the area known as "Bon Coin," I recognized, affixed to the wooden bulletin board of a closed café, the small yellow notice, the same as every year, announcing the Hector and Isabel Dioblaníz concert. As every year, I had received an invitation. Where could I have put it? Behind the Saba, it seemed to me.

Night was falling. On Avenue Ampère I had to switch on my headlights. My old red Dauphine worked well, except for its lights, its lights and its windshield wipers, afflicted with hyperactivity. The lights (for reasons that the most clairvoyant of mechanics were unable to explain) illuminated phenomenal distances. An overeffective contact somewhere, but where? As for the windshield wipers, they oscillated with such frenzy you could not see them at all and the windshield remained bone-dry, virginal, unblemished through the fiercest storms, for they sent the rain flying dozens of yards all around before it could even reach the windshield.

Avenue Ampère, short and ugly, flared up. Chemin du Regard, the horrible Chemin du Regard, running alongside the sinister Jonage Canal. I drew up in front of the house where I was born, almost my birthplace, a dingy wood cottage, not maintained, infinitely sad in this season and this light, with the old Cusset Cemetery nearby, the gloomiest of the gloomy, and the hydroelectric plant, straight out of a nightmare.

No other dwelling in sight.

I was late. I should have been here long before. My mother was watching for me from the second-floor window. But I pulled on the old-fashioned door bell just the same, setting off a small distant tinkling inside.

Liliane Tormes. Liliane, a young, healthy, supple, slender, luminous first name for an old person now graying but once young and healthy and luminous, to judge from the photos in the big red album she brought out so eagerly from the closet, to be frank too eagerly, Liliane Tormes, my adoptive mother, was a little crazy, lost in her own world from which she emerged only rarely, but (in my opinion) whenever she felt like it, and from which she would have been able to emerge more frequently had she but wished. Perhaps she was playing some sort of game, although admittedly with such conviction that she had grown used to it and could no longer tell the difference, any more than I could.

She opened the door. I went in. The ground floor rooms were closed. The first evidence of her strangeness, three years earlier she had condemned the ground floor, where she then lived. She had evicted the lodgers from the second floor and settled in there, thus giving up an important part of her income. Had her house boasted fifty floors, she would have ejected forty-nine tenants and taken up residence on the fiftieth floor. Then, within a month, she had lost or nearly lost the use of speech. And she had begun to eat too much, to kill herself with overeating, never desisting from the consumption or preparation of food, pondering recipes or the products of recipes, grumbling, dozing, dreaming of future meals.

I kissed my mother. She hugged me, quickly and hard enough to asphyxiate me, as was her custom. Her hair was all white. She was bowed, wrinkled, thin. Eating did her no good. Apart from her first name and mine, Liliane and Michel, the few recognizable words in the soup of syllables bubbling out of her were generally the names of dishes, as I followed her up the stairs I could hear her mumbling: breeda mada dama beelo, boovee booro alalavalalamala moomoooooo vri pouleenoo white bread gr gr gustafoochlo lolo gueu noodles in cheese sauce muha dixa chareeetramplonavadixa fll fll tropical fruit, when it began I had taken her five times to consult a famous speech therapist, five lessons of one hour each, with no success, around the middle of the third consultation she had suddenly demanded "quiche lorraine" and "beef cutlets with tarragon," and after that nothing.

The table was set. The television was on, as usual. A dumb movie. Liliane watched everything. And even when she wasn't watching the television stayed on.

"They still haven't come about the telephone?"

No, she gave me to understand, still hadn't come. No dial tone. Phone dead.

"I'll call them. This time they'd better show up!"

Gestures and mime from Liliane signifying her burning desire to see the telephone links between her and me restored.

We sat down to dinner.

She scrutinized me with a pitying gaze as she downed large forkfuls of tomato and cucumber salad and occasionally urged me with an energetic gesture to do likewise and empty my plate of its last molecule of edible matter. But my appetite was unruly, unruly and capricious, at odd times of night or day hunger would assail me, I would feel up to devouring an acre of steak, but if at such moments no food was at hand within a radius of a yard or a yard and a half I preferred to starve with my mouth hanging open, and in any case the sensation of hunger swiftly disappeared and eating became hateful to me.

That evening, eating was hateful. To please my mother, I lifted the food to my mouth and worked my jaws with gusto, alas, impossible to swallow. I had an eiderdown in my throat and three in my stomach. By the end of the meal my plate was indeed clean, and I had helped myself liberally to everything, but it was all still there in my cheeks swollen as two pumpkins, I managed to cram a few more stewed fruit in, then I was forced to go to the kitchen and spit the whole meal, soup to nuts, into the trashcan, better now than later, I told myself by way of consolation.

On my return Liliane turned a suspicious gaze on me. I managed to smile at her.

The dumb movie had given place to games of unbelievable stupidity. An idiotic host was plying moronic competitors with silly questions, in the program that followed it, I was unaware of any transition from one to the other, a tired tenor sang pretty songs, badly:

When the devil calls we fly away,
Faaar from the ones we looove,

or from the homes we love, I wasn't sure, but I believe it was the ones we love.

Liliane and I drank coffee. Liliane drank whole pots of it every day. Too much. She made wonderful coffee. Yet this evening I thought it had a taste of dead leaves.

We sat quietly, without speaking. Every now and then Liliane nibbled at a fruit. Her lips had kept a fairly handsome shape despite the wrinkles around them. More than usual, her mouth and eyes reminded me of the mouth and eyes of Isabel Dioblaníz, of the Hector and Isabel Dioblaníz concerts. It seemed to me. I had seen Isabel Dioblaníz only once.

Around half-past eleven torpor engulfed me. The two dining room windows opened onto a night so anonymous it might have been in a tropical bay. If I stayed this way till daylight, would the sun rise on a tropical bay? On the infinite sea, on vast expanses of virgin nature, on the first day of the world?

Yes, we might easily have been somewhere else. The trees and the Jonage Canal gave an illusion of coolness, and the little house that was almost my birthplace was prettier inside than outside, stylish even, in this landscape on the outskirts of Villeurbanne where it seemed to be the outpost or the last stop in a cursed land, but the inside, as I was saying, did not lack attractiveness, thanks to Liliane's maniacal care and thanks to my late father, a creative, meticulous, and tasteful handyman (had he, in the year and a half preceding his death, entered into a liaison with Mrs. Liliane Tormes? No, an absurd notion, Liliane had never known a man, I was certain of that), an authentic genius of a handyman who had built everything from scratch, starting with the house itself, who had installed everything, wiring, plumbing, gas heat, and the rest, who had decorated everything, paintings and tapestries, white or pale or blue, furniture bought at the flea market on the Place Rivière in the days when the flea market was held on the Place Rivière, repaired, cleaned, refinished, and upholstered by him, yes, an utterly delightful interior, particularly my bedroom, where I no longer slept but which Liliane kept intact, a jewel, with its toy closet, wooden toys made by my father, and . . .

The theme music for the news made me jump. Not my mother, who was nodding off without having swallowed her last segment of fruit, speared on a fork. How could she live this way? And how could I live this way?

I watched the news without seeing or hearing anything, but still with all my eyes and all my ears, as if the TV set were delivering me some secret of the greatest importance. My attention was at once frenzied and distracted. Dr. Perfecto Jinez, renowned Spanish ophthalmologist and graft specialist, was still missing, that was the only news item my mind caught as the information winged past me, the rest of it following a lightning trajectory from one ear to the other. If only this Perfecto Jinez had been able to operate on Bach (to whom, incidentally, he bore a distinct resemblance, his face grave and his hair worn long, like a wig, out of obvious vanity)!

I had not even known that Perfecto Jinez was missing. I knew nothing of the affairs of the planet. Had the Chinese unleashed a worldwide offensive, only the appearance of yellow faces at my semblance of a balcony would have alerted me to the danger. A European ophthalmological conference had taken place in Lyon on July 27, 28, and 29. On the night of July 27 to 28, Perfecto Jinez had disappeared from his hotel in Tassin-la-Demi-Lune. The affair seemed to tickle the woman reading the news, who was struggling to remain serious, who was even weeping with mirth, but without opening her mouth any wider, it was ugly, monstrous.

It was sign-off time. The station shut down for the night. The TV set crackled and an infinity of white dots shimmered on the screen. After ten minutes of passive rage I rose and turned the knob, putting an abrupt end to all this crackling and shimmering. Then I brushed the shoulder of Liliane, asleep or not. She opened an eye. "Bluegavooyoo," she said reassuringly, of course, Mother, bluegavooyoo, I told her I was leaving, thanks for the lovely dinner.

She tried to stand up. Suddenly she made a face, put her hand to her heart, whimpered, and fell back into her chair. I was frightened, very frightened, I yelled out (it had been a long time since I had yelled out in this way): "Are you in pain?"

Yes, she was in pain, but she indicated to me that the pain did not last, there, it was gone.

"Have you ever had this pain before?"

Yes, had this pain before.

"Why didn't you tell me? You must see a doctor!"

She shook her head.

"Yes! You eat too much. You drink too much coffee. You're wearing yourself out in this house, the stairs, the housework . . . You need someone to help you."

No, nobody. She didn't want anybody and she would never want anybody, she valued her privacy too much, I was the only person she allowed to violate it, she hated the whole world.

She rose without apparent effort. I took her in my arms.

"Don't be sick. You're all I have. Don't leave me. What would I do without you?"

Cowardly words!

Even as I gave way to my emotion I felt angry with Liliane, very angry (she said to me, whispering normal words: me too, you're all I have! and I was horrified to find myself shoving her back down onto her chair upholstered in pale fabric with dark flowers), I was angry with her for being the least fragile link between me and life, would I ever have the courage to send her that letter?

Yes, I would!

I knew I would!

Too much coffee. She drank too much coffee. It was probably coffee that gave her these palpitations, painful cramps of the cardiac muscle, she would have to be dragged bodily to the doctor's, no doubt about it.

•

She waved from the window, as always.

Not a sound, not a breath of wind. Would I see Liliane again? Once more, this boundless indifference. Not a breath of wind. The leaves on the trees were still. The night was empty and black. I switched on my lights. Through the empty black night their glare easily reached the Cordillera of the Andes, those heights in the distance.

It was 1:07 A.M.

At 1:10 I drove past the number 12 bus terminal outside the new Cusset Cemetery. A person who must have missed the one o'clock bus waved to me. I braked twenty yards farther on, reversed, opened the door.

It was a woman. A girl, young. I had thought so, but wasn't sure, she was wearing pants and I hadn't looked too closely as I went by.

"Good evening. Thanks. Which way are you going? Downtown?"

She was tall, with big eyes. Her shirt was untucked. She had long flowing hair. Her pants were very tight. Behind her, pasted to the wall of the bus shelter, a yellow leaflet announced the concert to be given on August 15 by the Bach Choir and Orchestra of Mainz, conducted by Thomas Lom, two Bach cantatas, no. 82 and no. 4, *Ich habe genug* and *Christ lag in Todesbanden,* at the Temple, Place du Change, in Old Lyon, an Isabel and Hector Dioblaníz concert.

"Wherever you like. I can drop you wherever you want."

At this hour, in this part of town, a person could wait for a bus for a whole lifetime. And such was the extent of my passivity in these days of dreary apocalypse that I would have stopped if someone simply waved, and I would have driven this so attractive being of flesh as far as Singapore if she had said Singapore.

She got in. "I'm going to Cours Gambetta, number 3. It's the first building, next to Place Gabriel Péri. Thanks. I missed the last bus. I didn't see any taxis or cars or anything. I was getting ready to go back to my friends' house."

I pulled away from the curb.

The Dioblanízes, Hector and Isabel, rich Bolivians who had lived in Lyon for the past twelve years, owners at Rillieux-la-Pape of one of the country's biggest pharmaceutical laboratories, were rabid patrons of the arts and doers of good works. Why? Because they had a blind son. People hounded pitilessly by fate often practice good works. All year round they organized concerts whose proceeds went to various organizations for disadvantaged children. The August concerts were something of an exception, prestigious, almost secret affairs despite the posters mechanically distributed by the Rabut Agency. Their audiences were made up mostly of invited guests, often distinguished ones. Could such gatherings be listed under the heading of good works? No. When the Dioblanízes, Hector and Isabel, brought orchestras to the Sports Complex at Villeurbanne, seating ten thousand spectators, on a Saturday night in mid-June, with considerable discounts for the needy and sandwiches handed out at intermission, that was indeed an example of philanthropy despite the inevitable explosions of bloody, even murderous violence.

At the Temple, in August, no. They sent invitations to many countries in Europe and, on the evening of the concert, the Temple was like a little Tower of Babel. Very few from Lyon. Since 1969, the year my book was published, I had received invitations. Yet I had not sent them my book. I had sent it to nobody. I had of course wanted it to appear, but at the same time wanted it to vanish forever from the face of the planet. I had chosen a small local publishing house on the brink of bankruptcy. It had been a limited printing. No copies had been sent anywhere. Rapid bankruptcy had indeed been the answer to my prayers. Many copies had been bought up by myself and destroyed in a mood of somber exaltation. I had kept only one.

In August 1969, Rainer von Gottardt, so niggardly with his public appearances, had responded to the Dioblanízes' appeal and played the first book of Bach's *Well-Tempered Clavier* at the Temple. I was sick at the time, something wrong with my kidneys, sometimes I had to wake up at four in the morning and piss, wait three hours, and then, at the end of three hours to the minute, piss again, this time into a little flask, in the laboratory they looked for all kinds of horrible things in the flask. Bound to my bed, I had been unable to attend the concert, which had made me ten times sicker. The illness had passed, not the disappointment. I had never really recovered from this missed encounter with the pianist I worshipped as a god.

Since February 1970 Rainer von Gottardt had not given a single concert, having lost the index finger of his left hand in mysterious circumstances, possibly a car accident due to the sun's glare.

•

The girl, next to me.

I felt like leaning across, opening her door, and shoving her out at the first reasonably sharp bend. Or keeping her with me as long as possible, both.

We did not speak. At Place des Maisons Neuves we looked at one another, but not at the same time, her first, then me, her nose a bit short, then her, long enough for the silence to become jarring and my reluctance to speak so oppressive that I finally asked her if she had not been away on vacation, but just as she was answering I interrupted her, she merely opened and closed her mouth: "No, you didn't leave."

"No," she said with a smile. "I'm going tomorrow."

"Where?"

I blurted this "where?" abruptly, awkwardly, without any special interrogative inflection, almost as if I had discovered a bat in the glove compartment and had exclaimed "Wha-a-a!" I couldn't even speak anymore, I then uttered another "where," more human this time, more appropriate, but inaudible, scarcely breathing it, a cat with its ear glued to my mouth would have perceived nothing, later that same evening in fact a cat or a little dog was to slip yapping between my legs.

Where was she going?

"I don't know. I'm going with friends, we're going to drive south, to Spain probably. What about you?"

She ran her hand the length of her thigh to smooth out a crease in her pants, to no avail, the crease remained.

"No plans. I'm staying in Lyon."

"It's a good idea sometimes, staying. Your headlights are really powerful."

"Yes. Even though they're dirty. The whole car's dirty, the seats, you're going to dirty your white shirt."

"No, it washes quickly. What about you, are you going to wash yours?"

"Ooooohweell . . ."

I could speak only in code.

We reached Place Marc Séguin, once but no longer the home of a small monthly music magazine, half of its articles written by me. The Cours Gambetta lay before us, wide, deserted, unthreatening. In the distance, on the far side of the Saône, the hills were blacker than the night. Was such a dark night the harbinger of a less hot day, of a less implacable sun, perhaps of an absent sun? It was in any case a hope one had a right to entertain, I told myself (my pretty passenger was sliding her open hand along her other leg even though there was not the slightest crease on it), a hope one had every right to entertain, so let us cling to it.

Cling to it.

I stopped in front of 3 Cours Gambetta and mechanically switched off the engine. A heavy silence followed, knotting chest, throat, and stomach. I was now anxious to be alone. I turned to the girl with very long hair. Her hand was on the door handle, but she did not push it. I wiped my forehead with my fingertips, the night air coming in through the open windows had dried my sweat but already the sweat was coming back, the girl smiled at me, she smiled readily, she had let go of the door handle, again I felt obliged to say something and I said the first thing that came into my head, did she bite her nails or did she play the piano.

"I bite my nails."

She put her hands down alongside her thighs. She was hiding them. A touching gesture, her big eyes, her slow and serious voice were touching. What could I do to make her leave, and what could I say to make her leave?

"Can I see you again?"

I was the first to be astounded by my words, tonelessly uttered. She answered with simplicity: yes, then, after a silence, when?

I reflected: now? No, not now. Now or never. Never. Sweat was tickling my spine, my navel. Although ignorant of the nature of my embarrassment, the girl saved me from embarrassment.

"Tomorrow afternoon?"

"Yes."

"Around three? At three?"

·

I parked my car in the same spot, Rue Stella, thirty feet from the Hôtel des Étrangers. The sound of the door, slammed shut loudly shut out of carelessness, shook the whole town and caused me pain. One of the rooms in the hotel was showing a light. Well well.

Slinging my blue wool and silk coat over my left forearm, I felt something hard. It was the postcard that Rainer von Gottardt, the mutilated pianist, had sent me ten days before from Hollywood, California. It was half out of my inside pocket. I stuck it back in. Then I folded the coat higher up, near the shoulders, so that the card, held in a vertical position, would not slip out and fall to the street during the walk from the Rue Stella to 66 Rue de la République.

Indeed it did not fall.

A light was shining in the windows of my neighbor, the loner. It was extinguished as soon as I raised my head and glimpsed it. Had the giant himself been extinguished, had he flown away, dissolved along with the light?

He had moved in a month and a half after us. He spoke a chaotic French, moreover he did not speak, or very little. For more than a year we had limited our exchanges to vigorous nods whenever our paths crossed. Then one day, at the taxi stand on the Place Bellecour, opposite the Royal movie theater, we had a small conversation that was at once awkward and warm. He was painfully shy despite being built like a barn, he was one of those people you like at once, and his name was Torbjörn Skaldaspilli. Of calamitous ugliness. An enormous nose, eyes at his temples or just about, making him peer at you from a three-quarter angle like a large bird. Simian arms trailing to the ground. "And before that, you rented?" I had said to him just to say something. He must have learned somehow or other that I wrote for the papers. "Yes yes, bevor I rendet," he answered quickly, his features worried, watching my face for a reaction to his Viking "rendet," but I had remained stone-faced.

A taxi had materialized. Although he had been waiting longer than I had, he insisted on yielding it to me, smiling and stubborn, yes, yes, yes, no, no, no, you, not me, he lived alone, the only family he had in the world was his old mother in Norway, he was going to spend the month of August with her.

And so, as I pushed open the door of my building, an animal, a small dog or a big cat, came boiling out of nowhere and slipped out between my legs, barking or mewing, I couldn't tell which. I couldn't tell anything anymore. Sometimes I felt ill, deaf, dumb, blind. I forgot everything, confused everything, thoughts, words, the meaning of words, it must be an illness, the beginning of an illness, dog, meow, cat, sheep, a rat's staccato wailing, a dray horse's plaintive chirping, a shit fly's persistent barking, it was all the same to me.

•

On my fifth try the refrigerator door opened. I took the remaining beer, after which it was empty, the cupboards too were bare, nothing to eat, oh yes, a few slices of stale bread, nothing to eat and nothing to drink, could I receive a guest in this empty apartment and offer her only the lukewarm polluted Rhône water coughed up by my yellow faucets to drink, and only the air, thickened and wrinkled by the heat, to eat?

I did not ask myself the question.

I poured the beer into a glass and drank deep gulps as I walked about. The telephone cord tripped me just as I was finishing the beer. The glass jumped from my hands, fell, and rolled without breaking. I had had enough of the heat, of the telephone cord, enough of the telephone that never rang, enough of the refrigerator door. Enough of everything.

The girl's name was Anne.

I undressed and fell on the bed in the back room, which despite everything was the least torrid place in the apartment by nightfall. I immediately got up again. Lay down again immediately. Got up again and paced around, leaving trails of despair behind me. I bumped into the wall, whirled around, felt as agitated and ill at ease as a jackal in a goldfish bowl, sleep had deserted me, alas, I said to myself, nothing like a good night of insomnia after a long anguished day to make you contemplate an ever-shrinking horizon with an ever-gloomier eye, I had given up sleeping pills which did not make me sleep and which aggravated the effects of insomnia.

Time passed in painful agitation.

I wanted to scream.

The little digital alarm made an unpleasant noise, the faltering beat of a tired heart, blip, blip, either its own heart or else the heart or the distant footfalls of a nameless enemy, always the same yet always more threatening. It was the only drawback of this highly accurate timepiece. I would gladly have hurled it through the window, with rage, into Rue de la République or even as far as the splashing fountain on the Place de la République.

Liliane crazy. How I loved her! How I loved Liliane, my adoptive mother!

I was alone.

I fell asleep at dawn.

TWO

The silence pressing on my eardrums when I awoke was of the kind that precedes disaster, and, although certain that no disaster was about to occur, I experienced a sort of disequilibrium, a sense of being pushed over the edge of a cliff, unable to resist yet not falling.

A most painful sensation.

And then — it was ten o'clock — something did indeed happen. The jangling of the phone pulverized this sensation of imminent fall, at once so impalpable and so concrete, and holding such dreadful promise of being eternal. The phone! Who, why? My heart leaped in gusts, sweat bathed me from head to foot — but my eardrums were liberated!

I got up, picked up the receiver.

"Hôtel des Étrangers?" said a man's voice.

Wrong number. It wasn't the first time. The two numbers were similar, almost identical in fact.

My pubic hairs, which I was combing with the spread fingertips of my left hand, were wet from the heat.

Wrong number. What I should say would not come. Refused to come. And an exchange of sterile words was likely to follow, since it was not me they were looking for. Hang up without a word? No, too much passivity stifled me, my thoughts raced, quickly, the shortest and the most passive response came to me, I had to say something, the shortest and the most passive thing, the laziest thing. And the thing that would keep me less removed from life for a few seconds? "Yes."

I had replied yes. I was relieved.

"Room 228, please," said the voice, tonelessly, without expression.

"One moment."

I set down the receiver, went into the front room, removed the other receiver, came back and hung up in the back room, went back to the front room where I picked up the receiver and said:

"Yes?"

"Mr. Lichem?"

Mr. Lichem.

"Yes."

"I was afraid you might not have arrived yet. Good trip?"

"Splendid," I said, scratching my bottom which did not particularly itch.

"Good. Your meeting is set for tomorrow morning at ten. The address: 129 Rue Duguesclin, seventh floor, second door on the right. There is no name on the door. Tomorrow, 10:00 A.M., 129 Rue Duguesclin, seventh floor, second door on the right. Got it?"

"Got it."

"Good. Have a nice stay in Lyon, Mr. Lichem."

"Thank you."

And he hung up, and I hung up too. A mistake. Wrong number. Slip of the dial.

I was thirsty. I rinsed out yesterday's glass, the one that had not broken when it fell and rolled on the floor in the front room, filled it with water, drank thirstily, set it down on the edge of the sink, too near the edge, and, since my movements in the mornings were even less precise than my movements during the rest of the day, I struck it with my elbow as I turned around to go see if I wasn't somewhere else and this time, falling onto the kitchen tiles, it broke into a thousand pieces. I picked up the pieces of this glass destined to be shattered, so numerous and so widely scattered that you would have sworn I had broken twelve glasses.

Outside, the sun beat down more savagely than ever. The clouds that had veiled moon and stars last night had fled. Today would be as hot, hotter than its predecessors.

The phone had deprived me of that transition period between sleeping and waking that I needed more desperately than ever, a transition during which I would thrash about as long as necessary, stretching and yelling like a man on the rack, arms and legs heading in their own private directions, sometimes I sent a chair flying into a distant wall, or else I set the building to shuddering by banging my head against a nearby wall, or else I hurled myself out of bed altogether and rose in a state of sharp irritation, but well and truly awake at last.

My fingers were shaking. I made coffee. I showered. I put on my white clothes, shirt and pants. Not much in the way of clothes, and well worn. Nothing to drink, nothing to eat. Like last night, the coffee tasted like dead leaves. So my taste buds were responsible.

•

To my boundless stupefaction, the owners of the little Arab grocery on the Rue Thomassin, people I could have sworn would open their store and be handing out change with webbed fingers the day after a general atomic attack, had closed. The car was a few steps away, it started easily, I gave scarcely a thought to Lichem, Hôtel des Étrangers, who must be waiting for his phone call, I took the waterfront route, quai Jules Courmont, quai Gailleton, I was assuredly not going to find a grocery store on those streets, but it was going so well, each light turned green as I reached it, I didn't have the sun in my eyes, the easiest and the least fatiguing thing was to keep on going, going, you can always find a grocery store, and I kept on going, going, under the influence of that same paradoxically passive mood that would have condoned my driving the lovely hitchhiker Anne to the remotest confines of the solar system, the gallant red Dauphine leaping from star to star, its deranged headlights flickering into the blackest and most distant nights of time, I had reached the Galliéni Bridge, red light.

Green light. I had had to brake, stop. Going straight ahead now made less sense. I turned left onto the Galliéni Bridge. Its continuation, Avenue Berthelot, was broad, straight, tempting, and I remembered an advertisement plastered over the walls of the city and claiming (and there was one of them now, on Place Jean Macé) that the giant Carrefour de Vénissieux department store and supermarket remained open in August. No need then for an exhausting search, I merely had to go there, passively, sure of my facts.

I roared away. Every light green. Bravo. Beyond Place du 11 Novembre 1918, Avenue Berthelot changed names, Avenue Jean Mermoz, without losing any of its rectitude, its width, or its green traffic lights, Boulevard Laurent Bonnevay, Vénissieux, the store. However, a red light stopped me five hundred yards short. On my left, a huge low-cost apartment complex, the color of a toad flattened four days earlier by a car, a graceless housing project, all its putrid shutters closed tight except on the ground floor six feet from the highway and therefore six feet from me, the shutters and windows of one apartment were open, I could hear the sharply raised voices of a couple: "If it wasn't for my leg I'd give you a swift kick in the ass," the man was saying.

"Shouldn't have broken it then," said the woman nastily.

Thunderous sounds of tableware being piled up and thrown around, then the woman's voice again: "Easy to see your mother's been here, can't find a single knife in this drawer."

"When your mother's been around, you . . ."

I stepped on the gas to get away. The rest of the dialogue was drowned.

The department store. Low, flat, square or almost square, a huge, vile, many-hued parasite battening on a hideous landscape of vacant lots, factories, graceless residential high rises, and highways.

I drove along the front of this eyesore, there, the letters IFH. Parking. God, the heat!

There were people there, many many people. The survivors of summer. After three steps you were gasping and dripping sweat, the store's air conditioning dated from the slingshot era and people gave off heat like kerosene stoves going full blast. I almost turned right around and left, but I was swept inside by the flood, a zealous store employee with very black hair and a glass eye even gave me a cart decorated with multitudinous abandoned lettuce leaves, it ran crookedly with an anguished whinnying.

Nevertheless I made my way to the clothing department. The cart tugged at my arms, moving forward in a succession of leaps and yaws as if the store floor had been the soil of Verdun after the battle. I abandoned it. The fitting rooms were under sustained assault. People had given up the idea of getting into them and were trying clothes on anywhere, straw hats, coats, shoes, but also shirts, pants, we might have been in a public bath, hairy legs, tank tops, heavy breathing, odors, screams and tears from children, quarreling from their parents, long one-legged hopping odysseys executed by some (their other foot being caught in a pants leg) in a vain attempt to maintain their equilibrium, colliding in the course of their bizarre trajectories with those unable to see them and revolving helplessly because their heads, shoulders, and upper arms were imprisoned in too-tight pullovers from which they were unable to extricate themselves.

Diverse items of clothing were flying through the air or being trampled underfoot. Others, neatly stacked only seconds before, were being heaped up like mountains of cast-off rags. By coincidence, by mistake, or by an act of human or mechanical ill will, the mawkish music percolating out over the loudspeakers suddenly blared out at full volume. The level of madness intensified, a little bit of this madness stole into me without my knowledge, in the heart of the general frenzy I surprised myself trying on, calmly, but all the same trying on, a white shirt that aha! suited me well, I tucked it into my pants and abandoned the old shirt, which I could therefore have avoided washing the night before.

On the other hand, I should not have been in such a hurry to tuck the new one into my pants: a pair of white pants, denims with the same label and of the same size, fell into my hands from heaven. Instantly, and for the next three seconds, a tiny grubby child wrestled me for them. This grubby child was covered with slap marks. The poor kid, I said to myself, he must get it whether he turns right or left. It was probably the abuse that had stunted his growth. He was redheaded. I gave a sharp tug and glared at him, then immediately changed my expression and smiled at his mother, an enormous woman ready to pounce on me with all the fervor of parents who murder their children yet do not suffer a stranger to offer them the tiniest reprimand. My smile disarmed her, she gave the little one's skull a blow with the flat of the hand that halted his growth for the next six months, and raised her eyes upward in confusion and languor (her languid air and the white of eye she revealed gave her a hallucinatory bovine look) toward a carnival bonnet she had just pulled down over her forehead to her eyebrows, doubtless a curiosity of the millinery trade spawned by a malfunctioning conveyor belt, a black pink and green half-straw half-plastic headpiece decorated with three feathers, one of them as high as a lightning rod.

Perhaps I would never have tried on the pants if I had not had to wrest them from the little martyr. Whatever the truth, I did put them on, concealing myself in the heart of the bathrobe section. They fitted me to perfection. Then I also put on a very well cut black leather jacket, the most expensive in the store, nor did I hesitate to change socks and shoes (some white ones caught my fancy), I succumbed to the lure of straw hats, slipped on white gloves, made myself a middle-age spread of underwear thrust between shirt and skin, stuck a priceless pipe between my teeth and on my nose sunglasses more efficient and more handsome than my own, and sped to the food section where the same disorder allowed me to enjoy, on the spot, a pâté sandwich wrapped that very morning in cellophane and to conceal two of them under my hat as well as a small country sausage, nice and firm, and a few small jars of preserves in the inner and outer pockets of the jacket, finally I granted myself the luxury of a cool lemonade, which gave off a great big sigh, psccchh!, when I opened it.

I was a thief.

At the checkout counter I paid for a bottle of orange juice, a case of beer, a bag of 100-percent arabica vacuum-ground coffee, and a $16 bottle of Scotch whose price label I had surreptitiously

replaced with that from a pineapple syrup at $1.79, the over-
worked and uncaring cashier didn't notice a thing.

A thief. An outlaw.

•

I was unrecognizable when I came out. Anne would be dealing
with a very different man this imminent early afternoon, a
different man dressed like a prince and fitted out like a nabob,
then I forgot about Carrefour-Vénissieux, I forgot about Anne
too, sufficient to the day and even to the minute the evil thereof,
before was before, after was after, I went back home where I left
leather jacket, hat, pipe, gloves, underwear, and food, and immediately left to keep my appointment with Rainer von Gottardt.

The Saône waterfront. Deserted. At the slow red light on the
Kitchener Bridge, I fumbled for the pianist's postcard in my old
coat, which lay rolled up, twisted, and squashed on the passenger
seat. Quite impossible to find the right pocket. I lost my temper,
grew furious, clawed at the recalcitrant fabric as if I were seeking
the key to the cell in which I had been locked with six towering
wild beasts, I heard the lining rip. Finally I managed to liberate
the card from its textile prison, but not before I had inflicted an
ugly central fold in it, all this exhausting activity just to reread an
address I knew by heart, the Saône looked like cardboard
cemented in place by strokes of sunlight and heat, the climb up
to Choulans along the Rue du Commandant Charcot, heat and
solitude, I drove alone and sweated in the great noonday sadness,
yes, my new sunglasses were more effective than the old ones, I
reached Francheville-le-Bas.

Nobody. I saw nobody.

The postcard, in Cinemascope and Metrocolor, painted by a
certain Ed Scarisbrick, showed a young man in a denim suit in
the foreground, back turned to the viewer. He had a bag slung
across his back and was looking at a handsome building on the
right of the picture, a hotel, the Château Marmont. On a lawn to
the left, a huge billboard. In front of the billboard, a parked
Porsche, perhaps the young man's. You couldn't see the front of

the car, the lights. The huge rectangular billboard showed the building just as it appeared in the postcard, only without young man, car, or billboard, just the hotel, the greenery, and on the left in enormous letters the inscription: "Marmont Lane, USA," and on the back of the card: "Château Marmont, home away from home for stars, producers, directors, writers, and business people," the address and phone number of this California paradise, and then a few lines most curiously and kindly addressed to me by my own personal idol. Once, these few lines would have thrown me into a state of nervous jubilation requiring a stout straitjacket to deter me from wreaking injury on myself.

When I received them, no.

How had Rainer von Gottardt known I would be in Lyon? Why had he not phoned me, or asked me to phone him? I had never really asked myself these questions.

Francheville-le-Haut, the countryside or illusion of countryside on the city's outskirts, Rue de l'Église, a little street born in the center of the village and dying I imagine far off amid stones and scrubland, a little street with houses new or not new, most in fact very old, I believe, on the edge of the road or else set back from it, those set back being more or less visible depending on the trees and bushes around them, I stopped in front of number 36 and switched off the engine.

Terrifying silence. Like something falling upon your shoulders as if from the heights of heaven. I got out of the car, just moving in these conditions was like a circus exploit, I imagined a crowd poleaxed by the summer, beyond applauding, beyond expressing pitying admiration by even so much as a fugitive gleam of the eye, the sun's glare killed everything. A healthy, balanced person, I told myself, would not be doing what I was doing. I must be running a temperature. Or have no temperature at all.

The house was old and sat back from the road. After pushing through a creaking iron gate you had to cross sixty feet of red-brown grass. The rain that had fallen on Lyon and its environs in the last months would not have filled the cap of a fountain pen.

Meteorologists were immolating themselves out of stupefaction. Natural laws no longer obtained.

Thirty feet of unparalleled striving.

Another thirty to go.

The door of the pianist's house was at the other end of the universe.

He appeared, tall, huge, bald, wearing khaki pants and a white shirt with vertical red stripes and the sleeves not rolled up. He stood motionless on the threshold. Until the very last moment we kept looking into each other's eyes. He dripped sweat, so did I.

All I knew of him was two or three fuzzy photos. Since the time of his short-lived public fame he had refused photographs and interviews, he had refused everything, no one ever saw him, he hardly ever played at concerts, he hid behind his piano, his dressing room was better defended than a crime lord's hotel room, he was rumored to be violent.

I recalled the two or three fuzzy photographs. How he had changed!

Wearily he pronounced my name:

"Miguel Soler?"

"Yes. Michel. Michel Soler. Hello."

He put out his hand.

"How do you do. So you did receive my card. And you came. I am so glad to meet you."

"So am I. Very happy. I cannot tell you how happy."

I should have liked to put more intensity into this expression of my pleasure, but by now this was impossible, my words, like his, expired as they were spoken, if someone had unexpectedly pierced my buttocks with a sharp, red-hot iron I should of course have said ouch, but a little ouch, stunted, toneless, characterless, an ouch without relief, I told myself as I grasped as best I could his thick, soft, hairy, sticky hand, he withdrew it at once, and I mine at the same moment, we continued to stare into one another's eyes, but without embarrassment, things were going as they were meant to.

After three seconds of silent observation — almost severe on his side — his eyelids, heavy, grainy, speckled, the lids of an animal antedating man's appearance on earth, his eyelids abruptly and slowly blinked, and he drew back a corner of his mouth in an expression of benevolence, finally he looked away from me, raised his head toward the infinite and blue sky, more infinite and bluer than ever in this month of August, and looked back at me: "Shall we go in? It is a little less hot inside."

His monstrous bulk filled the whole door frame. He executed a labored about-face and moved off down the corridor. I followed him. To set so much fleshy matter in motion he was obliged almost to throw one hip and one shoulder forward, then the other hip and the other shoulder. We entered a vast room with beams and fireplace and roughly plastered walls. Against one wall, a piano. He pointed to a black leather couch into which I slumped unceremoniously and at once sank right down to the floor, you wanted to fling your arms out in panic and clutch something to break your dizzying fall.

He remained upright, his breathing labored and noisy. He appeared so totally exhausted it frightened me. You wondered if he could live one day longer, and I would not have been surprised if he had dropped dead on the spot.

He hauled a metal garden chair out from under a big farm table and set about installing himself in it with many grunts and moans. What misfortunes, what implacable blows to soul and body, had reduced Rainer von Gottardt to this state of premature old age?

The index finger of his left hand was missing.

Finally he got himself seated. He offered me a small cigar, which I refused. He lit one and then offered me a glass of white wine. I accepted. A bottle and two glasses stood on the table, but he had already been drinking, perhaps accounting for what was missing from the bottle, at least half. An ashtray overflowed with cigar butts. I saw a pipe and tobacco jar on a shelf.

With careful economy of movement (he was understandably reluctant to take any chances with his center of gravity) he handed me a glass; I leaned forward to take it from him.

"No tobacco. No alcohol. No couch. If I sat down in that thing . . ."

Contemplating the consequences of his supposition brought a wheezy laugh to his throat like the spasmodic gobbling of a turkey with a head cold, ha, ha! he swallowed his glass of white wine at a gulp, almost reducing his cigar to ash at a gulp as well.

"I'm not going to change all the furniture around at this stage. I found this chair outside, it does the job. Any other chair I'd probably break. And hurt myself falling. Look what's become of me . . . it's my heart, of course. No, I'm not going to change anything. I haven't even had the phone reconnected."

"I wonder if there isn't something wrong with my mother's heart. She gets pains. Cramps, sort of."

I had thought out loud. He answered without surprise: "I have never had any pain. But she should see a doctor."

"Does this house belong to you?"

"Now it does. It used to belong to my mother's brother. To one of her brothers. It's my only possession. I have nothing else. Three suitcases. And enough to pay for my funeral. Not much at sixty. The plane fare was expensive. I got in from California the day before yesterday. I reread your book again on the plane. I asked you in my card to keep my presence here a secret, please do so. I lived the first sixteen years of my life in this house. Except for the first sixteen months, which were in Wiesbaden."

"I had no idea," I said.

"Of course not."

Talking made you thirstier. I drank a mouthful of white wine, almost lukewarm. As for him, so many words had made him breathless, his voice was hoarse, a whisper strained and fading, the voice of a man on his deathbed. He grew calmer, refilled his glass, drank, looked at me. In a wig he could have been a caricature of Haussmann's portrait of Bach, but even fleshier, softer, more lascivious, the curve of his mouth hinting at depravity, you could have sworn that at that second he was watching hideous tortures and delighting in them. Yet he seduced me, something in him (his eyes) seduced me physically, amorously, I wanted to please him, almost wanted to touch him, there are several kinds of disgust, ambiguous kinds of disgust.

Batting of eyelids, drawing back of lips, just as before in the doorway, approval, benevolence. Rainer von Gottardt, the Maestro, unique interpreter of Bach, dispenser of spiritual joys without which my soul would not have been the same! Memory gripped me, stifled me, clawed me, I could have wept for nothing, but this was not nothing. I got up, I had to move. I took two very deep breaths. The pianist's pleasant manner persisted. He waited for me to speak. His eyes did not once leave mine, my emotion vexed me as I stood there leaning forward speaking to the Maestro suddenly unable to believe he was really there in front of me, as I addressed him as if in a violent burst of hatred or of passion: "I loved you very much," I said, my throat constricted. "I loved you very much. And I still love you very much."

The silence that followed this declaration was protracted.

"I am very moved. Believe me, I am very moved. I felt this love in your book." (He smiled.) "It is mutual."

My throat grew a little less tight. "I nearly saw you in 1969, when you played for the Dioblanízes. I couldn't come. I was ill."

"A pity. What a pity! So they do invite you?"

"Yes. I never go. I am by nature rebellious and reclusive."

I had seen Hector and Isabel Dioblaníz only once, two sickly looking characters, nervous, with wild rolling eyes. They were sponsoring a concert at the Salle Rameau. I perceived a slight resemblance between Isabel Dioblaníz and my mother Liliane, the mouth and the eyes. I did not introduce myself. I had never sought to approach them despite their outstretched hand, and I had accepted none of their invitations, being of a rebellious and reclusive nature, very rebellious, very reclusive.

"Were you invited this year? Sit down . . ."

"Yes."

"So was I, of course. Isabel Dioblaníz gave me *On Bach's Fugues* just before I left. For a long time I did not read it. A very long time. I generally don't like to read such books. By music critics still less. One day, I read it . . . As I told you in my card, I wanted to convey my admiration to you. And—"

He broke off, crushed his cigar butt in the round ashtray so full of butts that grinding one out merely ignited another ten, asked me if I would go outside and empty this ashtray, a regular little factory, on the lawn, anywhere, I went, the sun struck me full in the face, a butt remained stuck to the bottom of the overturned ashtray, I had to dislodge it with a finger, I returned, he had lit another cigar.

One detail was absorbing me: he held his cigar between the middle and ring fingers, not at right angles to his hand but drooping somewhat toward the little finger. As for the Maestro's index finger (the one that wasn't missing, of course, but that which he perhaps favored out of deference to who knows what sense of symmetry), it squashed his nose into a cauliflower shape every time he raised the cigar to his mouth. I had almost persuaded myself that this mannerism had a secret meaning that eluded me, then I forgot about it and thought of other things, but it is true that this summer my mind was constantly sifting through external circumstances, making connections between them, weaving them as it were into a network, into a spiderweb (he held his cigars in such and such a way, his telephone did not work and neither did Liliane's, I had received a phone call and it was a wrong number but I had agreed to meet an unknown person, and to meet Anne, the stranger who had stopped my car in the dark night, so late and still so hot, and to meet Rainer von Gottardt, the Maestro, from whom I had received a postcard to the utter confusion of my idle, lazy, mailbox, wounded in the virginity it had recently derived from the fact that nobody wrote me anymore): were these obsessions meant to hold me back, however ineffectively and despite myself, from the fatal slope I was on? To help me survive this joyous beginning of August, to prevent me from fleeing this vale of tears where I was drowning without dying, to force me at cruel intervals to keep my head above the lachrymal stream, neither dead nor alive?

I did not know. In the extreme confusion of my mind, I could not have said.

"Why did you never send me your book?"

"Ooooohweell . . ." I said, exhausted, falling effortlessly into his weary, moribund tones.

"Yes, that is your business." (He drained his glass of white wine.) "I have never read anything so good on Bach. Nor about my performances of his work. I probably speak with an accent, don't I? I do not often have a chance to speak French. Do I speak with an accent?"

Yes, a little. I rocked my head from side to side to signify yes and no.

"You are a pianist, of course?"

Another head movement, a kind of disjointed spiraling that meant yes no yes no yes no, one of those graceless tossings of the head favored by bulls when they are assaulted by stubborn flies, a little longer and an imbecile's drool would stream from my lips.

"Yes," I said at last. "I have played a little. A lot, in fact. I stopped when I wrote that book. Since then I don't think I have touched a piano."

"Why?"

"I don't know. A mystery. A broken spring. And therefore broken fingers too. Stiffened by handling a pen. I didn't want to anymore. I couldn't. I gave up."

"That is a pity. Several clues even lead me to conjecture that you have played in concerts?"

I emptied my glass. He was pressuring me with words. After each one he could have dropped stone dead, so great was the effort of articulating them. His prodigious bulk was wracked by spasmodic heaves. The sudden urge to flee, to get up, to tell him again how much I loved him and kiss his craggy furrowed brow and flee and forget everything, this urge was powerful.

"A few attempts," I said. "Crowned with failure. A disaster from which I have never really recovered."

"Crowned with failure!" (Once again he emitted the catarrhal gobble of a moribund turkey. Then the near-laugh stopped short.) "Would you like to play a few notes? This is quite a good Töhdeskünst."

He indicated the piano with his chin. Above the piano were two engravings.

"No, ha, ha!" I answered, wrenching a cackle out of myself the way you might rip a healthy tooth out with pliers. "What about you?"

He emitted a similar cackle, poured himself a third glass, did not reply.

"How do you earn your living?"

"Journalism. I have gone on writing. Music reviews in several small magazines."

"Does it pay well?"

I nearly laughed again, but it was too tiring. "No. Not well."

He was silent, hesitated, made up his mind: he wanted to tell me how much he admired me, and . . . "Before I die (for I have returned to Lyon to die) I wanted to talk. To meet you, the author of *On Bach's Fugues,* and to speak to you. Here is my idea. A limited but by no means negligible readership, in the United States and also in many other countries, would give its right arm for my memoirs. Limited, but not negligible — and loyal. For you, in any case, a small fortune, if you agree to listen, to record, and to write."

"Yes," I said without thinking.

"I am not asking you to reply at once. Think about it. Besides, I no longer have the strength just now to hear anything, much less to talk. I am exhausted. Jet lag. I shall sleep, sleep. If I can. I won't see you out, forgive me. Would tomorrow at five . . . ?"

An abrupt dismissal. I rose.

In the fuzzy photos he had looked slim, handsome, his face smooth and pure. Now his face was yellow, puffy, covered with tiny wrinkles, his thick lips too red, too glistening. His body, in which death was already making itself at home and monstrously disfiguring him.

He had returned to Lyon to die.

"Fine. Tomorrow afternoon at five."

Would I myself still be alive at five the next day? And would I remain alive for the number of days it would take to record the story of his life? I did not know. He was in a hurry, so was I. Rainer von Gottardt, the greatest interpreter of Bach since the beginning of time, even deader than I was, I loved him and wanted to see him again, I was sweating so profusely as I crossed the lawn that nothing would be left of me by the time I reached the car.

I started the engine. I forgot. I had dropped carelessly onto the broken seat in the Dauphine, my body hurt, for a long time my buttocks were sore.

·

She had said three, at three there was a ring at my door, it was her, Anne, the 1:10 A.M. hitchhiker, number 12 bus terminal, a bag in her hand, today she was wearing a little red dress of lightweight fabric, the flimsiest of scraps, a feather-light red dress that suited her wonderfully and showed off her pretty arms and legs, her pretty flesh, Anne was pretty and I knew I was going to make love with her.

I kissed her on the cheek, hello, she said hello back. Our faces returned to their rightful relationships with the axes of our bodies. A delicate moment, but her large dark eyes were examining me without malice, without a trace of malevolence, on the contrary her gaze was reassuring, she seemed to guess everything.

In the room facing the street we came across the Bach poster, this poster must have made me seem somewhat of an overgrown student.

"This poster must make me seem somewhat of an overgrown student," I said. "But—"

I attempted to explain myself no further, she made no further comment.

"How have things been since last night? And thanks again."

"Fine. Sit down. You're welcome. What about you?"

"I'm fine." (Flopping gracefully onto the couch, her bag flung down next to her.) "I'm glad I'm leaving on vacation."

Her smile was bright and cool in that stifling gloom.

"This heat!" I said. "Even though I never allow the sun to poke its nose in here. Isn't it killing you?"

"No. Yes, a little. Not too much. Have you done interesting things today?"

"A few errands. I saw a friend, well, someone I was supposed to meet, I tried to eat, I tried to sleep, I phoned the phone company to get them to fix my mother's phone, a little house-cleaning in your honor, twenty minutes in the shower. And I waited for Anne. What about you?"

It was true I had done some housecleaning, a vague attempt to put things straight, a spot of vacuuming, I even owned two vacuum cleaners, never mind the exact details of how I had come into this dual possession, alas! one was as ineffective as the other, one of them, the older one, forcibly disgorged from its rear end what it had swallowed through its mouth, the other, a newer and more sophisticated model, neither sucked in nor blew out, nothing, it would not have disturbed the stillness of the gos-samer down you sometimes find on eggshells, nothing save a fearful din, the din of a bomber squadron taking off before a decisive attack, the kind of din that wears out men's nerves and makes them pull the throttle all the way back, that particular one was extremely noisy as well as incapable of inhaling dirt, my ears were still hurting and I had had to finish the job with the dust broom, on all fours like an animal.

I sat down in front of the fair Anne on a chair with its back turned to the big wooden table, my legs crossed, shoulders slumped, the place where my hair came down to a point at the back of my neck flirting with a drop of sweat which had formed or had dropped on the first protruding bone in the area (the atlas), it tickled, I was sprawled, clean, well dressed, drawn, weary.

"Well, I did manage to eat and sleep. I got up late. I started packing. Nearly finished. And I came to see Michel . . ."

She smiled. So did I. Or at least an attempt, something approaching, I preferred not to know exactly what, an inhuman alteration of the facial lineaments I instantly concealed behind my right hand.

"What do you do in life?" I asked to give myself a quick change of face.

Her shoes were red like her little unbelievably light red dress, almost immaterial on her so-material flesh, ten such dresses thrust down a sparrow's throat would not have hindered the little creature from inhaling the air it needed to cleave the skies, her black bag, lying open, kept trying to slip off the sofa, she caught it by its underside, a cassette spilled out of it and tumbled along the floor amid a great clattering of plastic, case to one side and cassette to the other, Anne bent down quickly and retrieved it all.

"I play the violin in a jazz group. There are five of us."

"In Lyon?"

"Yes. At the Blue Note. Do you know it?"

"Not really. I believe I spent an evening there a few years ago."

"We've been playing there for six months. Seven. Before that we were in Barcelona. And you? What do you do?"

"Nothing exciting. Particularly right now. I write stories for magazines. But I haven't done too much recently. For the last six or seven months."

"What kind of stores?"

"About music. Recordings, classical concerts."

"Really? Then come hear us when we get back, OK?"

When we get back.

She had put the cassette back in its case. I turned my head toward the window as if something there demanded my urgent and passionate attention, stroked the back of my neck with my fingertips to still the persistent tickling, finally I emitted a furtive yes, the small yes of a sick child docilely agreeing to swallow leek soup at a time of day when he usually gorges on hot chocolate.

"Is the stuff you play any good?"

"Me or the group?"

"Both. You."

"Depends. Depends on the night. I started out playing classical violin. We have a good pianist, and a really good lead singer. That's where I was last night, at his place. He's decided that when we get back we'll make our fortune. We're going to try to write hit songs. Big winners. I think he's off his head. But you never know. He's recorded a cassette just to inspire us."

"Like a drink? Beer, orange juice, Scotch, coffee?"

"Orange juice. Can we play a bit of the cassette? I haven't listened to it yet."

Yes, I said yes, the way I had said yes to Rainer von Gottardt and to the man who phoned this morning, I was always saying yes.

The bizarre idea swam into my head that Rainer von Gottardt was perhaps not Rainer von Gottardt, the real pianist, but someone else, an impostor.

The bizarre and mysterious idea went away.

I busied myself with the cassette, Anne also rose, went to the window, lifted the curtain, looked down at the street, let the curtain fall.

"Nice place to live. Right in the heart of town. I love that fountain. In the very heart of town."

She took obvious pleasure in saying the word "heart."

"It's almost stopped beating," I said.

"There are more people around than you think. It seems to me."

Anne was simple and calm, she soothed me. I went to the kitchen. A singer with a Spanish accent began a sentimental song.

I tugged at the refrigerator door, pushed it, hard, gently, nothing happened. I was alarmed. Then I deployed a brand-new subterfuge: I pulled on the handle and at the same time landed a hefty kick low on the door. It opened. Phew! Perhaps I had found the key. Perhaps. But I wasn't going to shut the door again to find out. Some other time. I took out a beer and the orange juice. To assert that these bottles froze the palms of the hands would be a falsehood, but at least picking them up did not involve third-degree burns.

A quick swivel of the pelvis, boom! a blow of the hip, the door slammed shut and I turned away without giving it another thought.

Anne was looking at my books.

"You have a lot."

"I used to have a lot more."

I set the bottles and the two glasses on the table and drew nearer to her. She was fairly tall, and slender. We were face to face. I was looking into her big eyes, dark and deep. I raised a hand and slipped it between her left cheek and her hair, which tended on this side to fall forward over her face, to hide it, and I kissed her, three quarters on her cheek and a quarter on the corner of her lips, a simple, sweet, pleasant kiss, toward the end of it she pushed her head forward so that the pressure was stronger for a second, then she moved back, so did I, and with my hand stretched out I stroked her long hair on this same left side, and said sit down, I'll get you your drink.

The singer was singing his song. It was all about a carnival night, people were dancing, a man was in love with a woman but she pretended not to care, she danced without paying any attention to him, she even tried to make him jealous.

Anne stretched out her arm and took the glass of orange juice.

"I don't know why, my fingers look red today. The tips. Perhaps because I bite my nails. It's ugly. What about you? Do you play an instrument?"

"I did once. The piano. It's obviously frostbite," I said to make her laugh, not even looking at her fingers.

She laughed, yes, frostbite from the heat, she said, I bent over her and this time it was her mouth I kissed, very quickly.

Another song had begun.

I poured out my beer and sat down on the couch beside Anne.

Through dark and stormy weather, we'll stroll through life together, the words of the song were appalling, through the stormiest of oceans, we'll still share those sweet emotions, etc.

"Your fingers aren't red at all."

It was true, her fingers weren't red at all.

Appalling words to the song. Anne, examining her spread fingers to see whether they really were red, an idea she had put into her own head, sensed I felt appalled and said: "If you don't like it we can change. Do you listen only to Bach right now? Or no music at all?"

"You guess everything."

"Sometimes. That one was easy. Are you going to spend the whole of August in Lyon?"

"I think so."

"Wait a second, I'll switch off the tape."

"No, I will."

We got up, she took out the cassette. I put on the Fugue in B Minor from the first book, in the brief intervening silence there was a tsplokh! as a piece of Scotch tape came unstuck, and immediately after, drrinngg-drrinngg, the insect drone of the phone in the next apartment, it rang throughout the first sixth of the fugue, I had put my arm around Anne's shoulder to bring her back to the couch and we sat that way, my arm around her shoulders, when the phone stopped she laid her head on my chest, raised it only to give me a kiss on the cheek, laid it down again, my God how bad I felt, one foot already in the grave and here I was going to make love for the last time, one foot in the grave and the other in a wolf trap, at such moments you realize how difficult it can be to move along life's paths with enthusiasm and harmony, you are pulled back, you stumble.

You are afraid.

At the last notes of the fugue Anne raised her head, her face leaving my chest, in compensation she took my hand, and said of the music that it was beautiful, that it sang. She was right, Rainer von Gottardt made that fugue sing.

She got up, still holding my hand, pulled me toward her. I held her tight, my nose in her hair, kissed her, she was cooler than the world around her, she was the coolest thing in the whole world, her mouth and her tongue were cool and delicious.

It would be like the first time, and the last.

In the other room, the room facing that joyless adjacent wall, Anne quickly and easily slipped off her dress, I clumsily removed my shirt, ripping off two buttons and scratching my left forearm, we lay down on the bed.

I listened to her breathing.

"You are very pretty," I said.

"So are you," she said.

I wanted to cry.

I put my elbows on the couch and looked at her, wholesome, smooth-skinned, her breasts, hips, knees, shoulders well formed. I kissed shoulders, breasts, knees, then laid my head on her warm, cool belly, I slid her little pants downward a little, my heart was beating very fast, five hundred pants such as these would not have sufficed to sponge away the blood resulting from the most superficial of pinpricks, five thousand perhaps, I was moved by the graceful motion of her legs as they freed themselves from the cloth, the left bent back, I bent it still farther back after taking hold of it by the ankle and I kissed Anne between her legs one stretched out the other bent as I have described, a long kiss on her soft brown sex, a little later she told me my pants were difficult to unzip, I told her that wasn't surprising, they were brand-new, bought that very morning.

They were unzipped.

They were unzipped and released into the room an avid and turbulent object belonging to a suicidal madman continent for eons and firmly resolved to muster the energy for one last revolt, impossible to remain too long impervious to the kisses and caresses showered upon it, the jeans acquired that morning had remained stuck at mid-thigh but not for long, rapidly reduced to the state of a reef knot by my twists and turns they were ejected from the bed, almost from the apartment, with a wild kick, Anne was a treasure of sweetness and naturalness, I felt at once completely present with myself and completely absent from myself as I penetrated her with dreadful slowness and she spread and spread her legs ever wider with equal slowness, the pleasure of both of us preceded only by slowness, by an attentive slowness, the most attentive of slownesses, and the pleasure itself so violent that it scarcely ruffled our relative immobility, had it expressed itself with the frenzy required by its violence she and I would have exploded into fragments in the room, her long moans drove me to devour her face with kisses.

She opened her eyes.

She rose a little. I thought she wanted me to leave her. No. Then I thought she wanted to kiss my neck, or some other tenderness of that kind, and, yes, she did kiss my neck, but she also reached out and took the sheet, pulled it up to my shoulders, pressed her hands down on my back and slid them up and down to dry my sweat!

Ah!

Such gestures and the look that went with them almost filled my breast with tears. But later, the tears, gestures and look rekindled a desire that had no need of rekindling for neither recent satisfaction nor the imminence of death could at that moment have denied it life, and there had to be thousands of kisses given and received and thousands of unbearable sensations (Anne lending herself wholly to my madness and gradually falling into a state of nervous expectation rivaling my own), and thousands of mutual joys just to bring us back to mere everyday frenzy, until, with twilight fallen, we lay stretched out side by side, hand in hand.

Blip, blip, blip, rasped that other damned thing.

It was hot enough to kill you. Silence and heat suffocated the city, as if treading down on it with a gigantic sole, soft but murderous, you could feel it.

From time to time Anne let go of my hand, stroked the back of it, then took it back again.

•

"You haven't forgotten your cassette?"

"No, it's in my bag."

I kissed Anne standing by the door, the same kiss as when she arrived. You would have thought she was arriving.

"Have a good vacation. And thanks." (How tactful!) "Don't mind me saying thanks, I . . ."

"No. I wanted to say thanks too."

She did too? Good God, why? But when your belly has been opened up with an axe and your entrails spill out steaming and shimmering, you are apt not to examine your neighbor's sore throat with the requisite solicitude.

She told me I could call her in September, after the vacation. Or she could call me, if I preferred it that way. Yes, I muttered. She left. I closed the door.

A second later, I had scarcely taken two broken steps, there was a knock at the same door. Anne.

"I'm sorry . . . I couldn't work up the courage to tell you, but . . . I don't mind not going on vacation, if you'd like. I don't mind staying in Lyon. I wouldn't mind at all. If you want."

The cunning little devil! I should have thrown her out of the car last night! Get her out, get her to leave me alone! With my eyes, for weeping! No, I did not want her to stay! No one. Alone. Just my eyes, for weeping.

"No," I said, perhaps a little curtly. "No," I said more gently. "Thanks. You are adorable. Adorable."

This time, not a word, either from her or from me. She smiled, turned with the quickness of a child and started down the stairs.

And that was it. All I had now was eyes for weeping. I went and rummaged in the bottom drawer of the chest for the bottle of Alymil 1000. The moment had come, one possible moment, to swallow all the tablets and the packaging along with them, the bottle and the yellow and white box, but first it seemed I had to weep, my chest was filling gasp by gasp.

I threw myself face down on the bed, the Alymil 1000 clenched in my right hand, my left forearm folded under my forehead, and sobbed out great sobs, all the tears of my body and all the tears of my life, thus completing the transformation of the mattress into a washrag, the tears stung and my skin stung, I was sweating without Anne to dry my back, but Anne was already sliding into oblivion, the sobs became so violent and so lacerating that I had to thrash about to give them full expression, I rolled over onto one side like a hunting dog, then over onto the other, then onto my back, scowling and whimpering, bending and straightening my legs like a frog or a newborn child.

The crisis passed.

The spiderweb did not break, not that evening.

I felt sleepy. I felt like taking a quarter tablet. I took it. A buffalo dose.

I drank a beer, showered, crouching stunned in the tub, pupils dilated, at least I assumed they were, came back to the bed.

I slept. This time, taking sedatives worked. I slept twelve hours.

THREE

I awoke more relaxed than on the preceding thousand mornings, and, for that very reason, ready to die at once, why, because there was nothing to conquer, nothing to overcome, I mean none or very little of the tumultuous apathy of anguish interposing itself between me and my wish for death, but, for that very reason, I no longer felt the usual urgency either: it was easy, death was there, within reach, whenever I wanted, fine, conclusion: why not keep the ten o'clock appointment?

Thus my floating thoughts wandered. They astonished me. The astonishment soon passed.

An easy awakening then. I had squeezed the packaging of the Alymil 1000 so hard in my right fist it was crumpled. I uncrumpled it and put it back in its place in the drawer. Liliane Tormes would never have received the letter, if last night . . .

A stamp! I had looked so hard I had finally found a stamp!

I also dug up the last of some jam in the bottom of a jar without either label or lid squeezed into the rear left-hand corner of the vegetable bin of the refrigerator where it had eluded previous searches, the refrigerator whose door had swung open all by itself during my long night. I sniffed, it seemed to be apricot, I decided to scrape out the bottom and transform it into a surface by spreading it over my aged bread and soaking the whole in my coffee, why not? Which I did.

My nose over the steam, I sucked pensively on an apricot pit. Rue Duguesclin, number 129, seventh floor, second door on the right. Everything was retreating into oblivion, but a particular kind of oblivion whose cage was glass or transparent mist. I found the pit curiously soft. If you bit down a little, it gave beneath your teeth. I removed it from my mouth and examined it. Horror! It was not an apricot pit but a black insect, legs drawn up beneath it, and stuck to its abdomen, preserved vermin, that was what I had just been sucking and nibbling on so thoughtfully as I cogitated with my nose in the coffee steam!

A powerful wave of nausea lifted me from my chair and took me to the bathroom where I clutched the edges of the toilet bowl as if tomorrow every single toilet bowl would vanish from the surface of the planet.

I did not vomit.

I returned to throw monster and jam into the trash and coffee into the sink, eat four sugar lumps and drink water, a lot of water, uuughgh! great tremors of disgust still shook me.

I shaved twice in a row. My features were drawn, even more than before sleeping. Hair long, very long. I combed it carefully. Gaze somber, almost evil. Long hair used to suit me. Still does. I was tired. Every movement slow. Dressed in white. I used to think the mobility of my features made me ugly. But I was unable to master it, except at the price of even greater ugliness, for instance when I was photographed. My present impassivity, admittedly the product of despair, suited me: with the light switched off in the bathroom, I caught a glimpse of myself in the poor mirror as I was leaving, a light filtered through thirty obstacles bathing my cheek, in a single flash I knew myself handsome, of unbearable beauty, the beauty of a god, so I directed at myself a hideous and destructive scowl, which left my tongue in considerable pain I had thrust it so hard against the inside of my cheek while slitting my eyes, baring my teeth, and wrinkling my nose, which from the wrinkling assumed the aspect of a small red tomato.

At the foot of the stairs I butted absentmindedly into the chest, or rather, despite my height, into the navel of the asymmetrical former firefighter Torbjörn Skaldaspilli. He bore a basket full of bottled drinks. He dropped it, nothing broke or shattered, his arms were so long the basket almost trailed along the ground, he at once seized my shoulders protectively and asked if he had hurt me. No, I told him, he had not hurt me.

Neither one of us moved aside. I had never seen him from so close up. And I had never seen a man with eyes so far apart, one on his left temple, the other on his right temple.

"You are vell, despite hot?"

There was so much benevolence in the face that leaned over mine, the better to examine me! I sensed that he was ready to hoist the building bodily and turn it to face north if I complained too loudly about the heat.

"I'm fine," I said. "And you?"

"I like hot."

I took a step backward. "So you leave tomorrow? Are you glad?"

"Eight tomorrow morning. My mother. Yes. I leave the city. And you? Still not leave?"

"No."

"Shame. You are vhite. Tired. Tired?"

"A bit. The heat, you know."

The imminence of his departure had laid bare his feelings of natural kindliness toward me, feelings he had long repressed. He wanted to do something, he didn't know what. He said nothing and ruminated. He had an idea: "Ven I return, you vill do me the honor of eating in my house?"

"With pleasure."

"Norvegian food."

I was not about to tell him that by the time he got back I would probably be eating French soil, ha, ha! this image, my mouth full of earth, tiny teeming white worms sating themselves on the soft flesh of my armpits, this image afforded me a kind of atrocious joy, I said again: with pleasure.

He beamed contentedly.

What ugliness!

"Have a good trip. My respects to your mother."

Again he seized my shoulders, perhaps on the point of kissing me, then released me, said farewell and I will see you soon my dear, he really said "my dear," went away forgetting his basket, came back to get it, left again, stumbled on the bottom stair, turned around halfway up to give me another wave, which I returned.

Torbjörn Skaldaspilli.

The street, the housefronts, the sky.

The sun stunned you. It hit you behind the ears like a sandbag swung from afar on a cable attached to earth's tallest crane.

You were surprised not to flounder and sink in the burning, shimmering asphalt.

You sweated.

Rue Stella. Hôtel des Étrangers. Lichem. Or Lychem. Lychemme, Lychaimme . . . Could that be his car? In front of my Dauphine, stretching (that was the word) all the way to the corner of Rue Grolée, was a red Ferrari, brilliant red, glistening, sleek, immaculate, a beautiful new model Ferrari Mondial Quattro, probably one of a kind or numbered. Lychemmh had the stuff all right. Unless it belonged to someone else and was parked there by chance.

I didn't care. I got into my Dauphine, also red, but washed-out red, a pockmarked wrinkled old bag, I was careful to slam the door gently to protect my skin, so sensitive that a simple noise could sometimes set it hurting.

I did not so much as glance into the lobby of the Hôtel des Étrangers.

I drove.

Place des Jacobins, Rue du Président Édouard Herriot, along the waterfront, Lattre de Tassigny Bridge, the Rhône irritating in its timelessness, Rue Duquesne, my own four open windows, the streets, the housefronts, the sky so blue, it could be said that the sky was blue, and that there weren't too many people in town.

Nobody.

And yet here was a couple approaching me from Rue de Sèze. I got out of my car, parked in front of 129 Rue Duguesclin, exactly in front, it would have been impossible to be more exact, a couple plus dog, one of those extremely low dogs that wear themselves out at the end of their leash as if they had the whole world to haul along, the woman held the leash, a blond beauty with a haughty face. Her companion, on the other hand, his arm wrapped around her, was a disjointed dwarf, hairy, thick-chested, neckless, with arms gnarled as vine branches, spindly corkscrew legs, hair flattened on top and sticking out on the sides, nose big, purple, and spongy, one cheek cavernous, the other bulging, one eye protruding as if ready to leap from his head, the other sunk somewhere deep into his brain, and an anarchic gait, the gait of someone whose component parts had moments earlier been poured from a mechanical hopper, and who, despite the speed of his fall, or perhaps because of it, had succeeded in reassembling the whole and making it work more or less as it was supposed to, for each graceful movement of his companion he executed a thousand contortions. A couple so disastrously mismatched from an aesthetic standpoint that I automatically sought the flaw in the woman, a mutilation, something that branded her, a hand, an ear. I found nothing. Some inner ill, then? A urogenital complaint devouring her pubic zones despite the deadliest of antibiotics? Perhaps. I did not know. I could not say.

Mr. and Mrs. Lichem? No. Blond beauty and clothed ape passed by without paying me heed, without seeing me.

Every shutter on Rue Duguesclin was closed.

The elevator went no higher than the sixth floor. One floor on foot to reach the rooms under the roof.

Second door on the right. It was exactly 10:00 A.M. I put on my coat, removed my glasses.

I knocked.

A man opened, medium size, shifty eyes. He put out a hand.

"Mr. Lichem?"

"Yes."

I dared not ask him how it was written. How to spell it. The room, small and overlooking an inner courtyard, was empty. No furniture, not even a chair, on the ceiling a naked light bulb. No telephone. Just one picture hanging to the right of the window, a picture in very low relief, which immediately struck me (and I turned out to be right) as a collage of vegetable peelings and dried fruit.

A black leather briefcase leaned against a wall.

Number 129 Rue Duguesclin. Here or elsewhere, I told myself. Besides, wasn't I here, elsewhere, everywhere and nowhere? Yes, I was. And master of my own life and death. And master of the lives and deaths of others, for instance I could kill this shifty person who had greeted me with his gaze riveted to my ankles. Or else he was armed, or an unarmed combat champion, and it was he who would kill me?

We stood there in the room, six feet apart. I had not yet seen the eyes of this man who was without distinguishing characteristics, who was average in every way, height, dress, thickness of hair, quality of suit, shine on light brown shoes. But he had cut himself near the mouth shaving. And sunglasses, sticking like my own from the top of his coat pocket, had pinched his nose and reddened it at the bridge.

"Mr. Lichem, I am simply one link in the chain, as you undoubtedly know. As are you, the most important one at the moment. I do not know the identity of our employers, nor will you. And we will never meet again after today. The child's name is Simon de Klef."

I understood immediately.

If he had not looked at me until then, he made up for it in the second following his statement. His eyes suddenly bored into the depths of my being. I felt what was almost an internal tickling, first inside my head, then in my whole body (the way Gulliver felt, except he felt it on the surface of his body, when the Lilliputians loosed their thousands of arrows at him). Naturally I stood firm under this scrutiny and maintained the impassivity of an inanimate object. If he was testing me, he was wasting his time. Had he asked me to kidnap fifty children and hang them in a cluster from the tip of the metal tower of Fourvière after painting them yellow I would not have turned a hair.

When the second was up he went on speaking and looking at everything except me. I was sure I had made a good impression.

I liked listening to him. His voice was soothing. I listened.

"Simon de Klef." (He spelled it.) "He is ten years old. Son of Colonel Simon de Klef. The mother is dead. They live at the Impasse du Point du Jour, number 12, a villa. Point du Jour

neighborhood in *district 5* of Lyon. The colonel is a total quadriplegic. He lives in a wheelchair. Totally paralyzed, blind, mute.
Deaf. A body, nothing but a body. The person who looks after
him and the child for most of the year is on vacation. Her place
has temporarily been taken by the colonel's daughter, Simon's
half-sister. That's all. Take your time. Our employers insist on a
flawless job. As soon as you have the child, call 812–2121. Until
then, no unnecessary contacts. If you still agree, I am required to
give you the five thousand dollars, in cash, necessary for your
immediate expenses. As for the rest, it will all be handled the way
you specified. That's it. Nothing more to tell you. For that matter
I don't know any more."

He stopped talking. He looked at me, a second look. He was
waiting. I gave a simple nod: yes. He walked to the black leather
briefcase, took another black leather case from it, a very slim one,
and handed it to me.

"Do you want me to repeat what I've told you?"

I did not hesitate: no.

A professional of my caliber didn't need to have things
repeated. Besides, I had retained everything, nothing like not
trying to retain anything for helping you retain everything, and
even the things that I quickly forgot and yet didn't forget, and
that stagnated within me, weighed on me.

I approached the picture by the window. It attracted attention
both on its merits and because there was nothing else in the
room. It depicted a crowd, at once grotesque and threatening, of
identical and highly stylized characters, a banana peel for the
bodies and the tip of a squash, I believe, for the heads. The
ground was made up of orange peels blackened by the treatment
meted out to them by the painter, with here and there fine bright
splashes. The sky, painted yellow just above their heads, turned
blue as it receded. It was the sky of a religious painting in the
ancient style. The characters seemed to be looking at you despite
their lack of eyes, to be delighting dispassionately in your unhap-
piness, in your suffering, in your death throes. This looking
without looking left you uneasy.

In the corner on the left, initials doubtless: DPH.

"Original, isn't it?" said the other link in the chain, who in my opinion had a more important part to play than he chose to divulge. "I examined it before you arrived. Very original. Peelings, no? What do you think?"

"Oranges, bananas, squash," I said as I turned toward him. "Well . . ."

I was putting an end to the meeting. I wanted to leave this room. Putting the finishing touches to a good, strong impression.

"Mr. Lichem . . . I'll let you go first. Good luck and goodbye."

We shook hands. He looked at me, the third look. Perhaps he had the fleeting urge to prolong our conversation by a few words. I had no such urge.

We left one another to our respective fates.

Surprisingly, the elevator was no longer on the sixth floor. Someone who had not fled the city? And who lived in this building? Probably.

I pushed the button.

I waited, a long time, a very long time. The elevator was slow (although this had not struck me on the way up). Or my perception of time was getting twisted. Or the machine was on its way up from the antipodes.

•

I threw the slim leather case into the glove compartment. Five thousand dollars. A good morning. Still no Mr. Lichem, the real one, in sight. No doubt he was straining to locate the next link in the chain. A difficult task. I wished him luck and drove away.

I drove down Rue Duguesclin until Avenue Félix Faure.

Right onto Cours Gambetta. I passed the apartment of Anne the fairy queen. Where was she at this minute? Traveling the roads of summer, laughing uncontrollably in the company of her musician companions, careless, suntanned, delighting in new horizons . . .? Every now and then, though, the attentive observer detects on her face the shadow of a care: is she thinking of me? But soon, we may rest assured, she will think of me less. And then not at all? Or yes, still? I could not say.

It didn't matter. My body was that of a living person, I moved, I articulated words like a living person, but I was rushing more swiftly than ever away from the realms of the living. Some secondary effect of the Alymil 1000 was in all likelihood influencing my perception. Rue Stella, Hôtel des Étrangers. Lichem's hot rod had disappeared. No, it was not his. A specialist in dirty tricks would never draw attention to himself by parking a hot rod in front of his hotel.

Climbing the stairs drained the last of my energies. I closed the door of my obscure dwelling and leaned back with my shoulders to the wood, shaken by great tremors, my head sawing back and forth like a horse's, my arms describing speedy and complex figures in the air, all movements permitting me to dominate somewhat the frantic irregularity of my heartbeats, would I never again have the strength to set one foot in front of the other but have to hop along with my feet together, I asked myself in jest.

I stowed the slim case with the fortune in the bottom of the chest of drawers, same drawer.

Then I went straight to my bed and dropped into it like a felled tree. And I went to sleep.

Ten minutes later I woke up. But I had to sleep. Nothing else to do in the next few hours except sleep, since I was so sleepy and there was nothing else to do.

I undressed, set the quartz alarm (blip, blip, blip) to go off at 4:20 P.M., and then, to force fate's hand and to turn me into someone sure to knock himself out until 4:20 P.M., went back to bed. Why this awakening after only ten minutes? I had thought I was burying myself for eternity in the black hole of sleep, and here I was tossing and turning, with sleep as distant and inaccessible as some far mountain peak!

I was tired, so tired! I had an idea. I pretended I had succumbed, that I was already asleep, flat on my back, lids shut, closed fists emerging from the sheets on either side of my face, and doing my best to reproduce the noisy breathing of one sunk in the most bestial of slumbers.

It worked.

At 4:20 P.M., the accurate quartz alarm unleashed its wicked stridulations, low-powered but insistent, piercing, carrying for light-years. It was my total undoing. The world turned upside down. Impossible to find the alarm in order to end the sonic torment, I merely sent flying a bedside lamp, two glasses, and an empty bottle that happened to be there, with a sweeping uncoordinated gesture that damaged the back of my hand against the wall. To hell with the alarm, let it ring! To shake myself out of my sluggish, clumsy state I resolved to hurl myself out of bed, but my foot became tangled in the sheet and splat! a belly flop into the middle of the room, I seized the occasion to snatch a few more moments' sleep but pain obliged me to rise, I had hurt my ribs, my sluggishness returned, with half-closed eyes I went and urinated in the kitchen thinking it was the john, unusual sound, now flush, I gripped the naked ceiling bulb and gave a sharp tug, nothing, not working, then I had trouble pulling my shirt on upside down, telling myself these department store pants had turned out to be badly cut after all, then I slipped a shoe onto each hand, astonishing, I couldn't have laced them if I had tried, and crawled away on all fours thinking that usually your only contact with the ground is through your shoes, so I began to shoot my legs out to the right and left in order to achieve this goal and then, yes, then I really hurt myself badly, on the nape of my neck, I cut short my vaudeville acrobat act, shook myself and started all over again from scratch.

Ice-cold shower.

•

Ferrari not there. The cannonball from another world had left for its other world.

Rue du Commandant Charcot.

Accidentally paying attention to a phone booth some jokers had half painted red, I braked suddenly: the police. Perhaps I should inform the police, before this matter of kidnapping vanished beneath veils of mist thicker even than the misty cage of oblivion in which I kept all things?

I stopped at a total of five phone booths along the length of the Rue du Commandant Charcot. In the first (the red one) the machine wouldn't take my coin. It would not go into the slot although nothing appeared to be obstructing it. In the second booth I managed to force a coin into the machine. But that was all. Nobody would ever again force a coin into that same slot. The third machine spewed forty-three dimes into my hands and then immediately stopped working. The fourth booth was not a phone booth but some other kind of booth, I left it mad as a hornet. My coin easily entered the slot in the machine in the fifth booth. Easily. I heard it tumble and clink around as if it had plummeted into the depths of a washing machine, then nothing.

I gave up. Later. Besides, I had temporarily — and perhaps more than temporarily, perhaps even permanently — thwarted the plans of the kidnappers, who would not have any idea what was going on. Or Colonel de Klef would pay the ransom. I was truly, outrageously furious. My old Dauphine had to take the consequences, but sensing that it would be pointless to oppose me it climbed the winding slope from Francheville-le-Bas to Francheville-le-Haut with the precise passionate swiftness of a Ferrari.

I loved it, it was a good car, and its headlights lit up the road like no others.

●

Same distance to cover between the creaking gateway and Rainer von Gottardt's almost bucolic dwelling, under a sky as blue as yesterday's, halfway there, like yesterday, the Maestro appeared, dressed the same as yesterday, perhaps he was about to say the same words, and yesterday would begin all over again, no, this time he came to meet me, a few steps, a hip a shoulder, the other hip the other shoulder, with the gait of one who has forgotten the instinctive movements necessary to a human being's forward progress.

His hands were those of a monster of the deep. He switched his cigar from his right hand to his left and held out his right to me. He seemed less dead than twenty-nine hours earlier. Sleep, probably.

"Happy to see you again. What heat! I have traveled a lot, I have seen many countries, but I do not believe I have ever been as hot as I am in Lyon at this moment. On the second floor" (his head twitched half an inch in the direction of the second floor of the house) "it's unlivable. In the middle of the night I came downstairs to sleep. From now on I will sleep downstairs. And anyway, those stairs . . . It takes me a half-hour to pull myself up . . . Come, dear Michel Soler."

I fell into the couch where he must have spent the night, for the soft black leather was only just reverting to its earlier form, resilience, and elasticity, bent out of shape by unaccustomed and relentless pressures for which its manufacturer had not intended it. And how had the pianist managed to rise? In my opinion, he must first have had to roll onto the floor.

"What would you like to drink?"

"If I might, a coffee, I—"

"Of course."

"I can fix it myself if you like?"

"Don't be silly. I shall do it. Rest a little, you look worn out."

I had not yet shaken off the secondary effects of the Alymil 1000. Following my recent telephone adventures and the frantic motor climb up the hill, I had sunk into a gloomy lethargy which a few moments later had me replying as follows when the pianist asked me if I was still willing to take down the story of his life and retell it in my own way, making my own choices as to tone and style, he trusted me: yes, but a suffocated yes, awkward, throttled by a voice that I had already noticed in the course of the past few hours and that now thundered into my ears that I would not survive this day, that as soon as I got home I would go straight to the chest of drawers.

But I went on living just as if nothing was the matter.

He too drank coffee, one drink among so many forbidden him. Cigars, white wine. He was killing himself. I thought of my mother's heart.

"It is hot," he said, putting his cup down.

"Ooooohweell . . ." I said.

"Yes, it is hot!"

"Only because it's not cold out," I said.

My automatic remark tickled him, because it wasn't cold out, ha, ha!

"You are married?" he asked.

"No."

"Have you ever been?"

"No."

"Nor have I." (Suddenly:) "But you have loved women? You have loved a woman?"

"Maybe. I think so. I don't know," I said.

"You are still young . . ."

I thought I understood why he had given such a strange turn to the beginning of our discussion. I asked at once: "What about you? Have you loved a woman?"

"Yes. Yes, I can say that I have loved a woman."

The thought had set him dreaming. I had guessed right and had asked the right question. Rainer von Gottardt needed to say that he had loved a woman.

A silence ensued. I waited. Nothing more came forth. He had loved a woman.

I swallowed a mouthful of coffee. The coffee made me sweat, but it was good, free of that taste of dead leaves that had adulterated the recent coffees I had consumed.

"Do you know the Dioblanízes well?" he asked at last.

"No."

"I recall that Isabel . . . Isabel Dioblaníz told me that you never sent them your book."

"I didn't send it to anybody."

"A remarkable book. A sort of interpretation in words, in no way like all those music books I detest so much. What wonderful moments I owe you! As for your not sending it to anybody, if you only knew how well I understand you! I should have liked to record *The Well-Tempered Clavier* for my ears alone. And for yours, dear Michel Soler. I am so glad I wrote you that card from the Château Marmont. I must confess that I hesitated. I even hoped it would never reach you. That you would not appear here at noon yesterday. And yet I hoped for your arrival with all my strength . . ."

He was beginning to speak with greater difficulty, in a slower, lower voice. An interpretation in words! When you are incapable of an interpretation in music, I thought, but without bitterness, for the time of bitterness had passed myriads of decades ago.

I did not know what to say. "Thanks. Thanks. And you . . . do you know them well? The Dioblanízes?"

Wrong question? Unwittingly indiscreet? It seemed to me his tone was only slightly livelier, more composed, less natural, when he answered, "Yes. Quite well. But I have not seen them since 1969, the year of the concert."

"In 1969 you . . ."

This time a shadow of severity took up residence in his fine intelligent eyes, attractive despite the eyelids which were those of an old iguana, so much so that I did not persist and besides in my confusion forgot the meaningless words I had been on the point of uttering. It was after all von Gottardt (the player of genius, the object of my long-standing and unshakable veneration) who had first mentioned the Dioblanízes, if mentioning the Dioblanízes annoyed him, he had only to avoid mentioning the Dioblanízes.

I could not go on. How long would it take this accursed and delectable coffee to complete its work of stimulating mind and body?

"In 1969? Yes . . . ?"

"Nothing in particular."

"In 1969," he said, affable and good-natured from one second to the next, "I lived for some time with Hector and Isabel. Two lunatics, believe me. Particularly her. The birth of Jésus, their blind son . . . But you know the story?"

"Yes," I said.

The Dioblanízes had long believed that they would never be able to have children. Then one day in Lyon in 1967 there was born in Isabel's shrunken womb a small being of the masculine sex and with dead eyes they had named Jésus, like his grandfather who had died in Bolivia as a consequence of being kidnapped by a revolutionary group who had exchanged him in pitiable condition for a hundred of their own people. After the birth of the blind child, they had succumbed to a form of madness that had kept them cut off from the world, Hector for four months, Isabel for more than a year. Their wealth was great. They were already rich and manufacturers of pharmaceuticals in their own country. A handful of capable and devoted lieutenants, Bolivians all, kept the laboratories running smoothly, they devoted themselves fanatically to music and to their baby Jésus.

Rainer von Gottardt had been silent for some time—stopping short on the road to some confession? Then he said to me: "Will you go to their concert this year?"

"I don't know."

"Nor I. I don't know. Back then I could not help feeling a certain affection for them. Particularly for her. If you like, we can begin."

Begin? Had he not already told me the most important thing he had to tell me today? He had loved a woman. Isabel Dioblaníz? I was wearing myself out with questions. I forgot.

Begin. Yes, I wanted to begin. To listen to him, not to speak anymore, just him speaking, forever.

•

"I was born on September 11, 1917, in Wiesbaden, at 66 Blickstrasse, that's the house in the painting above the piano on the left. My father was a general and my mother an opera singer who gave up her career to raise me. Only son. She died shortly after my father abandoned her. She was sick, of course. I listened to music very early. And I made music very early, the violin first, even when I was tiny I loved the violin . . ."

His small silent Saba cassette recorder was on. We had moved to the lawn behind the house, rusty metal chairs and table, ashtray emptied but dirty, white wine, cigars, index finger squashing the large nose, in the shadow of big trees, which at this hour were beginning to mitigate the maddening power of the heat harrying the city.

Not a breath of air, however.

The lawn was like a miniature plateau. In the distance below you could see Lyon.

Sounds of insects or other creatures. Buzzings, dronings. Whisperings, rustlings. Burblings, purrings, clickings, warblings. I was lost. I have already mentioned the unbelievable extent to which I was confusing things. A background noise had been almost interweaving with the pianist's voice, sounding more and more otherworldly, as the hours (three) went by, the coffee was not bringing me back to the slightest semblance of life, and there he was dying in my presence, the blood draining from his lips, he had recalled Wiesbaden, Lyon sixteen months later (his father, incongruously the friend of Liebknecht and compromised in the Spartacist socialist movement despite his general's rank, suddenly fleeing Germany), the United States in 1933, Philadelphia, he had been sixteen at the time. Musical studies, already an active quest for anonymity. War, travels, rewards everywhere and on every occasion. Disappearance of his parents, sorrow, youth, beauty, talent, and solitude, chastity (he stressed chastity), work pursued in an anonymity preserved as jealously as humanly possible . . .

By the end, Rainer von Gottardt was forced to hold the recorder close to his mouth, his speech organs no longer emitting anything more than long fffffs freighted with frothing saliva, weariness, illness, despair dispatched the words to his throat where they roiled with so much poor rage that they managed to hoist themselves to the edges of the bloodless lips, and there, on the brink of those lips, which could do nothing but remain open to grant them passage and which were drowning themselves in an excess of saliva, the words did not take shape, they grew feeble, they slipped back down to the pit of his intestines, beneath the heart whose beating was audible behind his shirt.

Clack! End of the second cassette. None too soon.

He fumbled in the pocket of his khaki pants, pulled out a bottle of white tablets, swallowed one of them with a mouthful of wine, brows hoisted high on his bald forehead.

•

The painting on the left, then, depicted the house where he was born, Blickstrasse, Wiesbaden, a large white house on whose front stairway a well-behaved child with the face of an angel stood with his hands behind his back, Rainer von Gottardt in person, he told me, at five.

"But you were no longer in Wiesbaden when you were five?"

"No. I was here. The painter, a friend of my mother's, came to visit us. He retouched the original painting."

A memory assailed me, distant, lost. I was a child. I was spending my summer vacation on a farm in the country with relatives of a friend of Liliane's, in an old rather handsome farmhouse. Sometimes I would read in the shade of the elders by the huge beam buttressing the right-hand wall of the farm facade. It was by no means uncommon for tourists, zealous Sunday painters, lured by the picturesque look of the building to come and draw it, nor that I should be depicted reading in some corner of their sketches.

Such was the memory that assailed me.

The second painting seemed to be the original of the postcard reproduction I had received from the pianist, Château Marmont, the young man, the Porsche, the billboard.

Rainer von Gottardt, calmer, proposed that I share his modest meal. The day he arrived a taxi driver had helped him bring in supplies, just standard provisions, but anyway he was amply stocked.

"Alas, tonight I cannot," I said. "A previous engagement. I am sorry. Thank you."

"Another time?"

"Another time with pleasure. If there is anything at all you need, I am of course at your service. Don't hesitate to ask."

"Thank you. Nothing for the moment."

We agreed to meet again in two days' time. The idea of a second session the next day terrified him. In the state he was in, he said, he had to measure out his efforts, carefully husband what vital energy he still possessed if he hoped to reach the end of his story. And he wanted to.

I parted from him as if I were really going to see him again.

I reached the gate. I knew he was watching me from his front door.

"And your mother? Her heart?"

The cunning devil! I made a whole series of faces and head movements intended to convey to him that all was well on that score, then I waved my hand (he waved his) and walked to my car, fast.

Click, click, click, the two cassettes rattled together in my right pocket, I should have put one in each pocket.

•

I raced to my mother's.

Yes, God deliver us from the sun, all the way I had the sun full in my face, it had set fire to the house where I was born, my almost-birthplace, it looked as if it were in flames.

On the second floor Liliane was swallowing a cranberry tart. There was a rugby match on television. They were crashing mindlessly into one another. The sound hurt me. I lowered it.

We kissed.

I found Liliane livelier than usual. She raised the clustered fingertips of her right hand to her mouth and arched her eyebrows inquiringly and I replied that yes, yes, I had had dinner, nevertheless racadoo vram tur tur turt cranberries ooeem ooeem blookh meecado uttered most vehemently, I was obliged to taste the tart.

No, no coffee, I said.

Coffee could no longer do anything for me.

"You drink too much of it. Had any more heart pains?"

No, no more pain. She gave me a pretty, reassuring smile that effaced the vertical wrinkles from around her pretty lips and reminded me of the young Liliane, the Liliane shut away in the big red album.

"They're coming about the phone. Tomorrow around six. It's definite this time. Are you really watching the rugby game?"

Neither yes nor no. She went over and turned off the sound.

Then I heard her rummaging in the closet in her bedroom, yes, the photos, she loved looking at them with me. I could not refuse her this pleasure. Photos of her and of me at different stages of our lives went past without too much effect on me.

I took my leave of Liliane Tormes three-quarters of an hour after my arrival. Her too I left as if I would soon be seeing her again.

"Promise you'll call a doctor if you feel bad again?"

She raised her right hand, she swore. She gave me to understand that she felt well, but that I had as much color in my cheeks as a corpse from the last war.

"The heat," I said.

When she hugged me hard, I hugged her harder, my nose in her white hair, I hugged her hard enough to crush her, Liliane Tormes, my adoptive mother, yes there was one person in the world who would have let herself be ground into bits for me without a whisper, and I was going to abandon her, to leave her alone!

I drove away. She waved from the window. She was smiling. That was rare. Such was the picture of her I carried away with me, standing at her window, smiling, her raised arm now still.

•

Rue Stella. I switched off the engine.

A man emerged from the Hôtel des Étrangers. Roughly my size and age, gray suit, long hair, self-confident walk. He carried a black suitcase.

He walked past the Dauphine and looked at me I believe just as I, removing the key from the ignition and automatically slipping the five thousand dollars into my pocket, had stopped looking at him.

He did not look around. Would he turn right at the end of Rue Stella and go straight to my place without a second's hesitation? Ridiculous. He turned left.

I walked into the Hôtel des Étrangers. I asked the man behind the reception desk if Mr. Lichem was staying there. The clerk, old, sour, bilious, cackling, one of those jokers whose witticisms sow consternation all around them and simply accentuate their author's biliousness, said no, no Lichem here. Are you sure, I said. Certain, he said, since Lichem had that instant paid his bill and left the hotel, so no Lichem here, ha, ha! you poor stupid sod, I said to myself as I thanked him.

I delayed the hour of my death for a few moments. I granted myself a stay of execution.

I reached the Place de la République. Lichem was turning right into Rue des Archers. I heard music, an American song. Where was he going? To his car, parked for one reason or another away from the front of his hotel?

Rue des Archers. The music was coming from there, the jukebox of a brilliantly lit bar was blaring out full blast. Lichem had slammed the door of a little metal-gray Fiat Uno, not a Ferrari, after dropping his suitcase into it. He hesitated, then headed for the bar.

Passively I followed him in.

He was sitting in a booth against the right-hand wall, I sat in a booth against the left-hand wall. He glanced idly at me for a second. He had an animal jaw. He was not ugly. He ordered a Scotch, I ordered anything, a vermouth. You had to raise your voice because of the jukebox.

Mounted high up in a corner on my right, a television flickered without sound. The booth seats were reddish in color.

The bar owner, tall, thin, bald, impassive, no more and no less present or absent than a ghost, brought our drinks. He walked with curious little awkward steps, his legs stiff. Lichem paid then and there, emptied his Scotch with one swallow, and left.

I heard his car start up.

He was fleeing! Astonished and worried at not receiving a phone call the other day, he had attempted to get in touch with his closest contact, had succeeded, though not without difficulty, a series of phone calls had followed with the dials spinning so feverishly the phones took off like helicopters, a series of calls at the end of which Lichem had learned, had just learned, that his presence at the Hôtel des Étrangers was known and that he had better bug off, and he was bugging off! They must all be completely in the dark! I had thrown the malevolent machine off course!

Should I nevertheless inform the police before I went home to gorge myself on my five Alymil 1000s?

The vermouth was heating up fast, soon a reddish tea would be slopping in the bottom of my glass.

Night took treacherous possession of the city. The bar seemed to be the only place on the planet that still harbored life, an endangered life that had chosen this site to muster the remnants of its luminous forces. At least the owner did not grudge us light or noise, I heard the beginning of the song Anne had played on my Saba, the carnival night, the stricken lover, his indifferent love.

The owner disappeared.

I was alone in the world, dull lifeless nightmare, in this glowing red bar on the Rue des Archers, at night, with death very close, when (wretched last twitch of destiny, wretched attempt by reality to free itself of the pull of nothingness and conform to the words of the song if only as a memory, however ludicrous, of life!) a girl, a young woman made her appearance.

Well, well, I said to myself.

It was obviously not an exultant "well, well" uttered in gleeful support of the kind of strong notion that can impregnate a dialogue, impose a definite direction on it, arouse the admiration of listeners; no, it was a morose "well, well," uttered in no particular tone of voice in support of nothing in particular, impregnating nothing in particular, imposing direction on nobody in particular and halting the monologue in its tracks at no particular juncture, that kind of well, well.

She sat down two tables from me.

Now this very young woman . . .

She sat down not far from me, in a corner, so positioned that I had only to turn my head to have a frontal view of her.

This young woman . . .

We are all waiting for one face in life. We wait for many things but we wait for a face. I cackled, I raged, I wanted to get up and hurl my glass and metal table against the glass windows of the establishment, I cursed myself, one word leading to another I flung every insult at myself, to no avail: that face was the one I was waiting for!

A face destined for me.

Perhaps. I would soon know. For I had just arrived at an unbelievable decision.

The young woman was not tall, rather slight in fact, and carelessly, almost badly, dressed. She tugged a crumpled pack of brown unfiltered cigarettes out of her pocket. She lit one. Her marvelously sensual and alluring lips pulled thin as she sucked them in to draw on the cigarette, making her ugly. Her nails were bitten. When she stared at her lighter flame she squinted, and after her first long drag on the cigarette her left eyelid twitched slightly before blinking open a little late, it made her seem like a child, you wanted to kiss that very endearing left eye.

Sometimes she looked very young. At other moments you guessed she was closer to thirty than to twenty-four or under.

Her short hair was blond, not a very light blond. Not curly but tangled, twisted, rebellious, abundant, thick, a kind of helmet, light all the same, framing a face sparkling with light in spite of her dark eyes. Like me, she had two creases linking the wings of her nose with the corners of her mouth, the kinds of creases caused by years of bitterness or hilarity, or both, but hers were hereditary, I told myself, from birth. But mine too maybe. She was pale, very white.

I lost myself in contemplation of the young woman. Perhaps because of this, embarrassed, annoyed, she had not so far as I was aware given me a single glance since coming in.

I forced myself to turn and look at the television for a moment. A news bulletin. No sound. The announcer's composed features, then in black and white the grave face of Perfecto Jinez, the missing Spanish ophthalmologist, with his cockatoo crest of hair, then the announcer again, a night of carnival, of light and of music, thundered the glittering jukebox, then you came to the ball like a magic hurricane.

Magic.

A Coke, she asked the owner, the enchanted owner, plebeian ghost that he was, enchanted to the point of risking a joke: nice and cool? Ah! she did not answer yes, she did not shake her head, she merely gave him a smile, but what a smile! The smile of an angel, a smile of childhood, of beauty, of eternity, her soul spoke through that smile, emerging gaily from its envelope of flesh to lay me low, to plant in me the mad urge to kneel on the tiles before her table, a night of carnival, of folly and delirium, in that infernal din I saw only your smile, shuddered the jukebox, the owner hurried off and came back with the Coke, the coldest Coke on earth, I was sure, she poured it into her glass, a little soul still floated about her face of light, the owner left once more, walking with tiny steps, legs stiff, as if clenching his buttocks, which forces one to walk with tiny steps and stiff legs, the jukebox abruptly ceased its clamor.

It was now or never.

An unbelievable decision, an unbelievable risk.

Had someone told me before I entered that bar on the Rue des Archers as if in an ill-starred dream that I would do what I was going to do, I should have collapsed into helpless ill-bred laughter right in front of him, striving like a child to conceal my helpless laughter, my scarlet face averted, hidden behind open palms, breath hissing through clenched teeth, nasal snorts, viscous rattles shaking my breast (although it is obvious that not only do such maneuvers fail to conceal the attack of hilarity from one's interlocutor, that not only do such constraints fail to stifle it, but they also unleash it and make of it the sole object of everyone's attention).

I had decided to speak to her. To beg the favor of a conversation. If she did not disappear at my chaste and reverent approach, I would not die.

No more Alymil 1000.

Unbelievable decision.

"Miss . . . would you allow me . . ." To talk a while, and pay for your Coke (I could afford it, my pockets weighed a ton). Smile at me. Save me!

"Please, leave me alone." Her voice was firm, indifferent. And lower than you would ever have believed. She had replied at once, without hesitating. Naturally, after all those months I had spent staring at her, she must have thought here comes trouble, a sickie who . . . "I wouldn't want you to think . . ."

Not a word. Not another word would come out of my mouth. Help me, help me!

"Please!" Voice extremely irritated, almost hostile. And she had not looked at me.

Without having to be asked again, I left her. Death had just suppressed my last rebellion. I was like a dog, its bounding exuberance cut down in mid-stride by a command, renouncing the sizzling sausage platter and returning with measured little steps to its master's side. I left without paying for my vermouth, without turning around, walked straight ahead without seeing anything, went back to my apartment and swallowed the first tablet.

A minute later, the second.

Strange, dreadful, subtle product, this Alymil 1000. Taking two at once got you nowhere. The stomach, in full flight, rejected them.

Nonetheless, the first two had no more effect on me than Lifesavers.

I had stretched out on the couch in the front room, the one I liked best when all was said and done, my head raised, glass in one hand, tablets (three left now) in the other, my coat on the ground, I was lying down because I knew you had to lie down to take all five, otherwise you might stagger, you might fall . . . anyway you had to lie down.

But the suspicion that I could easily get up and dance a flamenco number nagged at me. And the third pill, the one supposed to bring on drowsiness and the beginnings of paralysis in the lower limbs (that was it, that was why you had to lie down), merely brought on a dazed sense of generalized and not unpleasant fatigue. It was worrying. I must have slept too long this afternoon and last night. And was it conceivable that certain organisms might resist to the point of . . . No, not to the point of. All you needed was a little patience.

But I wanted to get up. To see, to check whether I could stand. I got up. I could stand.

I went to the kitchen in the clutches of a kind of calm panic. I wanted to shut myself in there and turn on the gas. I was not in the mood to wait for death forever.

Just past the kitchen door I felt myself weaken and sat just in time on a chair. A little water spilled on my right wrist.

I took the fourth white tablet.

The fifth was supposed to lead fairly rapidly to deep coma. Should I go back and lie down? But I might fall on the way. I might be unable to take it, that fifth tablet. Yet nothing suggested that a deep coma was on its way. Unless you had to have already taken the fifth tablet to really feel the coma coming on?

Time ceased to pass.

I gripped the chair. No question anymore of walking. My thoughts began to blur. I was scared. Of not dying, of dying, I couldn't tell.

I turned all four gas burners full on. And I had the strength to swallow the fifth tablet.

I couldn't see much anymore. My vision was askew, distant. I was paralyzed, yet everything was moving around me. But nothing mattered much anymore, I could fall off my chair, I did fall in fact, a sort of long forward tumble, I had not mailed the letter to Liliane Tormes, I thought of Anne, and not of the girl in the bar, yes, I did think of the girl in the bar, of Rainer von

Gottardt, my head hit the open kitchen door and sent it slamming against the wall, I hurt, I was scared, I hurt, my God! I hurt
in my body and in my soul, so much pain was not possible, death
came all of a sudden.

FOUR

I coughed.

Coughing woke me.

"What do we do now?" asked a woman's voice.

"He's coughing so he can breathe. To be expected. He's made it. We can take that out now," said a man's voice.

"That" was a grease-smeared tube sticking into my mouth and linked to a machine that had made it possible for me to breathe for the last three hours.

I opened one eye. To glory in the life to come? No, I had grasped the situation.

A smiling nurse said to me in a gentle voice: "This won't be pleasant, but it'll soon be over."

And with infinite care she began to extract the tube.

Beside the bed stood a young doctor, bearded, robust. He wore round glasses with black wire rims. He too spoke gently to me, and with a smile. And he took my hand, the cunning devil!

"Everything's OK. You're at the Hôtel-Dieu. You're doing pretty well, considering what you swallowed. We even got to you before you reached deep coma, thanks to your upstairs neighbor the fireman. He found you right away. My name is Patrice Pierre, I've been taking care of you for the last three hours. And that's about it!"

He finished up with an even broader smile, and let go of my hand.

The tube was removed.

"Thank you. Thank you."

Two hoarse, thick thank yous, one for the nurse, the other for Dr. Patrice Pierre. Then I became aware of a terrible urge to piss, an urge whose relief would, I sensed, suffer only the briefest, the very briefest, of delays, the urge of a babe in arms, to tell the truth I wondered if I was not going to flood my bed incontinent, that was the word, I cackled inwardly with that part of my being that would have cackled through the horrors of torture, through the most horrible of the horrors, time continued to pass, I mentioned aloud this urge to piss ("I would very much like to pee"), of course you would, said Patrice Pierre, the nurse slipped a bedpan under the sheet and looked in the other direction, absolutely to be expected, said the doctor, as soon as you arrived we put an IV into you with lots of liquid just to make you pee.

The nurse took back the bedpan.

"Where is he?" I asked.

The doctor understood, indicated the door with his chin: "There. I'll go tell him. He's tearing his hair out. He ran all the way to the hospital carrying you in his arms. He put a piece of cloth under your tongue so you wouldn't choke. He showed us the bottle of Alymil. He even thought of looking to see what you'd been eating. Nothing, huh? You didn't have much in your stomach."

"May I see him?"

"Yes."

"I'll come back to take your blood pressure in a minute," said the nurse, young and very dark, still sweet, accompanying the doctor to the door.

Torbjörn Skaldaspilli came in, his features ravaged by anxiety, then, under the effect of Patrice Pierre's soothing words, ravaged by a smile.

He was by the bed in one stride.

"Why . . . ?" he asked.

"Thank you," I said. "Thank you."

Two thank yous, just for him.

Torbjörn the Timid was a man who, in circumstances he considered serious enough to warrant it, did not shrink from revealing, openly and abundantly, the inner mechanisms that controlled him. Right now he had to do something.

He did something.

He knelt by the bed, one knee on the floor.

He knelt (on his knees he was almost as tall as the doctor standing upright), his face now so tormented by the agitation of his soul that it seemed as if its sundry components, eyes, nose, mouth, ears, eyebrows, were shifting and twitching and working their way into unaccustomed locations, I mean more surprising locations than usual, an eye under his chin, an ear on his head in place of his hair and his hair covering his left cheek, he knelt down beside me, I had a brief, violent urge to die but I knew in the same second that I was finished for a long time with the urge to die, Torbjörn emitted a sigh that gusted clear across the room, and (this is how the extreme tension that had been building up in this near-saintly personage over the preceding hours resolved itself) took my hand, my right hand which lay there like an offering, abandoned, and pressed it between his own, and when he raised it a little I believed, hoped perhaps, that he was going to kiss it.

He did not kiss it.

I too tried to squeeze but managed only to tickle his palm, because I was very weak, and because his hands were as big as a ship's decks.

Thus Torbjörn Skaldaspilli knelt, took my hand, and almost kissed it.

Then he rose.

It was over.

My two saviors stood there, dumb, no one knew what to say. I noticed I had a big dressing on my left wrist.

"You vill vell now?" asked Torbjörn.

He meant to say: you will be well? I answered yes.

"If you like . . . I stay vit you. I do not leave tomorrow, I stay vit you, if . . ."

The cunning devil! He would have abandoned his mother! Even sick and dying!

"Leave," I said to him with all the valor of which I was capable, that is to say the valor of a rabbit caught out in the open in direct view of the guns. "If you do not leave, I do not want to see you or speak to you again. Leave. I swear to you . . . I swear to you that we will meet again when you return. You will make me Norwegian food."

"You svear?"

"I swear."

He relaxed, so did the doctor, who was watching him with curious and benevolent interest.

Torbjörn Skaldaspilli had seen me enter the building. He had been taking a stroll to enjoy the less hot night air. He was on his way back from Place des Terreaux, he had recognized me from a long way off. Then he had smoked a cigar, sitting on the edge of the fountain on Place de la République. On the way upstairs to his apartment, he had smelled gas. ("Luckily you had turned the gas on," commented Patrice Pierre, wiping his glasses with raised face and blinking eyes.) He had knocked at my door, in vain. I had not locked it, a detail that in any case would not have deterred him, suspecting something he would have entered the apartment shoulder first as if the door had been made of paper, but anyway I had not locked it.

He had put a roll of cloth under my tongue, telephoned the hospital to warn them of his arrival, picked up the tube of Alymil 1000, looked for the traces of a possible meal. "Because of noodles," he told me. "Specially noodles, very bad," I did not understand, "because pumping out the stomach makes pasta swell," explained Patrice Pierre, for Torbjörn, noodles meant pasta.

He had taken me in his arms and raced swift as lightning to the Hôtel-Dieu Hospital, a three-hundred-yard sprint.

On the doctor's advice, my colossal and kindly neighbor left me. He backed out of the room, dumb, his speech faculties temporarily exhausted, all his goodness in his eyes, and waving at me as if we were parting on a railroad station platform.

"Thank you," I told him again. "I will not forget you."

He shook his head, which meant: neither will I.

He was gone.

The room seemed empty.

I raised my left arm. "Why?"

"Three-quarters of an hour of dialysis. The nephrology department is next door." (Patrice Pierre jerked his thumb like a hitchhiker.) "A tube in two big veins and the blood is fed through a machine that purifies it. It's fast. Five liters every three minutes."

"I've never had that but I've heard of it," I said. "I had acute nephritis when I was a kid."

"Oh yes? Completely gone?"

"Yes."

Apart from this luxury treatment, I had of course been treated to the common or garden variety stomach pump, stretched out on a board with my head lower than my feet so that the water would not go down into my lungs, a quart and a half at a time, siphon, start all over again, twenty quart in all. Twenty quarts!

He explained it to me. His explanations were clear and calm. He was proud of his handiwork, proud of having brought me so skillfully back to life.

"We even splashed a little arnica on your face and forehead. You're going to have quite a bruise."

He was silent. I guessed what was worrying him now — my future life, if one could so express it, the long summer days ahead, and the weeks.

"As for other things . . ."

"It'll be OK," I said.

"Sure?"

"I promise you. Do you believe me?"

"Yes. I don't want to interfere. I'm at the hospital every night."

"Thank you. It will be good to know. When can I leave?"

"We'll keep you under observation for two or three days."

"What time is it?"

He studied his watch. His wrist was hairy. He raised his head. His glasses enlarged his eyes and, perhaps because they were round, made his eyes too seem round. He looked like a surprised child.

"Twenty past one in the afternoon."

"I would like to leave."

"When? Right now?" he said, more and more a child and more and more surprised.

"Tomorrow morning."

Not for a second did he play the doctor. He understood. He understood that I was going to leave the hospital as soon as I could stand upright.

"You really want to?"

"Yes. It's depressing here, isn't it?"

He smiled.

"You'll have to sign a release. I'll make sure they don't give you a hard time. They can be a pain in the ass about that. From a . . . physical point of view, I don't honestly see a problem. But wait until you can stand up . . ." (As I was saying: he understood everything.) "I'll give you a prescription. Do what you want with it. Do you feel like sleeping now?"

"I think so."

"Then sleep."

•

And I did sleep.

I was roused from slumber several times by the nurse stopping by to check my blood pressure, but I went quietly back to sleep each time, it was a night of peace, the nurse was so gentle she might have been caressing my arm and at daybreak she even laid her hand on my forehead, it was sweet and pleasant, that nurse was sweet and pleasant.

At ten in the morning another nurse, less sweet, came to take my pressure again. I woke up for good. I told her I intended to leave at once, perhaps Dr. Pierre had . . . Yes, he had, she nodded and left.

I dressed. My hands were shaking.

The less-sweet nurse came back with three sheets of paper, a form to fill out so they could send me the bill later, and then the release, I the undersigned, in case I might dash my head against the front of a building once outside the hospital, laying myself out for the count, or squeeze myself forcibly down the nearest sewer manhole to drown amid rats in fetid subterranean waters.

A prescription from Patrice Pierre. He had scribbled his personal phone number in a corner.

The nurse asked me in a neutral voice if I would like somebody to see me home. I said no, I would not.

I crossed the nephrology department. To my surprise the main ward was full, every bed occupied, much too close together, one patient's hand (with large dressing on wrist: dialysis) reaching out to grasp a flask of tea and closing instead on the nose of another patient who raised loud protests, various groans were audible, a cart was going the rounds picking up urine samples, propelled by a black male nurse broader than he was tall, the urine of the dying was of all shades, some having filled their flasks brim full with a pallid pinkish liquid, others having scarcely tinted the bottoms with bright red or black, in one of the flasks there was even a kind of quivering greenish soup that attached itself to the sides and clung with the stubbornness of living matter.

Then an old man raised his head and brayed: "Orangeade, mint, lemonade, pomegranate" (a refined joke I had often heard during the distant time of my own kidney ailment in the hospital at Antiquaille), gave a laugh that would have chilled an Eskimo's spine, and fell back on his cot, lids closed, mouth fighting for air, sick, wretched.

The male nurse (not black after all, he was merely dark of hair and skin), I swear the male nurse was running a race, as he left the ward he nearly squashed me against the wall with his cart, I let him go ahead of me with bad grace, didn't have a choice, I was full of anger, an anger no longer directed at myself but at the world.

I could have killed the whole world.

The peace, the serenity, the grace, the love of last night were no more, and the night itself was already retreating into oblivion.

·

For a quarter of an hour I roamed the twisting corridors of the old Lyon hospital before I found the exit.

I found it.

I emerged onto Place de l'Hôpital, small, restored, white-washed, beautiful. I stretched my body in the burning sun. Then I crossed my fingers and turned my hands palms outward, thrusting my arms as far forward as possible in this twisted posture, which stretched my fingers without making them crack, my joints do not crack like certain people's.

My left wrist hurt.

The shaking in my hands persisted.

Above the entrance to an apartment building, next to a café with lowered shutters, a plaque commemorated Louise Labé and her amorous writings.

A short stretch along Rue Confort led me out almost opposite Rue des Archers. I realized that I was perambulating with big slow strides, torso leaning forward, arms dangling to the ground, but with my head held up straight to avoid hitting one obstacle or another.

I rectified my gait.

The Bar des Archers was still open. I was hungry. And I owed the owner for a vermouth. Could I eat? Assuredly, if I was hungry.

I sat down in the same spot as yesterday. The owner arrived. As soon as he saw me he rushed to the jukebox. Too late. The reader will not long wonder what I mean. At the very second he bent to insert a coin, his back toward me, in the ten-thirty stillness of that summer morning in Lyon, he emitted an incongruous intestinal noise the likes of which I had never experienced, the likes of which I would never have suspected to exist, an urgent rattle of thunder, copious, larded, unequal, chaotic, astounding in its abrupt variations of pitch, rhythm, and intensity, a monster of sonority that swelled from a bird's sigh to the roar of a coal mine explosion, running the gamut of the drumroll, the coughing fit, the throaty laugh, the sound of a book being riffled quickly under the thumb, the hoot of an owl, a Gregorian chant, and a grenade assault bubbling out of the trenches. The wretch waited in rigorous immobility until his bowels called an acoustic halt, which supervened after one last boiled hyena's mew, then he turned to me, hand clapped to mouth, eyebrows raised, like a child caught in a naughty act. He was painful to behold.

"Forgive me," he said to me. "How mortifying! It's a sickness, a real sickness. I suffer from uncontrollable wind. That's why I keep the jukebox going full blast. The TV isn't enough on its own. Forgive me . . ."

He was disgusting, pathetic. I forced myself to adopt a civil attitude and civil speech — and of course made no mention of this sorry matter of wind.

"My head must have been in the clouds last night. I left without paying for my vermouth. Do you remember?"

"Yes. But it's on the house, don't you worry about it. Woooooow! This heat! I'm the owner's brother. I came to replace him yesterday. He knows all about my infirmity. But he doesn't want to leave his bar closed for a minute. He's a miser. If you only knew what a miser my brother is! Mind you, there are more people around than you'd think. And it doesn't bother me. Might as well be here as anywhere else . . . My wife has just left me." (He said all this rapidly and without changing his tone of voice, and went on in the same way without breaking stride:) "What can I get you?"

A café au lait with croissants, which I eagerly devoured, then another, I was hungry, a hunger that demanded rapid and complete satisfaction, the hunger of someone who had never eaten, of someone who had never been hungry.

Most eagerly. It was delectable.

From my rear pocket I removed the worn billfold Liliane had given me on my thirtieth birthday and paid the owner's brother, a ghost in broad daylight, his babbling attack of guilt somewhat abated. I rose, he moved away, seemed about to make a stop at the jukebox, decided against it, went around the counter and vanished into a back room with tight rapid steps, his backside in full voice.

•

The shutters were closed on Torbjörn Skaldaspilli's seventh-floor windows. At this very moment the cunning devil must be embracing his mother in cooler latitudes.

I am still calling him a cunning devil because he had left me a note which I discovered on pushing my door open, a few lines in a child's large regular hand, an exhortation to love life (the Norwegian giant with the face like a tidal wave was going to get under my skin pretty soon, him and the others, Patrice Pierre, the dark-haired nurse, and Anne, and Liliane, and everyone), a reminder of my promise, the joy with which he would very very soon be seeing me again, he wrote very twice, perhaps on purpose, perhaps not.

His signature enormous.

I folded the note and put it away in the chest, bottom drawer, next to the sealed and stamped letter never sent to Liliane.

No more Alymil 1000.

I was alive, completely happy and completely unhappy.

I undressed, washed my clothes, treated myself to a full three-quarters of an hour of washing at the end of which I was as clean as a new penny, I had new blood in my veins, they had hosed down the interior of my being with floods of water, and I had just scrubbed the exterior of the same being as though important inscriptions would appear if I put enough elbow grease into the job!

And then, sitting at the table in the room looking out on the street, I began to write — in my own way, free in both style and tone — the story of Rainer von Gottardt's life, I was born on September 11, 1917, in Wiesbaden, my little Saba (I did find the Dioblaníz invitation behind it, and had put it away in the drawer at the bottom of the chest) kept turning, click, I stopped, clack I turned it back on, click, I wrote, time went by, I drank two cups of coffee. I was writing, but badly. I mean the handwriting. I was having trouble with the act of writing, almost sticking my tongue out like a schoolboy. The sheets of paper didn't look the way they were supposed to. I worked hard but (could it be the trembling of my hands? because my mind wasn't trembling) in spite of myself I was forming letters that were either disproportionately elongated, sometimes vertically (as if frightened by some dreadful sight they seemed poised to escape by speeding upward like arrows or by being sucked downward suddenly like a sword in the water) and sometimes horizontally (moved by the same fear, they seemed anxious to grow slender, to flatten themselves, even to efface themselves for good); or else enormous both vertically and horizontally (taller but also bloated, complicated, as if stricken by a disease that wasn't content with swelling them up from inside, but had also latched onto each tiniest imperfection and turned it into a hideous excrescence, only ceasing its ravages on the brink of a veritable explosion); or else reduced, stunted, just short of invisible, forming shivery lines that sometimes went up or down at the most variegated angles with such rectitude and decisiveness that they did not halt until pulled up short at the very edge of the paper; sometimes on the contrary hesitating, daydreaming, dawdling, backing and filling, throwing fits of temperament, changing their minds, taking their pleasure in idle meanderings, in truth little caring whether or not they would reach that edge with which they nevertheless must sooner or later inevitably collide.

It was strange and uncontrollable, the source of boundless astonishment within me.

I reassured myself: later, a good session with a typewriter would tame and regiment these disturbing fantasies. But I had to have a new typewriter. Mine was decrepit. There were keys missing. If you weren't careful you could bruise your fingers, even make them bleed, on its bare metal spokes. Other keys had no spring in them, when pressed, they raised their arms and fell back with a small ironic plook! without of course printing anything at all. There were still others that printed no better, since you would have needed a hammer and a blacksmith's brawny right arm to depress them. Moreover, with the passage of time the machine had started to type any which way and any old how, there was no longer any point in hitting the right key, you were just as likely to get a logical response by closing your eyes and pounding with clenched fists on the echoing keyboard, but no key gave the same sound, the sounds were so varied you leaped in your seat with surprise.

A new typewriter.

Next I listened to Cantata no. 82 for the Feast of the Purification, and the Prelude and Fugue in B Minor.

Rainer von Gottardt was a genius, pure and simple.

At five o'clock I removed a large sum from the slim case and went to the Carrefour-Vénissieux department store, at the traffic light by the housing project I heard the same warring couple voicing the same reasons for their battle in the same loud and aggressive tones, a shattering din of cutlery being piled up and shoved around, the woman's voice, grating: "Easy to see your mother's been here, all right, can't find a single knife in this drawer."

"When *your* mother's been around, you can't find the drawer," the man replied in equally grating tones.

I stepped on the gas to get away, I would pick up the sequel, I told myself, on my next visit to the Carrefour-Vénissieux, ha, ha! Carrefour-Vénissieux, a vast, flat, verminous creature boring into the ground and sucking unspeakable substances from it, where I bought many items of clothing and food, paper, pens, an electric typewriter, and several other articles whose usefulness suddenly appeared glaringly obvious to me.

The people were calmer, the shoplifting less frantic. All I did was stuff a few cans of white shoe polish into my pocket and knot a blue silk tie around my neck before making my way to the checkout counter.

The little Dauphine was loaded to the brim.

•

I took it all upstairs and put it away.

War, bitter and unrelenting, could break out, it would not catch me with my pants down.

I pulled on blue jeans, a light blue shirt, and the white leather summer shoes. My long hair concealed the splendid bruise on my forehead that Patrice Pierre had foretold. In the complex lighting of the bathroom, I judged myself once again of godlike beauty, but this time there was no scowl; on the contrary, my chest swelled with false pride and with hatred for the world.

The phone rang next door, drrinngg-drrinngg, incredibly irritating.

I went back to my car. I needed to keep moving. The old fool from the reception desk at the Hôtel des Étrangers was standing outside on the sidewalk, idle, fatuous. He did not or would not recognize me. I started up. I was tempted to climb the curb and drive straight at him, forcing him to scuttle back to his reception desk with the hideous swiftness displayed by certain spiders, which is how he probably would run.

I wanted and was afraid to see my mother. Fear was stronger. Too many violent feelings would assail me. Not today. I would just drive around.

But I would be seeing my mother before the end of this day. A singular event would bring this about.

As follows.

●

I drove around, then, with no destination in mind (at least, that is what I thought, for I realized later that I was really conforming to a plan that must have taken root in my mind while I was carefully putting away my purchases from Carrefour, opening and shutting drawers and closet doors, shaking the refrigerator door the way you would shake a lemon tree to make it rain lemonade: victory, awed and tamed, it had offered no further resistance), cruising the waterfront route along the Saône and the Kitchener Bridge, where I turned right and tackled the stiff climb up the road to Génovéfains.

Colonel Simon de Klef, quadriplegic. His son by a second marriage, little Simon de Klef. Well, the child could play in peace. The kidnappers must be in some dark corner pondering their defeat and turning yellow with fear at the slightest unusual sound.

I drove to Impasse du Point du Jour.

Why? Just to be going somewhere rather than nowhere? Did I really think I was just going to ring the bell and say be careful, they wanted to kidnap Simon? Maybe. I don't know. In any case, things turned out differently.

Avenue du Point du Jour.

Just past the Impasse du Général de Luzy there was a small Codec grocery store on the right-hand side, empty but with music blaring. And between Rue du Docteur Edmond Locard and Impasse du Point du Jour I passed a gray Ford Scorpio going in the opposite direction, brand-new, slow, immaculate except for its headlights, which were broken—not smashed to pieces but both of them split, cracked. The only noteworthy items thus far encountered on my semi-bucolic excursion. There were trees everywhere, grass, flowers. The thermometers must have been registering one whole degree lower here than in downtown Lyon.

I parked just short of Impasse du Point du Jour.

I walked a little way down it. At the end of the street I made out a white Lancia. The bright sun-filled little cul-de-sac had an unspoiled, attractive charm, like certain unspoiled, attractive paintings you would like to enter and dwell in because you establish a connection between their unspoiled forms and colors and the kind of life you would lead there, a life that couldn't help being unspoiled and naive, that is why as a youngster I loved to contemplate the lids of certain boxes of cheese purchased by Liliane Tormes, my adoptive mother, a blue sky, candid and cloudless, the tender green of a meadow, a little yellow and red house, a russet cow to milk every night . . .

I reached number 12, the last house on the little street, closing it off to pedestrians: a two-story white wooden house, unusual, in the colonial style or in what I imagined was the colonial style, with a low-pitched roof ending in a porch supported by three columns, a balcony on the second floor, and on the first floor a similar balcony, or at least a kind of balcony you reached by walking up three steps.

A white wooden gate, a flagstone path leading to the three

steps. I turned aside and veered toward the tall spindle-tree hedge so as not to be seen from the house.

Piano music rose in the silence. I at once recognized Granados's second *Spanish Dance,* which I had heard and played so often in my youth. What I was hearing made me think of Alicia de Larrocha's peerless interpretation, but it was not a record, someone was playing, and playing well.

Through a little hole in the hedge I could see the lawn in front of the house. Two people sat there, one old, in three-quarter profile, in a wheelchair, the other a young child sitting in a wicker chair: Simon, father and son, both frozen in a waxlike immobility that was frightening. The child wasn't playing. He was looking straight ahead at nothing. He had long smooth black hair that came down over his forehead in a fringe. His father, body tucked in, protected by a plaid blanket despite the heat, was the picture of advanced decrepitude, face sunken, one eye closed, the other barely open, lower jaw sagging, hair thin and white. He seemed not to be breathing.

Quadriplegic. Defective and paralyzed. A body, nothing more.

The music came from the second floor.

The music stopped.

There was the sound of steps on the balcony, then a woman's voice spoke without tenderness: "Simon, take the shopping bag from the kitchen and go get us something to drink. There's nothing left in the house."

Simon did not speak, did not move, shook his head. The woman must have been looking elsewhere, because four seconds went by before she repeated her order, time for me to move a yard or so, duck down a little, and get a look at the second-floor balcony and the young woman leaning her elbows on it, in pants and blouse, a freshly lit cigarette in her mouth . . .

My heart took several savage leaps in my breast and vaulted into my head where it caught fire, triggering a conflagration that burned my eyes, my forehead, my ears, then descended in free fall to the pit of my stomach where it set about squeezing all my blood down into my toes. I burned, I froze, I trembled.

The person with the rather low voice giving the rather terse orders was the young woman from the Bar des Archers.

The child rose sullenly and wordlessly. He walked to the door of the house. The quadriplegic did not move an eyelash.

"Don't forget to take the empties for the deposit."

She straightened, breathed out and went back into the house.

I could have thrown stones at her. Big stones that would hit her on the back, between the shoulder blades, she would stumble and fall forward, arms upraised, hurting her face, her breasts, her knees!

No, I could not have thrown stones at her.

My plan to take a look around Impasse du Point du Jour had been thrown out of gear. No sooner had Simon the younger and his half-sister disappeared into the house, no sooner had the first notes of Granados (my beloved had returned to the piano) rung marvelously out in the silence of these luxurious and moribund semi-bucolic surroundings, than I had formulated another plan, precise, pondered, insane.

FIVE

I moved away from the house with long strides. I got back into the Dauphine. I drove a little distance down the avenue. I made a U-turn. I waited.

Little Simon emerged from the cul-de-sac.

I started forward, stopped with windows lowered when I was level with him. He was carrying a red shopping bag in which empty bottles clanked. I smiled at him.

"Hello, Simon!"

He looked at me.

God! I was stunned by his beauty (for he was beautiful, he looked like a darker version of his sister), but also a second later by a fleeting glimpse of mischief, disconcerting, painful, this child was inhabited by baleful forces, that was how I put it to myself at the time, there I was looking at the most beautiful little boy on earth when all of a sudden a wave crossed the dark eyes, a swift ripple of spite, of wickedness, altering his face, etching a shadow on his cheeks, making the lines running from the base of his nose to the corners of his mouth almost painful to behold, a swift ripple of wickedness disfiguring everything around him as if with an imperceptible yet enduring sneer!

Such was my first impression of the loved one's half-brother. In all likelihood an exaggerated impression, and one that faded in the minutes that followed: Simon was a serious, somber child who smiled little, laughed little (except in fierce bursts I would successfully strive to provoke at every opportunity), and whose gaze sometimes made you uneasy.

"Do you know me?" he asked, without too much surprise.

"No. But I know your sister. She's told me about you. She's shown me photos."

"Are you on your way to see her?"

"Well, no, I don't have the time right now. It's a pity, it's a long time since I heard her play the piano. Another time. I'll phone her. I recognized you at once so I stopped. You headed for the Codec grocery to get drinks?"

"Yes."

"Want a lift?"

"It's not far."

"The less you walk in this heat . . . Well, whatever you say. But hop in if you like."

My heart was beating fast.

He came!

Whether naturally passive, or just glad of the distraction, he walked around the car. I opened the door.

He got in and slammed it shut.

"Of course," I said, "it's not as pretty as the Lancia."

"Ooooohweell . . . I like old cars. This is a Dauphine. I've seen pictures of them. What's your name?"

"Michel."

"Oh, like my sister? Do you live in Paris too?"

"Yes, just like your sister. Yes, I live in Paris. I come to Lyon once in a while to see my mother. And to work. I'm a reporter. I write stories in the papers. About music. That's how I got to know your sister. Tomorrow, for instance, I'll be working."

The details of my plan were falling cunningly into place.

"Tomorrow? You work even in August?"

"Sometimes. A famous pianist is on vacation near Lyon, tomorrow I'm going to interview him and the story will come out in September. My mother's sick. I'm taking advantage of the job to spend a little time with her. A little bit like Michèle with your father."

Like his sister Michèle who lived in Paris. I got into first gear. I was finding out what a good actor I was. Would he grasp the perilous hand I now held out to him?

Second gear.

"Did Michèle send you out to the Codec?" (I grinned and gave him no time to answer.) "She's a bit bossy, isn't she? Strict?"

He grabbed my outstretched hand with both his, I had hit the right spot, exactly the right spot, he concurred most eagerly: yes, bossy, who did she think she was, why didn't she go to Codec herself?

He was a grumbler.

"Well never mind, we like her just the same," I said.

This time he reached out a small hand to me: "You like her?"

"Oooooweell . . . yes, I guess I like her. It depends. She's a good friend. She can get on your nerves."

"Me too. It depends. She can get on your nerves."

"In any case, she plays the piano well."

"Do you play?"

"Once. Not anymore. What about you?"

"Me? No."

I had pulled up behind a car. The gray Ford Scorpio. Seeing a grocery store open, the driver had probably felt the need to ingurgitate ten quarts of ice-cold liquid before going on his way.

On the sidewalk, a phone booth.

"Here we are! Well, Simon . . . I'm glad we got a chance to meet. Tell Michèle I'll call her. Right now I'm in a hurry, I have to go to my mother's, and later I have to meet some friends."

There was no more I could have done to win his trust. Take my leave. What if he said good-bye, opened the door? Should I yank him back in by his collar, put my foot down, speed away?

I toyed with images of violence.

No. It would suffice to hold him back with words, more words. There was in him a little of that indifference I knew so well, leaving him passively obedient, an indifference disturbed only, perhaps, by that bossy half-sister who got on his nerves.

But more words were not needed. He did not move. He wanted to prolong this unexpected distraction. We considered one another. The heat was murderous. It was impossible to keep your mind off it. He sighed from the heat. I plucked at my shirt to unglue it from my skin. He was wearing a little white short-sleeved shirt and navy blue shorts. His pretty arms and his pretty legs were tanned. He had his sister's straight, rather short nose, and her dark, deep eyes, the same sensual mouth, the same lines.

"The snow'll be melting if this keeps up."

"What?"

"The snow'll be melting if this doesn't let up."

He got the old joke. He had never heard it. It made him laugh, a brief burst of laughter. He repeated it: "Yes, it'll be melting."

He went on looking at me. I amused him, I interested him. I was a change from his sulky sister and his living corpse of a father.

I laid my hand on the gear lever.

"Well, this is good-bye, old buddy."

He tried, not very hard, to open the door. He fumbled it. I helped him.

"I hope we meet again soon. Vacation can get really boring, can't it?"

"It sure can!"

"Same with me. Luckily I have a little work."

I let go of the door handle and the door swung closed again.

"What if we pulled a joke on her, on Michèle? If you'd like to, that is."

He would like to. There was nothing he would like better. His eyes sparkled. He dropped the handle of the red shopping bag with the faint white checks and it sagged shapelessly from the weight of the bottles inside, settling down at his feet like an animal about to doze off.

"Yes, but what?"

"I have an idea. We could pretend I've kidnapped you." (He listened gravely and attentively.) "I could take you to my mother's . . . Naturally we wouldn't tell her it was me. We'd demand a ransom. I'd fix it so she's not too worried . . ."

I stopped for a second. He reacted to my tentative little pause in unexpected fashion: "So what? What if she is a bit worried . . . ?"

I protested with a captivating smile: "No, we mustn't. Not too much. We'll just tell her she has to pay a ransom tomorrow.

She'll have to drop off the money where we say, like in the movies. Later we'll tell her it was all a joke."

"She won't recognize your voice?"

I pinched my nose: "No, I'll talk this way."

Renewed burst of laughter, not joyful, not truly joyful. Letting go of my nose, which I had pinched too hard out of nervous tension, so that the nostrils seemed glued forever shut, I went on: "What kind of ransom?"

"She's rich. She has all Papa's money."

"Well, I don't know. Two thousand? You think we could ask for two thousand? We'll spend just a bit of it, enough to buy her a present so she's not mad. And tomorrow night we'll be together again, all three of us, then she'll see it's me and we'll all have a good laugh. OK?"

"OK. But I think she'll be mad all the same."

"No, you leave that to me. It'll be fun. A lot more fun than sitting in a chair all day waiting for it to get a little cooler, right?"

"You bet!"

"Wow, it's hot! Do you agree then?"

"Yes."

"Well, wait for me here, I'll call her right away. We don't want her to get upset and call the police, do we?"

"I don't know, the police might be fun as well . . ."

"No, no, no police. I don't have my address book, what's the number again? 812 . . ."

"812–5347."

"That's it! I'll be right back. You wait here."

He did not move.

Phone booth outside the Codec. The machine took my coin but, as I confidently began to dial the number, 812–5347, it shot the coin back out into my face. I hung up and stepped out whistling nonchalantly, it was either that or flatten the booth and afterward level the ground around it so no one would dream a phone booth had ever been there.

I smiled at Simon, well-behaved, obedient, passive, and signaled to him (jerking my left thumb at the Codec) that I was going to phone from inside the store.

I absolutely had to call.

My mind was working swiftly and clearly.

Not a single customer. Yes, one old lady, a spaghetti sauce aficionado, pushing before her a cart heaped with jars of spaghetti sauce, a tottering mountain of spaghetti sauce jars towering up to the fluorescent lighting, I of course had other fish to fry but I was nevertheless dumbfounded by the sheer quantity of spaghetti sauce jars, there were enough there to season a lifetime's worth of pasta, one old lady and, in the cold-drink aisle, a fair-haired man of about fifty with very broad shoulders, German-looking, who seemed to be hesitating over the nature of the liquid he would shortly be tossing back behind his necktie.

Hastily I snatched two cans of soda and a packet of frosted cookies, the word "frosted" being automatically irresistible in this furnace heat, and some mints, all in the same aisle, and hurried to the checkout lane to get there before the lady with the spaghetti sauce jars, if I reached it behind her and the checkout girl began to count her jars of spaghetti sauce young Simon would be of marriageable age by the time I left the store, there was dull but not unpleasant music playing, the slow romanza movement of the Concertino in A Minor, opus 72, for guitar and orchestra by Salvador Bacarisse (1898–1963), soloist Narciso Yepes with the Spanish Broadcasting Corporation's Symphony Orchestra, conducted by Odon Alonso, I knew this dull but not unpleasant music well because David, an old conservatory friend, played it, I had known three excellent guitarists at Lyon, David Aurphet, Gérard Roy, and another, Marc, whose family name eludes me, from my association with them I had retained a most lively appreciation for that instrument, the guitar, David, Gérard, and Marc, lost touch with all three of them, completely lost in David's case since he had committed suicide, but at least he had achieved his objective, he had blown up half of Lyon in the Boucle Bridge area.

Absent friends, Salvador Bacarisse, cookies and mints, the Scorpio driver, the lady with the spaghetti sauce, quick, the ckeckout lane.

Call Michèle de Klef.

A man in a white smock, probably the manager or his heroic replacement, had left his glass cubicle and was chatting with the checkout girl, a very young girl who didn't look anything like a checkout girl. I paid, then told the manager or his heroic replacement that I had an urgent call to make, the booth outside didn't work, for that matter no booth in this whole city worked, would he be so kind . . .

He would. I called from his office, 812–5347. It rang six times. Michèle was exactly the kind to play a few extra bars, to finish her musical phrase before deigning to be disturbed . . .

Well, I would pay her back in kind, and teach her to be a little more prompt in replying to calls!

Six times! Answer, damn it!

"Hello?"

"Michèle de Klef?"

"Yes."

"I have just kidnapped your brother Simon."

I sensed her mortal fear. The change in her voice was spectacular.

"What do you want?" she said after a silence.

I was ashamed. I did not speak at once. Nothing would come. She said again:

"What do you want? Money?"

Could there have been a note of hope in her question: money?

"No," I said.

No more hope, mortal fear once again, I could tell by the quality of her silence! Or was I imagining things, constructing arguments with myself the way I argued with my confused feelings?

"What do you want?"

"You."

Silence. (A certain relief on her part? No, that was my imagination.)

So it was her I wanted.

She had refused to say good evening to me, yes, of course, let's chat, why not? Now she would have to submit to my bed and to my presence beside her, inside her, I would throw her down across the aforementioned bed and I would use her body as I saw fit, then I would return Simon to her, bow deeply, and up and away!

"You, I want you, until tomorrow. You will see Simon again after that. You must not worry about him, I told him it's all a joke. He's having fun. Nothing bad is going to happen to him, I swear. Nor to you," I added a little foolishly. "Be at the Bar des Archers, Rue des Archers, just off Rue de la République, at ten tonight."

"You're crazy, I . . ."

I broke in:

"Yes or no?"

"Yes . . ."

I hung up.

•

The Ford parked outside the Codec dwindled in my rearview mirror. The sturdy fair-haired German-looking man was a blizzard of indecision. I switched on the windshield wipers to cheer Simon up. They cheered him up. The absence of rain and the filthy state of the windshield in no way inhibited their manic activity, or very little, the worn black rubber wipers merely writhed wildly out of shape as they scoured the glass with the frenzy and the high-pitched squalling of a disturbed nest of vermin, Simon let out his half-sad burst of laughter.

"This old Dauphine goes like a bomb, apart from the windshield wipers and the headlights."

"What's wrong with the headlights?"

"You'll see when it gets dark. They light up the road at least fifty miles ahead."

"Why?"

"I don't know. They do, that's all. We can give up this joke now, if you like, huh? Whenever you want."

"No, it's great!"

He drank his soda. I had told him that his sister had agreed to the ransom and that the handover would take place late tomorrow afternoon, I had answered all his questions, I had given him all the details he wanted.

Tomorrow was tomorrow.

We drove past the Saint-Irénée University residence hall with its thousand closed shutters.

We began to drop down into Lyon.

You could see the city.

The sun was everywhere.

"Still doing well at school?"

I wasn't taking much of a risk. And yes, he was still doing well. You had to extract words from him. He did not talk much.

"Now where's your school again?" (The tones of someone who has the name and address on the tip of his tongue.)

"Sainte-Croix Academy, at Saint-Just."

"Oh yes!"

Poor kid, a boarding school! And a tough one, I had heard all about it. I ruffled his fine black hair. He did not move, did not let himself be coaxed. He even stiffened, secretly. But perhaps he had been on the verge (even more secretly) of not stiffening?

"Where does your mother live?"

"By the Jonage Canal, in a small wooden house just like yours. You'll see, it's really nice inside. There's a television. My mother isn't really sick, you know. She's just a little bit odd. She got sick once, and ever since she hasn't been able to talk too well. She talks horse."

He began to laugh, then hesitated. "What does that mean?"

"It means speaking all wrong, mixing up the syllables. You can't understand what she's saying. But she understands everything you say. She's very nice."

Suddenly I remembered the insect in the jam. I had to quell a heaving in my stomach. Uugghh! I'd been sucking on it! I told Simon about the episode.

Liliane's phone repaired. Phone her to announce our amazing arrival.

In no time at all we were on the waterfront route along the Rhône. Simon became a little more talkative. He asked me if I had hurt my arm.

"A cat bit me the other night. I dropped my car keys, I bent down to pick them up, and pow! In my bedroom there's a closet stuffed with toys. My dad made them. They're wooden. Want to see them?"

"Yes."

"We're going to eat well. I hope you're hungry? My mother is a very good cook."

Opting against sidewalk phone booths, I headed for the main post office on Place Antonin Poncet. I left Simon in the car. He did not protest. He obeyed. He always said yes.

There was a busy signal. Poor Liliane must be going crazy trying to call me.

One ring. She picked up at once. My heart leaped. My mother's voice once again! Into my ears there came a whole outpouring of onomatopoeia indicative of her gratification at the restoration of her line, I told her how deeply I too was gratified, then I launched into my story: by the most incredible coincidence I had come across an old girlfriend who was headed south on vacation and had stopped off in Lyon with her ten-year-old brother Simon; I hoped to spend the night and the next day with the girlfriend; but her brother would be in the way, his sister and I had cooked up a story for him (which I made up on the spot for Liliane's ears, a kind of story-within-a-story) about a lost wallet and handbag which meant the two of them could not spend the night in a hotel, I couldn't lend them the money till tomorrow (and even then it would be tricky), but that by tomorrow they would surely have found the handbag, I usually lived in Paris, but I was a reporter, I had a job to do in Lyon and I was taking advantage of it to visit my mother, I would let Simon have my bedroom, at my mother's place, friends of mine about fifteen miles from Lyon would put his sister up for the night, we had just dropped her off there, other friends I was seeing tonight would take me in, I was working next day, in short, the kid—his mother was dead—had agreed to stay at Liliane's until tomorrow evening, was dying to, in fact.

I added a few refinements of detail.

Good actor. With a skilled hand I juggled the several false-hoods I had harnessed together. And I was giving Liliane plea-sure, and at the same time reassuring her, with this matter of an amorous adventure . . .

But would Simon have the good luck to be liked by her?

"Naturally I made no mention to my mother of kidnappings or ransoms," I told Simon later. "She wouldn't have understood. And then, the fewer people in on a secret, the safer it is." (He approved gravely.) "I just told her . . ."

And I told him what I had told her, which was just fine with him.

Lafayette Bridge, Cours Lafayette.

He was eating mints.

Every light green along Cours Tolstoï, except the last one, on Place Grandclément.

This time the gray Scorpio with the cracked headlights was not dwindling but growing in my rearview mirror as it turned in off Place Albert Thomas and raced the whole length of Cours Tolstoï to pull up alongside me at a red light on Rue Blum. Its fair-haired driver was rummaging in his glove compartment, I started up before him, he let me get ahead.

"Recognize that car?" I asked Simon. "I think he's following us."

An accomplice of Lichem? The possibility had fleetingly occurred to me. A mind game my mind was playing without me. Obviously an accomplice of Lichem would have taken care not to let on he was tailing me. So the German driver was not following me.

"You think so?" said Simon. "You think that's how he'd act?"

"Sometimes you would. If you're tailing someone who doesn't know you or who doesn't suspect he might be tailed. You pretend to overtake him, then you let him go ahead, then you overtake him again . . . Understand?"

"Then he is following us?"

"No. There can't be more than five cars on the road in Lyon right now, so it's natural you notice each other."

"Can we pretend he's following us?"

He was waking up, getting excited. All the better. I seized the opportunity: "You mean try to shake him?"

"Yes."

"Let's go!"

The Ford accelerated and overtook me just before Rue Pierrel. Instead of going ahead I turned left into this same Rue Pierrel, nobody knows Villeurbanne as well as I do and from this moment on no vehicle on earth could have caught me, at the end of the street I drove the wrong way up Boulevard Eugène Réguillon (a one-way street), a hundred yards in the wrong direction up Boulevard Eugène Réguillon, on the sixth floor balcony of number 80 I glimpsed an elderly couple drawn from the twilight of their apartment by the shrieking of my tires, hello there! like a haggard and elusive fire-breathing dragon I raced left onto Rue Olivier de Serres, crossed Cusset in the same way, took Cours Émile Zola, Boulevard Laurent Bonnevay, Rue Marcel Cerdan, at long last, on Chemin du Regard, I resumed the appearance of someone not pursued by a thousand demons hellbent on his undoing.

Simon was in an extremity of bliss, if it was possible for Simon de Klef to be in an extremity of bliss.

The mints had made him thirsty.

"They're tricky, mints," I told him. "You think they're cooling you, but they're still candy, they leave your mouth tasting like cardboard, unless of course you eat them all summer long, one after the other, without ever stopping."

Number 21.

My mother was at one of the dining room windows, her arm raised, just as I had left her. My heart beat three times faster.

Liliane Tormes! I was seeing her again!

"Shall we wave too?" I asked Simon playfully.

Liliane Tormes was rebellious, she had to be charmed, I knew her madness, I didn't think she would be able to resist Simon.

We each waved a hand from our respective windows.

"You know I can take you back to Point du Jour whenever you choose right?" I told him, switching off the engine.

He didn't choose. In fact, these remarks of mine were starting to worry him. As we climbed from the car with a pleasing symmetry of swinging legs and swaying torsos he was frowning. "Why? Do you want to?"

"Not me. After the ransom. We'd look silly if we did it before."

"Well then?"

We slammed our doors in unison. Simon's gestures were decisive, determined.

I got him to work the hand-operated front door bell. He had not known such bells existed, at least he had never used one. And he had never been in such a drab and out-of-the-way section of town.

From the moment I first spoke to him ("Hello, Simon!") he had loved everything we said and did.

Better still, Liliane and Simon liked each other at first sight. I was relieved. Why did they get on so well? Perhaps the mysterious attraction of one being for another, one madness for another, one weirdness for another — not that their weirdnesses were similar . . . But I could have spent ages attempting to sift the reasons for what happened when I introduced them to one another, I could have dug for eons and vanished down the hole I had dug in the heart of the crater of removed soil and only reemerged later, much later, in the antipodes, in the most distant and perhaps hostile land, so far from my mother, from Simon, and from Michèle, and I did not want to leave them, I did not want to, nor did I want to make connections between appearances and in so doing build castles in the air that mingled so readily with cages of oblivion tall as castles, suddenly you could see nothing, or so little, and then only when you looked beyond these monuments of illusion, the way certain groups of stars dissolve if you stare straight at them, in the same way whatever had formed in my mind would have meant nothing to me but would have crumbled between my fingers as soon as I tried to frame it in words — no, at this blessed moment of the declining day I contented myself with noting that my mother ruffled the child's hair and the child did not stiffen, and that the

comical language of the white, gray, and skinny Liliane Tormes
did not disconcert the son born late in life to Simon de Klef,
quadriplegic, flesh without memory or desire, did not inspire
mockery in him, that he even gravely punctuated the truncated
babble of my mother's words with yeses, noes, and other well
chosen words at exactly the right intervals from the standpoint of
the rhythm and the resonance of the babble thus uttered, and
even of its meaning, for meaning could be ascribed to it, Liliane
and Simon seemed like two musicians harmonizing well, even
though this harmonizing took place against a background of
deception (but of well-intentioned deception), each of them
believing he knew what the other did not, which was of course
false, myself alone knowing everything, the master of truth, the
wicked master of the world and of events!

So Simon and Liliane liked each other, I introduced Simon
to Liliane and Liliane to Simon, hugging my mother as hard as
she herself hugged me, murmuring to her how happy I was to
see her again, no! she could have no idea how happy, I insisted to
her almost with severity.

"Boroloo maro deedeedee bad advicemastoof?" she asked
me anxiously when we were upstairs.

"A cat bit him," Simon answered very naturally and
seriously.

She could not believe her ears, she gave him her warmest
smile. He charmed her! Then she pushed back my hair, having
noticed the bruise, highly visible despite its baptism of arnica.

"Walked into a door. Nothing serious. I'm going to change
the dressing on my wrist, a small one will do. Simon is dying for
a drink," I said as I went into the bathroom, and therefore
speaking in a much louder voice, almost bawling in fact, time was
passing most happily.

I unwrapped the interminable bandage. The arteriovenous
fistula artificially created to allow the introduction of tubes from
the kidney (artificial as well) had flattened. All that remained was
two ugly marks and a huge bloodstain with strange outlines
darker than the center of the stain. I wondered about the curious
shape of the outlines, suddenly I thought of them no more,

swabbed the place clean with alcohol and covered it with two Band-Aids.

Dinner was a pleasant halt in everyone's destiny. I almost forgot Michèle. My mother gloried in guests who did such honor to her fillet of veal in harness. She spoiled Simon, petting him like a second son, or like the son I did not have and she wished I had, and she never allowed herself to be threatened or impressed by the wickedness, the true wickedness that danced at certain moments in the child's eyes, for instance between two bursts of laughter, for I made him laugh, I was getting better and better at it, a wickedness that was perhaps more threatening to Simon himself, you told yourself sagely, Liliane realized as I had realized that Simon was not a bad little boy, an evil boy, but a boy inhabited by evil, if that actually meant anything, and I was to know later on that it did indeed mean something.

No one was interested in television that evening.

"Still have my toys, you know, up there, in my bedroom, hmmmmmmmm?"

My insolently interrogative mannerisms (mumbling, lips pursed like a chicken's backside, brows knit, chin thrust out) brought new laughter from Simon, his laughs could be painful, like the laughter of some heart patients whose chests seem to be bursting open when they laugh out loud, my wooden toys, you know, up there, hmmmmmmmm?

We moved into the room where I had slept for so many years and where Simon was going to sleep. We examined and fingered the many toys made by my late father, the creative handyman, the man who in my opinion never was the lover of Liliane Tormes who never had a lover, wooden toys painted sometimes with childlike colors, animals, houses, entire communities, or gratuitous constructions that lurched into eccentric motion when you pushed a certain spot with your finger. It was years since I had brought out these relics, but there was not a speck of dust on them, Liliane saw to that. They fascinated Simon.

"So you prefer living on the second floor to the first?" he asked her, more talkative by the minute.

"Chtraleefoumee," answered Liliane.

"Me neither," said Simon, "if I lived here, I would prefer the second floor."

And Liliane ran her fingers through his long black hair, several times, while he examined the toys with the intensity of a connoisseur, craftsman, or dealer.

His eyesight astounded us. He could pick out details at first glance, could spot, for example in the ear of a little wooden cat, flaws or peculiarities so small that I had to hold the ear in question an inch from my nose and squint at it to see the flaw or peculiarity at all. He told us he saw better than most people, much better than twenty-twenty vision, he was born that way, with exceptional eyesight. He was modestly proud about it.

Then it was time to show him the photo album, our three faces bent, me with one hand on the back of his neck and one on Liliane's.

•

The time I had set for my departure (9:30) drew near, my nervousness returned and in the last quarter-hour assumed disturbing proportions, I had to fight not to knock things over with sweeping blows of the flat of my hand, or even bounce around the whole second floor on the top of my head with little hops, as natural and graceful as a star dancer on both legs, or sit on the floor greedily eating my toes, or suddenly sag to the ground in a nerveless heap like a creature deprived of a skeleton, or move heaven and earth to enter a flask by its neck, or by a thousand movements of the head see my eyes without the aid of a mirror, or by a thousand others speak into my ear.

My hands were beginning to shake.

"Weren't you supposed to be meeting your friends?" Simon said to me at 9:28, as if the wickedness that then flashed across his eyes at comet speed allowed him to guess everything, everything, and everything.

"Yes, I'm leaving now. How late I am! Never mind, I was really glad the three of us could have dinner together this evening. Weren't you?"

"Yes. Me too. Is it far where you're going?"

"Rillieux" (the first place name that came into my head, probably because of the Dioblaníz Pharmaceutical Laboratories, DPL, Alymil 1000, madness, blind child, benefit concerts, useless yellow signs, I told myself I would go and hear the *habe genug* cantata, that is if Michèle de Klef did not bring charges, if she did I would rot in the bottom of some jail) "Rillieux-la-Pape, do you know it?"

"A little bit."

I had prepared Simon for this state of affairs: no furniture on the first floor at my mother's house, just one bed upstairs besides his, I would prefer to go and sleep with friends and come back for breakfast.

"You're sure you don't mind sleeping here with Liliane, and me coming back for breakfast?"

"He can bring us back nice freshly baked croissants," Liliane suddenly said to Simon's surprise, this time he nearly burst out laughing, as for me I laughed out loud and deposited a gentle kiss on the old lady's forehead.

Everything went well.

We went downstairs.

I switched on the headlights. They set the torrid night aglow from Villeurbanne to Casablanca, those rampartlike constructions in the distance.

"With your eyesight," I told Simon, "you can probably see Michèle writing out the check, two thousand, make sure she remembers all the zeros."

I winked conspiratorially at him, he winked back conspiratorially, then he took my mother's hand as she gave him hers, as if to console her for not being in on the secret.

A child possessed by the devil, but a good little child just the same, who kissed me on the cheek, and whose face I covered with kisses, and who let me kiss him, his eyes closed, a half-smile on his lips . . .

I left them. See you later. I called him old buddy again.

Yes, everything went well! Rot in some jail? Later was later, I told myself, and I told myself too, cunning kidnapper that I was, that I was Simon's captivator not his captor, ha, ha!, the witticism pleased me, I moved up through the gears in my ragged Dauphine, almost a wreck, I had to admit, and yet appearing to benefit from the heat, roaring away evenly the way the heat roared in the hot hot night, and I forgot my mother and her new adoptive son and, between the Jonage Canal and the Rue des Archers, hatred and contempt for the world choked me several times, but I breathed all the better for it, I raced into the night transformed into day by the sick lights of my rattling wreck, I raced as if I were on the road to immortality, one end of the Band-Aid came unglued, I stuck it back by pressing my wrist against my chin, I had not opened my veins to give myself death but they had opened them to save me from death, I was tormenting myself with questions and racing as if I were on the road to immortality!

Michèle.

SIX

I was fourteen minutes ahead of time when I entered the glowing red, noisy bar, the only one in the world, on Rue des Archers. The jukebox was playing a wild, aggressive, tenacious, obsessive paso doble (a rhythm for which, doubtless because of my origins and the infinite number of paso dobles heard during childhood, I was not without affection), forcing you to listen, you had to exert a correspondingly greater violence on yourself not to walk in time to it, elbows in, legs flexed, buttocks pointing rearward, barely repressing an idiotic simper, in order to proceed according to your own interior rhythms, I saw myself in a mirror, tall, thin, dressed in blue (blue coat, shirt, and jeans), hair wildly unkempt, I had never studied myself in mirrors so much as at this time of my death, of a godlike beauty, dark eyes filled with forgetfulness, love, and hatred, nervousness possessed my whole body, as I took my usual place on the seat against the left-hand wall I bruised my hip painfully on the marble edge of the table.

The round marble tables were elegant, dainty.

End of the paso doble, start of another paso doble. The owner's brother, bald, bowels in purgatory, appeared, drew near, smiled.

"How are you since this morning?"

"Very well," I said.

A coffee. A huge one, in his deepest cup. And if he would be so kind (his smile was getting on my nerves) as to turn off that jukebox, I had a date in this very bar with a beautiful friend, it would be nice to hear ourselves without having to yell our heads off. He spread his hands, wagged his head, raised his eyebrows, his way of saying: as you wish, but you have been warned.

He turned the thing off. What a relief!

The television was off.

The Band-Aid came unstuck again. It must be damp, or old, or both.

I drank the coffee too hot and began to sweat and sweat, as Michèle would have said, her mannerisms were already infecting me, she always always repeated words at least twice for emphasis, I looked at my watch every second and a half and at the street the rest of the time, at the sidewalk just outside the bar, I had not parked directly in front so that Michèle's white car would have room.

Nothing guaranteed that she would accept my covert invitation.

She was contrary enough to park a mile away.

But at five to ten, that was exactly where she parked, swiftly, deftly, skillfully, in a twinkling the Lancia Thema lay parallel to the sidewalk, handbrake set, door opening and shutting, she appeared, she made her appearance. My heart launched into a gymnastic routine whose diverse steps I shall not relate here, in truth as many steps as it could possibly take without actually shattering against its cage of ribs. Michèle appeared, entering the bar with a resolute step, almost a swagger, in which her whole body seemed to participate, or rather she swung her shoulders, imperceptibly yet perceptibly, there was something of the boy in her, a slight touch of the tomboy, ah! that this frail young woman should swing her shoulders in this manner, shoulders a little too broad for a woman, imperceptibly, that she should have a touch of the tomboy in her, it sent the tenderness inspired by her celestial prettiness soaring to the very heavens, my excitement was enhanced, rekindled, not diminished or halted by any earth-bound obstacles: the way she walked, certain attitudes, things, everyday details to be seen all around, but which she made her own and which undid you, undid me, for I was grateful to them for making this celestial prettiness more precious to me and for raising ever higher the emotion that impelled me toward her — the way she walked, certain attitudes, certain unchanging inflec-tions in her voice (but she would one day tell me she used to sing alto in a choir), her hands, not perfect (scarcely was she seated than she would light one of her cheap brown unfiltered cigarettes), I had decided not to get up, Michèle was wearing the same canvas pants with the same shirt sloppily tucked into them, she was wearing boots, she had looked at me four times, a half-second each time.

She sat down and immediately lit a cigarette, she grabbed at the pack, lit a cigarette, lips pulled thinly back, eyes squinting over the flame, the left eye. Her dark eyes seemed pale. They illuminated her face and were illuminated by it.

Tangled blond hair, a helmet, a frame, an adornment, a jewel-casket isolating all that beauty from the rest of the world.

No: the whole world was a jewel-casket for that face, that face destined for me!

The owner (his brother) appeared, forcibly clenching his buttocks, his skull and even his ears white from the effort.

Naturally he recognized Michèle.

"Miss?"

"Nothing."

"Yes she will," I said. "An ice-cold Coke, please."

Michèle had her back to him, I judged the wretch to be on the brink of an onset of flatulence, buttocks clenched most desperately to allow him to contain himself before his customers, indicating the jukebox in plaintive pantomime, I glared pitilessly at him, no, no jukebox, sullenly he switched on the television so as not to have to admit defeat, defiantly almost, but the sound was not very high, and suddenly, losing all semblance of control, he rushed behind his counter and disappeared, at least two doors slamming behind him.

Michèle and I were locked in an ocular war of nerves. Every now and then she gnawed on a nail.

I did not know what to say, or in what tone of voice to say it. Neither did she.

I had not been wrong: seconds after the big bad windbag's flight there came to us despite the closed doors what sounded like the barely muffled echo of a naval engagement played out against a high-seas gale, a polyphonic din of roaring broadsides and splintering rigging amid the howl of elements gone mad, the farter was farting hard enough to rip muscle and pulverize bone, but you had to be aware of the nature of the noise, otherwise you wondered, you could think anything you liked of course, perhaps fifty construction workers had decided to renovate the building in record time and all set to work at exactly the same moment on this August evening at two minutes to ten.

It was violent but short-lived.

Not a word from Michèle or me while the owner's replacement, so recently abandoned by his wife, emitted farts that might easily have split his scalp. Michèle dragged so hard on her cigarette I thought it would disappear down her throat as I, unable to say a word to her, struggled to contain a presence of mind seeping out the way water seeps into a hull holed in a thousand places, you bale and you bale, but the hull settles in the water and the boat sinks.

The master gunner returned, relieved, features relaxed, stomach flat, hollow even, with sweeping gestures he set a Coke before Michèle who gave him a luminous smile, although less luminous than yesterday's.

"One Coke coming up! The coldest Coke on earth!" (To me:) "Is the TV bothering you? Would you like me to turn it down?"

"No, no," I said. "A little background noise stimulates verbal exchange. A world war in the next room might be a nuisance, if you get my meaning. But the low murmur of TV? Ah no. And I'd like a Coke too, after that coffee. Please."

The waiter and I were trading jabs.

"Coke? I've heard that coffee and Coke don't go so well together. Bad for the liver."

"Don't worry about me," I told him. "I've got the Liver of No Return."

I cackled briefly, two ha's, loud, loud but dry and forced, instantly recomposing my features to lend them the fleeting air of an ancient and bilious ascetic, Michèle did not smile, I had not expected her to, yet I would have wagered that a smile was almost born in the nethermost depths of her complex soul, and that this aborted birth, if you can call it that, did not leave her features totally unaffected, those features fated for me because (I told myself) I had survived the Alymil 1000.

Ten o'clock sharp. The precise and consecrated hour of my date with Michèle, the hour of really speaking to her.

"Ten o'clock sharp," I said. "We have a date."

She examined me at greater length. At greater length than before. A hideous suspicion clutched at me: what if she did not like me? What if I was not her type? What if she did not at once fall in love with me? No, I said to myself, impossible. For several score hours my powers of seduction had known no limits. No woman could withstand them. No woman? No man either! No child, no animal. At the sight of me, animals would suddenly start to walk on their front paws and utter unnatural cries. Not even the vegetable kingdom was immune to the insanity of my charm, forests would shudder as they felt my steady tread along their leafy pathways, tulips and daffodils would writhe idiotically at my approach, sunflowers would avert their faces from the sun.

Violets would turn completely yellow.

Weeping willows would stretch their branches heavenward in imitation of poplars. Swamp grass would catch fire. Daisies growing in dandelions would devour the dandelions, using their petals as teeth.

"I suspected it might be you," said Michèle. "But I didn't really believe it. You are insane."

I drew myself upright, arms rigidly outstretched, and gripped the edges of the table. Master of the world. I stared at her.

The owner's replacement, his brother, set my Coke on the table, glass against marble, click-catacluck, awkwardly, it was not his profession, and besides there are some in the profession who shatter buckets of glass. Looking at each other (Michèle and I), being unable to speak to one another because of the presence of this resounding man, created a sort of complicity between us, it was better than nothing, proudly the noisemaker withdrew after proclaiming: "A good program on TV tonight!"

Abruptly I renounced my haughty attitude, leaned forward,

poured Coke into my beloved's glass and poured some for myself as well.

"What do you want?" she asked.

"I told you: you, until tomorrow night."

"You are crazy. What will you do to Simon if I refuse?"

"Rip his eyes out with my fingers. Eat them and stick olives in the sockets. But have no fear for Simon, he's fine, he's having fun, he thinks it's a game, I was very careful. They're looking after him well, where he is. You'll see, he's going to put on ten pounds. He needs to. He's convinced it's all a game, so you just play along. Play along, I'll explain later."

"If I weren't afraid of you and your madness," she said, "the police would be here already."

"Just play along," I repeated with a certain pleasure, for those four syllables lost all meaning with repetition, seeming to belong to some strange and mysterious language. "With this game. Just play along."

"And if I tell the police afterward?"

"As you wish. After is after."

My indifferent wave was meant to be limp and disabused, the kind of wave with which you repel a mosquito too aged, too infirm, and too stupid to bite, but I failed to master this indifferent wave, my nerves were close to the fraying point, and plonk digadigadig! with a slap I sent my Coca-Cola bottle flying, retrieving it so swiftly in the same frenzied motion that not a drop of liquid escaped, I drank from the bottle, then went on speaking: "As you wish. After is after. But don't do it. Simon's going to gain ten pounds. He's skinny, that boy. Put on ten pounds or have his eyes ripped out and olives stuck in the sockets. As you wish. Tell anyone you like. But tell who? The city's deserted."

Bitter buffoonery. I wanted to be hard with her, to send her flying to the bar floor with a slap, to tell her she too was skinny, that her shape and her proportions were far from perfect, that Coke made her burp, she had burped once, she drank too fast, a burp she hadn't quite stifled, not that it had actually risen to her adored lips, so soft when you imagined your finger brushing them, or your own lips, or when you imagined not just brushing but licking, sucking, devouring with love (the love I had felt for her in the first second of that first evening had returned to me intact), and not to be compared as a physical symptom (needless to say) with the loathsome bubbling sounds emitted by the temporary master of the house, so arrogant this evening—no, it had been the merest tremor in her adored tummy, followed by the merest hiccup—yes, my love for her returned to me intact despite her unfriendly attitude toward me, true her brother had been kidnapped and if she wanted to see him again with eyes instead of olives in his sockets she must grant the use of the most intimate part of her person for a period of twenty-four hours, enough to put anyone out of sorts, and yet despite these circum- stances something of the evil inhabiting the half-brother was legible in the half-sister's adored face, in the flash of her eyes, in the ill-tempered facial lines already noted (from the nostrils to the corners of the mouth).

I adored Michèle de Klef.

"There's dancing on TV," I said. "I once knew a dancer" (I had never once known any dancer) "with a phenomenal leap. In fact she could perform only in the open. At least once every performance she amazed the crowd with an incredible leap, a leap so high that intermission was always scheduled between the time she left the ground and the time she fell graciously back to earth in a rustle of frothy taffeta. Have you made arrangements for your dad?"

A rustle of frothy taffeta. Just play along.

Arrangements for her dad.

The Cokes were a dull blood-red in color that seemed to splash all around, so that once we had drunk them the Bar des Archers seemed less red, mollified, relieved, drained of a little of its evil.

My ill-timed sallies (the Liver of No Return, the "just play alongs," the frothy taffeta, the slap that sent the bottle flying though not a drop escaped it, the leaping dancer) came close to amusing Michèle despite her best efforts, a smile, I noted afresh, somewhere far-off inside her would have liked to see the light of day, moreover my question caught her off guard so that she answered me without anger, "Yes, I have made arrangements."

Perhaps she was going to question me in her turn, perhaps, but the owner's brother suddenly bolted past at breakneck speed, elbows tucked in, knees pumping, I realized that this time seeking to restrain him would be useless, he fiddled with the knobs on the jukebox more feverishly than if he had been defusing bombs about to detonate, and then retreated elsewhere with the speed of a hunted feline to undergo his own detonation.

The captivating Spanish singer's captivating voice filled the glowing red bar.

"Let's go," I said to Michèle.

•

Yes, let's go. We had to go, to forget (I was already forgetting) those first flickering afterthoughts almost fanned into flame by the breath of remorse, hastening me toward a reappraisal of my course, when Michèle had said to me: yes, I have made arrangements. We had to go forward or die (and I did not want to die anymore, ever), rush forward into the folly of a business from which there was no longer any drawing back, to draw back would have been to die, would have been to sit at my table at 66 Rue de la République and drop my head on my folded arms after thrusting away pen and paper, no letter to Liliane or to anyone, but in the eternal expectation of death, without the artificial help of Alymil 1000 or of asphyxiating gas or of thrusting steel or of burning fire or of drowning water, at home with Michèle I drew the heavy maroon curtain in the front room and opened the french window to allow a maximum of the lesser nocturnal heat of the still-young night to waft in, but scarcely any of this lesser heat wafted in, I rested my buttocks against the rusting rail of the semblance of a balcony and gazed at Michèle in the light of the room, beautiful in the light, discountenanced, tense, and to fill the silence the apartment suddenly came alive with all the sounds of which it was so often the theater, tsplokh tsplokh, two pieces of Scotch tape at the same time, then the neighbor's phone, six rings, only six, the obstinate caller, if it was the same one, but I am sure it was, had got the picture, but even now hadn't yet got it quite clearly, and then the powerful, even sigh of the refrigerator door opening all by itself in the kitchen.

My voice, which I scarcely recognized: "You play the Granados dance well. At first I thought it was a record. Alicia de Larrocha."

She was discountenanced, tense. Full of hate.

I came and sat on a chair and (a thought for the wonderful Anne flitting across my mind) waved Michèle to the couch.

"Sit down. Would you like something to drink? I have everything. I went shopping recently. A beer? I just heard the refrigerator door open. We'd better take advantage of it. Often it refuses to open even if you tug at it with all your strength. Even if you yoked oxen to it. They'd snap their calves like elastic bands."

She sat down.

"Did you follow me the other night?"

I hesitated, nodded.

"Don't you want anything to drink?" (She shook her head.) "What arrangements for your dad?"

"What business is it of yours?"

"I hope it didn't cause you too many problems."

"I have a friend who works in a medical center at Sainte-Foy-l'Argentière. She was off duty. She hadn't left on vacation."

"Once again, you need have no fear for Simon. Nevertheless, obedience! Come here."

She rose. She came. She followed me into the back room. I switched on a small bedside lamp.

"Now we get undressed and we get in bed."

I got undressed and got in bed.

She got there before me. Obedience. She pulled the sheet over her.

We lay there side by side for at least half an hour.

My body was suddenly a stranger to desire.

My body was a stranger to desire, whereas I believe that back there in the middle of the Bar des Archers, I admit it now, right in the middle of the Bar des Archers where we had been sitting at a table thirty minutes earlier, I could have made love with Michèle under the goggling gaze of the master gunner, the ghostly replacement who could not set a glass on a marble surface without everything, glass and marble, being dashed to fragments — or out in the middle of the street, crossing Place de le République, offering the imaginary stroller the spectacle of an animal unknown even in zoos well-stocked with rare animals, or right on the stairway, why not, but here, now, in my burning bed, no, after half an hour I slipped my hand between the sheet and Michèle's body, taking care, almost, not to brush her flesh, then set this hand on her sex, gently, nothing more, and I conceived the frightening impression that I was touching someone else's sex, that there existed on the one hand Michèle de Klef the object of my instant and total love yesterday evening in the thunderer's bar, her soul as it were, and on the other hand this body, this body I wanted to see, I pulled the sheet aside with unwitting violence, I saw it, less thin than imagined, pretty, but pretty the way others were — and which was not Michèle!

Quickly I pulled the sheet back over us.

Her eyes were closed, her jaws clenched. Was she afraid? "Are you afraid?"

She opened her eyes, the left one a little later than the right, eyes dark and pale at the same time.

"Yes, I'm afraid. You're going to be sorry for what you're doing."

"What am I doing?"

"Anyway . . . I have an infection. You'll be sorry about everything."

"An infection?"

"Yes, an infection."

An infection! Still she did not understand! All the infections in the world would not have deterred me from devouring her with love, from penetrating her with my hardened organ from here to eternity — but that was just the point, it hadn't hardened, I suddenly did not perceive Michèle's body as animated, the soul on the one hand the body on the other, this body was not her!

An infection!

"Please don't be afraid. Please!"

"May I get a cigarette?"

I did not even reply. She got it, her cigarette, stretching an arm out of bed to reach the pocket of her pants, which lay crumpled on the floor like a dead cat, I got up with no thought for appearances and went to get the feather-light ashtray from the chest of drawers, bottom drawer, and came back to slide between the sheets beside her, she had already smoked half her brown cigarette.

"Don't be afraid."

"Well, I am afraid! You frighten me."

She finished her cigarette, crushing it out almost forcefully enough to pierce the thin aluminum, put the ashtray down next to the bed, tugged the sheet up so as not to show me her back, and then tugged it up over her small breasts and under her chin.

"We could cover our heads as well," I told her, "then it would really look like a wake."

Nothing. Time went by. She smoked a lot. Almost without stopping. Blip, blip, sighed the accurate quartz alarm that nothing could have dissuaded from uttering its gloomy blips, each blip sounded like a dying breath yet another blip followed it, the same one you would have sworn.

I looked either at Michèle or at the ceiling.

The heat was murderous. The sheet was unnecessary. The bed soaked up our sweat. Sometimes I thought of Anne.

I did not know what to say. "Would you like a drink?"

"Yes."

"What?"

"Water."

"Right, with lots of ice."

I got out of bed naked, still without the slightest concern for appearances. First I went to pee. I pulled the chain to flush. It didn't work. Worse and worse. Instead of drowning a little pee in a lot of water, it drowned a little pale pee in a sort of muddy deluge, a slow deluge of rust-colored liquid shot through with black, this was something new, you had to yank the chain three times to restore a human face to the damned toilet bowl.

I went into the kitchen.

Three ice cubes, more round than cubic, bobbed shame-facedly in the ice tray. I sloshed them into a glass which I filled with water for Michèle. I took a beer for myself. Gently, I closed the door of the noisy and inefficient appliance, not permitting myself to pound it to jelly, just as I was not permitting myself to shatter Michèle's skull with blows of my fist.

She drank her water, I drank my beer sitting on the edge of the bed with my back to her, then I lay down beside her again beneath the sheet while she lit another cigarette.

"Is music your profession?"

"Yes," she said.

"Speak to me," I said. "Speak to me! Are you a piano teacher? Do you give concerts? I heard you, you play very well."

Silence.

"Why won't you speak to me? What difference can it make to you? What's wrong with your left eye? Back in the bar—"

"I had an operation. I can hardly see out of that eye."

"Not like your brother then."

"He told you about that? He told you about his eyesight?"

"Yes. We're great friends."

I was resting on my left elbow, she on her right, we studied one another almost face to face.

"I don't know what happened with you, last night. I started to love you at once. I started at once to love you. I don't know what happened."

Phew!

But from that to kidnapping her brother and . . . What was she going to think now?

"Please don't be afraid. As for your infection, if you have an infection, I couldn't give less of a damn about it. Until tomorrow evening, try to be nice. That's all I ask."

Not another word.

We looked into each other's eyes for an hour. I had not known you could look into someone's eyes for an hour.

And the hour went by quickly, and it saved the night, for Michèle must have realized that there was no real danger in my house, and that to be afraid of me now was like being afraid of a sparrow nailed to a tree half a mile away, its beak tied up with thread. True, most of the time her eyes and her whole person gave off hostile waves, but sometimes indefinable waves as well.

The hour had gone by.

"If you want to pee it's next door to the kitchen. I'm sorry about the flush, it's not working too well. You have to pull it several times. I'll call a plumber tomorrow. The day after tomorrow. Go on, if you want to. I won't look."

She got up. I looked anyway, the way she walked, her little woman's body with a touch of the tomboy, her buttocks were most alluring, great uniformity and softness in her back, a pretty woman's body, of its kind, pretty and pretty for me, the most handsome of them all, a quick hypocritical glance during which my desire returned, then instantly vanished. Instantly.

I heard her pull the chain twice. Then a third time.

Call a plumber! What scandalous dishonesty! Indifferent and uncaring as I was and as I would probably remain for a long time yet, maybe forever, that damned plumbing would really have had to spit fire up the user's backside before the notion of a plumber made the slightest impact on any volitional area of my being.

Call a plumber tomorrow! The day after tomorrow!

Faucet noises. She was washing her hands, or drinking, or both, when she came back her mouth looked moist, her so-sensual mouth, the sheet was pulled right up under her chin, I told her again that I loved her, however astounding she might find such a declaration, and that she should not be afraid of me, I wouldn't hurt a fly, well, let's say a wasp, she nearly smiled, but she hated me too much, encouraged by weariness and sleepiness I dared to stroke her face, lift her hair and kiss her forehead whose curve I saw was flawless, kiss her left eye, and the right one, snuggle up against her although making sure the sheet was between us, and I dared implore her (in vain) for a look, a word, a gesture of kindness, implore her to stroke my cheek the way I was daring to stroke hers and to kiss her forehead and eyes and to snuggle up against her in the most total chastity.

•

Morning drew near. Scarcely cooler. Humid, exhausting. Michèle de Klef, whom I loved, fell asleep without realizing it. I slept too and woke before her. An infection! I frightened her! The police! I was crazy!

I waited for her to wake.

As soon as she opened her eyes, hatred thrust us light-years apart. It was unbearable. It was something to be fled at top speed. Stop the game now? No! The waves of hatred flowing over me would ebb. And Michèle would remain my prisoner until the end of this new day.

But in the short term, how was I to stay with her without doing her an injury? Without splitting open her breast, spreading her ribs, devouring her heart, lungs, and liver? Making mittens of her stomach and slippers of her spleen? Exploring her abdominal wall with my teeth, unraveling her intestines, rolling them back up into a ball and knitting myself a shroud in deepest gloom? Tearing out her hair, uprooting her teeth, sharpening her head and using it as a pencil? Take that! I longed to yell at her, here's something to addle your wits, you obstinate little bitch! Bam! And see how you like this slap across the eyes, think you can raise those eyelids now, hmmmmm? Ha, ha! And watch out for your ears! There! Just try undoing that knot I've made in them! And here, why don't we stuff the sheets of our disunion up your nostrils? Open your mouth! Shlop, shlap! Can you speak? No? I didn't think so. This cement sets hard and fast.

Yes, how remain in Michèle's presence?

"I'm going to be busy this morning," I said to her as I got up and dressed. "I have to go out. I'll be back either late this morning or right after lunch. I will have good news of Simon. Until then, take it easy. I'm going to lock you in. No, I'll leave the door open. But the slightest false move from you and I'll gouge his eyes out and send them to you in the mail. After I've bought some olives. You can wash, read, eat, or listen to music while you're waiting. I hope I'll dislike you less when I return. I understand why Simon loathes you."

"You understand nothing," she said from under the sheet.

I took the straw hat stolen at Carrefour.

"You can tell me what you mean later," I said. "Good-bye."

·

My mother was up and alert, but also whiter, paler, more wrinkled than ever. She had already drunk two cups of coffee. Simon was sleeping. I put the croissants on the table.

"Everything OK?"

"Deefoo meeloo mac viscous," she said.

"Great. Good. Fine."

I went into Simon's room, my room, the room with the closet containing the wooden toys made by my father, undemanding companion of Liliane Tormes for the year and a half preceding his brutal death. Simon was sleeping.

I saw myself as a child. I stood paralyzed, thunderstruck. Lightning flickering in from the distant past, twelve thousand zigzags, yet losing none of its extraordinary sharpness. The feeling passed.

Slumber had not disturbed his black silky fringe. I approached the wooden bed. Simon stirred, shifted onto his back with a whimper, as if in pain or afraid. I knelt. I could not help myself, I stroked his forehead, pushing back his fringe.

He opened his eyes.

His gaze on first waking was not so different from Michèle's three-quarters of an hour ago. The evil powers inhabiting him must have played at leisure while he was sleeping. But as soon as he really saw and recognized me, he smiled the way any other child brimming with joy would smile, or almost. I put my arms around him. We hugged each other with equal fervor on both sides. Then I stuck the straw hat on his head, he laughed.

"Slept well, old buddy?" I asked him, my heart overflowing with a liberating fondness.

He had, and he breakfasted heartily, and I did too, affected by my fondness for the child and despite the strange night I had spent, Liliane with alarming voracity, the table was heaped to the ceiling, she had prepared a breakfast that would have brought blissful satiation to a great army ravaged by privations, there was nowhere to put your elbows.

The heat came in unfettered through the windows of the beloved dwelling that was almost my birthplace. Sweat erupted immediately after a sip of the coffee in which, thank God, I no longer detected the slightest taste of decomposing vegetable matter.

Everything was going as planned: I had work to do but I would be back for lunch, I told them, with you, mama, ("beelee fluk meel mol, Michel black arcoo!"), and with you, old buddy, glad you slept so well, and at the end of the day everyone would be let in on the joke and we would all die laughing, we would go together to pick up the ransom, which had been left on the pedestal of the statue of Louis XIV on Place Bellecour, the satchel would not be visible at eye level, was Michèle worried? no, a bit annoyed, just annoyed enough (all this said as Liliane went into the kitchen to get four slices of toast that had leaped angrily from the toasters, chackachackachackachack!), yes, everything was going as planned, soon the circle would be closed, the sphere would be flawless — but hollow, empty of Michèle's love — and what would become of me next, a captive of the sphere of appearances, without love or the wish to live or to die ever filling it to the bursting point and thus setting me free? Hmmmmm? I did not know. Next would be next.

"Your mama said we're going for a walk this morning."

"Glad to hear it, you young rascal. I mean my old buddy! Glad for both of you. It's country around here, sort of. Have you ever seen the Jonage Canal?"

"No, never."

"When I was little I used to make slingshots. With a slingshot I could get right across the canal, from one bank to the other, you'll see, it's wide."

"You crossed the canal with a slingshot? Like with a boat, except it was a slingshot?"

Little smart aleck! I grinned at him.

"That's it, you've got the picture. No, it was the stones that crossed the canal. Sometimes I picked big heavy stones, I don't know what happened, the stone stayed where it was and I flew across the canal like an airplane. They're fun, slingshots. You can cross rivers in ships or planes, any way you like."

Simon laughed, but the freest and most spontaneous laugh he was capable of never quite banished from his face and eyes a tension, a torment, an anxiety, a fear, fleeting but perceptible flashes of fear and anxiety.

As for Liliane, the woman who would have moved into the hundredth floor of her house had her house contained a hundred floors, she watched us, Simon and me, as if we had been her own two children, and sometimes, between slices of bread or swallows of coffee, she smiled a smile that wiped away the wrinkles around her mouth, and this smile from my adoptive mother hurt me less now that I had renounced death.

"Plastackar bloom viroolette!" she suddenly said when breakfast was done.

I did not understand. And she refused to explain further. She was blushing like a bride, she smiled again. Usually I understood her. Not this time. It must have been the expression of a pleasant thought, for she looked pleased, almost happy.

Simon wore the straw hat, it was too big for him.

•

"I speak Spanish fluently," said Rainer von Gottardt.

He had an accent, but indefinable, neither American, nor German, nor Spanish.

"I learn foreign languages quickly. I studied Spanish for pleasure. And I lived in Spain a little, I'll tell you about it later. And you, do you speak that splendid language?"

"Alas, no."

"But Tormes is a Spanish name?"

"Yes, but my adoptive mother always spoke French to me. Never Spanish."

We were sweating in the piano room. The little recorder was already at work. The maestro had wished it so. He had not sat down, for we would soon be moving out to the lawn, and he wanted to avoid too many grunting passages from sitting to standing and from standing to sitting, passages that were, he said, hastening his demise.

"Now she speaks an unclassified language. An original creation. You have to be very used to it. I adore my mother."

"And her heart?"

"It doesn't hurt anymore. I hope it's not her heart. She won't see a doctor. But I'm going to take care of it."

Rainer von Gottardt was attired in a light yellow shirt and less light yellow pants that might fairly be judged unsightly, the same yellow as the posters announcing the Dioblaníz concert at the Temple.

"I used to like yellow," he said. "Not so much any longer. I did a little laundry before you arrived. It is the first time in my life I have ever washed my own clothes."

"I do my laundry all the time."

A kind of silent noise from the Saba, recording everything.

"You can put down that kind of detail, if you like. Laundry. People love details. We all love details. Our minds like to make connections between them. I am thinking, by remote association, of what you have to say about embellishment in your book, my dear Michel . . . or Miguel? Was it conceit that made you sign the book Miguel?"

"Idiotic conceit," I said. "If it wasn't so hot I'd kick myself."

"Ha, ha!" he went hoarsely. "How funny you are! But you look very tired . . . You allude to certain interpretations with embellishments so numerous and excessive one hears only them. And they end up being perceived as the very soul of the music."

"Yes," I said.

He laughed again, ha! just one ha! perhaps because my answer was certainly not overloaded with embellishments.

"A fine book. Once again, my compliments."

The compliments left me ice-cold, if you could remain ice-cold in that sweltering smithy. The rustic house retained yesterday's heat. You felt like enlarging all its apertures with a pickaxe.

The Maestro approached the piano with his look of someone who has had a cactus thrust into the foundation of his being and is walking in a manner to avoid all friction. He stretched out his hand, took a glass that was sitting on the instrument. Had he been playing before my arrival?

Speaking of details, I noticed that he had hung a third painting, no, a photograph, just to the right of the two others.

"Will you have lunch with me?" he asked in his expiring voice.

He downed the white wine remaining in the glass.

"Alas! Once again I can only tell you: alas! It's impossible, and please believe that I am sorry. As of tomorrow, yes. But until tonight my mother and I have an unexpected guest, a child, the beautiful, delightful, and troubling Simon, who would die of disappointment if I were to be away at lunchtime today. No, I can't do that to him!"

Two things: first, I experienced a new upwelling of tenderness merely from pronouncing the name of the child who must at this moment, hand in hand with my aged and beloved mother, be savoring the decaying charms of the outskirts of Villeurbanne, the desolation of its little houses, its joyless footpaths, the grimy vegetation along the banks of the Jonage Canal where desperate people come to drown. Second, I was speaking to Rainer von Gottardt with a mixture of grandiloquence and familiarity that astonished me.

"Simon. Simon who?"

He had not turned around. I could see his face in the piano's dark veneer. Why this question?

I hesitated. Why this hesitation?

"Simon de Klef."

Rainer von Gottardt, already motionless, grew more motionless still, not a fold of the light yellow shirt nor of the less light yellow pants stirred, but his face, oh! his face! Perhaps because just then it was reflected in a surface not exactly knotty but possessing a less-than-regular grain, his face seemed inhumanly deformed, the face of a monster. Was it a skull, I asked myself, that yellowish membrane pulsating like a dying bird and darkening each time it touched the damp brain beneath it? Were they eyes, those protruding abscesses surveying one another in deepest gloom? Were they ears, those rumpled gray folds into whose recesses my words, "Simon de Klef," had burrowed? Was it a nose, that protuberance mined by two nostrils dead to all save a mouth, that twitching wound in which words grown too weak to be uttered would slide back down his throat into the pit of his stomach where they would no longer speak to any but him?"

These things I asked myself as he turned around, face normal, neither more nor less ravaged than usual. Yes, some flaw in the wood, some trick of reflected light in the lustrous veneer, some optical trick on the surface of things. My thoughts became calm.

"Shall we go outside?" he said.

Yes, let's go. We had to. I rose.

"Is that a photograph?"

"Yes. A small Berlin townhouse. Renaissance. I lived there for a few days. In that small townhouse. In 1974. I shall be mentioning it to you again later."

He seemed almost satisfied that I had noticed this small Renaissance townhouse in Berlin. At all events I thought I detected a ghost of satisfaction in his voice.

•

And, in the course of the morning, the pianist's increasingly weary voice became harder to distinguish from the sounds of nature. The shade of the pines, if they were pines, but I think they were, could not stop you sweating, his hairless forehead bristled with drops of sweat, it was as if his forehead, no, it was as if the white wine instantly transformed itself into sweat that was hoisted up to his skull by his eyebrows, rising at every swallow.

A calm and wholly interior life until 1967. In 1967, although he had given very few concerts and had turned his back on the pleas and alluring offers of a score of recording companies, Rainer von Gottardt, at the age of fifty, recorded the two books of *The Well-Tempered Clavier*.

"In 1967. One of the two most beautiful years of my life. I am pleased with that recording, even today. I would not change a note. The other most beautiful year . . ."

The level of the white wine sank, the cone of cigar and cigarillo butts in the ashtray would soon challenge the towering pines, the city, Lyon, was distant and silent. At each puff the index finger of his right hand collided with the end of his potato of a nose, about the absence of his left index finger I confess I would have liked to question him, but he would get there on his own, I thought.

"And 1969. My second most beautiful year. The year of Ana. Bolivian, a redhead. Very rare, a Bolivian redhead. Magnificent dark and pale red hair. Ana de Tuermas, encountered in 1969 at the Dioblanízes, those two lunatics. Particularly her. Do you know that they may have fled Brazil after a scandal? A revolutionary group accused them both — so people say — of taking part in a massacre of rebel prisoners after the group had kidnapped Isabel's father."

"Er . . . was it true?" I said.

"Neither true nor false. Take your pick. A secret rumor. No one will ever know."

He fell silent. He was panting like a frightened monster, disgusting, pathetic. Once again I realized that he wanted to talk, but (aside from his fear of the respiratory effort it would cost) he also wanted me to urge him to talk. Ana, the woman he had loved. And not Isabel!

"Ana de Tuermas . . . ?"

"Ana. A friend of Isabel's. Much younger than I was. It is ages since I had news of her. Simon de Klef, that name means something to me . . ."

That name meant something to him? Signifying? Was he really trying to make me talk? No, I must be crazy. Sick in the head. Ready for a padded cell and a well-upholstered straitjacket. I calmed down.

"That's not impossible," I said.

"No, it is not impossible."

"Not impossible. His sister's a pianist, perhaps that's the connection . . . She's the one I really know, Michèle."

"Perhaps. Ana and Isabel knew each other in Bolivia, before Isabel's marriage. Ana was passing through Lyon at the time of my concert . . ."

A new bout of silent expectation. His lids of dried clay masked half his eyeballs. How could he bat his eyelids without scraping away cornea, pupil, and lens? No, their undersides must be soft and lubricated, like the eyelids of the mass of mortals. He examined me, waited.

"And . . . did you fuck?" I asked, seized by an incredible attack of vulgarity.

"We fucked our brains out," he instantly replied, all in one breath and without showing the slightest surprise. "Here, in this house."

He swallowed two white tablets, I a mouthful of black coffee, and the conversation continued as if nothing unusual had been said.

I repeat, incredible.

Then he described Ana to me, body like a goddess of old, beautiful as the muse Erato (he cackled, ha, ha!) whose likeness he had once contemplated in the Vatican Museum, with one major difference, Ana had long hair charged with sunlight that you never forgot.

Even hearing the word sunlight made you hotter.

Ana de Tuermas.

Of no definite profession.

He would talk to me of her again.

•

He did talk to me of her again, a couple of words, just before I left, I had gone up to the photo just above the piano, suddenly the small Berlin Renaissance townhouse recalled something to me, two floors, four windows on each floor, one straight gable one arching gable one straight gable one arching gable, seemed to recall something to me although I had never set foot in Berlin.

"I spent three days there with Ana. Beautiful place. The summer of 1974. You have mentioned me to no one?"

"No one."

"No. Plenty of time after I am dead."

"Are you really going to die?"

"Yes. My heart pounds, if you could only feel it pound! It can't go on, it wants to shatter my ribs, probably to feel freer. But of course it can't hope to shatter ribs. It will be shattered first. My body will be transported to Wiesbaden and buried there. I have family there still, nephews. They will find all the instructions in this house or on my person. Give little Simon a hug from me. Simon de Klef. You told me you had been sick? Once?"

"Yes. My kidneys. I missed your concert in Lyon. A terrible memory. If only I had met you then!"

"Yes! If only!"

He began to get up to see me out. I begged him to remain seated.

"You have started to write?"

"A little."

"Going well?" he asked simply.

I was silent about my handwriting problems, which did not affect the essentials and were bound to be resolved. "Pretty well. I'll show everything to you at the end."

"Agreed. Everything at the end. The only thing you will still have to report on will be the very last hour. Perhaps you will be by my side at the very last hour? Those will be the lines that I shall never read, the last ones in your book, ha, ha!"

"Dear Rainer!" I said in a burst of compassion and familiarity.

I could add nothing else, he could do nothing else but reply. "Dear Miguel . . ."

I withdrew reflectively and sadly from 36 Rue de l'Église, Francheville-le-Haut, in my melting, boiling Dauphine. I was not thinking of Michèle, and yet the thought of Michèle occupied me totally.

•

"I was scared, she was sitting down and couldn't get up, her face was all twisted, her eyes were closed . . ."

Simon and Liliane had strolled a few hundred yards, the scenic route, along the Jonage Canal, an open-air sewer, the hydroelectric plant, a complex mechanism for the mysterious processing of drowned bodies, the old Cusset Cemetery and its damned souls galloping in silence among the tombstones, when they got back Liliane had sat down and closed her eyes and had been unable to get up, and it had even seemed to Simon — either I dreamed for a third of a second, or else his gaze flashed malice for a third of a second — that she was about to topple over, unconscious, perhaps dead.

"This time I'm getting a doctor," I said to Liliane despite a flood of ferocious syllables. "Yes, mama, yes. Whether it's nerves or not, whether it's serious or not, we have to take care of it. I'll feel happier."

I tried Patrice Pierre whose prescription I had kept in my wallet in case I needed advice, no reply.

A thousand other phone calls with no more success. The doctors were away, or were refusing to answer. Or had given up the practice of medicine for ever. Or were sick, or dead.

At last a certain Morvan Tormavel, of Vénissieux, agreed, but only after the direst threats, to call on my mother in the course of the afternoon. He scarcely listened to what it was all about, what kind of pain, click! he hung up.

We lunched.

•

Liliane and Simon waved to me from the window. My heart lifted at no longer seeing Liliane alone at the window.

Nervous disorder. In my opinion, she had nothing wrong with her heart. I put Simon in charge of her.

"I like you, old buddy . . . When the joke's over we'll stay friends. OK? I'll give you a whole bunch of wooden toys. All of them."

He kissed me spontaneously. It was the first time. He hugged me.

But was it possible, just possible, that Simon de Klef, my old buddy from hell, had guessed everything, and was really saying a silent "sure, sure!" when I told him I had to return at once to my reporting job, to my polishing-up task, to the final version of my written transcription, destined first for the printer and then for the reader, thoughts gleaned from illustrious artists passing through our city as it gasped in the summer heat?

I drove off.

I had barely been able to finish my dessert, a quarter-ton of cream puffs apiece. With no intermission. My hatred of Michèle, which had gripped me all day, had gone, and love and the need to see her again suddenly hurled me so to speak out of Liliane's house and I crossed the dead city in the twinkling of an eye.

The sun assaulted you personally. The red Dauphine was a fireball despite its open windows. After a time it seemed you would be less hot with the windows rolled up. Fine, you rolled them up. Then, ill with the heat, you lowered them. You no longer knew what to do.

•

"You can sometimes feel a little less hot on the semblance of a balcony. You could have read out there while you waited. Or in the back room, the setting for our night of love. I love you. Speaking of reading, did you read this letter?"

Michèle, standing in the room, had her back to Johann Sebastian Bach. The drawer, the bottom one, where the past lay, was open. She had opened it and had violated its secrets, my yellowing book, Rainer von Gottardt, and the rest, and the letter, the letter written to Liliane (a stamp!) and never sent, lying on the table, opened, read! Indiscreet bitch!

I sealed the letter up again, the glue still glued, and put it back in the drawer.

"You are insane," she said.

I hesitated, then told her everything. (Everything except the night of my death, my suicide and its immediate cause, my hostile silence last night, so near and already so far, in the bar with the gross physiological pyrotechnics.) Everything, my insane history (whose craziness was only beginning to emerge and would evolve infinitely in the hours and days to come) from its beginnings, the phone call, the wrong number, right up to the present.

My love for her.

A love not shared, I thought my fictitious mistress would die of hatred.

"Stop trying to look so sweet," I told her. "All I did was fix it so your brother wouldn't really be kidnapped. Obviously they'll have to give up their plan."

She barely managed to calm down.

"I'm afraid. Simon was kidnapped before, three years ago."

Kidnapped before, three years ago? My expression must have irritated her for she exploded in rage: "You don't understand, you dangerous madman, that they may have traced him, through the phone or the phone book, by following you, finding Simon . . . Perhaps at this very moment . . . Call your mother, quick! Quick!"

Should I slug her four five times? Dunk her in ice-cold water? Leave the room with my gaze elsewhere and a carefree tune on my lips?

"Call her!"

Very well. I dialed Liliane's number.

No reply.

They should be there. They should! Nowhere else they could be. I let it ring twelve times. At each ring, twenty pints of blood fled my body.

I hung up.

"Let's go," I said. "Let's go and see."

SEVEN

Unnerved, Michèle let me take the wheel of the elegant white Lancia. Being unused to driving shooting stars, I put enough pressure on the gas pedal to make even my tattered Dauphine turn somersaults, so of course in the Lancia, I wouldn't have been surprised if we had passed a helicopter as we took off, it cleared the ground, crossed Rue de la République (closed to traffic) midway between heaven and earth, landing an inch from an optician's window, cautious reverse, what I thought was cautious, all the same the needle showed thirty, forward again, another three hundred yards of pedestrian walkway avoiding displays of flowers, benches, streetlights, Rue Childebert, Quai Jules Courmont, brooooooooooooom!

Was Liliane's phone out of order again? If not . . . if not, I had been flippant indeed in my introspective appreciation of the kidnappers' state of mind, men of fine-tempered steel unlikely to be shattered into a thousand pieces by my unexpected intervention the way your run-of-the-mill kidnapper might have been, and, Michèle was right, merely by riffling through the directory and keeping their eyes peeled for a few hours they had pinpointed me and waited coldly, despite the heat wave, that was a measure of their mettle, for the right moment, the moment to carry out their mission at whatever cost, at whatever risk, that was what had happened, Simon kidnapped and Liliane shoved around, struck . . .

God in heaven!

"My mother's phone is behaving unpredictably just now," I said with immense calm. "It's just been fixed. I think it's out of order again. Did you say Simon had already been kidnapped?"

"Look where you're driving. Hurry!"

"Please, talk to me!"

Cours Lafayette.

God, how she got on my nerves! I longed to drive headlong into the front of a building, opening up a yawning gap, the spirited Lancia reduced to a heap of small pieces of scrap, us miraculously safe and sound, needing only to shake ourselves to pull free, a few strokes of a whisk broom on the sidewalk and there would be nothing left, what had been a car would mysteriously no longer be!

"What is going on between Simon and you?" I said with the same calm. "I get the feeling you can't stand each other."

I was taming the Lancia. I accelerated. The main thing was not to put your foot down hard enough to reach the speed of light, a stern look was enough, brooooooooommmmm!

And I managed not to let Michèle see how much her panic had infected me. My question was well put. Speak of other things. Bravo. Yes, well then, just what was going on between Simon and her, what was the nature and cause of this naked hostility?

"I don't know," she said in less sour tones, slightly less sour tones than those of someone addressing a dog of frankly unprepossessing appearance. "It began after he was kidnapped."

She stopped talking. I looked at her. She went on: "He has changed. He's become very jittery. Naughty sometimes. Bad."

"There's no need to worry, my mother's phone never works. When was all this?"

"Three years ago. In 1974."

"Simon doesn't have a mother?"

"No. She died when he was born. In childbirth."

I went on having luck with the lights on the Cours Tolstoï. You could see them all, all green. Fifth gear. The windows were down, you could hear the engine, the wheels, I crossed Villeurbanne in a soft swishing of velvet and silk.

"Did you have to pay?"

"No."

"No?"

She hesitated. "No. Nobody asked for anything."

Silence. But she wanted to talk.

Back into fourth to cross Place Grandclément where a black dog, lying as flat in the shade of a kiosk as it was possible for a dog to lie (which was very flat), looked like a patch of tar or of black blood.

"Why wasn't Simon more suspicious of me?"

"I don't know. You must have been convincing. A good actor. And you arrived at the right moment, he's bored stiff. And then . . . he's forgotten. It was such a shock to him . . . He has forgotten a whole week out of his life, a few days before and a few days after."

"Did they mistreat him?"

"Him, no, but my father, yes . . . They were both kidnapped. My father was hit with three bullets, two in the head, they left him for dead."

Surprise, horror!

"Where did this happen?"

"In Berlin. At the time we lived in Geneva. My father went on a trip, he took Simon. In Berlin they disappeared from their hotel. They were found three days later in a house in the suburbs, my father almost dead, Simon staring at him. The owners of the house were away for the weekend. My father was pronounced dead by the first doctor who saw him. Will we be there soon?"

"Soon. Simon is going to be disappointed. What you've just told me is terrible. At the end of this road. Do you know this charming residential suburb?"

Avenue Ampère was uglier than ever. All this sun was the final blow. The street looked ready to shrivel up, to burn, to decompose, to sink into the earth, to turn black, a tomb for the Lancia, to keep it from ever reaching Chemin du Regard even though the latter was very close now, forty yards, twenty yards . . .

I recalled my phone call to Michèle and her hope when she thought it was an ordinary kidnapping, a simple ransom demand . . . What was she afraid of?

Chemin du Regard.

"We're there. Tell me the rest later on, if you like. My mother will make us a snack you'll remember for the rest of your life."

But my mother, Liliane Tormes, would never make anything for anyone again, ever.

Flames were coming from the kitchen window.

The disaster, a long disaster, had begun.

Michèle and I—with not a shout, not an exclamation, not a cry—burst from the car and raced to the house.

Simon, Liliane's new adoptive son, had disappeared. My mother sat in a chair in the dining room, dead. I knew. I checked. The heart. Fright. Could she be brought back to life? She did not seem to have been harmed. Oh yes, possibly the arm, just above the elbow. But it wasn't certain. A note, a page from an appointment book, August 5, 19—, lay on the table, for the child's sake wait, do not inform the police, I put the note in my pocket.

So the fire had not been set deliberately.

I saw the straw hat on the floor.

The television was on.

Liliane had been surprised in her kitchen where she was preparing the evening meal hours in advance as was her habit, vegetables in a newspaper on the sink next to the gas, as far as I could see, for the smoke in the little room obscured things and choked people, the gas was on, they had taken her by the arm, perhaps even gently, the paper had been moved a little, the fire had licked at it . . .

Bring Liliane back to life.

I lifted her from the chair. How little she weighed!

"Call the fire department," I said to Michèle. "We won't mention Simon. Hurry, and be careful, the house is going to burn fast."

I went down the stairs like a sleepwalker, a ghost, a zombie, my mother held tight against my breast.

My fault, all my fault! I had killed Liliane Tormes!

I laid her on the grass. I tried artificial respiration. But I didn't do very well, it was my first time.

I heard the crackle of flames. Yes, the house was burning fast, very fast!

Just as Michèle came out there was an explosion, the propane bottle exploded in the kitchen, I hadn't thought of the propane, my God, Michèle could have been hurt, without lifting my mouth from my mother's as I crouched over her vainly toiling I watched Michèle approach.

"They're on their way," she said.

The heat was unbearable, fear, madness, shattered nerves, pain were all unbearable, I rose yelling that we had to have a doctor, right now, right now, I raised my arms to heaven and struck my hands together, hard, I hurt them, the pain stung, I clapped my hands as if to make a doctor appear, and as fate willed it a doctor did appear in the instant I clapped my hands together! Dr. Morvan Tormavel, I had forgotten all about him, a little bald man with a big head, almost a dwarf, fair of complexion, wearing a light-colored suit, who descended from his Ford, came up to Liliane calmly and uncaringly and said: "Is this the patient?"

Was she the patient! Most calmly and most uncaringly. Yes, you asshole, how I would love to hammer you into the ground with blows of my fist on top of your head, both fists, a relentless hammering, a drumroll of fistfalls, bada*boom* bada*boom* bishbashbashbish, this elderly person stretched out on the red-brown grass was indeed the patient, I even felt she might be dead, Morvan Tormavel bent, examined her, I tried, I told him, artificial respiration, what if . . .

"No," he said, rising. "Massive stroke. Nothing to be done."

"You're sure that artificial respiration . . ."

Sure. He indicated this to me by an imperceptible widening of his right eye. No. Might as well blow into a violin. Scrape bagpipes with the bow of a fiddle. Piss into an upright piano. Knead a trumpet into dough.

Nothing to be done.

I dropped onto my knees (bruising them, and apparently ripping the flesh on the soles of my feet) next to Liliane. I closed her eyes forever. I kissed her forehead. I stroked her cheeks.

I stood up again.

Michèle was beside me. Sweat was rolling off my body in torrents. Tears too. And Michèle's face was bathed in sweat, her short hair, a little bit too long for short hair, stuck to her forehead. Only the dapper homunculus was not sweating. He had scarcely noticed a house was on fire. I took Michèle's hand and squeezed it. She did not return my pressure. But, as they say, nor did she seek to avoid it.

I put my mouth to her ear:

"We'll take care of Simon. We'll find him. I'll find him!"

"Yes," she said.

"Yes!" I said. "I swear."

The house was certainly burning fast. At top speed. By the time the firefighters arrived there was nothing for them to do. Despite their most heroic efforts they were able to salvage only a door bell, two doorknobs, and three knife handles. I'm exaggerating. But it is true that the little wooden house, at that hour of the day, in that season of that year, writhed and burned up in a flash under the frightening sun as if it had been made of paper and a giant magnifying glass had been placed between house and sun.

I could have left Liliane to roast inside, in her poor will she had expressed the wish to be cremated.

•

No, because she had also expressed the wish for her urn to rest in the grave of my late father, Diego Soler, in the Cusset Cemetery.

•

The body was removed.

Monsieur Marc Philippon, of the Incorporated Funeral Home, a large sandy well-dressed personable man, demonstrated sterling tact and faultless efficiency. He took care of everything, contacts with the police, death certificate, burial permit and the other merry operations that make the disappearance of a loved one so much merrier. Barring accidents, the mortal remains of Liliane Tormes would be reduced to ashes at 4:30 P.M. the next day at the Guillotière Cemetery.

•

"How are we going to go about it?" I asked dully.

"Go about what?"

"Getting Simon back. What are we going to do?"

"There is nothing we can do."

"But just now you said . . ."

"That was just now, we said anything that came into our heads. There's nothing we can do. I'm going to wait at home and hope they will give me instructions, ask for a ransom. If only you had told the police, the police or me, instead of—"

I sensed that she was once again seething with anger. She was driving. I was hunched on my seat like an old insect. She had better take care not to address me in that tone, the little bitch, I might suddenly straighten up, deliver a barrage that would send her flying, despite the closed door, onto the speeding roadway, leap behind the wheel and drive all the way around the world without stopping, looking straight ahead, before returning her Lancia to her fit only for the scrapheap, liberated from my love for her, she who would be leaving the hospital disabled and incapable of ever again driving any vehicle whatsoever, but her tone changed: "You must get some rest."

Very good. So I remained hunched on my seat, renouncing my drive around the world after that murderous barrage. Sweating, shivering, unhappy. I said anything that came into my head: "Do you have a mother?"

"No."

"Is she dead?"

"No. She abandoned us. She ran away with a friend of my father's, a company sergeant major. We've heard nothing since."

The de Klefs, brother and sister, had had no luck with their respective mothers.

A company sergeant major!

We took Cours Franklin Roosevelt to the river. The last light turned yellow, Michèle accelerated and cornered smoothly.

"I'm afraid. If it was just a ransom demand they would have let him go, wouldn't they?"

"No. It just proves they're stubborn."

"I hope so. Otherwise . . ."

"Otherwise what?"

Yes, otherwise what? What was she afraid of?

She did not answer, tense and agitated, terribly nervous.

She got on my nerves.

It was a pleasure to study her small straight nose in profile.

Liliane dead!

Lichem . . . Where was Simon? I thought, I had already thought of the gray Scorpio with the cracked headlights and its broad-shouldered driver, probably German. Liliane dead, Michèle bringing me back home after my almost-birthplace had burned down, Liliane stretched out on the red-brown grass, Rainer von Gottardt with whom I was dining tomorrow night, good evening, Maestro . . . I was hallucinating. Lichem, the German driver. My mind refused to work coherently. Michèle said again, "I'm afraid."

I said nothing.

We crossed the Wilson Bridge. I asked her to drop me at the river. She stopped the car.

"It was in August last time as well. They found Simon on August 7."

"The day after tomorrow?" I said. "Then we'll find Simon the day after tomorrow."

I did not get out of the car. I found it hard to leave Michèle. Talk to me, I said to her, tell me about this first kidnapping, and tell me what you are afraid of. Rue Childebert was empty as far as Rue des Jacobins. The embankment too was deserted. Not a soul. The heat, the light, so violent and so uniform it looked like black night.

She was willing enough to talk to me, but she didn't have much more to tell me than before. She didn't know anything. No one knew anything. Yes, her father and her brother. But Simon de Klef the father, living corpse, was incapable of communicating anything whatsoever in any way whatsoever. And Simon de Klef the son suffered, it seemed, from partial amnesia. Which had greatly intrigued the Swiss doctors. Since at the time they had been living in Geneva for twenty years. The father had left Lyon and the house on Point du Jour in 1954, aged thirty-seven (Michèle was five), after retiring from the French army, officially early retirement, in fact forced to resign. Why? Michèle did not know. Was there a connection between this unknown reason and the kidnapping twenty years later? Perhaps. Perhaps not. Michèle did not know of one. In 1967, the birth of Simon, the father lost his second wife. (Yes, the father lost, and was, said Michèle, sad sad sad.) In 1974 he decided to take his son, whom he adored, around Europe. In Berlin they disappeared for three days. Mystery. No way of finding out anything about those three days. The police discovered nothing. They were found in the circumstances I have related. The owners of the suburban home, a childless couple, were at once absolved of suspicion.

Berlin. Ford Scorpio, German driver. No, Lichem was the one who had done it, no one knew that better than I did. And, I said to her, surely Simon's amnesia was known to interested parties? (A mad hunch came to me.) Had they kidnapped him this time to make him talk about something he might have seen or heard then? Was that what she was afraid of? She hadn't really thought about it. Yes, maybe, although it had probably been a baseless fear, that or something else, she didn't know, she was afraid, afraid . . .

She smoked, her hands shook. She bit greedily at her nails.

"I can try and find out about this Lichem, at the Hôtel des Étrangers. I can go back to Rue Duguesclin, try to call 812–2121 . . ."

"No!" (She almost shouted.) "It would not help at all. On the contrary. You've done enough stupid things already. I'm sorry. Forgive me. I'm really sorry about your mother. Really sorry. You must get some rest. I'll wait, that's all we can do."

"Will you keep me posted? May I call you?"

"Yes."

She smiled at me. You dripped sweat inside that car. Liliane dead. Simon gone. What a wonderful sad smile! Without that smile, would I have the strength to face what I was going to have to face in a few minutes' time?

I opened the door and got out.

The Lancia pulled away and disappeared in a frothy rustle of taffeta.

•

The reassuring presence of Torbjörn Skaldaspilli, standing up there like a poplar planted in a geranium pot, would have gladdened my heart.

Alas, no one.

But I did see — just — perhaps — a faint tremor of the maroon curtains at my french window. Not a breath of air to explain it . . . Had I really seen it? And so what? I was incapable of any kind of decision, of anything but mechanical effort, climbing the stairs, opening my door . . . The thick drawn curtain hung there by my companion, as given to cutting cloth as to staining the wood of chests of drawers, had it stirred? No.

And so what? I entered my building. In other words: better to fight a hostile horde of a thousand ghosts upstairs than to take a single step out of my way down here.

Nevertheless, a part of me was ready for war, the choleric part that had armed my hand with Alymil 1000 and municipal gas burners, and whose destructive rage had not obtained full satisfaction, far from it in fact, since here I was still dragging around my wretchedness, my bereavement, and my love without great hopes for tomorrow, that part of myself, then, made more choleric than ever by recent events, was ready for war and, when I opened my door and found myself confronted with Lichem's lofty form, long hair and gray suit, with Lichem holding a revolver, my surprise was so incomplete, my rage so blind, my suspicion that he had no intention of firing without obtaining explanations from me so blinding that I instantly landed a kick capable of dislodging a mountain range in the tenderest region of his groin.

He was surprised.

He fell to one side, his weapon to the other, he toppled backward, murmuring insults interspersed with most pessimis-

tic predictions of my future chances. I begged him not to
concern himself over much on my behalf but rather to savor the
new and pleasant caress with which I was about to favor him:
with these words, and putting a good swing into it, I dealt him a
second kick that would have opened up a deep valley in a high
rocky plateau. There escaped from his unpleasantly rounded
mouth a long high whistling, abruptly curtailed by another
offering delivered by my new shoe from Carrefour-Vénissieux
that landed squarely in his ribs.

Then I hurled myself down the stairs.

I had scarcely landed on the sidewalk when I heard him too
hurtling down the stairs. A tough character. And my determined
assault on his credentials had not won me a fast friend.

Rue de la République, empty, white. Fear, true fear, fear I had
not yet known, suddenly flooded me.

Fear. My promise that I would see Torbjörn Skaldaspilli
again had been a little premature.

I began to flee, racing straight ahead in the even light, so even
that it resembled the blackness of night, I ran, and not until I
reached Rue Grenette did I think of using my head and say to
myself: use your head!

I turned left onto Rue Grenette after darting a glance back
over my shoulder and seeing Lichem on my heels, not really
close but not all that far for someone whose thoracic cage had
been undermined and testicles flattened, reduced to nothing,
epidermis on epidermis, a paper-thin film of skin flapping at his
groin! Yes, a tough character. Rue Grenette. Use your head.

Rue du Président Edouard Herriot on the right, Rue Henri
Germain on the left, Rue de la République again where I no
longer saw him (taking a cautious backward glance as I rounded
the corner) and which I crossed at a run. One chance out of
twelve thousand that he would choose this route.

Place des Cordeliers. I swerved into Rue Grolée and ran
down it at top speed to Rue Thomassin, a lone man with fire
licking his backside racing through the streets in this heat was a
picture of pure madness, where the Alymil 1000 and municipal
gas burners had failed, fear and breakneck speed would prevail, I

was dying of exhaustion, but I also had the impression that I would die if I stopped, so I ran, I ran, as it were, beating out the flames at my backside with my own hands as they burned up the road under my very feet, in such conditions the risk of a fall was great, but as luck would have it I had once upon a time run well and memory came to my rescue, once my stamina, my speed, and my excellent technique had consistently guaranteed me first place, only the play of circumstance had denied me world championship stature, I would shoot from the starting line like a cannonball and the race was over, shortly after if not at the exact same second I breasted the tape in total solitude, and, in my thirst for motion, it was not unheard of for me to go on galloping long after the end of the competition, losing myself high in the mountains where they had to track me for days and days in order to award me the blue ribbon. Yes, a famous runner.

Rue Thomassin. Then fifteen feet hugging the walls along Rue de la République. Lichem would expect me to be anywhere except in front of my building and anywhere except in my apartment where I went for a minute to gather a few things, clothes (jacket from Carrefour), money (the wages for the kidnapping given to me on the Rue Duguesclin by the link in the chain whose striking absence of qualities I had by no means forgotten, nor the nose pinched by the wearing of sunglasses), quartz alarm, up you get! blip blip, radio-tape player, paper, pen, beginning of my biography of Rainer von Gottardt, cassette recorded that very morning at Francheville (God how events were crowding one another, fate was hastily tossing me whole acres of events, making of me its free prisoner!), a few things, as I was saying, a few things which I stuffed into my canvas suitcase, the canvas suitcase under the bed in the back room, next to which, when I stooped to pick it up, I discovered Lichem's weapon, it had been jerked away from him so swiftly after my so-swift kick that it had skittered all this way, not immediately finding it despite fifteen feverish glances to right and left he had decided it was wiser to dash off in hot pursuit of me.

Into the canvas suitcase went Lichem's weapon with the silencer screwed onto its barrel!

No, under my belt, hidden by my coat. I was less dead and more invincible and immortal than ever.

·

Moving along hidden back streets with the cunning of an Apache, in the process exhausting myself more than by the most frenzied straight-line trajectories, sweating, panting, foaming, I trudged along through the Perrache neighborhood, passing six hotels that were closed, the seventh time I was lucky, the Hôtel Quivogne, Rue Quivogne, not far from the railroad station, nor from Saint-Paul Prison, nor from the large and reassuring or not reassuring police headquarters, nor from the arsenal, nor from Sainte-Blandine Church.

The man at the reception desk, foreign-looking, probably a Turk, showed no surprise at my appearance, scarcely noticed it. I was the only guest. Would Room 1 on the second floor suit me? It would, perfectly, I wanted none other. That would be $12 a night plus breakfast.

Gray dust, even black dust, lay over everything in this Hôtel Quivogne. The place had probably last been cleaned before the establishment was even built. Luckily the sun didn't shine into Room 1, which had a direct northern exposure, I flung open the window and threw myself on the bed, which gave off what seemed like a cloud of gas and was so hard it broke as many of my ribs as I had broken of Lichem's.

Liliane dead.

I burst into tears.

·

My breathing, impaired by my desperate wanderings and by my renewed sobbing, returned to normal. I rubbed my eyes. I saw the ceiling, blackish. And I tried to pull together the shreds of thought entangled in the feet of my mind as I was plodding my way through stifling Lyon in search of a haven such as this gleaming Hôtel Quivogne about whose cleanliness the most nonchalant and easygoing of pigs would have raised a fuss. Lichem and his cohorts had kidnapped Simon and had next tried to take care of me. But why next? And would they have left a message warning me not to alert the police if they had intended to take care of me next — all the time aware that I myself was a kidnapper? No.

On the other hand perhaps yes, simply to be careful.

Or else, a mad and obscure idea, Simon was a child very much in demand just now, and two rival groups (not to mention Michel Soler), for similar or different reasons, had both simultaneously decided to get their hands on him . . .

I twisted and turned in tortuous speculation.

A mad and obscure idea, but an idea whose blandishments the facts did not resist without flirtatious maneuvering. Ford, German driver of the Ford with the cracked headlights . . . He had stolen Simon from me, believing me to be just a friend of Simon's family, he had left a message and had then lost interest in my person. Lichem was ignorant of this man's existence, ignorant of what I had done with Simon, ignorant of everything. He had only recently located me, and had been waiting for me in my apartment to learn more . . .

Maybe.

I removed Lichem's weapon from my belt, where it was suddenly weighing on my intestines, and examined it.

Where was that adorable wicked child? In Lyon? Far from Lyon? And what did his many kidnappers, successful or unsuccessful, want? A ransom? Something else? The basic questions remained the same. The only new factor: I was in danger. They wanted to question me and then perhaps to kill me. What should I do? Go to the nearby police headquarters and tell all? No. I would leave only as a prisoner, so to speak. Rent a Lancia Thema and flee the city? But I did not want to be away from Michèle. Nothing to do but wait, like her, with her.

Silencer screwed onto the tip of the weapon, quite bulky. It could only be a silencer. And as far as I could see handmade, the most reliable kind, perhaps Lichem had made it himself to avoid unpleasant accidents, for sometimes this foreign body designed to render death silent hampers the working of the whole, thus ironically occasioning the death of the person desirous of inflicting it.

Under the sheets with Lichem's weapon.

I seized the telephone and asked the silent Turk to get me 812–5347. This time Michèle did not take her time. She grabbed the receiver in the middle of the very first ring, it's only me I said, and I told her my recent adventure and the shreds of thought I had hoisted from my feet up to arm level but really not much higher.

And of course all I did was add to her anguish and her confusion, but I could not quiet her . . .

"Of course!" she said. "Oh, my God! How scared you must have been! I'm worried for you. You brought it on yourself but I'm worried for you. Be careful when you leave the hotel . . . for the funeral. If you want police protection . . ."

"No."

"And then you should leave Lyon . . ."

"No. Maybe there's something we can do. I'm sure there is. I don't know what, but I'm sure. You can count on me." (Silence.) "I can't stop thinking of you." (Silence.) "Could we go and see a private detective?"

"No. I'll wait. You stay hidden, and get some rest. Once again, I'm so so sad about your mother, so so so sad. You can call me. No, it'll be better if I call you. If there's news."

A lot of words, but her tone was matter-of-fact, matter-of-fact beyond a doubt. It was more than I could take today, I replied OK bye-bye take care, and we hung up together, at least she hung up, because the phone, sticky with varying degrees of dirt, remained glued to my hand, I flapped it and shook it, then I took advantage of my hold on it to call downstairs and order a pot of coffee and a dozen croissants for breakfast next morning. By the way, did he have any cold drinks? No, no cold drinks, I thought not, might as well ask for refined honey in a bait-and-tackle shop, I let the water run for five minutes in a bathroom where the most stunted of dwarfs would have bruised himself black and blue trying to comb his hair and as soon as it was lukewarm drank half a gallon.

A great emptiness settled on me, the emptiness of forgetfulness and of neutral despair.

I locked the door. I undressed. I threw myself carelessly on the bed, ouch! that bed of embossed steel on which a senile, sedated groundhog would have lain with eyes wide open all winter long in the vain expectation of sleep, the cloud of gas that arose was less voluminous, less dense, more swiftly dissipated.

But I slept more hours in a row than I had since tenderest infancy. Troubled sleep, though, I manufactured dream after dream, one of which stuck in my memory: I was in New York, in a small street no different I told myself from a small street in any city, I was walking and I came to a corner and yes, there it was, New York, a gleaming skyscraper actually scraping the sky, contemplating it gave me a sense of intense joy, of exaltation, the loftiest and handsomest of skyscrapers, in reality a townhouse, the smallest of townhouses over Rainer von Gottardt's piano, I was living there with two women, one of these women had brought along a change of clothes because of the heat, I hadn't, I envied her. No more women. A cat, a big cat or a small dog, a nasty little animal that sank its teeth into my wrist, I had to shake my whole arm to get loose, finally it fell to the floor where it instantly died in a pool of blood, I wanted to throw up, I examined the tooth marks, two black holes with sharp outlines which meant: if this cat (for it was a cat, small, young, almost a kitten) died so easily, it must have been stricken with a terrible disease. Maybe contagious, and already caught by me?

•

Several times in my sleep I bumped painfully into Lichem's weapon. Hip, knee. Ankle. Genitals. Ouch!

Next morning the Turk, whom I had summoned, slightly more outgoing than the night before if no less taciturn (although he wished me a hearty appetite as he left the room), brought me a big pot of coffee and a basketful of croissants. Surprise, the coffee was almost as good as Liliane's and the croissants were delicious. A good start to the day.

I would have liked, out of despair, to go back to sleep again until the cremation. But that couldn't be done. My body would have refused. Instead I sat down in my underpants at a small, square, grayish table that rocked and was much too low, put Rainer von Gottardt's cassette in the tape player, and wrote until 3:00 P.M. Absorbing myself in this task was no problem. And my writing was more disciplined, my letters better formed, and I was regaining the ability to keep them on the page.

Better and better.

From time to time I ate a croissant. At 2:15 I ate two in succession.

At 3:00 I packed everything away in the suitcase and took a sorely needed bath. Sorely needed too were the prodigies of contortionism needed to permit ablutions in a bathroom where a basset hound would not have been able to snap at a fly without doing himself mortal harm, and where by dint of unimaginable calisthenics I managed to give myself a close shave, brush my teeth, and bathe my person, hair included, in this heat your hair was dry the second you turned the shower off.

At 3:30 I went downstairs, the steps were carpeted in red faded to gray-black except on the edges, where it was piss-yellow.

Three calls to make. Full of affability the Turk showed me the phone (this one had always been black, the phone in my room had once been cream-colored but had darkened and was now blacker than the one in the lobby), and full of tact he magically vanished.

I called Marc Philippon in case he had called me at my place on Rue de la République: no, no change, everything would go ahead as planned, with no problems from doctors or police, a natural death, accidental fire, the supernatural and the essential remained hidden to medical, municipal, and judicial official-dom, fine then, see you at the appointed hour, said Philippon, and keep a stiff upper lip, sir.

Then I phoned Satolas Airport, where I asked for car rentals.

Finally I called a taxi, the company closest to the hotel, without much hope, but they answered, replied in a hoarse voice, and said they would be around in ten seconds.

I went back upstairs. I took my money and Lichem's weapon. Safety catch, full chamber, six shells, trigger, nothing magical, child's play. Whoever tried too wholeheartedly to pick a quarrel with me would instantly get six bullets in his gray matter. Lichem's weapon thrust into my waistband. Coat buttoned over it.

I watched for the taxi from the window. Direct northern exposure, as I have already said. The only attraction of this Rue Quivogne, one of the least attractive of streets. The taxi arrived, shuddering and backfiring.

God was not delivering us from the sun. He was delivering us to it. And the sun burned out our eyes, amputated our arms and legs, rendered us liquid, sought to blend us into the black and sticky tar of the sidewalk. It wanted to destroy us.

I sported the fine handsome glasses from Carrefour with their slender black wire rims.

I did not recognize the make of car with noisy exhaust pipe waiting in front of the hotel. I squeezed into the rear right-hand corner seat.

"Satolas Airport," I told the driver, old, bald, wearing an undershirt, afflicted with a bad cold.

He started up without a word. He was a private operator, independent. Belonging to no company. His financial problems must be serious for him to be working in Lyon this month of August. Both he and his disastrous vehicle of no apparent make or vintage reeked of poverty. The gears ground, craaaaackkk! the steering floated, to stay more or less straight at twenty miles per hour he manhandled the wheel as if he were negotiating a series of downhill hairpin turns at fifty, as for the suspension it was like driving on wooden wheels, square, iron-studded, attached to dissymmetrical axles, not to mention seats stuffed with assorted bricks, monkey wrenches, and metal bottle caps. Sometimes a jolt would throw the car spontaneously into neutral and the engine would race. Then the driver got back into gear, craaaaaackkk, simultaneously sniffling powerfully enough to obliterate his features and coughing so desperately he threatened to tie his bronchial tubes in knots, a poor unlucky devil, really, gears, engine racing, sniffling, coughing, it all suggested a storm descending on the city, but alas no liberating storm came, only sun, discomfort, tension, I had my eyes peeled for Fiat Uno and Ford Scorpio, the Ford I had playfully shaken with Simon but perhaps it had really been tailing me and I had really shaken it that day, and another day it had tailed me invisibly, I kept my eyes peeled as I chewed over dark thoughts, Michèle, my enigmatic and disastrous love, Liliane, my mother gone forever, Simon, poor child I longed to find and rescue, only one cause for rejoicing: the driver with his cold was the kind who never once opens his mouth during the ride nor once examines you in his rearview mirror but leaves you free to sweat in despair and wring your hands on the back seat without afflicting you with observations and questions so pointless you long for a mute mankind, every tongue severed, Boulevard Laurent Bonnevay, highway.

The highway was soothing. You are nowhere on a highway. You might be far from Lyon. You might even be out of this world and on the road to paradise.

Brief respite. After a couple of miles and at the cost of a bitter struggle with his barely circular scrap metal steering wheel, my rheumy driver took the Satolas exit.

Airport. The meter showed close to two thousand dollars. A mistake somewhere. Greasy notebook in hand, half-inch pencil stub, black nails, the cougher plunged into a series of calculations at the end of which the sum had been brought back down to $19. I let him have $25, no no, it's I who am grateful to you, he looked at me for the first time, even smiled at me, he no longer had teeth, lifelong habits of poor hygiene plus lack of money, such people still exist.

The car, abandoned by Attila after the barbarian invasions and overhauled any which way by its mute driver, jolted away amid reports and shudderings. I would not have been surprised had it exploded, I was ready to duck my head down between my shoulders.

The air conditioning at Satolas, better regulated or more sophisticated than at Carrefour, rekindled a tiny spark of life. A few deplorable specimens of the human race were taking advantage of it, settled on benches, gnawing at crusts of bread and draining lukewarm beer dregs, a weather eye alert for the uniform that would move them on.

At the car rental desk a truly ravishing girl greeted me. I removed my glasses.

"Hello. I phoned a little while ago."

"Yes. Hello. Your car is waiting. First I need . . ."

I left the airport in a white Lancia the image of Michèle de Klef's.

Only the license number was different.

Go back along the highway by which I had come? Flee, no matter where? No. I returned to the city with a certain degree of pleasure, perverse pleasure, as if I had to drain Lyon's cup to the bitter dregs and even — as the future would show — beyond!

•

At 4:22 P.M. I parked at the Guillotière Cemetery. Following Marc Philippon's directions, alone among the graves, I made my way across the cemetery to the crematorium. The sun beat down more pitilessly than ever. It took advantage of my presence in the land of the dead to try to decompose me, disperse me, destroy me where I stood.

It would not succeed.

Marc Philippon, in a well-cut dark suit, was waiting for me at the incineration site. He gave me a firm handshake, no affected gravity in his attitude, a sober sympathy, that was all. Well done, Philippon. We went into the room reserved for the families of the deceased, a large, circular, almost bare hall. Organ music drifted out over an invisible loudspeaker, at least you had to assume it was the organ, and assume that it was music, it sounded more like the cries of terrified turkeys against a background of buckshot peppering a tin roof. And above all, an incredible thing, but heard by me on that day, from afar my mother burning, pops, explosions, crackling, as merry as chestnuts roasting around a fire of damp wood. I mentioned it rather sullenly to Philippon.

"I know," he said. "Sometimes the music doesn't cover . . .

But it's over now. Did you know that some people ask if they can watch . . . We'll have the urn soon."

We had the urn soon. It was handed to me. As arranged, I was expected at the old Cusset Cemetery for the burial. Another firm handshake from the rather handsome sandy-haired fellow in the well-cut dark suit.

I went back across the cemetery sadder and deader, I told myself, than in the worst of November days.

Would November never come? No, impossible to believe in November.

So urn in hand I went back across the cemetery, but did not turn right toward the parking lot just before reaching the main gate, for at that main gate stood the young and pretty Michèle, with whom an enigmatic and disastrous love had linked me the instant I raised my gaze to her face one epochal evening.

EIGHT

I went to her. She was smoking. She was very white, not tanned at all. She wore a black dress. I didn't see her Lancia.

"Any news?" I said.

"No. I wanted to be at the cemetery with you for the funeral. Since I knew you'd be alone. If you want me here, that is."

"I do," I said. "It's nice of you. I'm very touched. But what about the phone?"

"My friend from Sainte-Foy is staying with us for a few days. I told her to answer the phone as if she were me. If they phone . . . Was it awful?"

Yes, it had been awful, awful.

"Awful," I said. "I'm trying not to cry. They play music, but there's something wrong with their public-address system, you can hear the bodies burning. I'm trying hard not to cry. Let's not stay here. No need to be dead and cremated to be reduced to ashes in this weather. Another three minutes out in this sun . . . You have to be careful."

"My car wouldn't start. I came by cab."

We walked to the parking lot.

A few more steps and she would see the Lancia.

"Wouldn't start, eh?" (Clap! Setting my mother down, I clapped my hands.) "Well, what's this then?!"

Miraculous apparition of the Lancia.

Bitter buffooneries, the ill-timed jests of wretches wandering between life and death, seeking out and fleeing the one and the other, summoning and dismissing the one and the other!

"It occurred to me that you should rent a car," she said. "I tried to call you at the hotel, but you had already left. It was an intelligent move. Your red Dauphine – "

"I know. Conspicuous. Might as well wander around in – "

I resisted the temptation to make an ill-timed jest. "I liked driving your Lancia so much I rented one."

I opened the passenger door, she got in, permitting a better look at her white legs, shshshfrooooop! the door swished shut, I walked around the car, reached through the lowered window to drop my mother on the rear seat, and got behind the wheel.

I drove off.

"Add to that the money I have coming to me," I said. "A small inheritance, the insurance on the house . . ."

And the five thousand dollars for the kidnapping.

I left Guillotière Cemetery by Boulevard des Tchécoslovaques. Michèle was pale, she had dark rings under her eyes.

"Did you really want to kill yourself?"

"I don't know."

"You're not going to?"

"No."

"You promise?"

"Yes."

She might have thought of it sooner. Like yesterday, for instance. Not leave me alone for a second. A wave of hatred made me sweat harder than ever.

"Do you play the piano?"

"No. Once, yes, once I played."

"I haven't read your book, but I've heard about it. I'd very much like to read it. I just flipped through it at your place."

Read my book! Hah! She could go scratch her private parts with a holly branch. (Good golly Miss Molly gimme that holly, I hummed to myself.) I did not reply.

"I'm sorry, it was most indiscreet of me to go through your things. I was out of my mind."

After Avenue Félix Faure came Place des Maisons Neuves, Rue Jean Jaurès, Place Grandclément. . . .

"If I understand correctly, Rainer von Gottardt contacted you, he's in Lyon now, and you're writing the story of his life?"

"Yes."

"That's good. That's wonderful."

"Yes. Don't tell anyone, he doesn't want anyone to know."

"Of course not."

She had made no more mention of my troubles yesterday, or of Simon.

•

At 5:00 P.M. on the dot the ashes of Liliane Tormes, the woman whose son I had been without the agency of defilement, these ashes were inhumed in accordance with her wishes in the grave of Diego Soler. Together they would rest in peace.

I myself consigned the urn to the bowels of our planet, and a worker armed with a shovel restored the surface of things to order.

My mother was dead and buried.

Six tears flowed from my right eye. None from the left. Henceforth we must contemplate life without Liliane, without her delicious meals, her craziness, her limitless love for me, her horse language, neerva boolimi meeasmess meeasmess cranpateeloo bottomless misery, bllll bllll vvvvvv . . .

Dead and buried.

•

"What you were saying about a detective . . . . I've been thinking. Not the police, but a private detective . . . I'm so afraid this is the end of Simon. What happened to you yesterday . . ."

Aha! So that was it! Compassion alone (and even more than that, in the depth of my bereavement I had hoped for more, why not?) had not impelled Michèle to seek me out, to materialize before me at the cemetery gate, an apparition, an illusion born of the excessive harshness of the sun and the excessive violence of my emotions!

"Right," I said. "We'll find one."

"Today? At once?"

"Yes."

"It won't bother you?"

"No. On the contrary. We'll stop at Place des Terreaux. The Alexander the Great Detective Agency is there. Let's hope it's open in August. Above all this awful August, above all this awful August" (the first "above all this awful August" pitched noticeably higher, with the "this" representing the peak, than the second, which was perceptibly lower, monotonous, duller). "You'd have to be really bitten by the investigating bug to do any detecting this August. Anyway, let's hope. Alexander the Great. It's fairly well known. You must have seen the ads."

"No, I don't think so. I haven't lived in Lyon much. Why are you living through this awful August here?"

"Ooooohweell . . ." I said ("this awful August," she had repeated it, the little minx!). "'There be a Phoenix living here all awful and unknown,' I remember that sentence from a school grammar book. Do you live alone in Paris?"

"Yes."

"Do you come to Lyon often?"

"No. Never. Only in August. Simon spends July in Grenoble with a sister of my father's who has lots of children. And I come here in August. It's been that way for three years, ever since I've lived in Paris. Since the Berlin episode. I couldn't stand being with my family anymore. Or with what was left of it. I couldn't stand seeing my father in that state. And Simon . . . I told you how he has changed. In any case I had to go to Paris for my music studies. Only I would have come back more often. My brother started to frighten me . . ."

"How?"

"I don't know. He's become . . ."

I never thought I would one day take corners as fast as I was now circling Place Maréchal Lyautey in order to reach Quai de Serbie from Cours Roosevelt, you were unconscious of your speed in this Lancia, a quick glance at the dashboard as Michèle talked to me, ouch, too late to brake, I would never reach the Morand Bridge, we were going to water-ski across the Rhône, no, immense relief at the realization that we had remained glued to the road, such relief that for a fleeting moment it brought relief from all pain, leaving in my heart a yearning for an arduous endless journey that would be child's play to the magical Lancia, relief then would be eternal.

"You have also," I said nastily, very nastily. "You have also become."

•

Place des Terreaux. I pulled up in front of the Zoom movie theater.

As I got out of the car my coat flapped open and I inadvertently displayed Lichem's weapon.

"What is that?" said Michèle.

"Lichem's weapon. It skittered under the bed. Our bed, remember? I decided to hold onto it as tight as my own right arm."

"Do you think that's wise?"

"Wisdom itself."

"But what if you're stopped, if you're asked . . ."

"I won't be stopped. By anything. Do you know the Saint-Pierre Palace? It's pretty, all white . . ."

She looked at the Saint-Pierre Palace on the opposite sidewalk, all white and pretty. Looked at me, hesitated. "They say Old Lyon has been considerably restored too," she said.

"That's what they say. But I haven't set foot there in ages." (Just as I had not set foot in Berlin, I told myself, thinking of Rainer von Gottardt and the private townhouse where he had stayed.) "Shall we call on our detective?"

Schblonk! A pigeon. A pigeon crashed to the ground at our feet. It was disgusting. I should mention that Place des Terreaux is a pigeon-infested square. In these temperatures some (a lot) of them were dying of heat and falling from the roofs, schblonk! on Place des Terreaux you had to plot a zigzag course to avoid being bombarded by heat-struck pigeons plummeting from the roofs, schblonk!, schblonk!

Schblonk!

The Alexander the Great Detective Agency. We went into the alley to the left of the Zoom and to the right of a café on the corner of a street whose name I can never remember, a dingy, dirty, bumpy alley, a muddy intestinal tract, on the left were two long uneven rows of battered mailboxes of varying materials, shapes, and colors, a kind of wall-disease, a monstrous fungus, a bubonic eczema, a scab-encrusted urticaria, a carbuncular psoriasis, Michèle said to me: "The agency may be well known, but this area is — "

"Yes, it is indeed. Never mind, the agency has the best-looking mailbox."

I had just seen it, Alexander the Great, fourth floor left, the adjacent mailbox on the other hand was the ugliest of them all, the filthiest and most fetid, besmeared with tomato sauce and toad drool, a piece of carelessly torn shopping-bag paper pinned in place by a twisted thumbtack bore in ravaged letters the inscription: Dr. Clève-Simonnet, diseases of the mouth, ha, ha! you might as well chew manure to disinfect a canker as seek this Clève-Simonnet's opinion, see that? I said to Michèle as I walked ahead of her suppressing a sick laugh, one of those laughs you hear in the seediest asylums for the incurably insane on days of storm and of medication strikes.

At the end of a long, dark, winding climb, the landing lights giving off less illumination than a firefly on its deathbed, we reached the door we sought. I knocked, knock, knock, knock.

"Come in," said a barely audible voice.

We went into a large sumptuous room with three windows open on Place des Terreaux, after the dark fetid squalor of the courtyard and the stairway your mind and eye were tempted to rejoice.

We took four steps forward. Only then did a man of my age who had scarcely glanced at us remove his feet from his desk and rise to greet us with a lack of enthusiasm he did nothing to conceal.

He motioned us to sit down across the gleaming desk from him, and sat back down himself. He was shorter than I, stockier, and his hair was so like mine, length, waviness, cut, that I had to fight the urge to raise my hand to my head to make sure my own was still there. He smoked the same brown unfiltered cigarettes as Michèle, apparently in the same extravagant quantities.

"We were afraid you might be closed in August," said Michèle.

"We are, almost. I'm filling in. Keeping the flag flying. I've been sent down from Paris. I'm just getting started in this business."

His accents were vulgar, and vulgar too the twist his words imparted to his mouth when he spoke.

"Do you live in Paris?" asked Michèle.

"Yes."

"So do I."

"It's my first time in Lyon. What heat! Seeing how crowded the city is, I have to admit I wasn't expecting customers."

"You have to expect anything," I said.

A pointless comment, vain and hostile. Hostile because in the second he replied yes to Michèle's question (which I held against Michèle) whether he lived in Paris, in that second, looking more closely at her, the summer replacement at the Alexander the Great Agency fell in love with her.

That at least was what I concluded.

It must be admitted that with that black dress against her white and delicate skin, her slender but not bony figure, her luminous visage, with her perfect blend of perfection and imperfection, of grace and lack of grace, she would have induced a dead dancer to execute heavenly leaps of sentimental ecstasy.

"Right. You're absolutely right." (This said in the tones of one who would gladly have driven his fist between my eyes in immediate and vivid illustration of my claim that one should expect anything. To Michèle:) "Well, then. How may I help you?"

"My brother has disappeared. He's been kidnapped."

She handed him the note, the page from the appointment book left beside Liliane.

And she told him about her brother Simon and the first kidnapping.

Then, as we had agreed, she let me recount more recent developments. Naturally I told a truncated version of the story, presenting myself as a friend of the family, a version that was silent on my own sorry role, the story without me, I invented, I mainly left things out, indeed I limited myself to the most detailed description I could manage of the two people I suspected, Lichem and the German driver, and advanced the theory of rival sets of kidnappers, a theory conceivably borne out by the attack of which I had been a victim. (But in truth the victim . . . the victim had been Lichem, who to avoid giving vent to the howling of a wolf must right now be soaking his private parts in an analgesic and emulsifying solution.)

His vulgar countenance twisted in a grimace, the investigator did not once take his eyes off Michèle. He offered her a cigarette, which she accepted. A light, she accepted that too, she even waited to be offered one, although she was holding her own lighter (of yellow plastic) in her hand. I was sorry I had come.

I was jealous.

He asked several questions.

Every now and then a pigeon slain by the heat plummeted past the window, the right one or the left one, or the middle one, or past two windows at once, two pigeons, it was like a game, then you heard a distant schblonk!

"I don't really know what to tell you. There's no trail here to speak of. We'll just have to wait. Your brother is either in Lyon, or in Berlin, or somewhere else. If he's somewhere else or in Berlin, I can't do a thing for you. If he's in Lyon . . . I still can't do all that much. Drive around, walk the streets on the chance of spotting one of the two men described by . . . by this gentleman. I can try, if you like."

He pushed the ashtray across the table so that Michèle would not have to reach over. He was paying her shameless court. Cheap, insistent. He disgusted me.

"Yes, I would," said Michèle.

She would like! My anger rumbled.

He had her fill out and sign a form, they traded phone numbers ("My name is Renaud Lossaire, I live here, at the agency"), and finally he asked her for $75, she hastened to write out a check with a pen he handed her. This verbal agreement between them ("If you like," "Yes, I would"), which had brought a gleam to Lossaire's eye, these signatures, these figures, this money sealing their pact all drove me mad.

I noticed as we left the agency that my rival's face was not so ugly in repose.

We reached the Lancia.

Schblonk!

"Maybe we should have trusted him and told him absolutely absolutely everything," said Michèle in the car.

"You're absolutely absolutely crazy! For one thing it wouldn't help at all, I don't see how it could. But I do see how it could have ugly repercussions for me. And for another thing . . . for another thing don't you realize the guy has the brains of a bird, he's as sharp as a cow? He couldn't find his own mother in a broom closet. It's obvious he's as thick as two planks!"

"Not to me it isn't." She immediately forced a smile to soften the harshness of her remark.

What game was she playing? Did this Renaud Lossaire really inspire trust in her? Had she been aware of his disgusting advances, as subtle as a jailbird propositioning the lowest prostitute in town after three years of celibacy? Due to a stint in the desert? Or was she digging the heel of vengeance into me after I had declared my sacred love for her, and on the day of my mother's burial? How I regretted taking her to the Alexander the Great Agency! A private detective! Had I really believed in the usefulness of such a step? A little, probably. The tiniest hope had to be cultivated, the slightest chance explored. But so slight. No, for me it had been an excuse for seeing her, for spending time with her . . .

Had it not been for that softening smile I swear I would have pulled out my weapon and killed her.

But, just like yesterday morning, I suddenly felt (as we drove past a Codec grocery store and I craned in vain to see some inoffensive German tourist beside his Ford with a trunkful of groceries) the painful need to flee from her and then, alone, to recover some of my strength in order to face anew this disastrous love that was consuming me even more efficiently than the fire of the sun.

But when I pulled over in Impasse du Point du Jour, with my white Lancia's nose an inch from the nose of her white Lancia, and she proposed a cool drink, I accepted, saying to myself, come on, the day can still be saved.

We got out of the car.

"Do you know anything about simple repairs? Just in case it is a simple problem . . ."

"Very simple, then," I said. "Empty tank, jammed hand-brake . . . Do you have any gas?"

"Yes. A full tank."

"Water in your battery? In this weather . . . Did you check?"

"No."

"Let's check. That might be the cause . . ."

That was indeed the cause. I lifted the hood, unscrewed the six plastic caps on the battery. Bone-dry. Not a drop of water.

We walked by the spindle-tree hedge.

"Strange house," I said.

"Built by my paternal grandfather four years before his death. He spent a lot of time in the colonies." (Ah! colonial style!) "It's always been looked after well."

"It looks brand-new," I said. "Just sprouted from the ground."

Michèle pushed the wooden gate open. Her father was in the same spot on the lawn, covered with the same plaid blanket, in the same intricate metal and leather chair that must also be his bed. Michèle stroked him on the skull, with no more effect on the quadriplegic than if she had dealt him an axe blow. So much stillness, so much insensibility were not of this world, they made you uneasy. Still. Insensible. A body, nothing more. But he lived. He lived, and he knew.

"If we pulled the pin from a grenade and tossed it in his lap," I said to her, "are you sure it wouldn't extract a few words from him that might help us to . . ."

"That's really clever," she said.

"I agree," I said. "But you irritated me, with that detective. Forgive me." (I looked closely at the unfortunate man, his sagging jaw, his closed eye, the other one half open, in any case he couldn't see a thing, his skeletal hands.) "What kind of wounds could have . . ."

She told me. He had taken a first bullet in the base of his spine. The second full in the skull, small caliber, from the right temple to the left temple, stopped by bone after severing the frontal lobe but without touching a major vessel. Horrible. The third, fired from the side, had fractured the vertebrae at the base of the neck, burning and bruising the marrow without totally destroying it. Horrible horrible.

At that moment a young woman came out of the house, tall, dark, well built, with long hair. She held a book in her hand, one finger slipped inside to keep her place.

"Michel, Annie," said Michèle.

I shook hands with Annie, the nurse from Sainte-Foy l'Argentière. She studied me with a permanent air of surprise I was unable to account for.

"Hello. What are you reading?" I asked, just to be friendly.

She showed me the cover, losing her place in her timid haste. I saw the title, *Our Kingdom Come,* and a photo, it looked like Place Bellecour.

"Is it good?"

"Yes, it's a novel, it takes place in Lyon."

Then there was an awkwardness, I'm reading in the living room, Annie finally said and left, her white dress flying.

A little later Michèle and I were drinking Coke in her bedroom on the second floor, that's where the piano was, a Töhdeskünst much smaller than Rainer von Gottardt's. The house was indeed well looked after, with handsome wooden furniture piled with many-colored cushions. Surprise: on one wall hung a menacing throng of merrymakers made of fruit and vegetable peelings.

"DPH, isn't it?" I said to Michèle. "There was a picture by him on Rue Duguesclin."

"Really?"

"Who is he?"

"Phil Dreux. A Lyon artist. He's dead. Don't you know him?"

"No."

"His stuff's in lots of homes in Lyon."

"We should really have taken a quick look at Rue Duguesclin, just in case . . ."

"What we really should have done was tell Renaud Lossaire about it."

"Oh, please! Please don't mention that . . . But I'll shut up out of respect for your father . . ."

"Out of respect for my father?"

"What if his hearing were miraculously restored just as I let fly with an appropriate flood of curses, the shock might be too much for the flicker of life left in him. What bullets in the marrow and the brain couldn't do, my vile language . . . You play the piano really well, you know."

"You're crazy. You're truly crazy . . . What about you? Have you given it up altogether?"

"Yes. I gave it up when I was very young."

(Hah! She could always . . . holly branch, good golly Miss Molly.)

"And you, you teach, you . . ."

"Yes, I teach at a conservatory just outside town. And I'm making a record of the Granados."

"Very good!"

"I was lucky. I met the right people," she said sulkily.

"I'd love to listen to you. Whenever you want . . ."

She did not answer. She was sitting up very straight on the edge of her bed like a well-behaved child. I was lost amid the cushions of a chair with splayed wings. A bird lighted on the windowsill, looked at us, flew away.

"In a couple of hours I'm having dinner with the fallen genius Rainer von Gottardt. Could I see you later tonight? I don't want to be alone for a second."

Suddenly I was sure she would accept. But she refused, quite offhandedly, with a simple shake of the head and one of those smiles that make you want to lash out.

I instantly left her.

"Are you angry?"

"Yes. Boil water and pour it in the battery, the car will start."

I descended the stairs rowdily, saluted the father with a gracious sweeping gesture, fingertips almost touching my fore-head, although a goat trotting on its hind legs and singing in a soprano voice would not have left Colonel de Klef less impressed.

I turned around before leaving the garden. Coat buttoned. From now on Lichem's weapon condemned me to be hot.

No one on the upstairs balcony. She must have remained seated on her bed. In place of a heart she had a sharpened axe. Annie, on the other hand, appeared at a ground floor window and responded with surprise to my good-bye wave. She was a person I filled with surprise.

Three steps took me to the car.

We survivors of the city would have paid heavily to have God deliver us from the sun — from the pitiless eye of God, I suddenly told myself, suddenly conceiving the notion that God, His gaze necessarily riveted on us, could not deliver us from the sun unless He ripped one of His own eyes out!

•

"You've come into a fortune?" asked Rainer von Gottardt.

"No. I rented it for a few days. A small indulgence. It's not as hot as my Dauphine. And more comfortable. Sometimes my whole body is in pain, I hurt everywhere."

In truth my body had stopped hurting.

"You were right. And soon you will be able to buy it."

The pianist with the missing finger had prepared an extremely simple meal requiring only the opening of cans. Old, doubtful cans. It would be best for me to say as little as possible about the salad and the omelette. The fallen genius had given the cab driver who had brought him from the airport a list of purchases as long as a landing strip, for this cab driver lived in Saint-Genis-Laval where his wife's brother had a grocery that stayed open in August, and so, when the trusting von Gottardt confided his concerns over provisions, the driver said well, there's my brother-in-law . . . of course he will deliver, anywhere, you bet, and so forth, good business for the brother-in-law in question who had thus unloaded a large part of his stock and got rid of some canned goods just a few minutes short of their final shelf date.

Only the white wine was excellent.

"Why haven't you reconnected your telephone?" I asked my enormous, puffy, mottled host.

His Saba cassette recorder was on, sitting near my left hand on the big farm table. I ingurgitated a last forkful of grated carrot. The grated carrots were from a jar that had bleated like a goat when its lid was unscrewed, they were far too vinegary, they were far too everything but they were too vinegary, and this last forkful made me cough, sneeze, shudder from head to toe.

"I am ashamed of this meal, my dear Michel, believe me, I am ashamed. I am so unaccustomed — "

"I assure you it doesn't matter. Speaking of grated carrots, my mother Liliane Tormes used to claim, at the time when her powers of speech were still like those of the rest of us: when the carrots have been grated the vitamins too have been grated."

I could mention Liliane without collapsing more dead than alive at the foot of the table. Moments spent with Rainer von Gottardt were moments out of time.

"Ha, ha! Your mother is funny, like you! The phone . . . Why do you mention the phone?"

"I don't know. Has your experience ever included the possession of a telephone?"

"Ha, ha! Yes."

"You might need a doctor . . . Your heart . . ."

"Don't you worry. What has to happen will happen when it is supposed to happen. A phone, even a solid gold one, will not make the slightest difference."

Having uttered these words he raised his head and his brows, looked me straight in the eye, stuck out a thick furred tongue and ran it around his red and unwholesomely glistening lips, a series of operations that put the crowning touch to his looks, giving him the air of a fairground freak.

I understood. I imitated his maneuver with my own tongue, and en route encountered a fragment of grated carrot.

"Thank you," I said.

"Pray do not mention it. My God! The omelette, the pasta . . ."

"I'll come with you. Yes, I insist!"

We went into the kitchen, which looked out onto the back of the house and was quite well equipped. The green salad—it was in fact gray, and badly washed—was ready. We were supposed to eat the omelette first and immediately afterward, with the gray salad, consume canned beef chunks in gravy with baby potatoes, baby potatoes that the maestro, fearing they would not be a substantial enough accompaniment, had decided to reinforce with extremely large macaroni. Alas, unaccustomed as he was to the execution of household tasks, he had not foreseen that it would take longer for very large macaroni to cook than for eggs to become an omelette. Moreover, while I was preparing the said omelette (with eggs that must have been laid decades earlier by a sick hen), he was shaking an excessive quantity of very large macaroni into an excessive quantity of water, so much so that after the omelette we waited endlessly and would have had time to eat endless omelettes, every hen on earth would not have sufficed to make enough omelettes to fill this long wait.

The omelette.

"Don't force yourself," said Rainer von Gottardt. "Leave it if you like. I prepared a lot of food. It seems to have some kind of aftertaste . . ."

He was panting. He was exhausted. He was drinking too much. He smoked his cigars while eating.

"Perhaps even a slight foretaste," I said. "I believe I will leave it. From now on, please, don't get up, I'll go to the kitchen, I'll take care of everything. And please don't worry, eating this dinner with you gives me great pleasure."

"Me also." (After a short silence:) "Apart from making your acquaintance, two events make me regret that I shall not live longer. My recording of *The Well-Tempered Clavier,* made at a time when I did not have this horrible missing finger. And my discovery of the sacred joys of the flesh with Ana de Tuermas. For it was with her I discovered those sacred joys. At fifty-two. What I knew before that did not exist. Before or after. Is the pasta not yet cooked?"

"Assuredly not," I said. "I don't believe the water has even begun to simmer."

"I leave it in your hands. I did not see Ana again until 1973. We had not spoken much in Lyon. We had spent a few days together here in this house in Francheville, without telling the Dioblanízes. She was very secretive, even with her friends. She spoke little. Would you believe that despite the intensity and the suddenness of our passion she left Lyon without giving me her address? I was in despair. But sure I would see her again one day . . . In 1970 I lost my finger."

I considered him with a less jaded air. More inquisitorial. He smiled.

"In circumstances I would prefer to keep secret. They are of no importance. One of the dramas of my life. For two years I devoted myself to teaching. And for those same two years, to alcohol."

Rainer von Gottardt had acquired a distaste for teaching, but not for alcohol, whose praises he sang so impressively to me that I downed my white wine in one gulp and refilled my glass to the brim.

The father of one of his pupils suggested that he try a detoxification cure. An ordeal that reduced the pianist, as he put it, to the timorous condition of a newborn child. The same pupil's father, who greatly admired him, then invited him to come and rest at his house in Cadaqués in Spain.

"It was at Cadaqués, which for me is the most beautiful place in the world, that I saw Ana again. She lives there. Same violent passion. I shared her life, more or less, until 1976."

"More or less?"

"She often kept me and her other activities apart. She would vanish and reappear. Borderline activities, the activities of a high adventuress, of an outlaw, this I knew. But she did not tell me much. She was lovely, intelligent, secretive. And crazy. She needed danger, intrigue, secrets. The last I heard of her, which was a long time ago, she had settled down. But you have not taken off your coat?"

"No, it's all right, I'm not too hot, thanks."

He was silent for a moment, then confessed to me that he was attracted by virginity. The few women he had known were virgins, or very nearly so. Ana of course was not. She had slept all over the world with everything that had balls, and even with some that didn't, for instance with Isabel Dioblaníz, that lunatic, in Bolivia, and perhaps in Lyon as well, yes, the relationship between the two women was also physical. And yet . . .

"And yet I loved her as though I had been her first lover. Incomprehensible. Earthly paradise. We traveled. After Spain, North America, South America, North Africa, Berlin, the summer of 1974, a few days in the little townhouse a friend lent her. On Wahrscheynstrasse. The photo. Over the piano."

The little Renaissance townhouse, four windows per floor, one gable straight the other arched, a building to which he was drawing my attention, a building I felt I had seen before. Where? It couldn't be, I was imagining things.

"You mentioned the rumors surrounding the Dioblanízes' departure from Bolivia . . . Your friend Ana de Tuermas must have known the true story?"

"Perhaps. If she did, she did not want to talk about it."

I did not insist. He was telling the truth. The word piano still hung in the air.

"I would very much like to hear you play. Even just a few notes," I said.

"I too would very much like to hear you play."

"One of these days?"

"Yes. And you?"

I did not hesitate: "Yes."

"You must start to play again, my dear Michel. As soon as I am dead. I believe in you. Do not ask why. It is a question of faith."

"I think I hear the macaroni boiling over," I said. "No, don't get up. I'll be right back."

The macaroni was indeed boiling over. I put a low flame under the canned beef, which was more or less warm by the time I had finished draining the pasta and putting about one-fortieth of it into a dish with a big lump of nicely rancid butter.

"Voilà!" I said.

"Thank you. Sit down, sit down. I am hungrier and eating more tonight than at any time since I arrived. Probably your company. I would also like you to tell me about your own life. But you do not seem so inclined. What is that on your left wrist, those two distinct marks? And on your forehead, that bruise you are hiding with your hair?"

"It's a secret. I'll tell you if you tell me about your finger."

"Ha, ha! Too bad! How funny you are! The American company that will be publishing my memoirs, Smikel and Keyelgod, will do a good job. They are very rich and internationally connected. The public has lost sight of me a little, but my recording of *The Well-Tempered Clavier* will be in the window of every record shop in the world the day after the book comes out. And the press, not just the trade press but the press in general, even the scandal sheets, they'll dig up all the old dirt, they'll recall all the mystery surrounding my life, the obscure regions, and they'll announce that all is revealed in Michel Soler's book. Before you know it you'll be sitting on a nice little fortune. Eat! This macaroni looks like a tapeworm convention, ha, ha!"

He was being lavish with his thick labored laugh today.

"What obscure regions?"

"Those three days in Berlin, for instance, August 1974."

Berlin again, August 1974. The Renaissance townhouse. Had Simon father and son been held there against their will for three days and had they then, after one or more hideous scenes, been taken from there and abandoned in a suburban house whose innocent owners, it will be remembered, had been away for the whole weekend? A mad hunch.

This hunch of a connection between Rainer von Gottardt and the two Simon de Klefs had of course already occurred to me, but I had tucked it away in the bag of invincibly mad and mysterious hunches that had been so eagerly assailing me since the beginning of this tropical August, appearances at once explored and linked, interconnected along impalpable networks of mist, bridges, roads, spirals of mist, but these ideas, how shall I put it? I seemed more or less to have been born with them, they dwelt in the shadows, gaining strength in secret, lurking, waiting for the right moment to attach themselves to something, anything, with the object of taking shape, of being caressed, of being praised, and — triumph — of being recognized as triumphant!

Such a moment was upon us. Would it not have been better if my soul had kicked that mad and invincible, and innate, hunch all the way back to its state of dreamy nonbeing? But wouldn't such a kick have meant sending myself back as well, and thus annihilating myself? I asked the fatal question: "What happened?"

"I do not know."

"But you were . . ."

I broke off. Rainer von Gottardt hesitated. Perhaps he had nothing to say? And perhaps my unframed question was forcing him to . . . to say what had truly happened?

"Nothing. Neither actor nor spectator." (He hesitated again. My silence was cruel. He hesitated, then:) "But an accomplice, alas, yes . . . A distant and unwitting accomplice."

I could no longer turn back. To turn back would have been to die, not to speak would have been to remain forever silent.

"And if what happened then, or something like it, were to have happened again, recently? In Lyon? You would know nothing about it? You would have nothing to say about it? Neither you . . . nor Ana de Tuermas?"

"No. No, certainly not!" He was astonished, sincerely astonished. But he did not question me.

"You swear it?"

"I swear! I swear!"

Together we sighed with relief, as if Madness, Horror, and Aberration themselves had brushed us with their tattered wings and spared us for that evening. And we chatted, lightly, of other things.

The meat inedible. Hails of bullets fired by the most pugnacious armies would have flattened themselves against the chunks of beef in gravy with baby potatoes and been reduced to dark blotches of uncertain contour or else by a supreme irony would have ricocheted and winged back toward those who had fired them, unless, poorly aimed, they veered and cut short the lives of the thousand slugs clinging to the salad leaves, of which incidentally by tacit agreement we did not touch a single leaf and from which our slightest breath, faint though it was, detached and sent flying broad fringes of graying decomposed matter. As for the querulously yellow potatoes, they either exploded when we pierced them with our forks or else collapsed with a sigh of deepest melancholy on our plates where they shriveled up in one last spasm before flattening out anew, this time for good.

Two and a half cassettes recorded.

A last bottle of white wine and good strong coffee helped our digestive organs recover from the nutritional aberrations we had inflicted on them.

•

On the threshold, Rainer von Gottardt took and held in his hairy wet hand the hand I held out to him.

Our relief had endured, so much so that instead of telling him thank you, good-bye, get some rest, I'll see you the day after tomorrow, I spoke to him unhesitatingly and unthinkingly of

Liliane: "I buried my mother this afternoon . . . She died yesterday."

"My God! My poor friend!"

He squeezed my hand tighter. Showing no surprise that I had delayed this moment of revelation so long. Guessing perhaps — his own mad hunch, the twin of mine — the nature of the words that came unhesitatingly and unthinkingly to my lips: "She was keeping little Simon de Klef for two days. Simon de Klef was kidnapped in her house, in her presence. She was not brutalized, thank God, but her heart must indeed have been diseased; it did not withstand the fright. And since I had asked her to look after the child, I feel I bear the guilt both for the death and for the kidnapping . . ."

He merely said, in his nationless accent — and I expected no more, neither astonishment nor questions, we both knew now what we wanted to know, the rest was unimportant: "The guilt! My poor Michel Soler! I am with you heart and soul. But alas, I can do nothing! Except to tell you again how much I love you! And how much I regret that we did not meet in 1969!"

"Please believe that your love is important to me, and that it is returned."

Then Madness, Horror, and Aberration again flapped their wings, but from afar, furious, powerless: "What you told me just now . . . What you told me just now, do you still swear it?"

"Yes! I still swear it! On my soul, on yours! On your mama's soul!"

He took me in his arms, his elephant cheek pressed against mine, we hugged one another for half a second.

"What loneliness, my friend," he gasped out all in one breath.

"Yes," I said, "what loneliness!"

"If you like you can sleep here. Stay here as long as you like. I sleep downstairs. The two bedrooms upstairs are empty. We would not be in one another's way. Our interviews would not be any more frequent, I need rest, rest . . . You could live just as you pleased."

No. My regular visits to the Maestro stood out against the backdrop of my life in just the way a character is repeated at regular intervals in a tapestry, I could readily perceive my life as a character and my visits to Rue de l'Église in Francheville as backdrop, and thus I saw more clearly the mysteries of my life, even if the key to these mysteries remained hidden to me, hidden within the general plan, but perhaps it would be given to me if I persisted in these games of perception.

"No," I said. "Thank you. From the bottom of my heart."

•

I returned to Lyon tortured by a stomach ache and very tipsy, and determined to get even tipsier before going to my cast-iron bed on Rue Quivogne.

More from melancholy than from caution, I decided against the Bar des Archers, pointless I told myself aloud to put all my baskets in the same egg, which made no sense and sent me into helpless laughter, but laughing hurt my stomach, I concentrated on holding my stomach still and forcibly assigning to my face alone the task of expressing all my nervous hilarity. I turned purple, my lips swelled and thickened, my eyes screwed up and vanished, their former location was flawlessly smooth when you ran your hand over my face, sweat flooded my forehead, my nose flowed like a fountain, two jets of what must have been water vapor steamed hissing from my ears, and sounds never before heard from me escaped my mouth and filled the car. But I held on, the crisis came to an end without a muscle in my abdomen so much as twitching. Bravo.

A few seconds later I was to laugh less. As follows:

A bar was open on Place Carnot, a vast bar, empty, depressing. No. I accelerated. On Rue Mercière, perhaps, where a memory of the life and high spirits animating that street on other nights of the year might still linger. I hurried to Rue Mercière.

Stupid goddamn construction made it impossible to park there. I left the car on the corner of Rue de Brest and walked, click click click went the cassettes in my pocket.

Wonderful, the bar lights were on, the usual dull glow from its diffused lighting.

A couple came out.

It was Michèle and Lossaire.

Michèle and the detective! Michèle de Klef and Renaud Lossaire, Lossaire, the hated rival, the vulgar and incompetent detective who, if hired to solve a case of jealousy, adultery, and murder, a white woman married to a white man having given birth to a yellow infant with slanted eyes and the white man having been poisoned with opium, would not have interrogated the man sharing a landing with the couple, an oriental, the only one in the district, until months had elapsed, and even then only because of a denunciation!

Michèle and the detective!

At first they did not see me, nor, because of the noise of the door, did they hear me. Michèle came out first, still wearing her little black dress, he closed the door behind her. They took a few steps along Rue Mercière, slowly, each lost in his own thoughts, like people who know that something amorous is about to happen between them.

Renaud Lossaire drew near to Michèle.

He took her hand.

And — a terrible hatred lifted me clear of the ground while a terrible pain sought to nail me to it so that I continued to walk forward like an automaton — he took her hand, and Michèle did not withdraw her hand, she yielded it to him, they walked in silence a few feet from me, hand in hand!

They had put a red-hot iron to my heart — how I would have preferred them to put it to my eyes! — and they were pressing it hard.

Michèle stopped. She freed her hand. She looked around. She saw me. Her face became as full of pain as mine.

Lossaire looked at me without pain. A mocking sneer of triumph twisted his mouth into an ugly line.

Not a word. Not from Michèle, not from me, not from him.

Then I turned and walked quickly away.

·

I walked unseeing past the car and onward with steps now
faltering. Suddenly it was hotter and heavier than during the day.
And such powerful, uniform heat seemed suddenly like winter
cold.

I was cold.

I did not recognize the city any more.

I was trembling, my lips were trembling, as if a constant
stream of misshapen words were escaping them and bruising
them on their way out.

Suddenly it was raining, with a dense mist settling wetly on
the streets. Bent double by pain, pulling my threadbare blue
wool and silk coat tight around my thin shivering torso, I
entrusted my fate to luck rather than to memories as shapeless as
the words ceaselessly battering my mouth. Everything combined
to make my progress difficult, the gnawing of my intestines, fear,
which constantly obliged me to twist my neck and make 180-
degree turns of such impetuousness that my rotary movements
were poorly controlled and I drilled into the sidewalk like a
spinning top to assure myself of the absence of who knew what
pursuers, the rain, probably of long standing I told myself, since
the ground had been transformed into a veritable quagmire from
which you had to extricate yourself by brute force with the result
that at every step my knee shot up into sharp and violent contact
with my chin, this collision triggering a dry crack immediately
followed by another dry crack triggered by the rattling together
of my jaws, all too often followed closely by a yelp as my tongue
got caught between my teeth, the resulting sharp pain standing
out for a second in clear contrast to my abdominal pain, not to
mention the accidental falls, I pitched head first into flooded
potholes, veritable wells where I remained immersed to the hips,
arms pinioned, head submerged, foaming with rage and project-
ing into the bowels of the earth uninterrupted strings of curses
that rose in bubbles to the watery surface of the potholes, and I
cursed, swore, yelled, and raved even more when I bumped
against a sidewalk, trod on a cat, lost myself at the end of a blind

alley, stumbled over a turd, or lurched face to face into a cunning pursuer unless it turned out to be a companion in misfortune, at whom I then frantically clutched in order to catch my balance or to overpower him, I wasn't sure which, in a series of furious maneuvers whose only upshot was that I more often than not managed to hurt myself, my hands having clawed only at my own body and the thick mist!

●

I came to, amid heat and light, in the bar on Place Carnot.

The waiter was bare-chested. I had never seen a waiter bare-chested. He had black brows beetling so low that at first sight they looked like a pair of mustachios. I saw that I was not the only customer. A man and a woman were sitting side by side at a booth, the man had his arm around the woman, the woman was blond and very beautiful, the man small and ugly as a circus freak: the couple from Rue Duguesclin. They were not speaking to one another. They had tied their small dog to a slender metal pillar, and the small dog was tugging, tugging, in clear hopes of hauling the bar, the Perrache neighborhood, and all Lyon toward latitudes that were cooler and more conducive to life.

I sat as far from them as possible. I ordered white wine, white wine, white wine, and, don't ask how, all that white wine cured my stomach ache and put my thoughts back in order, no, drove every thought from my head.

As we had murmured, Rainer von Gottardt and I: what loneliness!

●

At an advanced hour of the night, almost at dawn, I went back to the Lancia and drove to Rue Quivogne.

Michèle was sitting on the curb in front of the hotel. She rose as I parked.

She was waiting for me.

NINE

"I was waiting for you," she said.

"Yes. Everything all right?"

"Yes. What about you?"

I looked at her beautiful dark and pale eyes.

"I squint worse when I'm tired," she said.

"It's pretty," I said. "I adore your eyes. Did you know it's tomorrow already? The seventh?"

"So?"

"So we said we would get Simon back on the seventh."

"That's true, we did. Let's hope we do."

No one at the reception desk.

"He just left," said Michèle. "A little while back I called Annie to give her the hotel number."

We went up to Room 1.

"It's not exactly four-star, but it's discreet," I said as I closed the door.

I turned. The hour had come. I went up to her as she reached an arm out to me, and we kissed each other and remained standing for several minutes kissing each other and touching each other's bodies, backs, hair, foreheads, cheeks. At one point I stepped back from Michèle because I wanted to kiss her in the hollow of her arm, inside the bend, and I caught a glimpse of her face whose expression she had not modified even when I pulled away from her and it was an expression of happiness, of peace, of luminous joy, with lowered lids she was smiling a half smile, the hollow of her arm later I said to myself, bringing my face close to hers I caressed her lips with my fingertips, she kept her eyes closed, mad with love as I was mad with love, I forgot everything, in fact I had forgotten everything the instant I saw her sitting on the curb — forgotten everything except our first night of love.

Without letting go of her waist with my left arm, without interrupting the long kiss conjoining us, impelling her to stoop, to follow me, I bent, with my outstretched right arm removed her shoes, then slid her petticoat down the length of her legs, she lifted one leg, the other, presto, no more white petticoat under the black dress, I straightened up and held her to me as before, as if she still had her white petticoat on, no need to hurry.

I was much taller. I removed my own shoes by shuffling and rubbing my feet together and hopping from foot to foot, it was like a dance, then I raised the black dress with one hand, two hands, and caressed legs and buttocks, belly, soft and blond sex, the dress caressed the back of my hands, I knelt, Michèle held her dress above her waist legs spread while on my knees I kissed her with a real kiss of the kind with which I had been devouring her mouth, I rose still caressing her, she sighed like a baby, eyes closed, half smiling . . .

I took her black dress all the way off, it came off over her head, seizing the opportunity to kiss her small breasts, it looked as if the dress would fall back down but Michèle got rid of it, presto, the dress was on the floor, pity, I really liked that dress, but I was wrong, I realized later that during my absence our Turkish host had cleaned the place most conscientiously, so the dress was not irreparably sullied, Michèle undid the top button of my jeans, the toughest one.

I helped her. I was able without too much trouble to break free of the prison of cloth these new jeans constituted, I ripped off my pants in the same movement, Michèle stooping pulled the jean legs, left, right, while I rested my hands lightly on her shoulders so as not to fall, without too much trouble but it would not have done for a fire to break out at that moment and for me to be forced to flee at a gallop, presto, off with the jeans, rolled into a ball like a baby bear, my hands slid from Michèle's shoulders to her head as she suddenly took my sex in her mouth before rising and crushing herself against me with all her might, we were naked and I was certain, and would still be certain later, that she was encountering pleasure for the first time, I don't mean the actions but love, the sacred joys as Rainer von Gottardt had expressed it, my dinner with him seemed remote, even remoter the day that had just passed, and the days that had preceded it.

I lifted Michèle and set her down on the bed, her white flesh, her body so perfect and imperfect, I set her down on the hard bed of Room 1 in the Hôtel Quivogne, Rue Quivogne, delicately so as to spare her months of immobility in a cast, motionless as a statue, as a subject in a photo, as a wax figure, and on that bed of stone we lay enlaced, my face buried in her tangled light hair.

"I think . . . I think my infection is better," she said in a small voice.

I looked at her. That endearing left eye was closed. I was about to protest, to say no, to let her know I didn't care, that I didn't care about anything, that all that mattered was this love, and that for the following reasons such a love did not concern itself with . . .

"No, wait," she said. "I really think it's better. I'm almost certain. But I haven't been taking . . ."

She broke off, my kisses on her mouth prevented her from speaking. She hadn't been taking! OK. She wasn't absolutely sure she was cured, and on the other hand she had not been taking anything to counter procreation? Conception? The same silent protest from me: that was exactly what I was going to tell her, no, to make her feel — but in my opinion she knew it as well as I did: so far would we go in the communion of pleasures of the flesh that flesh itself would be left behind, powerless, powerless to damage and destroy itself or to quicken and proliferate, frozen for eternity in its sacred joy of the moment, to die or to procreate after simultaneous and most exquisite gratification of our genital organs, this night, did not count, better still: could not be, death and life did not exist so united were we and so united would we be, no I had not forgotten our first night of love, the night of our greatest separation when only our souls had been joined, but on this night the body and soul of Michèle were but one and suddenly she and I were but one, neither zero nor two nor three, one.

One.

And, having experienced ourselves as one, we devoured one another with love, dawn drew near — but had night ever really fallen? you might have asked — the night became almost gentle — a result of the direct northern exposure of the unprepossessing Rue Quivogne? — with dawn drawing near we devoured one another with love, I used each point of Michèle's body as if it had been her mouth or her so soft blond sex for the first time so alive to the love of a man, she likewise used each point of my body in the same manner and indeed sometimes it was our sexes that our hands caressed or our mouths kissed, our moans at such moments of heightened pleasure filling the bedchamber particularly when it happened that the caresses were most rapid and violent for a few seconds, for however long was needed, and the kisses of a deep unflagging voracity, which transformed our moans into cries, sometimes our eyes met during a halt in which desire was not appeased but rather was gathering its scattered forces in the recollection of the moments just past and in the expectation of those about to be and which would be without peer, yet recollection and expectation were one in the intensity of this gaze, I responded with a smile to Michèle's happy smile, thus our eyes met again and immediately after, furiously, our mouths, time passed unmeasured, daylight or the memory of daylight piled up at the window, after one of these kisses came the moment when I slowly penetrated Michèle and was wholly in her and she wholly in me, and then, my face in her neck and hair, we lay unmoving, as if savoring for as long as needed the terror of never satisfying the infinite hunger we had one for the other, the terror of a death that would then supervene and whose shadow weighed ever more on us, then Michèle spread and spread ever wider her pale legs — at the window the darkness or the still-tentative dawn bathing the world with gauzy softness — her pale and soft legs in which the void left by her spreading called me to the most carnal pleasure there was, I started to move inside Michèle without taking my eyes from her, I did not take my eyes from her, our waiting was both supplication and trust, I moved faster, then very fast and very far inside her, endlessly, our moaning was unbroken, then she held me very tight in her arms, I abruptly stopped and looked at her one last time, she was beautiful, supplicating and trusting, our moaning ceased — finally there was a slight movement of our bodies and a cry, one same cry that would never cease issuing from both our mouths, and our movements, although they now became convulsive, did not shatter the preceding immobility, on the contrary we were at the center of it and they extended it to the confines of the heavens and set it afire, ever more infinite and ever more afire, and we were consumed by it down to the last atom of our flesh.

•

Despite the direct northern exposure the heat was oppressive.

A tiny room, no getting away from it. And much thrashing about. We took turns peeing in the tiny bathroom.

Part of the day was spent in dozing and in new lovemaking and caresses. Michèle told me she loved me, that she had loved me at first glance. But that night you didn't even look at me, I said. Yes I did, she said. I did look at you. An immediate and incomprehensible attraction to the other person. The certainty of knowing the love we had just lived. But that night she had been out of sorts, upset as she was every year when she met her father and brother again. Upset, out of sorts, worse even than in other years. Why worse? She didn't know. She had felt so bad in her birthplace at Impasse du Jour that she had jumped into her Lancia after a shouting match with Simon and looked for a bar that was still open so she could drink a Coke alone and in peace. And she would not have responded if God Himself . . .

She asked me to forgive her. And, she added, to forgive her for everything. I did not pursue it. The past was the past. I did not want to discuss the past. I had forgotten it.

She noticed the bruise on my forehead and kissed it a thousand times.

The phone did not ring.

Heartstrings taut in the uncertainty of dawn, if only they could be loosened, if only the new-breaking day would foil its own old tricks, if only promised windfalls would befall and dawn's promises would hold, if only love and Simon could both be recovered, new life, grant me new life, I implored as I took another pee in the bathroom where a fly would have been hard pressed to rub its forelegs together in comfort.

We made love and caressed as often as it was possible for our bodies to take lovemaking and caresses. One caressed the other deep into semislumber, and sometimes true emergence from slumber was almost instantly followed by orgasm, then it was tendernesses and kisses that never ended and soon we made love again, questing in our innermost depths for the pleasure that no longer consumed us at once, like a diffuse, voracious, and already vast fireball, but marked out in our bodies the linear advance of its conquest, linear but all the more ardent for that, and better perceived and monitored by our senses in its subtle, slow, but harrowing and in the end invariably lightning-swift progress, and we would go back to sleep still moaning in our slumber or semislumber.

At one o'clock, the mild discreet Turk brought us coffee and croissants. We remained under the covers while he set down the tray. He attended to what he was doing and to nothing else.

"He is perfect," I said to Michèle. "He cleaned the room while I was away. You should have seen the state it was in when I arrived!"

After the coffee and croissants, and a last embrace, we slept until five.

At 5:15 I paid the Turk. A big tip. I was rich. I congratulated him and thanked him for the excellence of his service and his croissants.

"And thank you for choosing my hotel," he said in a fine voice without an accent and tones bordering on distinction, which surprised me. "I don't think I will have many new guests for a while . . ."

He smiled, so did we. He wished us a happy August and shook hands with us. Then his face resumed its closed look.

•

"And there we are!" said Michèle, strong and slight, lively, bright, smiling and pretty. "A double bed!"

We had moved a single bed next to her single bed, in her bedroom, a double sheet spread over them and there we were, the two beds were but one.

I shaved and bathed in a real bathroom, changed, and joined Michèle and Annie downstairs on the lawn with the military man, fallen and drained of life, his head crammed with the secret details of the grim story, but a story he was incapable of expressing, a god without power, mute.

If only he could have spoken!

Annie studied me with the same look of surprise. She had finished her book, *Our Kingdom Come,* and was reading another by the same author, *The Phantom,* also set in Lyon. She liked this author. She was looking forward to the appearance next January of a third book, *The Realm of Shadows.* Annie had a splendid body. She seemed to be very attached to Michèle, who did not seem to care so strongly about her.

Next January! Would January ever come? Could you believe in January? No, no more than you could believe in November. Even less than in November.

•

"Do you still hurt?"

"It's better now, like this."

We were lying in the bed made of two beds, eyes in each other's eyes, hands in hands. The second I left the Hôtel Quivogne my stomach ache had returned to remind me of its presence and was assailing my guts with successive waves of stabbing attacks. I had gone upstairs to lie down.

"Did you put distilled water in your battery?"

"No."

"I'll look after it in a moment."

"Fine. I'll go and make dinner with Annie."

"I love you," I said.

"So do I. So do I, I love you!"

•

I boiled a saucepan of water, poured it into the Lancia's battery, turned the switch, RRRRRR! roared the resuscitated Lancia.

After dinner — how doleful to watch Michèle thrusting a spoonful of nutritious liquid between her father's teeth and holding his chin up so that the old and mysterious colonel would not dribble, a doleful and disgusting spectacle that killed my appetite, already the victim of cramps and waves of nausea, the well-built and surprised Annie noticed my disgust and flashed me the shadow of a nice smile — after dinner I said to Michèle: "I can't keep still. The phone isn't ringing . . . It's now or never if we're going to do something. Doesn't matter what. Drive around town, walk . . ."

I was repeating what Lossaire had said yesterday. I knew it. Almost the same words. Renaud Lossaire, the man whose name Michèle and I had not once mentioned since meeting again, the detective who would have launched a grueling investigation to search for the monocle screwed into his own eye, the man Michèle had paid to drive and walk around town, whose name we had not mentioned and about whom I had stopped thinking but about whom I thought then, and the powerful claw of jealousy drew near my heart but I turned away in time, it closed on emptiness, gashing its own palm with its razor-sharp nails! I went on: "Maybe Lichem has decided it's a waste of time to go on looking for me. Maybe I can find the man with the Ford Scorpio. Let's look for the ones who are looking for us, or looking for each other. It would be a miracle, but . . ."

"The detective is taking care of that."

She mentioned the detective casually. And I replied casually, "That'll make two of us."

"It's dangerous . . ."

"Oh I don't know . . . In a car . . . I can stay in the car."

"A white Lancia. They must know I drive a white Lancia."

"Exactly. So they're not going to expect your brother's kidnapper to drive around in your Lancia. Anyway, mine has a Lyon license plate. I'll give it a try. I'd rather do something than nothing. I feel responsible."

Michèle removed from her mouth a cherry pit nicely polished by the pretty organs of her mouth, teeth, lips, tongue, and threw it into the trashcan.

"Well, I'd rather do something than nothing too. Let's go."

"What do you mean, let's go?"

"I'm coming with you."

"No!"

•

Give or take a few yards, as I have already said, I lived right in the center of the city, and, following what must ultimately have looked like a series of concentric circles, we approached this center, my apartment on Rue de la République next to Place de la République. Accompanied by a woman, clad in my sharp black leather jacket and driving a big-shot's white car, I bore scant resemblance to a loner in a threadbare blue coat and a disreputable red Dauphine, I drove calmly, on the alert, along Rue Childebert and on Place de la République we saw nothing, not a suspect vehicle or human being, in fact we saw no human being.

Finally, however, we spied one, a big dirty ragged young man who was drawing on the sidewalk, you wondered where he thought his public was, in my opinion he had to be deranged. I stopped.

"Stroke of luck," I said to Michèle. "I'll give him a coin and ask if he's seen anyone hanging around. I won't be a second."

I put my right hand on her imperfect knee, with my left hand I opened the door. Michèle opened hers.

"No, you stay!"

"What difference does it make? I'm going with you. I don't ever want to let go of your hand."

We smiled at each other across the roof of the car.

She took my left hand. I felt strong, and ready to grab with my right for Lichem's weapon. But there was nobody for leagues around, and the mad artist was a real artist.

And this madman was drawing a goat, a gigantic goat, on the cement of the sidewalk! Generally, sidewalk artists do the baby Jesus, or the Virgin Mary, or the Virgin Mary holding the baby Jesus, or fields, suns, sheep, rabbits, in short they do soothing upbeat scenes, but not this one, a goat, gigantic and hideous, its head haloed in red, with three horns and a fox's ears!

He paid us not the slightest attention but went on rubbing the cement with his colored chalks.

Michèle did not miss the box of chalks I only just managed to skirt, she kicked it. The box overturned, the chalks spilled everywhere. The crouching artist rose like a madman, bore down on Michèle with a somber fiery gaze, seized her arm, her pretty biceps where a vein showed, showed almost too much, and roared — his voice filled the space between Terreaux and Perrache, "Why don't you look where you're going, lady? Look! Now pick them up!"

"Just one minute," I said, "you — "

Vloop! A punch full in the face! He was mad! He had let go of Michèle and punched me smack in the face. Vloop!

Michèle screamed.

I grabbed the arm that had punched me and took a step toward the bearded man, he was tall and standing with his legs apart, I hooked my right leg behind his left and pushed to throw him off balance. He resisted the push, straining to return to his vertical stance. I exploited this effort in the following way: I glued myself to him, backside against his stomach, flexed on my legs and threw my right hip as far as I could to the right, seized him by the waist with my right arm, and, pulling with my left hand on his right arm, which I had never let go, I swung him across my hip. His legs left the ground. Then I straightened up to give maximum speed to this rotating movement, he found himself with his legs in the air and his head down, continuing his full circle until he landed flat on his back on the hard cement where his body bounced most sickeningly.

Michèle's hand tightened on my shoulder.

He had broken nothing. He might have, his fall was terrible. He rolled onto his stomach, moaning, then up onto all fours, then he rose. His gaze frightened me.

Enough of these exhausting calisthenics, I told myself: I yanked Lichem's weapon out of my belt and aimed calmly between the goat-painter's eyes. It was his turn to be terrified. He sprinted away, holding his sides. Thirty yards away he turned around to check on the situation.

"Get thee behind me, Satan!" I yelled, stamping on the ground the way you scare off a dog.

He took off without turning again and was soon reduced to a gesticulating dot near Place des Terreaux where he would have to look out for falling pigeons, schblonk!

"That didn't get us far," I said to Michèle.

"I was scared! You kept that talent hidden!"

"Well, you know . . . It's the first time I've had to use it. And it's the only trick I know. Anyway, it worked. A goat!"

"But you wouldn't have fired at him, would you?"

"I would."

"No!"

"No."

I had told her nothing about my suicide, about my anger no longer directed against myself but against the whole world. An anger that her love had done little to attenuate . . .

Just in case, I went and took a look around my apartment, sure of finding no one, unless it was Renaud Lossaire pursuing his inquiry with his back to my door, awaiting the enemy and prepared to wait until the end of time.

No, no one. I merely heard the phone next door ringing.

And near the Lancia I thought I heard the sound of the jukebox in the Bar des Archers. Masked for a second by something resembling the bursting of a dam. I put away Lichem's weapon, which alas did not fit into the pocket of my jacket, so that I still had to tuck it into my belt. I opened Michèle's door. My beloved was trembling a little. But she had insisted on going with me.

I drove in the direction of the Rhône.

My stomach hurt.

"Are you tired?"

"Yes."

"You're squinting a bit."

I kissed her on her left eye. She took my hand, squeezed it, I squeezed back. Squeezing any harder would have crushed the bones.

"I love you, she said. "I can't wait to make love with you."

"Nor can I," I said.

I drove along. I was following the waterfront.

"Why did you have an operation?"

"My left eye wouldn't move at all, at all. I was operated on by Perfecto Jinez."

"The one who's missing?"

"Yes. I hope nothing bad has happened to him. I was in his clinic in Barcelona."

"Why there? Why him?"

"His reputation. He'd been recommended to my father. Apparently Spanish ophthalmologists are the best in the world. Maybe he's just taken off into the blue. He's also supposed to be a great womanizer. Maybe the pretty young maid in his hotel attracted him and he took off with her . . ."

"Are you serious?"

"Almost. I found him very kinky. He liked me. We talked about music a lot. He has magnificent hands, I remember. Not as pretty as yours," she said, lifting my hand to her lips and smiling and squinting.

As for the powerful, hairy, claw of jealousy (Perfecto Jinez the great lover liked her!), its fingers opened and closed several times, but in vain. It closed on empty air. And the thought of Renaud Lossaire himself, conjured up anew, at once retreated.

"Once again, forgive me for being so indiscreet . . . I saw that you had been invited by the Dioblanízes. What an honor! Will you lend me your book? I can't find it anywhere."

"Yes." (Good golly Miss Molly I hummed to myself just to

keep my hand in.) "Well, will you go with me to their concert? And will you play the Granados for me?"

She put her head on my shoulder. Ah, what tenderness! We were warm together. We felt good. I tilted my head so that our hair was closer together.

It was true love.

•

I took the Galliéni Bridge and Avenue Berthelot. Suddenly I was no longer drifting along. Another mad and mysterious idea was taking shape, and had perhaps already taken shape the moment I felt the need to leave Impasse du Point du Jour for this strange ride through the lifeless city.

I headed for Carrefour-Vénissieux.

Night was falling. The air was unbelievably heavy.

"A Renaissance building in Berlin, is that possible?" I asked Michèle.

"No. No, I don't think so. Why?"

"At Rainer von Gottardt's, over his piano, there's a photo of a small Renaissance townhouse in Berlin. It must be a copy, no?"

"Yes, undoubtedly."

"I ask because I have the feeling that particular townhouse looks familiar. And since I haven't done much traveling . . . I've been trying to remember, racking my brains . . . I wonder whether it couldn't be in Lyon?"

"So?"

"So I'm going to the Carrefour de Vénissieux department store, the only place open today as far as I know where I might be able to consult a book on Lyon. Maybe. Their book section is quite well stocked. Lost memories scare me. I need to know. Drifting this way and that . . . Well, on the other hand I now think we're wasting our time. We can go back anytime you say. At once if you like?"

"No, let's go there."

Last red light before Carrefour. On the left, the awful hous-ing project, lights on in the ground floor apartment. You could see the couple. They were no longer fighting. You could see them clearly, fat and unclean, sloppy, the man sitting on a chair, his broken leg resting on another chair. The woman was leaning over him, she was kissing him on the mouth while her hands were unbuttoning the invalid's trouser buttons. The light changed to green just as she liberated and grabbed a sex the size of a chimney, and leaned forward further, I drove off, brooooooo, thus escaping the graceless spectacle.

"I know those two," I said to Michèle.

"You know them?"

I told her.

Parking lot. Cabinetmakers. IFH. Incorporated Funeral Home? My God, yes! I drove up to the window, the IFH coffins were made here, there in the glare of my Lancia's headlights was a whole row of them, lined up like big ugly animals at the back of the warehouse!

Liliane.

A fleeting urge to weep, instantly detected by Michèle, made swallowing difficult.

Liliane dead, Simon kidnapped, Michèle's love, Rainer von Gottardt and his Renaissance townhouse, a replica, the original I was about to hunt down in my own city . . . Everything was moving quickly and fate went on dealing me events endlessly the way a full-fledged neurotic deals cards on a big-winning night, I scarcely had time to pick up and sort my hand.

At 9:46 P.M. we penetrated the almost-deserted store, fourteen minutes before closing time. The romanza movement from Salvador Bacarisse's Concertino, a clear favorite on the shop floor, was playing over the public-address system.

"This is where my adventures as a thief began," I said to Michèle.

A detailed account of my pilfering amused her. The air conditioning had been repaired, or was better regulated, or perhaps it was just that — since the store was empty — human body heat was not counteracting its effectiveness.

"You're in pain, aren't you?" asked Michèle.

"No. Every now and then."

"I thought you had the Liver of No Return."

"Ha, ha! Right you are!"

She wrapped her arm further around me, and in this way we arrived at the book section, walking with our arms around one another just the way lovers' arms wrap around one another.

Fifty seconds later my faith in my mad hunch was rewarded by my discovery of a *History of Lyon* by Robert Ballestron (a prolific local writer of uneven talent, author of a treatise on astronomy, a little encyclopedia on the life of animals, a dictionary of symbols, a cookbook, a moral guide for everyman, a medical handbook, a collection of fantastic tales for children, *The Phantom* and *Our Kingdom Come* — the two novels Annie was reading — and of course this *History of Lyon*), on page 124 in chapter 12 was an old photo of a small Renaissance building.

"That's the one!" I said.

I had indeed seen it in Lyon, how many years earlier I have no idea, in the Saint-Georges neighborhood between Rue Bellièvre and Rue du Vieil Renversé, near the famous Café Soleil. I read the accompanying article, so did Michèle, her chin resting on my left shoulder, her adored breath filling my nostrils with balm.

The building did not date from the Renaissance but was built in the Renaissance manner in 1645 by the architect Simon Maupin, the man who built the Terreaux town hall between 1646 and 1652. Robert Ballestron congratulated the city of Lyon on its plans to restore the little building to its original interest and appeal; it was now almost in ruins (which would account for the haziness of my recollection). He concluded with an anecdote: so interesting and so appealing had the building been that a rich Berlin art dealer passing through our city had fallen in love with it and had had a replica built on Wahrscheynstrasse in Berlin . . .

I replaced Robert Ballestron's book.

"Shall we go?" I asked Michèle.

•

I parked on Place François Bertras, next to a red Dauphine so like mine it almost frightened me. I even had to check its license number. It was not mine.

I surveyed our surroundings. I made no move to leave the car.

"Want some gum?"

"Yes, please."

I took a pack of eleven pieces of mint chewing gum from the left-hand pocket of my jacket.

"I stole it at Carrefour," I said. "Just to keep in practice."

Michèle laughed. She had been studying me.

"Is anything bothering you?" she asked.

"Yes."

"What?"

On our way from the Hôtel Quivogne to Point du Jour she had asked me a thousand questions about my conversations with Rainer von Gottardt, a pianist she too worshipped of course, how could you not worship him? I had given her no inkling of my precocious and startling suspicions, nor of the strange conversation that had confirmed them last night.

I hesitated. I decided.

"This is a secret, beautiful and adored one. Von Gottardt, the God, the Maestro, the Genius, dropped out of sight, you know, after the loss of his right index finger and his various intoxications and detoxifications. He led a rather shady life. He's been revealing its vices and vicissitudes to me bit by bit, leaving me amazed. A mad affair (like our own, my love) with an adventuress. They spent three days in Berlin, in the summer of 1974, in the Renaissance townhouse mentioned in that book in Carrefour . . . And it was in that townhouse and during those three days that, here it comes, your father and your brother were held prisoner, that your father went through his ordeal, before father and son were taken to the suburban house where . . . That's all. It's a lot, amazing, incredible — but no more. What I mean is: Rainer von Gottardt was a chance accomplice, innocent of any real wrongdoing, he knows nothing, cannot help us in any way, is basically ignorant of those events and even more ignorant of recent developments. Both he and his companion. He swore it to me, I believe him."

Exclamations, kisses, further details demanded and given, kisses, faces caressed, Michèle and I loved each other, the minute spent with her in that car was so to speak a minute won.

A minute spent with Michèle was a minute won.

"That is why, beautiful and adored one, that is why I wanted to clarify my confused recollections, and why we are here now."

"Why?" she said, even though she was close to realizing.

"For no reason that can be put into words. Simon kidnapped in two cities . . . Two identical buildings . . . I want to check. Wait here, sit at the wheel and keep all the doors locked."

"I told you I don't want to let go of your hand. Please . . . I'm coming with you. In any case it's so insane . . . We won't find anything. Don't leave me here alone . . ."

I believed she was right. I let her come with me. But, how shall I say it? my faith in my mad hunch was secretly so strong that reality would be forced to conform to it and to bare its teeth in fury at the image of this madness — and in the quarter-hour to come it would indeed conform, and would indeed bare its teeth, in the terrible manner outlined below.

•

Our arms still around one another, we reached the short narrow Rue du Soleil. I had deliberately not parked too close.

Nobody in the street, nobody in the whole neighborhood, it seemed to be annihilated by a silence as heavy as the heat.

At 4 Rue du Soleil there was a scaffolding. They had whitened and refaced every stone surface and all the ornamentation (much of it incongruous on a Renaissance building, Doric, probably added on, absent if I remembered right from Rainer von Gottardt's picture, and I did not recall it from Robert Ballestron's book either, the triglyphs and metopes of the friezes, the moldings of the stylobates and statuettes). Everything wooden on the other hand was rotting, black-green and worm-eaten, the entranceway for example, held shut by means of a shaky crossbar that a determined flick of the thumb would have reduced to iron filings, but I eschewed any such flick, why? for fear of the noise.

I murmured to Michèle:

"We'll try the building next door. There must be courtyards in the rear."

The door to the building on the right was also locked, moreover the handle came away in my hands. I put it carefully on the ground. Building on the left. A round doorknob. I turned it the usual way, clockwise: nothing. I was about to give up when I decided to try turning it the wrong way: the mechanism worked, the door opened.

In the kingdom of keys, locks, and bolts, there are indeed mechanisms that work backward.

I closed the door behind us.

We went through the building, lived-in and decrepit like every building on this street, in almost total darkness. At the end of a corridor a small door opened onto the courtyard, separated from the neighboring courtyard by a rusty broken-down wrought iron grille.

Another scaffolding climbed the back of the Renaissance townhouse. No openings within reach except a fairly solid locked door and three small circular windows on the second floor.

That way lay salvation. Should we climb?

"Let's climb!" said Michèle. "It looks easy."

"OK," I said. "But be careful. You go first."

In fact it was an easy climb. And we wriggled through the central window, wider than the others, without any trouble, I went through before Michèle, legs first, then I caught her in my arms, lively and agile and pretty, and took a few seconds to kiss and caress her, buttocks and thighs squeezed tight in her pants, shoulders and breasts without the slightest cloth constraint, my hand slipped inside her loose shirt.

We were in an empty room. Opposite the circular window, a closed door that must lead to the heart of the building.

"What shall we do?" she asked.

"We'll open the door, take a tour of the building, see whether I'm as crazy as you keep saying, and then we'll go . . ."

Nevertheless, we were whispering.

We whirled around at a sound just behind us. Michèle's mouth opened to scream, our hearts stopped beating, I did not even think of reaching for Lichem's weapon.

Renaud Lossaire.

He was wriggling in through the circular window, also clad in a leather jacket. He showed little surprise at finding us here, having probably seen us climb in, and I must admit that I mastered my own surprise very quickly.

"We were here first," I said provocatively. "What do you think you're doing?"

He placed his forefinger against his coarse lips: shsh, silence, not so loud! He spoke in a very low voice.

"I located the driver of the Ford and followed him here. He's changed cars, he's driving a small Fiat. He was alone. He bought some beer in a bar and then he came in here. He's downstairs right now. I came round by Rue Bellièvre. I had to climb over a roof. I saw you come in."

"Why not through one of the courtyards? The building next door?"

"Locked."

"Sometimes all it takes is turning the handle the wrong way and you're in," I said with a hint of contempt, and as if it was an appropriate subject of conversation.

He paid no further attention to me. He went to the door, stroking Michèle's hair as he went past, a brief caress (she immediately pulled her head back — I nearly killed him, and told myself I would sooner or later), and softly turned the handle.

The door opened.

He had a revolver in his hand . . .

The door opened onto a gallery without a handrail; it completely circled the floor. The gallery was narrow and permitted a view of the floor below, a huge room, a sort of atrium with the sky blocked off, if that makes sense, like a central space designed for staging a show, and — and suddenly my mad hunch took robust shape! — a show there most certainly was!

Despite our refusal to believe our eyes, when Lossaire had opened the door wide enough we saw four standing wax figures, propped up in more or less vertical postures by pieces of wood doubtless picked up in the courtyards — and three of the characters thus depicted, strikingly lifelike, realistic, and well-drawn, three of these characters were known to me!

One was Simon de Klef the elder before he received his wounds. The second was a woman: beyond a doubt Ana de Tuermas. The third, Rainer von Gottardt . . .

The fourth was a fair-haired middle-aged man with bestial features.

Scarcely had we seen this than we saw more, but now hell was to break loose and bear us away in its talons: the door of a downstairs room opened and the broad-shouldered driver of the Scorpio (and then of a Fiat) came onstage, pushing ahead of him little Simon whose eyes he had bound, squeezing the back of his neck, probably quite hard, for Simon's head was lowered and he was wincing slightly.

I understood, I understood!

"We're going to try again, boy," the man almost shouted in a German accent, "we'll keep on trying until you remember!" (He ripped away the blindfold and shouted:) "Remember! What did you see? Just tell me what you saw!"

I stifled Michèle's scream.

Terrified, Simon stood as motionless as the wax figures. The man grew angry, shook him, suddenly pulled out a gun and waved it in the air, fired a round at the figure representing Simon the elder, and yelled out at the top of his lungs:

"Answer! What did you see? I know you remember! Tell me what you saw or I'll kill you! Remember! What did you see?"

But Simon did not remember.

Only a few seconds had elapsed since Lossaire had half-opened the door. Now he swung it wide, took a silent step onto the gallery, revolver in hand. And jumped!

Renaud Lossaire jumped, landing one floor down six feet

from the man, who let go of Simon, eyes wide, tried to squeeze
the trigger, but too late, the surprise was total, Lossaire, legs still
bent, hit him with two shots smack in the chest, straightened
up . . . and was himself hit in the middle of the chest, poor
fellow, toppling over in almost the same motion as the German
he had just killed!

For the street door, the door leading in from Rue du Soleil,
had been kicked or shouldered open with a loud crash, a man
had burst in and fired at Lossaire . . .

Lichem!

"Stay here!" I said to Michèle.

Lichem dashed up to Simon, hoisted him in the air.

I had left the gallery and reached the top of a stairway leading
straight down to him before he saw me.

I did not know what to do with my revolver, because of
Simon . . . But I drew a bead on Lichem, whose feelings for me
by now had to be devoid of warmth, and who did know what to
do with his revolver, who fired at once and hit me somewhere in
the middle of my body, stomach, hip, maybe the virile areas, it
hurt but I could still stand up, he was going to fire again when he
saw Michèle running down in spite of my warning, with a yell he
turned his weapon on her, a shot rang out . . . But he had not
fired, it was Lichem himself who was hit, in the neck, his neck
was red with blood: Lossaire, with the last of his life force and all
his energy, had found the strength to squeeze his trigger again!

I fired myself, three times, firing anywhere just as long as it
wasn't at Simon, Simon who wasn't struggling, who seemed to
see nothing, to hear nothing, who seemed lifeless wax, Michèle
was screaming my name, Lichem, overwhelmed and losing
blood, tucked the child under his arm and fled, vanishing in the
twinkling of an eye.

I leaped down the stairway and at the bottom fell half-
stunned.

Michèle bent over me. I grabbed her ankle:

"Stay here, don't move, he'll kill you!"

Then I must have lost consciousness, for a few seconds, not
for long.

When I opened my eyes silence had returned, broken only by sobs from Michèle who sat on the bottom stair holding my hand.

She stopped crying, her face was inches from mine.

Before I go on, two things: first, I saw a cold shadow flit across her loving gaze, a hostile distancing, a malevolence that had not been there for the past few hours. Then love, concern, compassion returned. Second, when I regained consciousness the very first picture that came back to me was that of Michèle yielding her hand to the detective on Rue Mercière — and the claw of jealousy finally managed to close on my heart and crush it.

"I'm going to call an ambulance," she said. "But I'm afraid of leaving you alone."

Virile areas hit? No. A bullet in the stomach? No, it wasn't that either, the stomach ache afflicting me was already familiar, I had been suffering from it since yesterday more or less. The hip, I had been hit in the hip, in the hollow of the hipbone. I was sitting. There was a small hole in my jeans. It was hardly bleeding at all now.

"Don't move!" said Michèle.

I raised the cloth over my wound.

"It's OK," I said. "It doesn't even hurt. I don't think it's anything at all. I know a doctor who's on duty every night at the Hôtel-Dieu, let's go there."

She had a little handkerchief, which I stuffed between my jeans and the wound.

I stood up. I could walk without any trouble.

Renaud Lossaire and Broad Shoulders were dead, good and dead. I forced myself to go through the detective's pockets. I found a key ring. ("The check you gave him," I said to Michèle. "The check in his desk drawer.") But disgust and a mounting nausea deterred me from going through Broad Shoulders' pockets for papers that might not have been there, that were unlikely to tell me anything, that would in any case have been faked.

In the room that this man — Liliane's murderer avenged by

Lossaire—had emerged from we found canned food, lots of empty beer bottles (and two full ones, the ones he had brought in this evening), an inflatable mattress, a blanket, a transistor radio. The man was patient, stubborn. He had skillfully reconstructed the setting of the drama Simon had lived through three years earlier in order to deliver a shock, try to reactivate his memory, try to get him to say what he had seen back then!

Poor, unhappy Simon! What scars would this new nightmare leave on his already unstable psyche?

"What should we do?" Michèle murmured.

"Leave. We won't touch anything else. No one will come in here before September."

We left the bodies and the wax figures and secured the door as solidly as we could, I was even able to monkey with and block the dilapidated keyhole so that the door would not swing open at the slightest touch.

Nobody in the street, nobody in the Saint-Georges neighborhood. Nobody anywhere.

I could walk without limping.

Michèle asked every second how I felt. Well. I felt well.

An unbelievable encounter with destiny! Incredible but simple. Lossaire, the detective who had almost been deflected from the aforementioned encounter with destiny by a doorknob not made exactly like the others, had picked up the German's trail. As for Lichem, had he somehow picked up Michèle and me? If so he was cunning indeed, for I had been extremely vigilant both in concealment and in reconnaissance. Or had he chanced upon Lossaire and followed him . . . mistaking him for me? Particularly if Lossaire was driving an old red Dauphine . . . ? Lossaire who could have been tailed by a whole armored division without suspecting a thing?

But who had been brave. And who had managed to stay on the German's trail.

But whom I hated beyond death.

Hand in hand! Stroking her hair!

Lossaire, his first assignment or very nearly. The Alexander the Great Detective Agency. Awaiting the harbingers of death on Place des Terreaux . . .

Schblonk!

The red Dauphine's engine was still hot.

"Renaud Lossaire's car?" asked Michèle.

"Possibly. Probably."

I had the keys. I checked. Yes, Renaud Lossaire's car. And on the windshield of this car, held down by the wiper, was a note. And another note on the Lancia's windshield, bearing an identical message: pointless and dangerous to tell the police if you ever want to see Simon again.

Two notes hastily written in black ink, one of them slightly bloodstained. Lichem, finding the Renaissance townhouse as crowded as a railroad station at the start of vacation, finding two cars with warm engines outside, wounded, frantic, not knowing who was who anymore, had left these two messages just to be on the safe side. It was lucky for him that we were not parked in the Carrefour-Vénissieux lot during the height of the Christmas shopping rush. Two messages, both of which I stuffed into my pocket.

Michèle drove me to the Hôtel-Dieu. I was in no pain. I kept reassuring her. We talked in hushed voices.

What did they want with Simon? What had he seen? Who was the broad-shouldered German whose looks and deeds had proved too much for Liliane's fragile heart? Some rival of the ringleader of three years ago, bent on reviving the affair for his own profit? And what affair? The German and French police, Michèle said again, had uncovered nothing. Who? How to find out? No way of finding out. A thousand ethereal possibilities arose. We would never know. In any case he was dead now, ethereal himself. That was the only reality.

No matter. What mattered now was Lichem. Was Lichem after Simon for the same reasons? No, I was sure he was not. Or was he? A ransom, or something else we would never have thought of? There were no certainties, no avenues in which to channel thought or energy. We were still more or less at square one. There was nothing to do but wait.

The small bloodstain was not spreading. The handkerchief was doing its job well. The pants held it flat against the wound.

"Here's what we'll tell Patrice Pierre," I said to Michèle. "Almost the same thing as Annie . . ."

Place de l'Hôpital, Louise Labé and her love sonnets, Hôtel-Dieu Hospital.

I pulled the jacket around me to conceal the wound.

"I would like to see Dr. Patrice Pierre. It's personal. He's a friend."

The woman at the desk blew her nose (she too had a cold), and pointed: "Corridor. First corridor on the left. Third door on the left."

It was a waiting room. A woman was waiting, dark-haired, young, with a smiling face. Michèle and I were scarcely seated when there was a sound of voices and of a door opening and closing in the adjoining room, then footsteps, the door opened, Patrice Pierre appeared.

He at once smiled at me (like the first time). He came up to us. I got up, so did Michèle, not the woman.

"It's me again," I said.

He shook my hand.

"Nothing serious?"

"No . . . Michèle, a friend who was nice enough to come here with me."

He shook her hand too, delighted to meet you, pointed to the woman who rose, her smiling face all smiles.

"Esther, my wife. She was nice enough to stay here with me . . . Good evening, my darling."

Mrs. Pierre, delighted to meet you, they kissed, kisses, hand-shakes, delighteds, it went on forever, after all I had a bullet lodged in my midriff, soon unwavering respect for the laws of polite society would be more than I could endure, Michèle felt the same, I sensed that she was on the point of shouting quick! he's hurt, do something, she was eaten up with anxiety — when Patrice Pierre suddenly noticed.

He looked at me and understood from my expression, the

cunning devil, that an allusion to the circumstances of our first encounter was not called for in Michèle's presence. He decided to see me alone. He took me by the arm: "Let's leave them to get acquainted, and come and tell me all about it."

•

"A problem, eh?"

"Yes."

What could I tell him? In a few days, in this dead city where it seemed impossible that anything could happen, where heat and the absence of people seemed to obviate all possibility of events, well, heat and the absence of people had produced very different results, in a week, seven days, I had passed myself off with persons unknown as a kidnapper and professional killer and had received a down payment of five thousand dollars, I had committed suicide, I had conducted several interviews with an internationally famous pianist, kidnapped a child, held the sister of this child prisoner with the intention more or less of raping her, buried my mother, who had been slain in effect by one of the true kidnappers, shared a few days of perfect love with the sister (speaking of which, a little gynecological exam, oh! just a formality, would perhaps be in order, in fact, Michèle, my friend . . .), the child had been kidnapped from the first kidnapper by a second kidnapper, who had killed the detective who had just killed the first kidnapper, and had wounded me (which is why I'm here, Doctor), wounded me in a Renaissance townhouse in Old Lyon of which there is a replica in Berlin, an identical building in which three years ago the same child had already been held against his will, along with his father, and where the internationally renowned pianist I mentioned earlier . . .

No.

No, despite his warm feelings toward me he would at once be on the phone to the nearest police headquarters, to Interpol, to the psychiatric ward of the Hôtel-Dieu, instantly fifteen male nurses would gallop up, all false smiles, hairy left arms reaching toward me and right arms folded behind their backs holding the syringe. No, I fed him a false and very abbreviated version of the story, cratered with huge omissions, tailored to justify my reluctance to inform the police and to hold his sympathetic and passionate interest: Michèle de Klef belonged to a wealthy family, we had been strolling in the city, Michèle, her young brother, and I, at one point the kid was twenty or thirty yards ahead of us when a stranger in a car, right in front of our eyes . . . I had hurled myself toward them, the hoodlum had fired, I had fallen, I had even knocked myself out. A ransom demand would doubtless follow . . .

A compassionate man, this Patrice Pierre! He turned pale at my story (although abridged — a full account would have rendered him incompetent to continue on duty), told me to lie down, lowered my jeans and pants with infinite care, lifted up my shirt, removed the blood-soaked handkerchief, swabbed, examined . . .

"My poor young man! Once again you've had the devil's own luck . . . You survive Alymil 1000 and bullets inflict negligible wounds on you! A small-caliber round in your pelvis, probably well lodged in the hollow of the bone there, on your hip . . . A very minor operation . . . We'll X-ray it just to be sure."

He swabbed and probed, the little balls of reddened cotton piled up.

"Do I have to be operated on right away?" I asked anxiously. "Just now I'd rather not leave my girlfriend alone . . ."

He looked again.

"No. No . . . A little Mercurochrome, a strip of Band-Aid and you can go on about your business without giving it another thought."

"Later."

"Yes. You won't even need stitches, look at this tiny hole. And no need for antibiotics, the bullet burns as it enters. Automatic disinfectant. It doesn't hurt?"

"Not really."

"Good. Let's wait for the X-rays anyway. Who would have

believed they kidnap children in Lyon in this day and age . . . It's incredible!"

"Incredible," I said. "Now what about the police . . ."

"What about the police, as you say. Don't think I wasn't thinking of them . . ."

"I can always make up a story. But I'd rather not. And then all that red tape . . . You know? I've had enough for tonight. I want to stay with Michèle. As soon as she's got her brother back . . ."

"You're asking a lot of me," he said. "Normally speaking I should inform the police, you realize that?"

The last cotton ball stayed white.

"Yes. I realize it and I realize I'm asking a lot of you." (I smiled.) "A small sin . . ."

Patrice Pierre halted for a moment on the broad road he had always traveled, the road of Goodness and Righteousness, halted for a moment at the fork of Evil, Vexation, and Doubt, indeed a pathway called Evil, Vexation, and Doubt did lead off the broad highway and drift away into the nettles. He took three steps along it and stopped at once.

"You aren't hiding anything from me? I can trust you?"

"You can," I said, with much heartfelt conviction and much treachery.

He stroked his beard, cleaned his little round glasses, and turned back up his favorite road, hoping that his three small steps had not held him back at all.

"OK. X-rays. I'll tell your girlfriend to be patient."

•

He took care of the X-rays himself, the pelvis, the skull, because I had been stunned no matter how briefly, any loss of consciousness called for an X-ray.

Nothing on the skull. And a now-harmless bullet lurking in my pelvis.

He saw me wince. I told him about my stomach aches. He asked some questions, probed: colitis. Nothing serious, of nervous origin.

I told him it was good to meet people like him, like him and my upstairs neighbor. ("He's in Norway, he's visiting his mother.") I told him these things while he was sticking an ordinary Band-Aid on my wound, neither more nor less than for a fleabite, it was almost annoying.

When we got back to the waiting room I had a plastic bag containing what I needed to change the dressing, some antibiotics, a medication for colonic spasms, another for the nausea that often accompanies such spasms, and tranquilizers for Michèle and me. A whole little pharmacy.

He made me promise to call regularly. I promised.

And in that waiting room, we experienced, the four of us, a small intermission of peace, of simplicity, of uncomplicated living. Esther Pierre was made of the same stuff as her husband, and by the same maker. Perhaps we would all meet later on, when our troubles were over, somewhere other than in a hospital? Yes, perhaps. We all hoped so.

•

At three in the morning I awoke from a first restless slumber. Michèle was breathing evenly. A small bedside lamp was still on. I stirred a little. I did not hurt anywhere. Small strip of Band-Aid. I was sweating despite open window, absence of covers, nudity.

My erect sex was hard as iron. Nerves, fatigue, the tranquilizers, a combination of all three. It was hard as iron and seemed determined to remain that way forever.

That kind of hardness.

It was August 8. We certainly had found Simon again on the seventh.

Nightmare pictures were dissolving in my mind. I thought back over the past few hours and days, the bereavement, the wounds, the disastrous setbacks. But the picture that tormented me most cruelly and held center stage was of Michèle and Lossaire walking hand in hand.

I decided to switch off the lamp. I leaned gently across my tormenting beloved. She opened her eyes. I halted in midmovement. I examined her, prepared to hate her — madness, I was mad! — if the slightest spark foreign to love marred her gaze. No, no spark foreign to love.

I wanted her to get on top of me and make love to me. But perhaps the wound, the little hole Lichem had made in my midsection, ruled this out? Did it really rule it out? No. Michèle got on top of me and made love to me, carefully, with a slowness and a care that aroused her and brought her swiftly to pleasure.

Then she caressed me. We were half-asleep. She put her head on my stomach and licked the sweat there while she went on caressing me, her mouth took in my sex, as hard as ever and forever, again licked the sweat off my stomach, for sweat that summer in Lyon in a bed with a lover did not take months to regenerate, and it provoked a pleasure that lasted and lasted, a long-drawn spiraling into satiety that carried us to the stars.

I held her to me.

Then suddenly I perceived that she was crying.

"Why?" I asked.

"For no reason."

I struggled against a kind of hatred.

"What happened with that detective?"

"Nothing. Nothing happened. Don't think about it. It's stupid."

•

In the morning, after swallowing a dozen assorted pills and capsules, and drinking fifteen pints of coffee, I went to Place des Terreaux and stole Michèle's check from Lossaire's desk, as well as the paper she had signed and the page from the appointment book.

Schblonk!

I was wearing my blue jeans, spared by the enemy's bullets.

From Place des Terreaux I hurried to the pianist.

TEN

"Did you know it was a copy of a small building here in Lyon? In Old Lyon? Which was also post-Renaissance?"

I examined it carefully. No Doric frieze.

"No. I did not know. I spent only three days there. I did not know the owner, nor anyone who knew the owner, who lived in Munich anyway. The house had been lent by a friend of friends of friends. Of friends."

I took a half-step to the right: Château Marmont, hotel, trees, the Porsche whose lights you couldn't see, the young man in blue.

"Is this the original?"

"Yes. Ed Scarisbrick gave it to me. We wove a warm friendship. Can you say weave a friendship?"

"Probably. Did you stay long at Château Marmont?"

"Two years. A bit longer. From my final and complete break with Ana until a few days ago. Illness did its work during those two years. The place, initially pleasant, finally became hateful to me. When I realized that my heart was beginning its last gasping sprint, I thought of Lyon. And of you, dear friend, of whom I had already thought a lot, to whom I so badly wanted to speak."

One-third of a step to the right.

"Your mother's painter friend was mighty skillful. There's no sign of retouching. Anyone would take you for a five-year-old on the steps of the little white house where you were born and which you had in fact left five years earlier. What an angelic expression on your face!"

"True. I kept that angelic face for a long time. It was only on the threshold of old age, let us say on the slippery slope of maturity, that my features coarsened and grew corrupt. Illness? Yes. But chiefly the loss of my finger, the physical impossibility of recording other works by Bach. Not to be able to record the Partitas was a blow that left me with my face ground in the dirt, with no chance of ever getting up again. So it's not surprising that it looks like an eggplant! Alcohol too. I've drunk as much as twelve bottles of white wine a day, can you believe it? Every twenty-four hours. I often got up in the middle of the night to fill up. That's slang, isn't it? My French is coming back from contact with you. And Ana. My soul was not prepared for the turpitudes of the flesh, as a result my body quickly began to bear their stigmata. We loved one another in purity and depravity. But Ana was as beautiful the last time I saw her as in her photos taken at eighteen. Amazing."

What a speech! His last ". . . azing" was lost in a winded gasp. At last I turned around. He turned too, for he was standing in the middle of the big room with his back to the piano and the pictures. We had been talking back to back.

"Why complete and final, the break?"

"And brutal. From one day to the next. I don't know. Nor have I sought to see her again. A mystery. Let us sit down, if you don't mind, I am exhausted. You exhaust me, my dear Michel!"

"Forgive me, forgive me!" I said.

I rushed forward and helped him seat himself on the metal chair. He was dressed the way he had been on my first visit, in khaki pants and white shirt with vertical red stripes, but this time he had rolled up the sleeves to expose soft, pallid, hairy forearms. Pants and shirt were unironed.

The tape recorder was on.

I slid down into the couch where you sank so deeply your very voice grew deeper, almost cavernous. An abyss of a couch, softer and deeper than ever since the Maestro had been sleeping in it, he would have made a dent in Stonehenge.

"These last few days," I said to him in deep and cavernous tones, "and this past night, I have lived through events beyond my understanding . . ."

Time went by. A long time. The events in question were already fading behind the bars of the cage of oblivion.

Rainer von Gottardt broke the silence: "Simon de Klef kidnapped, a similar Renaissance townhouse, events beyond your understanding, this past night . . . In this Renaissance townhouse? My God, what are you hinting at! You should have agreed to stay here . . ."

"What you swore the other night, the things you swore the other night still hold for any questions I might ask you?"

"Yes. Put such fears out of your mind."

"What Simon de Klef and his father may have seen while they were held prisoner in Berlin, and which certain people now seem anxious to —"

"My dear Michel! I beg you!"

"I am sorry."

"What Simon and his father saw, they were the only ones to see. They and one or more other persons, I have no idea, Ana and I saw not the shadow of a shadow of them. There are some paths you cannot retrace. The evil goes farther back. Too far, beyond reach. Do not think of it anymore, I beg you from the bottom of my heart! Ana and I kept the prisoners for the first two days. We cared for them with the greatest kindness. What happened on the third day . . . we know from what the papers said afterward." (In light conversational tones:) "Speaking of papers, would you be kind enough to bring me a few next time?"

"Of course, with pleasure."

"Thank you." (Resuming his stricken tone:) "Dear Michel Soler, I had intended to speak of it to you one day or another, perhaps you had realized? Your book, the communion it created between us, decided me. I had to speak to someone: it would be you. I have already told you that my apprehension was almost as strong as my desire to see you that noon on August 2. You appeared. And I spoke to you. And you pressed me, put me to the torture . . . yes, you did! But we are coming to the end. Fame and fortune await you, now you are going to have to stop."

What sternness in his comely gaze! He spoke still in response to my pressure, but he was now exerting an inverse pressure, so that the truth his words revealed, liberated from the murky zones that had once obscured it and kept it out of reach, now revealed itself to us with a clarity that was perhaps modest and circumscribed, but was utterly trustworthy.

I was done with him. I did indeed have to stop, or else go on alone despite his warning. Today we had reached a point in our conversations at which (if we wished to go ahead with the story of his life and finish it, rather than lose ourselves in it and continue to commune through sterile misunderstanding, confusion, and frenzy) we had only to retrace our steps calmly, to distance ourselves with measured strides from this point we had reached, and whose cunning snares he had so skillfully dismantled, or rather avoided, until the obvious end of the story — his death? His death, which alone would allow me to continue . . . ?

"I have a confession of another kind to make to you," I said. "The first time I saw you I wondered whether you were the real Rainer von Gottardt. Or a fake, an impostor."

"Ha, ha!"

"I know. I didn't really doubt. One of those mad hunches, you know . . ."

Rainer von Gottardt was no longer yellow but dead white from fatigue. It made the red of his lips brighter and more striking.

"Would you like us to rest," I said to him, "and you can tell me about those two painful but uneventful years you spent at Château Marmont?"

"I would indeed," he said. "But let's stay here. I would not have the strength to drag myself out into the garden. If you would be kind enough to bring the cigars and white wine . . . No, bring the pipe and tobacco jar, over there, on the table. I smoke the pipe now and then, just to give my lungs a chance to breathe."

•

"I have thought of something."

"So have I," I said. "I bet it's the same thing . . ."

I was at the wheel of the Lancia. Never had he come out so far into the world with me. His pipe rumbled like a double bass. His hands took up the whole width of the door.

"Let us put money on it. If my health permits . . ."

"It will. We'll go to the Dioblaníz concert together."

"Yes."

"I should be delighted. But what about your cover?"

"Oooohwell . . . At this stage . . ."

"And I should be delighted to introduce you to Michèle de Klef, my pianist friend. She's going to record Granados's *Spanish Dances* soon."

"Very good! You love her?"

"I don't know. I think so."

"I shall be most happy to meet her. It is not entirely certain," he went on dreamily, "that Ana will not be there. Isabel and Ana have been out of touch a long time, years, but . . . No, I don't think so. Well, let's just wait and see. It would be a miracle."

"Let's wait. This week I am going to do a lot of work on our book. Life is beautiful."

"I am convinced of it," said Rainer von Gottardt.

•

But with the closing of the otherworldly parenthesis that my visit to the Great Interpreter constituted, this time like every time, life seemed less beautiful.

The discreet Annie — whom the white Michèle treated a little bit too much like a faithful slave for my taste, a slave one scarcely needed to address — lonely Annie, Annie the well-built, surprised Annie, suggested during the course of lunch, just to be tactful, the Annie you neither saw nor heard any more than the shadow of a shadow, suggested that she depart if we had no more need of her. I don't think she wanted this, on the contrary. But she was polite, she needed to know, she was testing the water. She was performing a service and did not consider that this gave her the right to end her days under the roof of those she had been helping.

"Do as you like," said Michèle. "But if you're not bored and you don't have anything else to do you can stay. I like having you around. We don't see each other too often anymore. I was glad when you said you weren't leaving on vacation . . . Stay the whole month with us if you like."

Sincere and friendly words. They had met as children in a Geneva choir. Annie still sang in a choir.

"Fine," she said. "I like being here too. I just hope everything turns out OK for Simon . . ."

So she stayed.

(Two days later, as I was chatting with her on the grass while Michèle played the piano, and we happened to be talking of clothes and I was deploring the unusable state of my white jeans due to the unfortunate circumstance of their being torn, she offered me a pair, white jeans, new, sent to her from New York by an old friend, a doctor, doing his internship in a kidney clinic there, and which were much too big for her, she had realized it the night before while trying them on for the first time. I accepted, I put them on, they fit perfectly, just as well as the old ones, they needed just a small adjustment to the cuff carried out by Annie on the spot as we continued to chat, but about quite other matters than clothes.)

That afternoon, a much-needed rest, Michèle and I dropped off from two to four. From four to five we stayed in one another's arms without sleeping, without making love, without really talking, and without really knowing what was in the other's mind.

Then Michèle played me the twelve *Spanish Dances* by Granados. I changed my mind a little bit, alas, about my first impression. Or rather, her playing struck me as an uninspired imitation of Alicia de Larrocha, and, in the more difficult of these pieces, her technique was less than infallible.

She played the second one, my favorite, the *Orientale,* fairly well.

She stopped between pieces. I kissed her then, on the neck, on the hair, on the eyes, on the eye once molested by Perfecto Jinez's scalpel and which, after my kiss, reopened only hesitantly, a tiny and endearing hesitation, I had to fight not to kiss harder and to devour raw.

Afterward I paid her a thousand lying compliments.

"You're very nice, but . . ."

She started to cry. An attack of depression. Simon. Her recording coming up. She lacked confidence in herself, she was not far enough advanced. If she had not met people who knew people, and if an influential person had not been in love with her, however hopelessly, she had been clear and quite firm, but all the same . . . In short, the whole thing smelled of backscratching, she was ashamed, she didn't believe she deserved to make a recording, but she no longer had the courage to turn back, she was terrified of the sound sessions, they were going to be torture, torture, she'd have to start over and over and over, she was even afraid in advance of the sound technicians . . .

I did not know what to answer. "You're wrong. You — "

"I'm starting to feel ill again. Forgive me. Everything's mixed up inside my head. And Simon, Simon!"

She closed the piano, rose.

"I'm ready to go to the police and tell them everything," I said.

"You're crazy! They'd put you in prison! That's all you'd achieve. They wouldn't find my brother, what are you thinking of? And there's the message left by this Lichem . . . If only they wanted money! All we can do is hope and wait. But I don't believe anymore . . ."

Talking made her worse. She started to cry again.

I took her face in my hands. "Don't stop believing . . . Let's go on waiting and hoping."

In her dark and pale gaze was something I did not like to see there, something I thought had forever fled, something I had all the trouble in the world to dispel with sweet words and tenderness.

•

I wrote until dinnertime.

The phone did not ring.

Lichem's weapon was put away behind the piano.

My wound was visibly healing. That tiny piece of death nesting in my pelvis was a wonder of self-effacement.

No, not until dinnertime. A quarter-hour before dinner, I stopped and learned from Annie that Michèle had gone to the Codec grocery. To do some shopping, on her own. Now that she no longer had an adorable and possessed little brother to order around with extreme coldness, I thought, she went to Codec herself, but without letting the person who was her lover and in love with her know, leaving him to perish in the toils of abandonment.

I cut a diagonal path across lawns and gardens, taking me from the house to the opening of the Impasse du Général de Luzy. Depressing residential stretches lay before me.

Heat, silence, closed shutters.

And yet, shortly after crossing Rue du Docteur Edmond Locard, well-known Lyon criminologist, a street I had to cross in my diagonal path, to my surprise I heard children's voices. I saw them, two kids, behind a hedge. Squatting. I listened. They were playing a game probably just that minute invented and consisting of crapping without peeing, at least that's how they defined its rough rules, the one who managed it would have the other's dessert that evening, the loser claiming loss of appetite or sudden tummy ache. (Patrice Pierre's medication had cut down my own cramps and waves of nausea to almost nothing.) I crept away noiselessly, leaving them to their interesting and uncomfortable enterprise.

A man was using the phone booth outside the Codec. The area was certainly jumping all of a sudden. And that phone booth must work on an on-again, off-again basis, and that man had had more luck than I had. He was fat and I saw that he was laughing with his whole body, he was sweating, weeping, shuddering with laughter. So exhausting was the violence of his laughter that sometimes he could no longer remain upright, he tottered, sank, his back slid down the glass. And sometimes, unable to endure any more, he held the phone away from his ear. He immediately stopped laughing, his face assumed a vast gravity, he straightened up, gave a dignified little cough, adjusted his attire. Then he put the phone back to his ear, and at once laughter shook him from head to foot, and so it went on.

Such were my encounters on my way to meet Michèle.

I sneaked up behind her and took the basket from her hands.

"You should have told me you were going to the Codec . . ."

She smiled at me, lips closed. What sensuality in the curve of those lips! What a luminous face! How I loved, how in love with her I was!

I pointed to the office of the manager (or to that of his heroic August replacement): "That's where I called you from the first time. Supermarkets large and small are my preferred stations on the road to a life of crime."

She paid the checkout girl, as young as ever and looking unlike a checkout girl as ever.

We left.

"He was already there when I got here," said Michèle.

I turned three times to look at the man with the calamitous hilarity. He seemed to be imprisoned in his booth for eternity.

We went back in silence. Michèle was as taut as a crossbow, her body giving off negative waves of nerves, of anxiety, and, I very much feared, of hostility, which of course she could not control, little arrows of hostility whistling and raining down on the whole Point du Jour neighborhood and transfixing me, so close to her in space and in my heart, most painfully.

They undid me. Already in a jittery state, I abandoned myself to scenarios of calamity: I spun the shopping bag counterclockwise and sent it crashing to the sidewalk (bottles, jam jars, tomatoes, pickle jar) and yelled what the hell shit fuck and fled at top speed to the center of the city, to its heart, as Anne the hitchhiker who loved to pronounce the word heart would have said!

I stroked her shoulder, her arm with the slightly protruding vein, spoke to her very gently: "It's going to be all right. I know it's going to be all right."

But it was not all right. That evening, an initial amorous contact did little to bring us closer. Michèle drew me into her own circle of fear and I went on the attack again about Lossaire, the detective who would have had trouble making charges stick against Hitler. "What happened between you and Renaud Lossaire?"

"Nothing. I already told you."

"But what I saw . . . Why?"

"No reason. I don't know. Out of disgust, out of weakness. I felt ill. I've felt ill for the last three years. He called me, he was insistent, he was nice, he wanted so badly to help me . . . I agreed to see him."

"Did you sleep with him?"

"You're insulting."

"No?"

"No!"

"You swear?"

"Yes, I swear."

"Did he kiss you?"

She hesitated.

"Yes."

Oh God oh God oh God oh God oh God!

"Why? Why? Did you want to?"

"Absolutely not."

"But you let him?"

"Yes. Yes and no. I was . . . Believe me, you're getting upset over nothing. Trust me, that's the only way you can help me."

"Good God! Why did you let him kiss you? And why let him hold your hand? Didn't you know I was there, sick with love for you?"

No, I did not trust her! Yesterday jealousy, not content with closing its claw on my heart and grinding it to dust, had also deposited its quick and mortal seed there. Within me the floodgates of a torrent of questions burst open, always different and always the same, just like the whirlpools in a mountain stream: had he kissed her more than once? All right, OK, just once, but why? Once was once too much. Had it excited her at all? No, in fact he disgusted her. OK, but in that case what had she been after, and for God's sake why had she let him take her hand, an abomination to which I had borne maddened witness, I who had already declared my sacred love to her. Had she not been in love with him, even if only for one-twelfth of a second? And was it really Lossaire who had called her and not the other way round? No, OK, fine, but why agree to see him then, OK, see him, but flirt with him? What do you mean a big deal? When you kiss someone and give him your hand, what did she call that, picking daisies? Playing bridge? Sneezing? Cleaning her ears out?

And so forth.

A whole book would not suffice to convey my meanderings as I went over the same ground again and again. I drove her and me crazy mad. I made us crazier than we already were.

At 1:12 (blip blip, digital alarm), she got out of bed so abruptly I thought she was finally fed up and ready for some excess of word or deed.

No. A pee. She crossed the room, went out into the corridor. A touch of the tomboy in the body, in the not-quite-defined waist. The arms quite strong despite the impression of slenderness, a bit long too in proportion to the legs (quite strong despite the impression of slenderness), delicate little breasts of slightly unequal size on a thoracic cage with too-prominent ribs, small buttocks actually not so small and most alluring although not perfectly shaped and somewhat low-slung in relation to the line of the body. The hair grew fast and was more tangled every day. Complexion dull white. Eminently desirable flesh, when you had the urge to find it desirable.

But what use is it to pile up a succession of details that cannot possibly convey what I felt in her presence, cannot possibly convey the essential, which escaped me, I loved this person, this body, this face, she was beautiful to me beyond expression, and it was that beyond that had first of all dazzled me, Michèle was beautiful and luminous, with a beauty and a luminosity destined for me.

Flush, return from peeing.

She stopped by the piano. I thought she was going to reach her arm behind (an arm I could have gazed at all night long, touched, kissed, playing with fingers, wrist, elbow, shoulder, running my lips along that visible, slightly protruding vein, then grazing on the hollow of this arm folded around my face like a gag) reach her arm behind the piano and take Lichem's weapon, for she said: "I don't like it, knowing this weapon is here . . ."

"What does it matter, my darling? I'd rather keep it. Have it within reach. You never know."

She came back and lay beside me.

"I loved you at once. I love only you. I have never loved the way I love you. I never loved before you. But I feel ill."

"Why?"

"I don't know. Don't hold it against me. Don't reproach me with anything."

Silence. The crisis of words was over. We remained silent for ten minutes or so. During those ten minutes desire took hold of us, grew. Michèle touched me first, shyly. I came onto her, at once penetrated her, slowness, we knew, was not required, the convulsions of pleasure swiftly achieved and of devastating violence hurled us out of bed and out of the house bouncing from lawns to gardens all through the neighborhood.

"Why are you so sad?" I asked her in the morning.

We each knew the other was awake. She was twisting and turning in her anxiety.

"I love you and I'm scared that I don't love you. I tell myself that if I loved you I wouldn't be feeling this way. Everything's mixed up in my head. I can't stand it any longer. Why, why? I've felt so good with you, better than at any time in my life. I don't understand. Forgive me, please forgive me!"

Unexpected, cruel, harrowing, insane words, each of them embedding itself like a spike in my flesh, soon I would look like a huge porcupine.

She was twisting and turning with anxiety, the fever of delirium joined forces with the heat of the day, her forehead was flooded. I kissed it, that perfect forehead, from the eyebrows to the roots of the hair, several times, light caresses to brush away the sweat. Her gaze was remote, shifting, suspicious, empty. I turned away. I could not stand that look. "Calm down. It will get better. Don't get to the point where words lose their meaning. We'll talk about it again when you feel calmer. I love you, I know you love me. I promise — " I did not know what to promise her. Not forgiveness. That she had, in my presence, held the hand of Lossaire, the man who had died for me, for her, and for Simon, and whose lips twisted in such vulgar fashion when he emitted words, I knew I would never forgive her, never, never. Never.

Neither did I understand anything about anything anymore.

•

A week elapsed before the fateful evening of August 15, the night of the concert at the Temple, a concert announced in Lyon by a handful of dirty yellow pamphlets the Rabut Agency persisted in posting even though at most three tickets were available at the entrance for the uninvited, a concert organized by the Dioblanízes, Hector and Isabel, those two lunatics, particularly her, patrons of the arts, drug manufacturers worth billions (DPL, Dioblaníz Pharmaceutical Laboratories), passionate music lovers, and the parents of a Jésus blind from birth whose blindness had aggravated their lunacy.

Every evening I called Patrice Pierre, late, at the Hôtel-Dieu, the hospital of my birth and my rebirth. The wound? Perfect, as you predicted. The little hole in the middle of my body was shrinking day by day to a small, ragged, pinkish slit by no means unpleasant to look at. No, still no ransom demand, it was indeed astounding, we could only wait. Michèle, my friend? Well, in circumstances as trying as these, hardly surprising that she was losing heart somewhat. Me? No, I was holding on. And say hello to Esther, well, thank you, see you soon then, yes, with pleasure . . .

On the tenth, twelfth, and thirteenth, I visited Rainer von Gottardt, whose last and probably only friend I was. In that week he finished telling me everything I needed to write the book we had planned. Cassette piled up on cassette and, since I wrote quickly, page on page. By the morning of the fourteenth I held in my hands a 277-page manuscript, in good shape it seemed to me, pretty well definitive, and quite legible, I mean from a handwriting standpoint, my faculty for shaping letters, words, and sentences on a blank page had been restored to me, intact, my handwriting grew more disciplined with each passing hour, it was normal by page 70 and flawless by page 120 despite the speed of my writing. Good sound work.

On the morning of that very August 14, I stopped on the following passage:

On August 2, my heart pounding with hope and fear, I awaited the arrival of young Michel Soler, whom I had not sought to contact by telephone, so great was my fear of telling him what I would inevitably tell him if I met him, and he agreed to take down the story of my life, Michel Soler who I was not even sure had received my card from Château Marmont or would be in Lyon in this torrid month of August.

On the stroke of noon, a red Dauphine stopped in front of the gate of my almost-birthplace in Lyon.

It was he.

Emotion stayed me from going out to meet my expected and unexpected visitor, the emotion of finding myself in the presence of the author of *On Bach's Fugues,* that wonderful book, unique in musical writing of course by virtue of its wholly inner understanding of Bach's work and by virtue of its profundity, but a profundity born of surface effects bold and subtle, at once hidden and highly visible, of the closest scrutiny of notes considered almost in their carnal imprint on the score — I exaggerate — and I have already explained that — the structure of this analysis like a foundation platform, analogous to the play of fingers on the keyboard, no finger in any case being able to press lower than the key — a unique book, then, in that it constitutes a truly musical interpretation — and what an interpretation! — a book destined for worldwide renown, for there is not a musician in the world who would not profit from reading it. As for its author, he is a pianist: and one, I know, who will be heard from shortly. I know it, I sense it, and, on the threshold of death, I ask that my words be heeded.

As the reader probably suspects, it was Rainer von Gottardt who was behind this fanfare. It was on the afternoon of the thirteenth that he first dared draw my attention to the fact that his publishers, Smikel and Keyelgod, would leap at *On Bach's Fugues* as soon as his biography had satisfied its readers' initial appetite. Yet another small fortune for me. Or quite simply a fortune. And this notion of a fortune born of the reproduction and multiplication in broad daylight of what I had once sought to reduce to nothing and kill in its egg in the darkness of a cellar, this idea of a fortune that would make more certain, more complete, and more enduring what I sometimes called my mastery of the world, this idea, to my own gigantic astonishment, smiled on me for a few seconds that day.

Ferrari, checkbook case of supple alligator leather, studded with rare pearls . . . How much for this jewel? When I bought a jewel at a jeweler's, the jeweler would no longer secretly phone the bank to ask if Mr. Soler's account . . . , an episode I had actually been subjected to at the time of my cohabitation with the one who had finally wearied of my person and my ways — but that person and those ways, at that time and in relation to that one in particular, would, I repeat, have tried the kindness of a solid-bronze Buddha. Or again, if the jeweler did telephone, he would be told in tones of no uncertainty and of some severity that Mr. Soler's check could most certainly be accepted, that a check from Mr. Soler could not only be accepted in perfect tranquillity as payment for the jewel but also as payment for the jeweler's shop and even for the building the jeweler's shop was in, and for all the buildings in the long street where the jeweler's was located, whose facades Mr. Soler might take it into his head to face in gold plate, which would not modify Mr. Soler's phenomenal account in any appreciable way, and what is more —

faced with the jeweler's chagrin, the banker's tone might change from one of severity to one of haughty assertion — and what is more, speaking of buildings, the bank, after enlarging its offices in vain, had been forced to build an endless skyscraper (the one of my dreams, ha, ha!) to house the special computer alone capable of handling Mr. Soler's accounts, accounts comprising a number of zeroes of which the number of stars in the sky gave but a laughably inadequate notion, ha, ha! so laughably inadequate it was uproarious, it made you laugh so hard you couldn't stop, ha, ha! the jeweler would pocket my check in unbridled mirth, bent double, firing off spluttering salvos of saliva!

Then I forgot this idea of a fortune.

As for the allusion to a possible career as a pianist, it left me perplexed and discountenanced. But Rainer von Gottardt had asked me, as if I were doing him a favor, to transcribe his prophecy word for word, a condition perhaps, he told me with the waggish air he put on so well, of its coming true.

He believed in me.

Had I begun the piano very young? Yes. Had I attained a decent level, as he was convinced I had? Yes, I thought so. I even thought in all simplicity that my interpretations of the works of Bach and of certain Spanish composers, such as Granados, around my twentieth year, were not devoid of interest. Very well. Had I at that time played at the feet of a master, or even simply a teacher, but one of those teachers endowed with the highest musical and human qualities, competent, intelligent, kind, who tried to sever me from my madness and drag me, shove me, direct me in life and in a career? Hell no. Besides, I would have avoided such a calamity, had it presented itself, like the plague. Anyway it could never have presented itself, since I had worked alone and reclusively from the tenderest possible age, drawing a bead on all piano teachers who appeared. All this being the case, my three concerts crowned with failure meant nothing, since they had been played with soul in full flight and fingers trembling . . .

Good, and so?

Yes, so? Why not? Why, once the book was completed, not sit
down at a piano again?

He had faith in me. "There be a Phoenix living here all awful
and unknown," he had said to himself on returning to Lyon.
Like an archpriest he had so to speak checked my mind against
the glyph representing it in the high holy book of music, and had
found them to be indeed one and the same. And he had burned
the body of the old Michel Soler on the altar of the Sun, and now
he proclaimed his faith in the new Michel Soler!

"I'll think about it," I said. "I promise."

I promised him I would think about it. After the book, and
after . . .

After was after.

On each of my visits I brought him a few papers and
magazines, purchased at the newsstand in the Perrache train
station and tossed carelessly onto the passenger seat, where my
eye sometimes fell despite itself on the headlines. Of course it
picked itself up again at once, the retina virgin of any impression,
except one day (the twelfth) when the word Bolivia printed in
huge letters impelled me to read the article. A coup d'état. A
thousand dead. A handful of rather bloodthirsty generals had
been replaced at the nation's helm by a group of blatantly
bloodthirsty generals. A far-right regime (judged too mild, and
not responsive enough to certain external directives) had given
place to a regime of the very farthest right. Before they had
tortured guerrillas in dark cellars or hidden places, now they
would be slicing off their virile parts and gouging out their eyes
in the civic center on market days. The operation, meticulously
prepared for months, had gone off without a hitch. Bravo.

Also on the twelfth, after my interview with the pianist, I
hastened to Cusset Cemetery for five minutes' communion at
Liliane's grave. I called on her image and her presence with an
intensity rarely felt in life. And I wished her the eternal peace and
happiness that in my view she was very close to deserving.

I did not weep.

Also on the twelfth, returning from the cemetery to Point du
Jour and driving along Cours Émile Zola, I overtook the scarlet

Ferrari Mondial I had one day seen in front of the Hôtel des Étrangers. It caught up with me, or rather I let it catch up, at the red light by the Villeurbanne skyscrapers. Tiered buildings whose design dates back to the beginning of the century and illustrates most strikingly one of the major architectural currents of the thirties. Morice Leroux, the father of these skyscrapers, was undoubtedly influenced, like all European skyscraper builders, by a German intellectual movement, the "Bauhaus," and it seems there is a complex in Vienna, the Karl Marxhof, that resembles the Villeurbanne construction despite —

The Ferrari. Its driver was a dignified old gentleman of concerned mien sporting a bow tie and long white locks. Some Lyon burgher kept in the city, one speculated, by the grave illness of his spouse. He lived in a residential suburb. At the beginning of August he had paid a frantic private call in Rue Stella on the surgeon who had operated on his wife in order to learn more, much more. And today he was off to procure drugs in a pharmacy that had stayed open, or was coming back from that pharmacy. I did not know. I could not say.

I would never see him again.

That I received an invitation to the Dioblaníz concerts impressed Annie, to whom I talked guardedly of my past as a musician and of the book in progress on Rainer von Gottardt, all this as she altered her white jeans to fit my leg length and as we chatted of anything but clothing under the blind eye of Simon de Klef, a wax figure set out on the lawn in daylight hours and wheeled into the downstairs bedroom at nightfall.

Before singing, Annie had played the oboe. Once she had even played the important oboe sequence in Cantata no. 82, for the Feast of the Purification, the very same one I would be hearing at the Temple at 9:30 P.M. on August 15.

The jeans were fixed. I thanked Annie and returned to the living room to write. On the second floor the notes of the piano, which had fallen silent, once again rang out.

•

Before that fatal concert I must speak, with beating heart, of
Michèle. I shall abstain from describing the twists and turns she
so artfully put us through. I shall stick to the facts, that is if you
can really speak of facts. We had loved one another at first sight.
Fine. What such a sudden, incomprehensible love meant I do not
seek to understand. Michèle, unhappy and long troubled, had
not surrendered to this feeling until the day her brother disappeared, when, standing beside Liliane's body, I had taken her
hand and she had not pulled away. And she had not consented to
living and experiencing that feeling in her flesh until the day, the
night, I caught her hand in hand with the accursed Lossaire.

Facts, nothing but facts . . .

After a few hours of perfect happiness a nightmare scene on
Rue du Soleil. Michèle had been repossessed by her demons.
Why? Because she had once again seen her brother in hideous
circumstances and could imagine the martyrdom he must be
enduring? Perhaps. I suspect the reason was less simple. Because
she had lived in torment ever since the first kidnapping, and
Simon had reappeared at a moment when she possibly
dreamed . . . of being rid of him for ever? Mad hunch. I do not
know. I abstain from twists and turns. I simply note the fact:
Michèle repossessed by her demons.

I again raised the question of the police. One word from her
and I . . . Dangerous and pointless, she repeated . . .

More and more, those demons thrust us apart.

My strenuous work on the written interpretation of Rainer
von Gottardt's life was a not unimportant distraction for me.

We continued to make love. Without ever again knowing the
fabulous bliss of our second night in the Hôtel Quivogne, heart
of the city, direct northern exposure, beneath the sightless gaze of
the throng dreamed up by Phil Dreux, DPH, every night one
humped the other and the other humped the one most
bruisingly, most painfully, hard enough to separate flesh from
bone, to set fire to the house of wood and cushions.

And we continued heedless of procreation. Of conception.
Why? I had given a satisfactory explanation on Rue Quivogne,
but afterward? Michèle: because she fed on self-disgust and

cared about almost nothing? Because basically she loved me?
Me: because I had pridefully likened myself to the Phoenix (a
kind of eagle of notable stature fledged with gorgeous fire-red,
black, white, blue, and yellow-gold feathers by whose side the
king of the peacocks looks like a harried old crow), and because
the Phoenix is an unreal beast, which reproduces itself sin-
glehandedly and may therefore safely cram with seed everything
in creation sporting an orifice? Because when all was said and
done I loved Michèle?

We could not have said. We did not think of it. We did not
speak of it.

I must certainly have loved Michèle to suffer without nailing
her to the wall (bang! bang! a nail between my teeth to follow up
on the one already hammered in) to suffer certain of her
reproaches without nailing her to the wall (when all that I had
done, infected by her own nervousness, was quiz her for four
nocturnal hours on end about her relations with the late
Lossaire). She had waited 30 years for me (she who was destined
for me) and could not grasp why I was unable to deliver her at
once from evil. After that she fretted over the notion that perhaps
she did not love me, attributing her torment to the poor quality
of our love, sought and found (in me!) reasons for not loving me,
for in the end it was in me that she located the source of the
trouble! And even, whirled round ever faster and deeper in her
maelstrom of folly, of bad faith, of hostility, she raged at me for
not accepting her doubt with light heart and smiling lips, the
light heart and smiling lips that alone could assuage the distress
born of this doubt, if not actually dispel the doubt itself! In short,
she ended up hating me because of not being able to love me in
peace, and I, sick at my inability to convince Michèle, who loved
me, that she loved me, I —

The facts.

On August 14 at 4:00 P.M., I decided to return to my
dwelling. So strong was her desire for disaster and so hungry was
she for the pleasure of bitterness that she did not try to keep me.

She simply asked me if we would meet again. Simply, but
anxiously.

Of course, I told her. You know we will.

The two white Lancia Themas ran nose to tail along the short stretch of freeway.

Satolas Airport.

The truly ravishing girl behind the desk took the papers and rang up a new and enormous sum, with what I had paid for these few days' rental you could easily buy yourself one, ten, twenty Lancias, the whole Lancia assembly plant in Turin. She did not look kindly at Michèle.

•

"I'm going to miss you," I said to Michèle.

"Me too."

"It will soon be tomorrow night. It's almost here already. I'm looking forward to this concert. Afterward we'll see. After is after."

She gave one of those smiles (like the one she had given the noisy brother substituting for the owner of the Bar des Archers that first night) one of those smiles in which the soul, precisely because it had to struggle against demons black as chimney sweeps, and managing to escape them for a second and to wash hastily but energetically, gave expression to itself, relieved, free of its carnal envelope, with a purity, a radiance, a luminosity, and an innocence that were paradoxically incomparable.

I took my suitcase off the rear seat and got out of the Lancia.

"See you tomorrow night," I said and she said, we both said at the same time.

The car disappeared at the end of Rue Stella, Michèle waved, so did I.

I gave a friendly little kick to the right rear tire of the Dauphine, faithful vehicle whose headlights dispelled the darkness of the remotest night of time and whose windshield wipers would have conquered the Flood.

And so I returned to my dwelling.

Three letters awaited me. The bill from the IFH funeral home ($837.96, why the $37.96, ha, ha! why the 96 cents,

probably the box of matches needed to light the fire), a postcard
from Kristiansand, Norway, from Torbjörn Skaldaspilli, large
writing, a few words on the order of: soon I return, I hope that
you better, I am well, very cold here but I do not mind hot or
cold.

My mother and I embrace you.

And a card from Cuevas del Almanzora, province of Almería,
Spain, sent by Anne, who couldn't wait to see me, who was
exhausted, who had given up hit songs but had composed a
beautiful song she had just recorded on a cassette, who was
thinking of me and who sent me a big kiss.

I felt I was returning home after a long round-the-world trip.
I walked around the apartment. The heat both hit the body and
clung to it like a cloak of molten studded metal on whose studs
an army of little devils were flailing away with maces.

I opened the windows and everything that opened.

Four strips of yellowed Scotch tape had come unstuck
around Johann Sebastian Bach. Johann Sebastian Bach still
refused to look me in the eye. Tap tap tap tap, I stuck them back
again.

I unpacked my bag with a certain sadness.

Into the bottom drawer of the walnut-stained chest with
Lichem's weapon and the kidnappers' notes!

I went to pee and flushed seven times. The first three times
there was noise but no water. The fourth, a ball of water as big as a
melon leapt three feet in the air above the toilet bowl with a
splish and fell back in with a splash. The fifth and the sixth were
the most disastrous. You would have thought a herd of cattle had
wandered through my latrine. But the seventh time the flush
worked as well as on its best days.

An eyewitness seeing me run at the refrigerator door several
times shoulder first would have concluded that it was hard to
close and that I was irritated. Wrong. I was quite calm, and it was
a way of opening it. It opened. I drank a beer slumped on my
couch listening to Cantata no. 82, *Ich habe genug,* I have had
enough, said Hans Hotter in his fine bass voice, I cannot go on, I

rejoice in my death, slumber now, weary eyes, close in sweet bliss.

But since closing your eyes or letting tears drown them were just then out of place I turned off Hans Hotter's celestial voice and worked until the evening of the next day, 7:25 P.M., minus six hours of sleep, three-quarters of an hour for absorbing nutrition and twenty minutes on the phone, a call to Patrice Pierre ("no more dressings, no more antibiotics") and to Michèle before going to bed, another to Michèle at noon on the fifteenth.

"I love you," I told her at the end.

"I love you too," she said. "I'm glad I'll be seeing you tonight."

Yet her voice was not the voice of a woman happily in love.

"So am I," I said. "Until tonight. Until soon. Until right away."

No news of Simon. I believed the child was doomed. They would find his body one day, or perhaps never. However pointless it might be. I had once again told Michèle, I would soon have to tell the police the whole story, from beginning to end. She protested. But this time I insisted.

Soon. Soon was after.

My God, she was tense and hostile! And yet that August 15 at noon I loved her more than ever. And her pain hurt me. And I continued to seek refuge in my task of writing, which prevented me from giving in to hatred. I continued to write without hating her, without forgetting her for a single second, without her image ever ceasing to interpose itself between me and the paper.

At 7:25 P.M. I shaved, showered, washed my hair, put on clean and white clothes (Annie's jeans) and the black leather jacket, the most sumptuous fruit of my depredations at Carrefour-Vénissieux.

I studied myself in the bathroom mirror. I found myself more astonishingly beautiful than ever and flashed a triumphant, seductive, and wicked smile at myself. That damned mirror was deteriorating. The whole apartment was deteriorating. I'd soon have to make a change.

Before leaving I read the last lines I had written:

I had few freshly ironed items of clothing left. I washed
with my usual difficulty, ate without appetite but down to
the last canned pea (very sweet, with even a slight aftertaste
of cranberry), dressed myself for my last excursion into the
world in an old full dress suit with tails altered and
superbly ironed by my favorite chambermaid at Château
Marmont and not too rumpled by suitcase living, and
awaited the arrival of Michel Soler, my heart pounding
with hope and fear, as it had the first time.

Thus before dying I was going to see the Dioblanízes
again, Hector and Isabel, those two lunatics. Particularly
her. And would I see Ana again? No, that would be a
miracle.

Michel, recent friend and friend forever, arrived punc-
tually in his old red Dauphine and not in the lovely white
Lancia he had rented for reasons I feel sure he never fully
divulged to me. But I knew enough. The rest was petty
secrets. We each kept petty secrets from the other.

I had hoped that this evening, before leaving for the
concert, we would play a few notes.

We had promised one another we would.

•

"Yes, here I am riding around again in this red vehicle from the
days before there were red vehicles on earth. I like it. Here are the
papers . . . and" (I fumbled with my right hand in the right
pocket of the jacket my left hand held by the collar) ". . . here is
a pipe, a good pipe I believe, judging by its price . . . It has never
been smoked, of course, I merely held it between my teeth to get
out of the store where I stole it."

"Ha, ha! You shoplift?"

"No, never. It was an exception."

He put the pipe in his mouth, whee whee, drew on it. I

looked at the Töhdeskünst. The first book of *The Well-Tempered Clavier* lay on the lectern.

"Splendid. It does indeed seem splendid. Thank you. I shall start to use it tomorrow, or tonight as soon as I return. You are as elegant and handsome as a god, my dear Michel. A little thin and pale . . . but you can put some color back in your cheeks in September, as soon as the book is finished . . . If you go on working at this devilish speed you will have finished everything by the end of August?"

"Beyond a doubt," I said. "Very elegant and attractive yourself. An old set of tails?"

For his last excursion into the world, on the evening of his death, he had put on a dark concert outfit. His saurian eyelids rose and fell, it was a surprise not to see his eyes bloodily striated in consequence.

"Yes, indeed. Thank you for the compliment. What's this?" (He had opened a newspaper at random and come across a picture of Perfecto Jinez.) "Perfecto Jinez missing?"

"Yes. Do you know him?"

"By name. The Dioblanízes often took Jésus to see him. Nothing to be done, alas. His is one of the most authoritative voices in the world. They adore him. They had a blind faith in him, you might say, ha, ha! I shall read the story later. It's strange, I have enjoyed having the papers to read. My interest in the world's affairs has hardly been lively these past few months."

"Nor mine," I said, looking at my watch. "We still have a good quarter of an hour. Would you . . ."

"Willingly. I had the same idea. You too?"

"For you to play, or to play a few notes myself?"

"Both."

"Yes. I had thought both too."

"Shall we play together? The last fugue of the first book? You will be my left hand . . ."

"Let's try. Your left index finger?"

"Of no importance. Perhaps I shall tell you about it later on."

I regretted my question. He no longer spoke of Simon. He

no longer spoke of anything. He was not angry with me, he even smiled at me, mischievously.

Fugue in B Minor, BWV 869, I had told him often how much I loved it and how his interpretation threw me into ecstasy. I put two chairs together, opened the music sheet on the stand.

"Follow me," he said.

He began the theme so slowly that I was able to follow without error, laboriously, with a heavy touch, but without a wrong note. How long had it been since my hand . . . What joy! With Rainer von Gottardt!

I played. And in the last third of the score I even gained confidence. Rainer felt it. He accelerated the tempo, added embellishments, gave the phrases all their suppleness, their curvilinear beauty, their freight of gentle, stubborn, unfailing sensuality, he interpreted faster and faster in this way right on till the final chord without losing me, I had managed to follow him!

I had played with him, with Rainer von Gottardt, we had played together!

He closed the sheet, the piano.

Any word, any gesture, any demonstration would have been superfluous, would have diminished our emotion, which was calm, infinite.

Or else would have unleashed it, scattered it, sent it astray, so that we would have arrived at the Temple arm in arm, a bottle of white wine beneath the other arm, weeping like crocodiles, laughing like hyenas, and bawling out barrack-room ballads at the tops of our voices, roll me o-ver in the clo-ver, roll me over lay me down and do it again!

Silence.

He took out a box of white tablets. He swallowed two, put the box in his pocket.

"Would you mind stopping at a post office?" he said. "I have a letter to mail."

I had trouble squeezing him into the Dauphine, whose exhaust pipe sagged to the pavement under his weight.

I drove off.

We were full of a deep joy.

•

The fact that the Place du Change — wonderful, an authentic little jewel, restoration was much farther along here than at Saint-Georges, where Simon, not far from here, a few days ago . . . — the fact that the Place du Change was teeming with people in this month of August in Lyon aggravated rather than dispelled the strangeness of the urban landscape.

And meeting Michèle here, like a normal girlfriend, with whom you have a normal date — our first normal date — after what had happened, carried the strangeness to extreme limits. My heart shrank when I saw on her face the expression it wore in her darkest moments. But we kissed one another lovingly, on the cheeks, close to the lips.

"I am delighted and overwhelmed to meet you," she said to Rainer von Gottardt, in her voice that was rather low and without absolute distinction.

Mouth distastefully pursed, bitter lines, her glance hard and fugitive. And yet, all white in her black dress, speaking to the pianist, she smiled at him, and that smile lit up Old Lyon better than twelve thousand searchlights could have done. I still wonder how Rainer von Gottardt was able to bow low enough to kiss her hand. Doubtless he ripped muscles, splintered ribs and sternum, wrenched stomach and intestines: yet the fact remains that he bent before Michèle like a willowy youth and kissed her hand, his sea monster's mask suddenly seductively alight.

He thanked her. That was all. I believe that they did not speak to one another again after that, did not even look at one another when he introduced her to Isabel Dioblaníz.

The light of seduction died, so did Michèle's smile. Rainer straightened. Cracks, unwrenchings, hissings were heard. He coughed so hard his cigar flew from his hand.

On the steps of the Temple two sickly beings dark of skin and hair, a small man and a small woman, scurried in all directions at once (particularly him), shaking hands, raising arms heavenward, bending earthward, hopping, making hundred-

and-eighty-degree turns and talking, talking, ceaselessly talking and rolling their eyes.

Particularly him.

We approached them. At a distance of sixty feet we distinguished at least seven skin hues and a dozen different languages.

Isabel Dioblaníz almost swooned from unalloyed joy on recognizing (after some hesitation: how the Maestro had changed!) Rainer von Gottardt.

"Maestro! Rainer von Gottardt! Rainer! What a surprise! But why? Why didn't you let us know? I would never have dreamed . . . I knew that your health . . . Hector! Rainer is here!"

She could not help herself, she fell into his arms. He could help himself, resisted, then melted, stroked her hair. Making perilous little hops, Hector waited his turn.

Isabel Dioblaníz was more beautiful than I remembered. She did in fact look like Liliane in her youth. For a woman not spared by horror she had a clear, candid, free, and happy gaze. So did her husband. So excited was he at seeing Rainer von Gottardt that he could hardly stand still. He had become as mobile and elusive as a hummingbird, now standing beside you, the next second crouching behind you, or walking on his hands in front of the Temple door (admirably restored), or gesticulating from the summit of the building like a lookout announcing land. You ached to rap him on the skull with a hammer to restore him to a more human posture.

Rainer introduced us, Miguel Soler, you know, author of the book, his friend Michèle de Klef, pianist . . . Isabel gave various exclamatory shrieks, heaped me with friendly reproaches, at last you deign to show yourself, what a joy to meet you, what a book, at last I see you, I scarcely dare believe my eyes, and you, my dear, a pianist! what a wonderful couple, how young and good-looking they are, aren't they, Hector, etc. Tirelessly garrulous. Having found out who I was, Hector made a knot of his right leg. He spoke at the same time as his wife but this was not too disagreeable as his voice was less piercing than hers, and she spoke flawless French while he jabbered a mumbling pidgin that constituted a background noise and nothing more.

"And . . . Jésus?" asked Rainer.

"Alas! The heat has rather knocked him out, poor dear. He's sleeping. We would so much have liked to bring him tonight . . ."

"What a shame!"

Heavy sigh from Isabel and Hector, the latter grabbing one ankle and hopping crabwise away from us.

Then Isabel pointed out one or two of the musical celebrities surrounding us, a real success this concert, a more prestigious success even than in years past, if only because of your presence, dear Rainer, but you haven't told me anything about yourself, how long have you been in Lyon, you wanted to surprise us, so you know Miguel Soler, what's happening in Bolivia is terrible, isn't it (she said to my astonishment), but we shall be able to talk more easily after the concert, which is going to be superb, just you wait and see, despite his youth Hans Melchior is the finest bass voice around today, but you seem exhausted?

"Yes," said Rainer. "I should prefer to avoid too many introductions, if that doesn't . . . Any at all, in fact . . ."

"But of course! Please forgive my—It's just that I'm so happy! Come and sit down, come! Let me take you to your seat."

There was no mention between them of the absent Ana de Tuermas.

This absence disappointed me. Ana de Tuermas was missed.

Graciously, Isabel Dioblaníz took Michèle's hand and conversed with her: "Do you know that black dress suits you extraordinarily?"

"Doesn't it, though?" said Michèle, deliciously natural and pretty, Michèle whom I knew to be tormented by her demons.

"So, you're a pianist?"

"Yes."

That Isabel should be holding Michèle's hand was not without its disturbing effect on my state of mind. I was in a hurry for us to be seated and for me to be holding my beloved's imperfect hand.

"Michèle is preparing a recording of Enrique Granados's work," I said, mastering my annoyance and displaying more graciousness and charm than the other two combined.

"No! My God! Will you send it to us at once? And will you come and play the piano at our house?"

She had let Michèle's hand go. I had taken Michèle by the shoulder. Rainer von Gottardt had put his own hand on my shoulder.

Isabel was looking at all three of us. She astonished me. She made you like her.

There was a moment of calm, a moment almost of silence. I got the feeling we were posing for a photo.

That we were already in the photo.

Then they were all fidgeting and cackling again. Hector had managed to get his torso (although it was no thicker than a dragonfly's) caught between two lateral columns, and he was waving his arms and legs and rolling his eyes so wildly that they seemed to be protruding from his cheeks. We had to help him get free.

"I am happy," Isabel Dioblaníz suddenly said to us, "happy!"

ELEVEN

The Bach Choir and Orchestra of Mainz was already seated. Hans Melchior, the soloist, a pudgy, fair-haired, feminine-looking young German, was collecting his thoughts. Although his hands were not moving he seemed to be rubbing them together. The conductor, Thomas Lom, was about to raise his baton.

The Temple on Place du Change, a Tower of Babel in miniature, was packed and expectant. Hector contented himself with nibbling at one of his ears which he had pulled and tugged to its present length to calm his nerves.

We were in the second row, Rainer von Gottardt, me, Michèle. Rainer was sitting on the right of an old Tunisian pianist, Michèle on the left of a young Malian violinist.

As soon as he was seated, fearful of fatigue, of the crowd, the heat, Rainer swallowed three white tablets.

The conductor raised his baton.

The orchestra began. With the very first notes, the whole Temple rose from the Saint-Jean neighborhood and soared up into the sky like a huge hot-air balloon. And soon Hans Melchior, chest swelling, hands no longer pressed against one another but crossed tightly against his breast as if addressing a supplication to the earth we had just left beneath us, sang. The union of voice, organ, and oboe was a thing of magic, you rose, you were transported into uppermost heaven!

You were afraid.

I have had enough, I cannot go on,
I would depart this world below in joy.
Ah! if the Lord would deliver me from the chains of my body!

Slumber now, weary eyes,
Close in sweet bliss,
Slumber now, slumber now . . .

A magic union! I held Michèle's hand. We listened, together, with our whole heart, Michèle and I, and Rainer.

But Rainer, poor soul, was tiring rapidly from the strain of controlling his hoarse, rapid breathing. Before the second aria began I saw him take two more tablets and painfully swallow them. I suffered for him. The heat was truly vengeful. We were dying. I took off my jacket. You would willingly have stripped down to your skeleton.

I will not tarry here below,
There is naught in this world
Pleasing in my sight.
Slumber now, weary eyes,
Close in sweet bliss!

I did not take my eyes from my friend. A few people, inconvenienced by his noisy breathing, showed their irritation in various subtle ways, here the creaking of a chair, there the rustle of clothing, elsewhere the click of dry mucous membrane as a tongue came unstuck from a palate.

Isabel Dioblaníz, in the front row to our right, had been showing all the symptoms of ecstasy since the concert had begun. No longer among us, she rose ever higher and faster!

In silence, Hector nibbled at his other ear.

My God, when shall that wonderful moment be mine,
That moment when I will enter into peace
And rest in the sand of the cool earth?
World, good night!

During the recitative, Rainer von Gottardt took my hand. I leaned closer to him: "Shall I call a doctor?"
"No."

It was an order. I recalled that his features could express absolute severity.

He handed me a small notebook.

"Tell Ana de Tuermas. Tell her I have always loved her . . ."

There was nothing to be done. The details of his heart ailment were set out in my manuscript, he was going to die, I knew. I knew!

"I implore you . . . For my own peace of mind . . . You're sure you don't want . . . ?"

"Certain. I ask you only to stay by me."

"I'll stay by you," I said. "I'm not going to move an inch, I'll be by you to the end!"

He squeezed my hand tighter.

There were one or two clearly enunciated shushes. I looked at Michèle just long enough to shake my head, scowl, and frown, a mime intended to convey: no, nothing in particular, nothing that concerns you.

Hans Melchior embarked on the final aria.

I had given my right hand to Michèle de Klef, my left to Rainer von Gottardt.

I rejoice in my death,
Ah! would I had already found it!

Old Simeon is recalling his life of faithful service. Now his Lord has come, He is but a child, but He will be the Savior of the World, and the old servant can close his weary eyes, Hans Melchior sang it over and over again, then repeated it one last time:

I rejoice in my death,
Ah! would I had already found it!

End of the cantata.

I had not taken my eyes off Rainer.

The audience had been asked not to applaud between *Ich habe genug* and the following cantata, *Christ lag in Todesbanden,* "In death's strong grasp our Savior lay." There was a burst of sobbing. Isabel Dioblaníz had dropped from her seat to her knees and was weeping. "Thank you, God, thank you!" she moaned through her sobs! Hector had crossed his legs around the back of his neck and was tugging at his nose with both hands.

Rainer von Gottardt was trying to speak to me. I brought my face close to his.

"Thank you, dear friend. Thank you for everything . . ."

"And I thank you!"

He crushed my hand.

The pressure relaxed. His weary eyes closed in sweet bliss.

His enormous envelope of flesh, plated, pulpy, speckled, was so heavy it did not budge from the seat, it sat there, slumped and still, lids forever closed.

"He's dead," I told Michèle. "Wait for me."

I rose.

I approached the stage. Only then did Isabel come out of her ecstatic trance. Her tears, I said to myself in an amazement that froze my blood to ice within my veins, unaccountably, and despite the heat that threatened all the living in this temple with instant decomposition, her tears were tears of joy! Truly a passionate music lover! She deserved her reputation!

I believe I gazed on her with anger.

She saw me. She was bewildered. She wondered what was going on.

The soloists were ready to sing, the musicians had tuned their instruments. Arms spread, Thomas Lom deliberately did not look over his shoulder despite the sound of my footsteps and the audience's murmured disapproval of the person thus disturbing the ceremony.

I spoke to him, Thomas Lom, the conductor, in English.

"Please don't play. Rainer von Gottardt is dead."

•

The concert was interrupted.

I said to Isabel Dioblaníz: we must tell his nephews in

Wiesbaden. We'll find the instructions on him, in one of his pockets.

•

When I reached the Lancia my mind was made up.

"Can you lend me your car? For a short while. I'll leave you the Dauphine. Two days at most. I have to make a trip. To Spain, but just across the border. I have to go, and right now. A favor I promised Rainer von Gottardt. I have to give the news to one of his female friends. The woman he loved."

It was true and false. Michèle sensed it. Maybe she would have come with me if I had suggested it. Maybe not. I suggested nothing. She demanded nothing, asked no questions.

War raged between us.

"Of course," she said.

"Thank you. I brought you—"

I pulled from the left inside pocket of my jacket my only copy, a dirty yellow, of *On Bach's Fugues,* Rhône Valley Publishers.

"Thank you," she said.

"I love you and I know you love me," I said to her for the twelfth thousandth time. "I'll be back soon."

"Forgive me. Please forgive me."

Without thinking, something I had to say, I said: "And please forgive me."

We could not have remained together a second longer.

True and false. The last and the maddest of my hunches had come over me in the Temple on Place du Change.

A car that did not have Lyon plates suited my plans. And one that could hit 130: I might just be in a hurry.

It was 11:30 P.M. At my place I stuffed two or three things (including the blue silk tie lifted at Carrefour) into a small creased travel bag. I removed Lichem's weapon from the bottom drawer. With the silencer unscrewed it fit in my jacket pocket perfectly. Death, if death there must be, would roar loud as thunder.

I also took my anti-spasmodic and anti-nausea medication, for Rainer von Gottardt's demise had fomented mutiny in my bowels.

•

Soon I was winging down the Highway of the Sun toward Spain and Cadaqués.

I forgot Michèle.

Did I forget Michèle? My love was large. As large as the city, which seemed so infinite when you were pilloried within its confines by the heat? As large as the city. But what if you left the city? Well, let's say it stretched to the remotest suburbs, even into the surrounding countryside: beyond that, could you even talk legitimately in terms of the city? And in that case of love?

I forgot Michèle, I raced straight ahead, I fled, and this straight line of flight was like a line drawn through the knots and tangles of the map of the past! Of course, but would this flight sooner or later bring me back to her? And was I fleeing in her car? A car in which several particles at least of the soul of Lyon, the stifling theater of our love, were still trapped, still suspended (despite the cross-breeze I had created by opening all the windows), or still clinging to the fabric of the seats, to the leather around the base of the gearshift, to the rather sticky glass dials on the dashboard?

Stifling, painful contortions of my thinking, reflecting the painful contortions in my bowels—a sign that I was not forgetting?

God, what torture!

From time to time I raised the bottle of white anti-spasmodic tablets to my mouth, tossed two or three back between tongue and palate and swallowed them with the help of a good swig of anti-nausea mixture.

Spasms and nausea faded, disappeared.

•

I crossed the lower third of the country by night.

There was little traffic. No traffic at all. Little.

Between Nîmes and Montpellier I filled the tank. The Lancia gobbled up the highway without seeming to move, so straight and unswerving was the road.

It took me less than three and a half hours to reach the Spanish frontier. I would arrive in Cadaqués early, too early, in the middle of the night. I took the Perthus pass over the frontier. A very old customs officer kept sneezing, and when he wasn't sneezing he yawned. He had no teeth. He was of retirement age multiplied by twelve. He blinked continuously. Drivers license, Lancia documents, everything was in order, but he didn't really look at them. An old man. It seemed to me he saw nothing. It seemed to me you could cross this frontier with a week-old beard, a knife between your teeth, a machine gun in your belt, twelve cases of dynamite on the back seat, and thrust a wanted poster beneath his nose in lieu of travel documents. He waved me through, eyes closed, forehead wrinkled, mouth half open, momentarily stuck between a sneeze and a yawn.

So I went through.

A hundred yards farther on, I stopped. Up ahead on the highway to my left, where the lights from frontier post still carried, a man was bent over his car, hands resting on the hood. He turned his white-maned head in my direction. There was great distress in his gaze.

I had an urge to speak to him, to speak to a stranger. I slowed and stopped.

"Engine trouble?"

"No. Sick. Stomach. Oh God!"

He must have been about forty in spite of his snow-white hair and mustache. His car, a big Fiat, had Paris plates.

"Come over here," I said.

He never hesitated, he came over, circling the Lancia with small steps. I opened the door. He collapsed onto the seat.

"Oh God!"

"Does the pain come in waves, in spasms, and at the same time you want to throw up?"

"Yes. I nearly did, just now. I got out of the car fast . . ."

"Spastic colon," I said. "I have just what you need."

"Are you a doctor?"

"No, just sick. It's written on the label, spastic colon. Here, you take four tablets and swallow them with this mixture. It works. Anyway, it worked for me."

He complied like a child, paying no heed to what he was swallowing.

"You should start to feel better within fifteen minutes."

"Thanks," he said. "I'm on my way from Paris, I'm joining my wife and children on vacation in Madrid. That's where I'm from."

"I'm going to see a girlfriend in Cadaqués. I'm from Paris too. And I was born in Spain as well. I don't know how I managed it, I'm going to arrive in the middle of the night."

"Well, I'm going to be late. Do you know Cadaqués already?"

"No."

"It's beautiful, you'll see."

He bent double, arms folded across his stomach, and winced.

"It's best not to talk," I said. "Wait a bit."

We waited twelve minutes in silence.

He was shifting less, his breathing had grown more even.

"Getting better?"

"Yes, thanks. What luck meeting you! I'll give you my card, just in case. If you're ever looking for an apartment in Paris . . ."

We shook hands. He returned to his car with firmer steps. He was tall. I tucked his card away in an inner jacket pocket.

I pulled away. He waved, smiled. His name was Sebastian Miranda, he was a real estate agent.

I saw the sign for Cadaqués once, then got lost on complicated secondary roads. I got annoyed. I got even more annoyed when I reached a closed railroad crossing that stayed closed forever. Had the train already gone through? It was a crossing with no crossing guard, otherwise I would have killed the crossing guard. I would have tied him to the rails. All of a sudden, phtoooo! the train shot past, short, stubby, rust-colored, phtoooo! looking and sounding just like a vigorous expectoration, not only had I been waiting endlessly for this train in the night faintly touched with first light but I had scarcely seen it, phtoooo!

The countryside flattened out.

I emerged onto a minor road. Rosas and Cadaqués were signposted to the left, so I turned left (even though I would willingly have turned right and roared off at top speed out of rage and the perverse urge to cut off my own nose), a few miles before Rosas another left, Cadaqués, a narrow road that twisted through a deserted and again mountainous landscape, it was all too much for me.

The sea, out of sight but you sensed it was there, pushed deep into the heart of this hilly topography, and Cadaqués sat at the very tip, on the point of a narrow V, you felt as if you had reached the end of something, you couldn't go on, perhaps one of the land's ends of this world. The white houses of the little port climbed a mountainside dominated by a beautiful and very large church too large for either port or houses. I pulled up in front of the first hotel I saw, if not the first then the fourth, I believe, probably because of its name, Hotel Cadaqués.

It was ages since I had looked at the sea. I gazed at it for ten seconds, still and blue-black beneath the paler sky, then entered the hotel.

It barely crossed my mind that the weather was cool and that I was treading the soil of my forefathers.

A woman, neither old nor young, was sitting at the reception desk. Her posture and the semidarkness at first persuaded me she was asleep. Then I realized that she was staring at me with eyes that were absolutely unmoving, dead, no, something other than dead: counterfeit, eyes that were not genuine you told yourself, then suddenly — horror! — real eyes replaced the fake ones, in the twinkling of an eye, the expression was marvelously apt since she had merely raised her eyelids, it was just makeup, skillful original makeup, eyes painted on her lids!

Phew!

She gave me a big inane smile, I a big foolish one.

I forgot this woman and her painted eyes and I slept for four dreamless hours in a second-floor room looking out to sea. When I awoke, I thought for a few seconds that I was back at the Hôtel Quivogne. The room was as small, maybe smaller, but sprucer, as if the Turk, not content with a good cleaning, had also touched up the paint and put up new curtains.

I savored the charms of a leisurely toilet in a bathroom not big enough to house a spider unless its legs had first been cut off close to its body, and partook of breakfast, for which I had ordered mythic quantities of food, on the terrace across the street a half-inch from the sea, slap slap ripple ripple wooosh, went the wavelets dying at my feet. The woman with the painted eyes had been replaced by a young Spaniard, puffy and sleepy-looking. But he told me clearly and concisely how to get to Villa Madre de Osdi, on the Madrid Highway.

A fine bright sun.

The Madrid Highway started behind the church, you got to it by a narrow street so steep it seemed vertical, it then disappeared into the mountain. Villa Madre de Osdi was between the sixth and seventh bends a mile past the church.

I stopped a little way before the sixth bend. I took a few cautious steps forward until I could see the house from behind a rock, about three hundred yards away, on the left-hand side of the road, in the center of an area enclosed within high walls and dotted with pines, olive trees, and flowerbeds, white, isolated, its face turned to the sea — and with open windows, and I could even see a silhouette at a second-floor window. So there were people living there. Ana de Tuermas? Perhaps. Probably. I hoped so.

I had no intention of ringing her door bell and introducing myself, the pianist's little notebook my visiting card, saying: "Hello, Rainer von Gottardt is dead, I was his friend at the end, he entrusted me with a message for you, a message he gave me in hideous circumstances (even as he spoke death was bearing his soul away), a message so sincere and so intense it conjures up great geysers of emotion, geysers capable of splashing and even extinguishing the sun: he always loved you!"

No. I went back to the village, bought a pair of field glasses, the finest, and two cheese sandwiches, and returned to take up my station behind the rock, sixth bend, Lancia parked with its nose pointing to the sea.

And I waited. I waited an hour.

Sometimes I looked through the glasses. I saw nothing interesting. Nothing at all, to be frank, either at the windows or anywhere else. No car, unless there was a car concealed behind the house.

After an hour the door opened. A redheaded woman wearing a bathrobe appeared on the threshold. The very finest field glasses: I could have counted the lashes around her green eyes. Or admired the contraction and dilation of her pupil, even the harmoniously unequal lengths of the converging lines of her iris. She slipped off her bathrobe. She was naked. Tall, perfectly built. Body like a goddess of old, Rainer had said.

The wax figure from the Renaissance townhouse.

Ana de Tuermas.

He had always loved her.

She stepped forward, suddenly her feet left the ground, ploof! I thought she was plunging head first into the bowels of the earth, but little bursts of spray informed me that no, she had merely plunged into a pool invisible behind its screen of flowers.

In my opinion she was alone. But I still was not going to ring her door bell. If my mad hunch was correct . . . "Of course, your phone number is in the notebook he gave me, but since I happened to be passing by along the Madrid Highway, I thought . . ." No. If my mad hunch was right, I had to approach her quite differently, that was the problem. I would of course give her the message. Rainer von Gottardt, who must at this moment be watching me with a severe and disapproving eye, could rest easy on that score. But later. After I had found out whether my hunch was correct or incorrect.

Now began the most trying wait of my life.

Ana de Tuermas, with her long, splendid, amazing red hair,

often swam. She often stretched out in the sun (after swims). Then she set up a folding table between house and pool, put up an umbrella and ate a lunch of cold cuts and salad. Then she went back in and the shutters of a second-floor window closed for the length of a siesta.

Was she really alone? Yes, I thought she was.

I would willingly have taken a siesta myself. I ate my two limp warm sandwiches, taking ten minutes to chew each mouthful for want of liquid. Thirst was drying me up, shshshshshshsh, I would dry up on the spot and be reduced to the condition of an old stump barely visible in the dusty landscape, the more certainly because the sun was revolving about the rocks and I was more exposed and defenseless beneath its destructive rays than I had ever been in Lyon.

God deliver us from the sun! From the pitiless eye of God . . .

After her siesta she resumed her indolent routine, swimming, tanning, calisthenics, ingesting delicate little snacks and cool drinks, reading illustrated magazines . . .

She remained naked all day. Without the slightest self-indulgence, I became intimately acquainted with her body, which was displayed to me for hours on end and in effect but a few inches from my eyes — eyes reddened, smarting, assaulted by the sun and the pressure of the field glasses — her body with the perfect contours of a goddess of old, scant inches from my eyes, I even came near falling over backward when, following a calisthenic routine, legs spread and bust abruptly thrust forward, her ideal buttocks and their cleavage burst so to speak blindingly into the binoculars, the slight curve embraced by the line of the long thighs where they joined the outer precincts of her sex was flawless, one of the beautiful things the world sometimes offers for our contemplation.

I had not digested my two limp and warm sandwiches.

In the late afternoon she went back inside and did not come out again for an hour and thirty-four minutes.

This day was truly endless. I thought it would never end, and that I would wait for Ana de Tuermas until the end of time. And a thousand thoughts a thousand times regurgitated plucked at me: had she decided not to leave her high-walled enclosure for the next three days? Was she living with someone who for some unknown reason remained inside? Or who would soon arrive? Were friends coming to take her out for the evening? For a week? Forever? Was she packing?

No. As soon as she reappeared, at the end of the hour and thirty-four minutes, clad in a black T-shirt and green pants and carrying a small black bag slung from her shoulder, everything was fine.

She locked the front door.

She was out of sight for two minutes.

She was on the road.

I let the Lancia roll a half-mile in neutral. I parked in a little back street near the church. I walked back to the church and waited.

I heard the clicking of her heels draw near.

Draw away.

She was walking down the vertical street. At the bottom she turned left. I sprinted forward. For going down a street like this it was advisable to have a rope ladder rather than legs. I barely avoided exploding to popular acclaim into the public square in the guise of a human avalanche, an arm, an ear, and an eye bringing up the rear, another roar from the crowd. I spotted her at once on the terrace of a restaurant not far from the Hotel Cadaqués. She was going to have dinner.

I got back to the Lancia wheezing for breath, went around the top of the village, came back by the shore road and stopped in front of the Hotel Cadaqués. Did Ana de Tuermas notice me? I did not concern myself with the question.

I went up to my room. I put away the binoculars. Through the window I saw her consult the menu. I cooled down under the shower for three minutes and went and sat at a table opposite hers, my jacket under my arm, the blue silk tie round my neck.

Inside the restaurant a jukebox played the fashionable songs of the singer with the Spanish accent, in fact he sang them in

Spanish, a night of carnival, magic hurricane, wreck of the good ship Love.

I ordered the first thing that came into my head. Salad, chicken, fries. With the sandwiches still in residence in my stomach and nerves clutching my throat as delicately as a crab a jellyfish, I could get nothing down. But I was able to calm myself by drinking beer, triggering a few eructations carefully stifled and masked — for fear that if I allowed them too generous expression they would have made every diner in the place leap out of his chair — but liberating.

I would be hungry later. Later we would see. As I pretended to eat I looked at Ana de Tuermas as was natural, no more, no less. I mean the way any well-bred man may look at so beautiful and desirable a woman, taking care not to reveal more plainly than is proper that were it not for that breeding of his it would take the entire restaurant staff to stop him ripping the woman's clothing off and performing the carnal act with her on the sidewalk amid scattered, overturned, broken tables, some reduced to mere heaps of splinters.

I did not know if I desired her or not.

She, on the other hand, found me to her taste, I would have bet my life on it, she liked me, but how could she not, ha, ha! since the night of my death my powers of seduction had snapped their fingers at limits, everything in the world succumbed to them, subject to my seductive powers, beings and things at my approach forgot their subjection to natural laws, human beings doffed their souls the way you doff a cloak, animals thought they were in the circus and, without any particular training, strove ferociously against their own instincts, the mineral and vegetable worlds emitted audible sighs!

When dessert came, Ana de Tuermas . . .

Magpies lapsed into stubborn silence while carp had to be shot to make them be quiet. Camels called out for drink all along the trail and ravening lions let slender young gazelle toy with their muzzles. Live parrots lost the power of speech but once stuffed regained it.

Walls tumbled.

The railings around residential properties braided themselves of their own accord into clusters of three bars apiece to
offer me free passage between the braids, and the sea laid untold
reaches of its heaving bosom asunder to afford me ready paths of
coolness!

When dessert came Ana de Tuermas waved a mosquito away
from her face with the word, in English, "Bugs!" then smiled at
me. Fate decreed that the banished mosquito then immediately
sought new pastures upon my own face, I waved it away with the
identical gesture and answered Ana's smile.

"Bugs?" I asked.

"Insects. I don't like insects," she said with a faint Spanish
accent.

"Do you get a lot of mosquitoes here?"

"No. No, not a lot."

"They're hell in Paris. Would you object to coming over and
having coffee with me?"

My simple, direct approach, so simple and direct it mini-
mized any ulterior motives we might have had and leached them
of vulgarity much more effectively than a more roundabout
approach could have done, and perhaps even suggested that,
being persons of quality, we might let these motives remain
ulterior, and perhaps not, but perhaps we would, for the moment
the quality of our contact took no note of their existence, this
kind of approach bore its fruits.

"With pleasure," she said.

Simple and direct, she came to sit opposite me. What hair! I
ordered two cups of coffee. Ana de Tuermas was a little under
forty. Thirty-eight, I would have said. She looked it, and at the
same time she seemed young and fresh. She was suntanned. Her
skin was not a redhead's skin. Just a few freckles heightened by
the sun, freckles whose number and arrangement on the bridge
of her nose and her cheeks I knew by heart, freckles embellish-
ing the beauty of her beautiful woman's face.

For a second I forgot the nature of the mission that burdened
the shoulders of my soul and saw in her only the woman of
Rainer von Gottardt's life.

"Are you on vacation?"

Her reply almost bowled me over with astonishment. The ball stopped half an inch from my pins.

How naive I was! Oh, my seductive powers alone would have done the job, but . . .

"Yes and no," she said. (After a pause for silent, friendly scrutiny:) "I find you very handsome and very nice. And very naive . . . I'll be as frank as you: I'm a semi-pro. Forgive the squalid word. Let's say one-fifth pro," she added humorously. "I choose who I like and when I like. That's my profession and that's my way of practicing it." (She smiled:) "Which explains why I'm poor so often! So. I hope you have no regrets . . ."

"Regrets. Over what?"

"I don't know. The coffee, for instance."

A wide, mischievous, beautiful, warm smile, which I returned as best I could. So Ana de Tuermas had become a semi-professional. Or had always been one more or less? Well, that did not inconvenience me one iota. Was most convenient, in fact? I would soon be alone with her and would quietly try to find out. Quietly, or forcefully? I suddenly asked myself. Lichem's weapon between her large light-green eyes, I'm waiting, you'd better start talking or things are going to get hot.

That thought while returning as best I could her beautiful woman's beautiful smile.

"No. I wouldn't quite say on the contrary, but . . . I feel relaxed enough now to tell you I find you wonderful. And so miraculously beautiful. That I was dying to speak to you. And that I'm glad I did. Are you Spanish?"

"Thank you. No, Bolivian."

"You speak perfect French."

"Yes . . . I lived in France quite a long time. Near Cannes. And for a very long time in North America. I have traveled a lot."

"What's your name?"

"Isabel."

Isabel? Isabel. Nothing to be surprised at. Ana de Tuermas did not reveal her real name to everyone she met. To a casual customer . . .

"It's one of my favorite names." (She smiled again.) "No, I swear — "

"And you?"

"Renaud. Renaud Lossaire. I live in Paris. I'm on vacation. I've been driving all day, I've just checked into the Hotel Cadaqués, next door. I had a reservation."

"And what do you do?" she said with a smile.

"I'm in real estate. All year round I'm bored. Are you staying at a hotel as well?"

"No. I live in a house a little way from the village. I arrived two and a half months ago. I'm having a rest. At first I wanted to buy a car. I didn't. I sometimes rent one. Otherwise I walk. It's very pleasant."

"Are you staying with friends?"

"No." (She was silent, then added reflectively:) "The house used to belong to my sister."

"Your sister?"

Arrived here two and a half months ago? Her sister? Used to belong? A house which used to belong to her sister and where she had been staying only two and a half months? Everything was getting confused. How could I find out the name of this sister? Ask her? No. Tell her I had to go to the john or to slip back into the hotel for a moment and try to gain confirmation of what I was beginning to guess, say that I was looking for a woman named Ana de Tuermas, that . . .

But I was spared any further step.

"Ana . . . She died. A year ago. I'm glad I spoke to you too."

My mad hunch faded away, losing every last ounce of flesh. And it brought me real relief. I felt at peace with Rainer von Gottardt. I had gone on alone, but I had not gone far. So much the better. Isabel was named Isabel, sister of Ana. A wonderfully beautiful and desirable person, to whom I regretted lying, to whom I would willingly have transmitted Rainer's message with as much passion as if I had been Rainer and she Ana, I always loved you . . .

Later, perhaps. For I had resolved to spend the night with her. Going back to Lyon tonight was beyond my strength. Saying good-bye to Isabel and sleeping alone at the Hotel Cadaqués was sad and lacking in style.

And, let's be frank, I suddenly desired her.

"I am really sorry. I don't know what else to say, but believe me, I'm really sorry." (I really was.) "An accident?"

"No. She killed herself. In the house here. Exactly one year ago yesterday."

"Would you like to go and have a drink somewhere else, somewhere in Cadaqués?"

"No, I don't feel like it."

"Nor do I. Please let me pay for your dinner. If you like, and only if you like, we can go to your place. I would like to."

She smiled, laid her hand on mine which I turned upward at the soft touch of hers, a complete turn, our two hands were palm to palm, I squeezed her hand.

"So would I."

"I have to leave you for a second, a phone call. I have to call Paris. I'll be right back."

A real relief. And a sudden desire to speak to Michèle, whom I loved, to tell her I couldn't wait to see her again tomorrow.

I rose.

I had already dialed the first few digits when I changed my mind. I was afraid of hearing her voice. Afraid of the certain anguish and the probable hatred that would latch themselves to the airwaves and be immediate in my ears despite the hundreds of intervening miles.

I would make up a little lie.

Let us admit too that I was afraid to compromise the carefree nature, however relative and temporary, of the hours ahead. The joy of imminent reunion with Michèle whom I loved remained intact, my sudden desire to speak to her suddenly passed.

I hung up.

On the mailbox nailed to the front gate was inscribed the name Ana de Tuermas.

I stopped the Lancia near Villa Madre de Osdi after crunching over the gravel of an avenue lined with pines and bougainvilleas.

"I was bowled over when she left me this house. In a drawer I found a photo of the two of us when we were teenagers. We looked alike. We were practically the same age. She led a very independent life. We had scarcely seen one another since that picture was taken. She hadn't forgotten me . . ."

I kissed her on the cheek. The evening was peaceful and cool. I saw the pool. My exhausting day of lying in wait seemed remote. Now I was going to enjoy the places I had been spying on, the person spied upon, Isabel de Tuermas, almost-twin sister of Ana de Tuermas, who was holding my hand as if it were a child's and leading me from room to room, white walls, bright curtains, dark furniture, ending in the large bedroom on the second floor where I looked out on the sea lying prisoner of the mountains, very visible despite the gathering dusk beyond the village, the tall church, and the white houses.

She showed me the photo. The two redheaded girls were the image of beauty itself, fissiparously reproduced. They had begun studying music as children, Isabel the violin, Ana the piano. They had even played together, a little, very little, Isabel recalled. Later on Isabel had embarked on medical studies that had been broken off after two years. Their parents had been wealthy, then ruined. The father was dead.

"Do you live here alone?"

"Yes. Without a mate, if that's what you mean."

"You're not afraid?"

"No."

She undressed on the left of the bed, dropping her soft and clean black and green garments at her feet, in a heap on the parquet floor, which surprised me. Surely I had no right to suspect her of being moved, ill at ease, troubled? But perhaps I had. I did the same, jacket, jeans, tie, shirt, in a heap at my feet, on the right of the bed, being careful not to let Lichem's weapon thud against the floor. I was indeed moved, ill at ease, troubled for, another confession, I had never in my life known a professional, semi, one-third, or one-fifth. Nor, to heap confession on confession, a woman older than myself, even by two days, and so fully a woman as the wonderful Isabel de Tuermas.

And in this Villa Madre de Osdi, in the bed where doubtless Rainer von Gottardt had loved Ana, I lay down, naked, beside Isabel naked and fully illuminated, she had left four lights on, what white lie should I hand her to explain the small scar at my mid-section? The spirit of invention failed me. Had I scrambled across barbed wire pursued by three fighting bulls? Had I scratched too hard after being bitten or stung by a wasp or mosquito, by an insect, by a bug (every now and then an American word came naturally to her lips)? Had I fallen on a knife carelessly stuck handle first in the ground? Had I just had a fatty tumor surgically removed? Had I swallowed a rabbit bone which had emerged in that spot as I bent down to pick up a coin? Had I had it since birth, was I born that way, with that little slit not far from my member, had I almost been a woman?

But she made no comment, contenting herself with caressing and kissing that member and putting it through what was at minimum an infinite number of loving attentions without omitting a single one, and in the appropriate order and disorder, from a brushing with the tip of her tongue hardly more perceptible than the draft winnowed in from the next room despite the closed door by the flight of an insect or bug, but which nevertheless caused the whole of one's being to arch and shudder in febrile and panicky ambuscade as if a mortal enemy, frrrrrrrt! were perhaps scrambling down the chimney, all the way to a violent caress kindling a fire, a rage, a madness so all-consuming that the general of an entire army laying siege to the house would realize the wisdom of retreating with silent tread, carefully, avoiding clicks and creaks, and would issue instructions to this effect in a voice so low that his men would damage their eyesight attempting to read the words on his lips.

I was sporting in the bed of Aphrodite herself.

The infinite time having elapsed, she drew me onto her and I understood that she wanted me to flood her without delay, I understood and I complied with this desire without there being any need to express it through endless chatter, argument, or pleas, for in the fire, the rage, and the madness that then took hold of me, the muscular waves generated in my body by the mere blinking of her beautiful green eyes would have been enough to trigger the liquid outbursts, torrential in their capricious savagery but fluvial in the enormous volume of their flow, of a flood that was itself interminable.

Thus she willed it and thus I complied, and thus her own satiation, born amid the numberless amorous attentions (which were therefore its womb) she had inflicted on me and although she had at that time to my great surprise not wanted me to reciprocate them, thus her own satiation grew beneath the torrential and fluvial assault of the flood, and I again complied when I understood that she wanted me to remain within her to bring this satiation to fruition, and not only did I comply but I complied as if complying with a higher and more demanding order from her because my desire, intact and deathless, she had fortified it so well, awoke in her an infinite number of satiations brought to fruition, and even, made more fiery and raging and mad than it had by the amorous attentions previously lavished on it by hand and mouth but now lavished by the burning, convulsive and tortured body of Aphrodite herself, ecstatically stirred by her primordial ritual, it released a fresh flood worthy of the first ages of the world at the instant of her last satiation, brought for that reason to a fruition infinitely distant and unknown to her!

And finally I complied when she desired me to emerge from her.

I covered us with the sheet. She stroked my sweat-soaked hair, I kissed the discreet freckles on her nose and cheeks, and we went to sleep with all (four) lights on.

In the middle of the night I awoke. I was hungry, thirsty, hot, and I wanted to pee. I patted the bed next to me for Isabel's body. No one. She was no longer at my side.

I was instantly afraid.

A simple cloud had momentarily veiled, without completely blocking its inexorable rays, but nonetheless had veiled the sun of the nightmare, and this cloud still pursued its course across the heavens, leaving me exposed, trembling, afraid, watchful. What was I afraid of?

I half sat up.

The bedroom door had been pulled shut.

I bent down, removed Lichem's weapon from the pocket of my black leather jacket, pushed back the safety catch. Three rounds. There were three rounds left. I held the weapon under the sheet, against my leg. Why? I did not . . .

I heard stealthy steps.

Then suddenly no more stealth, a footstep hitting the floor hard and the door thrown violently open, a man came in with a gun trained on me.

About my size, quite good-looking, long hair. In shirt-sleeves. A large dressing on his neck . . .

Lichem!

No, I had never really left Lyon! Isabel — Ana! — stood in the doorway looking at me with embarrassment and perhaps pity. She had put on a white dress. Lichem, Ana! My mad hunch was reborn from its own ashes at full gallop. Isabel was Ana. Ana had lied to me. That story about suicide and an inheritance and perhaps about a sister as well, despite the photo, was pure fiction. A look-alike friend. Lies. Rainer von Gottardt had not lied to me. But he could not have known.

Only I could know! My mad hunch was right!

I played the rudely awakened sleeper.

Lichem's surprise was greater than mine. Then his eye blazed with animal ferocity.

"You!" he said in a low voice. "Again! I thought it might be you but I didn't really believe it. You followed me here! What do you want? Why did you say you were me? And all the rest? Why? What has that kid got to do with you? And what are you doing in this house?"

All fear vanished. I marveled at the coolness and aplomb with which I maneuvered to avoid a lethal burst of fire from our weapons. Despite my anger, no longer directed at myself but at the world . . . What was I doing in this house?

"My job," I said. "Getting information. I'm conducting an inquiry. We had the pleasure of meeting in my private residence, but my place of business is in Place des Terreaux. I work there under another name. I'm a private detective. That's why I said I was you: a professional tic, it goes with the job. I realized at once something fishy was up, and I was right. Tough luck, huh? Not that I was any luckier than you. There are others in this game, as you know. Complicated business. But what about you? Who hired you to kidnap the kid? You know what I mean: who is behind it all?"

I had spoken slowly and calmly. I had rattled him. Ana was drinking in my words. But Lichem's arm did not move, did not shake, and what he said next was not calculated to foster the hope that there would be no lethal burst of fire.

"I would gladly tell you. I don't think you'll ever have the chance to tell anyone. But I don't know, myself. And I don't give a damn."

I thought of my visit to Rue Duguesclin. One link in the chain. It was probably true that he didn't know.

"You would be unwise to kill me," I said. "They know where I am. Your position is bad enough already. Instead, why don't you tell me who your first contact was?" (I jerked my chin in Ana's direction:) "Ana de Tuermas?"

"Ana? Why do you call her Ana?" (To Ana:) "Why?"

So the fake suicide victim had also lied to the not unattractive animal whose virility I had so sorely assailed one day that it must have retreated in utmost pain into the recesses of his crotch, and who had in return nearly reduced my own to nothing on Rue du Soleil in Old Lyon.

"My sister's name was Ana," she told him in a firm voice. "He must take me for her and think I gave him a false name to be safe."

She was miraculously beautiful in her short, white, flimsy summer dress. And she kept her calm despite the confusing circumstances.

"That's right," I said. "That's exactly what I think. And another thing: don't forget to tell me how much I owe you."

"You understand I have no alternative," Lichem said to me. "Up! Out!"

"I am not leaving this bed," I said.

He understood that I would not leave the bed.

"Isabel my darling, I'm sorry . . . He's dangerous. He's nearly killed me once already. Leave us for a moment, please."

"No, Léonard!" she said, almost imperiously.

His name was Léonard.

"I have no choice. Leave!"

"No!"

Maybe she would have leaped forward. But Léonard Lichem was a resolute man, he was already tightening his aim on me, quickly, unhesitatingly, he was about to fire. Our third meeting would be our last, the road we traveled was too narrow, and on this third and last path too narrow for us to pass one another, one of us would go on alone!

At that point I was half sitting up in the bed, my back to the wall, my torso offered up naked, my hand hidden beneath the sheet and clenched on the weapon, his weapon, Léonard Lichem's Lyon revolver. Could a sheet deflect the trajectory of a bullet? No. No point in pulling the gun out. Besides, I no longer had time.

I didn't really aim.

A twelfth of a second before the instant he was going to fire, I fired, twice. Given my position, and the convulsive nature of the movement that then gripped my body, the first shot hit him in the groin.

The second smack in the head. In the skull. The noise, very loud, outlived my double pressure on the trigger, the leap of the bullets, their penetration of the adversary flesh.

Ana screamed. She stopped screaming.

Brutal silence.

Léonard Lichem lay at the foot of the bed, dead in my opinion after a last sickening convulsion that laid him on his back. The waxed floor darkened red around his head. Ana was paralyzed. I paid her no attention. I had leaped from the bed and was feeling the animal Léonard's pulse and his chest in the region of his heart. I knew thanks to old Simon de Klef that revolver bullets can travel about inside your head as thick and busy as bees swarming in a hive without breaking the heart's stubborn will to beat.

"Dead," I said.

I pulled the sheet off the bed and spread it over the body. Then I dressed, shirt, pants, dancing on one foot, then the other. Into the jacket pocket I put my revolver, Léonard Lichem's Lyon revolver!

"An eye!" Ana murmured in English, coming out of her state of shock.

"What?"

"A private detective!"

"Yes. A small-town detective. You've done a good day's work, Ana de Tuermas."

"Why Ana?" she said softly. "You're crazy. I am Isabel de Tuermas. My sister died a year ago, she's buried in Cadaqués. I have her papers, I can prove it to you, ten people here could tell you the same!"

She waited, as if I might have something to say. Nothing to say, or very little. My ability to give expression to any feeling whatsoever was impaired. I had been wrong. I was crazy. Hunch incorrect. I savored my error to the dregs: "What was your connection with this gentleman, who led me to you here in Ana de Tuermas's house?"

"I was . . . his friend. I met him on the plane to Barcelona. He has a little villa, a pied-à-terre, in Rosas. His sources of income were mysterious. Drugs, I think. That's all. I understood nothing of what you two said to each other, I swear. I am not Ana, and I have nothing to do with this business of yours, nothing!"

Crazed suspicions. They canceled out the corpse, the whole situation. And my mad hunch began to dance from side to side in pathetic embarrassment, wearing the sheepish look of a false witness, feet turned inward, fingers twisting and working at the ends of its arms, cracking the joints. But still it refused to run away and hide.

"Why bring him here in the middle of the night?"

"Because . . . poor Léonard! Are you going to call the police?"

"Yes. Self-defense. I hope you will be honest enough to back me up. Why?"

"Please, let's not stay in here . . ."

I followed her downstairs.

"So, why?"

"He was away for a week at the beginning of the month. All he said was that he was on a job that would bring him lots of money. I didn't even know whether it was in Spain or somewhere else. I've seen him twice since his return. He told me it went well and badly. He was wounded in the neck. But he had been paid. I would never have dreamed it was a kidnapping . . . and a child, was that it? Yesterday I wondered about you a little. Not right away. When you made that phone call. And later, when it looked to me as if you had a bullet wound in your hip. But I didn't really worry. But later, during the night, I was scared. I thought you might be here for Léonard. I didn't believe it, but still I started to get scared. Scared for me as well, to be frank. I called him because I wanted to make sure. It took me a long time to make my mind up. I was worried about you, I kept telling myself I was crazy. I would never have believed . . . that I had guessed so right!"

Disaster! Lichem had been hired by who knew whom to kidnap Simon de Klef, the first order had come from who knew whom, and now I would never know. And chance had brought them together, him and Isabel de Tuermas, sister of Ana. All the rest was the fruit of my madness. I flung myself upon my mad hunch, which fled like an arrow, losing all flesh in its flight and lodging in skeletal form if not in the form of powdered bone in the remotest recess of my skull.

"Do you have a beer?" I said.

"Yes."

She brought a beer, and Scotch for herself. She poured for me. She was shaking a little. So was I.

"I'll show you the death certificate," she said. "I received it in Bolivia. I had to have it to take possession of the house here."

"No," I said, "I believe you." (I drank.) "Your friend kidnapped a child in Lyon, in France. His relatives asked me . . . Never mind the details. I caught up with your friend, he escaped me the first time, I followed him . . . He was just a bit player, I'm certain of that. However, Ana de Tuermas was something more. She had a certain reputation . . . But you know that better than I do. I thought perhaps he had got this job through her, and that through her I could go higher. That's all. Botched investigation. Insufficient information: she's dead. I was wrong."

Yes, disaster! Without my mad hunches, I would not have had to kill Lichem. I attempted to mask my confusion. I succeeded. But what to do now? Isabel was looking at me, listening to me, astonished . . . What a miraculously beautiful and desirable and worthwhile woman! Good actress? No. My mind had explored all the possibilities. So much the better. A little of my relief endured.

She was drinking her Scotch in hasty little gulps.

"In any case, you're a good actor," she said. "Until Léonard got here, I basically thought you were for real. Were you going to try to . . . to interrogate me, later, tomorrow morning?"

"No. It's true I thought you were your sister, but I believed you when you told me she was dead. It was only just now . . ."

She was stricken.

"Then it's my fault . . ."

"No. Something like this was bound to happen sooner or later. Don't torment yourself." (I downed the last of my beer. Then:) "I wish . . . I wish you would go on thinking I was for real. I was. As soon as you told me your sister was dead I forgot what had brought me here. And I was happy with you all this past night. At peace. I'm sorry about your friend . . . I'm sorry for what I said . . ." About how much did I owe her. She understood.

I took her hand and kissed it, swiftly.

I let go of her hand. She was brave and nice enough to smile at me, quickly, a quick smile.

Yes, what to do now?

I knew what to do. I stopped trying to look stricken. I ran a hand across my forehead. I buried my face in my joined hands. I heaved a long sigh, a second even longer one, at half the volume. Concern was born in Isabel de Tuermas's beautiful green eyes.

"It bothers me to have killed a man," I said in a fading voice. "It's not really my line . . . And it bothers me to have killed someone dear to you."

"Dear is a bit strong. He was very nice to me. Present and discreet. But you had no choice. And I didn't know he kidnapped children."

"And good-looking and sexy too," I said. "I'm almost jealous." (With a hint of a smile:) "Don't listen to me, I'm crazy, you said so yourself." (Without a hint of a smile:) "I don't want any headaches from the Spanish police. If I report his death. They're godawful for that kind of thing. I'm not from Interpol, you understand. A small-town detective from Lyon. What's more . . . needless to say my investigation has been compromised. The people who hired him will learn of his death . . ."

"You're torturing me!" said Isabel. "If you only knew how sorry I am I called him. Don't be angry with me! Don't think I'm not afraid of headaches too . . . As you can imagine, my life hasn't been exactly . . . respectable. Could I be charged as an accessory?"

"You could, but it wouldn't stick. If the charge is false and if I help you. I'll help you, don't worry." (The moment had come:) "There is one other solution . . . If I were alone it's what I'd do."

"What's that?"

She said what's that, but she must have understood.

She even welcomed this other solution with a certain alacrity. But I did not question her on the absence of respectability of her past life, I rushed into the breach I had just opened: "Get rid of him." (Once the solution is formulated, treat it as accepted and instantly voice doubts and queries about its execution. I therefore

went right on:) "Does that seem possible to you? Did he know a
lot of people here?"

"No one. No one who will worry anyway. No long-term
contacts. Me. A bit. I have the feeling it was the same in Paris. He
was a loner. He . . ."

"He lived in Paris?"

"Yes."

"Do you know if he was thinking of going back?"

"No. We were supposed to spend a few days in
Morocco . . ."

Said as if it were an embarrassing confession, or almost.
Adorable Isabel!

"That's convenient. In fact, it doesn't matter much. The
main thing is . . . You must know the coastline here pretty well
and . . ."

"I know a place," she said decisively.

Silence. I pretended to hesitate.

"Don't do anything as a favor to me. It wouldn't exactly be a
disaster if I did call the police."

"No. Well, do as you like. But I've had enough of this kind of
thing. This is the last straw. And the worst . . ."

"You realize that I have to have your absolute discretion? Can
I trust you absolutely?"

"Yes."

I believed her.

"You realize too that I'm going to need you? As little as
possible, I hope, but . . . it's not going to be fun. Are you up to
it?"

"Yes."

She finished her Scotch. I stood up.

"Let's give it a try," I said.

The next hour could scarcely have been called fun. I had to
roll, wrap, and truss the corpse—this I took upon myself—in a
big blanket—the floor under the head was clean, the blood
around it had created a halo—the corpse whose bloody skull was
adorned with a sort of little central horn, whitish and swollen—
where brain, a little brain, had shot out frothing!—the body on

which every fold of skin or fabric at the midsection was like a ewer abrim with blood that overflowed, dripped, ran at the slightest movement! And on my own too I lugged the abominable and gigantic banana downstairs, and then out of the house.

And I took it upon myself to swab the blood from the bedroom floor: this I believe was the worst, there was so much of it (the whole sheet had turned bright red), the stains were so stubborn, and the cleaning equipment provided by Isabel so insufficient and inadequate, a sponge that was too small and absorbed little, tile-cleaning liquid, it was discouraging, I scrubbed and scrubbed like a condemned soul.

I might have been cleaning the Augean stables with a crumpled-up sheet of paper, a real labor of Hercules, but a Hercules most woefully mistreated!

Finally, abundant use of wax brought an acceptable result.

I wrapped the red sheet in two other clean sheets.

I washed my hands. I made sure I wasn't covered with blood. I studied myself in the mirror. I was transparent. Nausea had made of my bowels one enormous and painful mariner's knot. I fought back the impulse to throw up. But I peed at great length.

I went downstairs.

"You OK?" I said to Isabel.

"I'm OK. What about you?"

"OK."

I was in need of an oxygen mask, of cardiac massage, of drip-fed amphetamines, but I told her I was OK, and it was OK!

Lichem had parked his car, an almost new BMW 745 IA Executive, just before the sixth bend. We went there on foot, holding hands, hidden in the dark solitary night.

The sky was cloudy.

We brought the BMW to the front of the house.

"Go inside for a second," I said to Isabel.

The blanket was clean. Luckily, Lichem had not bled since being packaged. I worked the corpse onto the rear seat.

I also threw the package of three sheets into the rear seat.

We set out. Isabel went ahead of me in the Lancia.

Five miles outside Cadaqués, Isabel turned left onto a paved trail almost too narrow for two cars abreast. I was often apprehensive that some sharp-toothed rock would carve an unneeded base-relief in the Lancia's body, but no. The trail crossed other trails. I followed Isabel. At the end of a winding and bumpy trip of a mile or so, we came out onto a plateau high above the sea.

We got out of the cars.

A sheer drop and no rocks below, said Isabel. An excellent swimmer and diver, she had found this spot herself. It seemed to have been conceived for the secret jettisoning of coffins.

I locked the BMW.

The Lancia's front bumper bumped gently into the rear bumper of Lichem's coffin, and stuck. I accelerated. I accelerated faster and faster, in first gear, foot on the floorboard soon, for ten yards, fifteen yards.

Almost hitting twenty-five!

I braked.

Five yards to go. The BMW went on alone, flew for a moment above the waters, dipped its nose, and vanished after a short graceful fall . . .

There was an enormous kersplatt! followed by a monstrous gloogloogloogloogloof!

Isabel ran up. I took her hand, we went together to the edge. The BMW was settling. Only its roof was visible. Then nothing, calm sea, silence.

"It's very deep here," she said.

Reluctantly, for as long as it took to climb back into the Lancia, we released each other's hands. We were joined in matchless complicity.

"What are you going to do now?"

"Get back to Lyon as quick as I can."

"When?"

"As soon as . . . as soon as you want me to. And you?"

"Go back to Bolivia. That's what I'd been meaning to do all along. In a few days . . . I'll live with my mother. How long does it take to get to Lyon?"

"Four hours. Why?"

She thought.

"Would you like to take me with you? I can get a plane there. I couldn't spend a single hour alone in the house. I don't want to be alone until the second I climb into the plane. Would you mind?"

"No."

"It won't bother you?"

"No. Just the opposite. I don't want to be alone either."

"Thanks. When shall we leave?"

"This minute?"

"OK, this minute!"

We drove through Cadaqués. I reached the church, immense. I took the Madrid Highway.

Isabel hastily filled three suitcases and locked all the shutters, windows, and doors in Villa Madre de Osdi.

•

The woman with the painted eyes really was sleeping. I climbed the stairs silently, collected my two or three things (four things with the field glasses), came back down noiselessly. The woman raised her painted lids, uncovering her real eyes. I went up to her.

"I'm leaving," I said. "I can't sleep anymore and I have a long journey ahead of me. I'm going to Morocco. How much do I owe you?"

I paid her. She gave me a smile more inane than the last, I gave her one more foolish than the last.

I left the hotel. It was four in the morning.

I started the Lancia and drove out of Cadaqués, the most beautiful place in the world according to Rainer von Gottardt, with Isabel de Tuermas beside me, her hand in mine.

TWELVE

The night's events had reawakened in my mouth and in my soul the repellent taste of the preserved vermin I had reflectively sucked one day (so recent yet already remote) at 66 Rue de la République in Lyon, a taste I managed to banish by draining the last drop of Patrice Pierre's mixture and running my tongue greedily around inside the neck of the bottle.

The old customs man was not at the frontier post, having died no doubt of old age since I last came through, with his colleagues making ready for the funeral, passing the hat around, mulling over inscriptions for the wreaths, in short, nobody at the frontier post. I slowed down, swiveled my head in every direction in search of a living soul: no soul living, I did not stop, I pushed on.

With the frontier behind me I began to forget Lichem, the cunning devil Léonard. Isabel de Tuermas no. She remained in the shadow of the nightmare. At least it was to the nightmare that I attributed her silence, her reserved manner, her apparent distance during the early part of the drive. The complicity that had united us on the cliff was no more. I was sorry.

Each of us was lost in his own errant thoughts.

•

Not only did the still and silent Lancia gobble up the highway that leaped with relentless swiftness into its jaws, but I also had the impression the path of return was taking me ever farther from Lyon.

From Michèle de Klef

Between Montpellier and Nîmes I filled the tank.

Not long after our gas stop Isabel sighed, and, as if this sigh had dispelled the most troubling of her worries, she laid her head in the hollow of my shoulder.

She slept.

She slept between 6:00 and 7:30. Sometimes she frowned a little and whimpered, whining like a child trapped in bad dreams, whereupon I stroked her hair, her shoulder, drawing her closer to me without squeezing her too tightly so that she should not awaken this woman looking so new, so fresh, and so worthwhile despite a past life (longer, just barely longer than my own life) not completely respectable, a miraculous woman and miraculously beautiful and in great distress who was going home to live with her mother in the land of her ancestors, and who did not want to be alone until the moment she climbed into the plane for the homeward journey.

She did not even really awaken when we passed through the toll, but at 7:30, as we approached the dangerous Mulatière bend at the end of the highway and I slowed from 130 to 70, she whimpered and opened her eyes. She moved away from me without a word to check her hair and the state of her features in a small mirror.

"Home. You look wonderful, you look as if you've slept ten hours in the bed of a princess."

"Thanks. And thanks for the pillow."

At 7:40 I parked on Rue Stella. The heat in Lyon had not dropped one-twelfth of a degree. We expired of heat as soon as I stopped the engine. The old fool from the reception desk at the Hôtel des Étrangers was taking in a few lungfuls of less torrid air on his doorstep. This time he recognized me and greeted me with a big loud good morning, a big smile, a big wave of the hand. Damned yokel. Had we once called in the cattle together? No. I responded with the merest of nods. Maybe the Lancia and particularly Isabel (when you saw her red hair and her divine silhouette you lost interest in other things and succumbed to unhealthy speculation) had dazzled the poor imbecile. His sudden obsequiousness really got under my skin, I almost whirled and dispensed a couple of kicks. He came within an inch of hastening over to carry our three heavy suitcases, one in each hand and the third between his teeth, one look from me and he would have scurried over with the hideous swiftness displayed by certain spiders.

I took the two heaviest ones.

"It's hot in your city," said Isabel.

"The hottest place on earth," I said.

We walked slowly on.

Place de la République and its fountain.

"There it is," I said. "The door with the goat in front. Some lunatic drew a goat under my window."

"It's not badly drawn," she said.

She was right.

Upstairs in my place I went straight to the refrigerator. Discarding all previously exploited techniques for opening the door, I bent my legs, seized the apparatus around the middle in a bear hug and let it drop with a crash from as high as I could, almost transforming it into a one-way dumbwaiter shooting down through floor after floor until it reached the cellar where I would henceforth descend to eat in the company of the rats.

"It's nothing," I said to Isabel who came running in terror. "The door is often quite hard to open."

It had opened.

Sitting around the table in the front room, we treated ourselves to a breakfast whose individual components were all commonplace but taken together were most satisfying.

"Why Bach?" she asked in English.

"Why Bach? A souvenir of the days when I played the piano. I liked Bach. I still like him."

"You played the piano?"

"Yes, when I was young. Later I was a reporter. Then I took up this crass trade that brought us together, I'm thrilled with my decision."

She smiled, without joy.

After breakfast, I put away my two or three things. Four counting the field glasses. Into the bottom drawer went the field glasses and Léonard Lichem's Lyon weapon, a weapon with one bullet left. For Michèle? No, ha, ha!

I called Satolas information. A plane was leaving Paris for La Paz next day, Sunday the eighteenth, at 9:00 P.M. Twenty-six hours' flying time to Lima, long stopover, three hours from Lima to La Paz. From there Isabel would go to Sucre where her mother lived. She was listening in on the call, she nodded to me, I asked for the reservations desk and handed her the phone. She made her reservation.

"I can go to a hotel until tomorrow, if you like. I feel better than I did last night, I wouldn't want to disturb you . . ."

"You prefer a hotel to my humble dwelling?"

She smiled (without joy), hesitated: "No."

Her offer and her hesitation both surprised me.

"Then stay. I would rather you stayed."

"All right," she said.

Once again, I sensed she was far away. In the shadow of the nightmare.

My God, all that blood!

I forgot, she didn't. She certainly didn't seem better than last night. She was courageous and dignified. I kissed her on the cheek.

"Very well," she said. "You are very kind."

While she was bathing I phoned the Dioblanízes at Rillieux-la-Pape. The phone was picked up by a man who had an atrocious accent, but who wasn't Hector. I introduced myself and asked for Isabel.

"Miguel Soler! My poor dear Miguel Soler! What a cruel blow! I have tried to call you so many times . . ."

"Forgive me," I said. "An unexpected commitment. Quite impossible to call you myself although I very much wanted to. A whirlwind trip, my mother ill . . . But all goes well. False alarm."

"I'm so glad, so glad! So many sad tidings! Let me tell you what happened. That is why you are calling, yes?"

"Yes," I said.

"Well, our mutual friend's body was taken to Wiesbaden. The dear great man was very sick, he knew that at any moment . . . He had made all the arrangements . . . We found all the instructions on him, in one of his pockets, as you said we would. I got in touch with his nephews that very night. I took care of everything, I advanced the money, anyway by yesterday his mortal remains were . . ."

"What devotion! You have been wonderful," I said fervently.

"I loved him so much! You too . . . You had known him since . . . Had he told you anything of . . . of his strange destiny?"

I had piqued her curiosity. Was she jealous of her great men? Probably. I was lying. I continued to lie. I would have felt I was betraying Rainer von Gottardt. Later. Once the book was finished. Sent off. Even published. And I was of a rebellious temperament.

"No, not at all," I said. "He was simply anxious to meet me before he died. He also wanted to see you again, to attend your concert. I offered to drive him. He accepted. A great honor for me. All the same, I had no idea . . . It's terrible."

"Terrible!"

Her emotion touched me. A rebellious and reclusive temperament. Suddenly I felt guilty. "And while I'm on the phone I'd also like to apologize," I said to her, "for my attitude . . . for what must have looked like bad manners . . . All those years of reclusiveness . . . but also, believe me, of suffering. All those invitations left unanswered . . . What you must think of me . . ."

"Please, my dear Miguel Soler! Not another word! Life, sometimes . . . But we're going to make up for all that, aren't we? We'll be seeing you this year, you and your charming friend? A Granados recording? I adore Granados!"

"Yes, we'll be seeing each other. Absolutely! Is your son better? You mentioned that the heat had made him ill . . ."

"Oh! Jésus! Yes, he's much better, thank you. It's wonderful that you should remember, that you should think of . . . What terrible heat this summer! We're leaving in September. We must have a change of scenery. And as soon as we get back . . ."

"Yes," I said. "Again, thank you."

"What for? Goodness gracious!"

"For taking care of Rainer von Gottardt as you did. For your patience and your understanding . . ."

We hung up on excellent terms. It was easy to grow attached to this pretty, talkative, idealistic little woman. You forgot the rumors. You assumed she had at last heroically overcome the misfortune of her blind son. The weight of the past.

You kicked yourself for your mad hunches.

Isabel de Tuermas came out of the bathroom. She had heard me phoning.

"Do whatever you have to do," she said to me. "Don't do anything different for my sake. Work, if you have to . . . work."

"OK," I said.

It looked as if the morning was going to be a pain. And the rest of the day, and tomorrow. Because Isabel felt ill at ease with me, there was no denying it. Or with herself, or both. As for me, I had lied to her so much I no longer knew what to tell her. Certainly not the truth. What good would it do? She was leaving, vanishing, disappearing thousands of miles from Lyon.

She was wearing very tight white jeans and a ballooning shirt whose sleeves she had rolled up above the elbows.

Perfect arms, smooth tanned elbows.

What could we do or talk about? Wander around Lyon like tourists? Ha, ha! In this heat, with everything we had on our minds? Talk about having fun we could hire a band and parade around town at the head of it on our knees, wrapped in furs and flagellating ourselves. Visit the sewers. Plunge our laughing heads into their tainted waters and amuse ourselves by catching rats with our teeth, no hands.

Draw a bead on the goat and leap from the fifth floor.

We had nothing to say to one another. Or else the words stopped in midflight. I made an effort and asked her, "What's wrong? The shock of last night? Guilt? Fear of what might happen to us now?"

"All of it. No, not guilt. Léonard was and would have remained a stranger to me. Not like you," she said unexpectedly, without a smile, her tone unchanging. "Fear, yes, a little . . ."

"I already told you you have nothing to fear," I told her gently, brushing my hand along her perfect shoulder, her arm, her elbow smooth as a very young woman's. "Even supposing you are ever approached about it, you know nothing, you have nothing to reproach yourself with, you knew him, you'll be hearing the news, that's all. And in the worst possible scenario I'll be there to answer, you have nothing, nothing, to be afraid of!"

"I'm sorry. Fear as well of going back to Bolivia. And perhaps I need a little sleep."

"You want to sleep?"

"No. No, I couldn't now. After lunch."

"Are siestas your secret of eternal youth?"

The phone rang in my absent neighbor's, and at almost the same moment in my place. I picked up the receiver. The ringing next door also stopped. Their caller was beginning to get the picture. Or else had contracted an ear irritation, perhaps even an infection, from pressing the phone too hard against it.

Michèle?

No. Surprise, it was Anne, the intelligent and beautiful hitchhiker from the number 12 bus terminal, so essential and delicious one day to my flesh, Anne who had pulled the sheet over my back to dry my sweat, and who had wanted not to leave Lyon!

"Where are you calling from?"

"Close by. I'm at the Hôtel-Dieu. I had a health problem. Nothing to worry about, but they had to operate in a hurry. They flew me back from Spain under medical supervision. I waited until I was feeling a bit better before I called."

"Can I come and see you?"

"Yes. That's why I was calling . . ."

Frank, simple, adorable Anne!

"When?"

"Whenever you like."

"I'll be right over," I said.

Gynecology ward. She told me how to get there.

"I have this friend," I said to Isabel.

"Yes. I realized. Go on. Don't worry about me. I'm going to read a bit, take it easy, try to relax."

She came over and kissed me. She was glad to be at my place, with me. And glad I was going.

•

Soon every denizen of the little world at the Hôtel-Dieu would recognize me from afar, people seeing me would leap forward to greet me, why it's Mr. Soler, how are you Mr. Soler, what brings you here this time, Mr. Soler? Arsenic, a whole bag of it? Inhaled the contents of a warehouseful of propane bottles? Let's see now, an eye gouged out? No? Another bullet in the midriff then? A blast from a flamethrower, a knife in the ribs? Ah! I have it: you have just shot the hospital director and thrown his body into the Rhône. No? A friend of yours? Operated on for an enormous cyst in the right ovary, the only one she has left, which same enormous cyst exploded, to use the rough-and-ready expression of the resident gynecologist, causing a seepage of blood into the abdomen that required the positioning of a tube in said abdomen connected to a bottle that filled as the hours went by with a blackish liquid? A friend of yours subject since childhood to this kind of problem, to such an extent that she is condemned despite her tender years to childlessness? Ah, good, good! Well, so we'll look forward to the next time then, Mr. Soler!

I found Anne Miller, condemned despite her tender years to childlessness, pale and thinner. She smiled at me as soon as she saw me, like the ready smiler she was. A tube stuck out from under the sheet.

Her room looked out over the waterfront, the Rhône struck motionless by the heat, Villeurbanne in the distance. It goes without saying that I had gotten lost before finding this room. That against my will I had crossed the damned nephrology department, where the same patients in the same beds rasped out the same complaints as they filled the same flasks with different shades of urine, mint, pomegranate, orangeade, where the same dying clown or his twin brother bleated. That I had wandered like a lame and suffering soul down the dead-end labyrinth of identical intersections and blind corridors before finally realizing that the obstetrics-gynecology department was quite close to the main door on Place de l'Hôpital.

But here I was.

Pale, thinner, endearing. You saw only her dark eyes and the long black hair tumbling down the left side of her face. I kissed her, half cheek half mouth, just as pleased as she was at this reunion.

"Did you get my card?"

"Yes. Thank you."

"I thought about you a lot. How is your month of August so far?"

"Not bad, really. Quiet. I thought about you."

She told me in her serious slow voice about her long-standing troubles. And this business of a cyst. She had started to hurt badly at Jerez de la Frontera. Taken by ambulance to the hospital in Malaga. She had so little faith in the heavy-handed, indecisive doctor she saw there that she requested immediate repatriation. A few hours later they were operating on her here at the Hôtel-Dieu. A straightforward, safe operation, but unfortunately there had been this complication . . . No help either from the intern on call, a jerk, who had frightened her the day before by mentioning a second operation. She had felt depressed. She pictured herself as a prisoner here in this hospital for an unspecified length of time. She had called me . . .

Yet it bothered her for me to see her in this state, with this tube and this bottle by the bed. (I pushed aside her hair, which was brushing against her pretty short nose, and placed there, between nose and cheek, a tender kiss.) She was hoping for better news this very morning from the visit by the head of the clinic, who was not a jerk but who was never there. She thought the flow of blood had stopped, the level in the bottle had not changed since last night. And she no longer had any pain at all. Maybe it was over?

It was over.

I was getting ready to tell her about Patrice Pierre when the head of the clinic, a young bald man, suddenly came in accompanied by the jerk intern and a skeletal nurse. It did not immediately occur to me to leave the room when they entered, and after that, since no one showed any interest in me, I squeezed myself into a corner and waited. Not for long. The clinic head looked at the bottle, pressed down on Anne's stomach, asked some questions, each three words long.

"All over," he said. "We'll remove the tube and give you a prescription. You can leave any time after four o'clock. Don't stay in Lyon. Country air, for at least two weeks."

And bang! the door of the next room was already flying open.

Anne was transformed, her face relaxed, relieved.

"Not surprising, that flow of bad blood couldn't have gone on," I told her. "Pure and innocent as you are."

She laughed. "What would you know about it?"

"Nothing. Are you going to leave town?"

"Yes. With my parents. They have a house on the Bay of Biscay, they stayed behind here until I could get out of the hospital. It won't be much fun, but I need the rest. I've never been so tired in my life. They live in Mornant, twenty miles from Lyon. My father's a veterinarian. I'll call them and tell them to pick me up at my place tonight."

"Why tonight at your place?"

"I want to be on my own in my apartment for a while. I came straight from Malaga to the Hôtel-Dieu. My luggage is here, in that closet . . ."

"I can come over at four and help you go home."

"Do you want to?"

I wanted to. And I wanted to stay shut in with Isabel as little as possible.

"OK," she said. "We'll listen to the violin cassette and you can tell me what you think."

"With pleasure. Do you still have red fingers?"

She smiled, she laughed.

"No. I don't think they ever were red. I have some crazy ideas sometimes."

•

"It looks as if I may have to be busier than I expected this afternoon," I said to Isabel (pleased to see me back—and secretly relieved at what I had just said?). "And this evening I have to return the Lancia to its owner, a friend who lent it to me for the trip. I hope this won't bother you?"

"No. Yes, but don't change anything for me, I already told you. That would bother me even more."

After a rapid, silent lunch, she wanted to sleep. I offered her my bed in the back room, asking her to forgive the modesty of the view through the practically walled-in window, it offered but the palest reflection of the infinite vistas visible from the second floor of Villa Madre de Osdi.

"If you're still asleep when I leave, well, I'll see you later, then. Take it easy, sleep, relax. Forget. You'll forget, you'll see."

"You're an angel," she said.

"No," I said.

I set my quartz alarm to go off at 3:30 and lay down myself on the couch in the front room. I slept like a log despite heat and worries.

I awoke at 3:23, blip blip blip. And I cut short the hideous and piercing alarm before it could jerk into wakefulness all those for whom it was still night in the world at this hour.

Isabel was sleeping. She was beautiful in her sleep. I thought back to the photo. Lovelier than Ana? Yes, probably. She had thrown off the sheet. She was naked. I had not known that a woman so perfectly beautiful could exist. A wave of tenderness swept over me, from the fount of my being to the most epidermic layer of my skin, and to the most superficial layers of that same epidermis. I almost woke her to ask if I could take the plane with her next evening.

Then I dismissed the matter from my mind.

I had the pettiness to lock the bottom drawer of the chest to preserve my secrets.

•

"Remember the address?" asked Anne.

"Three Cours Gambetta. Between the baby-clothes store and the fuel-oil merchant."

"What a memory!"

"Damn right. This is better than the Dauphine, isn't it?"

"Ooooohwell . . ."

Anne lived in a restored three-room apartment on the sixth floor, two rooms facing the street and a big bedroom overlooking a courtyard with a huge leafy tree. She liked blue, everything was blue. Blue, clean, tidy. She had three violins, lots of records and cassettes, lots of hi-fi equipment.

She spent three-quarters of an hour in the bathroom. She came out wearing a very smart pink dress with black buttons, her hair washed, makeup on, pretty enough to eat, and tired enough to sleep for ever. She immediately went to her bedroom to lie down.

The tree was truly huge, not to say gigantic.

"That bath was heavenly after all those days in the hospital!"

And we listened to her composition for violin.

I had not expected anything so beautiful. From the very first I was flabbergasted by her playing, which was of astounding tautness and precision, and, my God, amazed by what she was playing! What she was playing made my amazement grow and grow! The theme was splendid, its appeal at once hidden and immediate. Each bar, each note stood on its own and amazed you. And Anne's invention (indifferently backed up by her pals) the variety of the developments, the obvious and surprising way in which she returned to the bare theme, equally obvious and surprising way in which she revived it, transformed it, just when you were beginning to believe it well and truly dead, and finally her way — my amazement kept growing, my wonder, I listened in dread for the flaw, the fault, the collapse, which never came! — and finally her way of resolving the pauses so skillfully summoned up through plays of melody and of rhythm was profoundly satisfying, without ever encroaching on what was a sort of deeper expectation, some more deeply buried secret one nevertheless sensed was coming deliciously nearer, an expectation and a secret that seemed to linger on after the end of the piece, after the last notes, that left the mind appeased and hungry, joyous and in pain, and that put the interior of my being to fire and sword!

It was beautiful, perfect.

I got up and kissed her on the mouth twenty-four times in succession with such ardor she was forced to bite back her wide smile of satisfaction lest my lips burst upon her teeth, she was flattered and pleased.

"Any record company will be happy to record it," I said. "Your pals, if you don't mind my saying so, are not — "

"I'm finished with them," she said. "I'm leaving them. They can get along without me. This business of hit songs is completely crazy."

"I think so too," I said. "You're much closer to hitting it big with this . . . Find two or three other good musicians and form your own group."

"I've been thinking about it for a long time. I'll try in September."

She was very emotional, excited, exhausted. She was suddenly very thirsty. I went and got some orange juice from the fridge. I drank with her, sitting on the edge of the bed, then leaning on my elbow, carelessly, then I lay down and turned to face her and she turned to face me. I felt good. I was resting.

She still bit her nails. She had passed the time in the hospital biting her nails.

I kissed her on the mouth.

The window was open. Not a leaf on the giant tree rustled.

I raised her smart dress and kissed her pants, and lowered my jeans and pants, and we caressed one another, I was infinitely careful, I did not want to disturb or perhaps tear off a dressing, reopen a scar, spill her blood, but no, she would have warned me, and the dressing was as small as mine had been, an insignificant operation, complications suddenly simplified, who could explain why on this late afternoon of unspeakable heat, August 17, astounded by very simple things, the tree, the sky, the open window, the color blue, I let myself go, Anne let herself go, more than an hour went by in sweet and uninterrupted caresses, and at long last we caressed one another to the fullness of pleasure.

·

She made a copy of the cassette for me.

"A pity you're leaving," I said.

"Come with me. The house is big."

"I can't leave Lyon for too long . . . I'll explain later."

Anne the fairy queen asked no questions.

"I thought so," she said. "September will soon be here. I'll think of you till then."

"Me too," I said.

·

My heart beating, overflowing, constricted, broken, I opened the little white gate. Michèle was alone with her father. She was reading. She put her book down on the reddish-brown grass, threw away her cigarette, and came to meet me, imperceptibly swinging her shoulders that were just a little too broad, pale, undone by care. The folds on either side of her mouth were ugly. I loved her and restrained myself from fleeing at top speed.

"Just got back," I said. "Anything?"

"No."

She proffered her cheek.

Léonard Lichem had been wise to write on the pieces of paper with which he had flooded the Lyon area that it would be pointless and dangerous to call the police. Pointless and more dangerous than ever for me. Nevertheless, the second that Michèle pronounced that "No," I decided to go to the police. Soon. As soon as Isabel had left. Why? To be doing something instead of nothing? Yes. And to dispel the hideous sense of God knew what complicity between Michèle and me that suddenly swept over me, a hideous complicity whose hideous consequences Simon had mysteriously suffered.

Mystery.

"Did you have a good trip?"

"Yes. Tiring. Luckily I had the Lancia. Thanks."

I hesitated. Should I tell her — ? I did not get time to wonder long. Nor to try to justify by means of two or three falsehoods my failure to phone during my absence.

I did not get time.

"I've been thinking," she said. "I think it would be better if we didn't see each other anymore."

We were standing face to face in front of Simon de Klef the living corpse. A thread of spittle ran down from his lips. Extraordinary. I had never seen him in the grip of such kinetic frenzy.

Not see each other anymore. I had been expecting, word for word, just such an incomprehensible declaration.

"As you wish," I said. "Let's not go on endlessly about it. We know it all. I love you. I will not forgive you for what you have just said. I will not forgive you for holding Renaud Lossaire's hand and letting yourself be kissed by him. I will never forgive you for it. Life everlasting would make no difference. Never. And I will not forgive you for not answering me that first night. That night I went home and killed myself. A neighbor found me in time. I spent the night in the hospital."

The news had no effect on her appearance, only on her voice, which became scarcely audible: "You are mad . . . I love you, I would like to love you, I can't, I can't. About that first night, I already told you . . ."

"That first night, you didn't answer me."

"You shouldn't have said to me . . . I can't take anymore. It will be even worse now."

"That's why I said it to you."

I thought she was going to kill me, and there was no neighbor strong enough, not even Torbjörn Skaldaspilli himself, to loosen the grip of her fingers on my throat. She was squinting. A hatred akin to revulsion marred her features. It was a moment of madness. I was ready myself to lash out with all my strength.

I fought the temptation. We both did. A different outcome became mandatory. I seized Michèle by the wrist and dragged her with irresistible savagery into the house, beyond the immediate range of the malevolent waves emitted by our drooling companion, I dragged her into the wooden house, to the second floor, into her room, and only there, beside her bed, did I release her arm bruised blue-black by my grip, and go round to the other side of the bed, my own hand was numb from gripping so hard.

We undressed in silence. Postponing until later all hope or despair, souls exhausted, forgotten, lost, we made love the way animals probably do in meadows, in rivers, in forests. On mountaintops.

·

In the pockets of my jacket I had Lichem's weapon, and the keys and papers of the Lancia. I returned keys and papers to Michèle.

"I ask only one thing of you, to let me know if you have any news of Simon. For my part, I have decided to go and talk to the police in the next forty-eight hours. I'll keep you informed."

"No!"

"I've made up my mind."

There was no room for argument.

She left me at the gate.

"Annie's not here?"

"No. Gone to stay with her parents for three days. She'll be back tomorrow."

"Even now, I would be ready to give up . . . everything for you, my sweet. My life. I hope we'll meet again."

Yes, I would still have given my life, what I still called my life, for her. I had spoken coolly and calmly, she answered in the same way: "So would I. I hope so too."

She turned her back on me.

I got back into my little red Dauphine, for whose prodigious headlights the hour of illumination would soon be at hand, but for whose fabulous windshield wipers the hour of operation seemed alas so distant.

I stopped in front of the open and deserted bar on Place Carnot. The bare-chested waiter brought me two grilled ham and cheese sandwiches, I drank countless beers, thought about nothing, and returned home at ten o'clock.

•

I listened to music with Isabel. She knew Rainer von Gottardt as a pianist and was vaguely aware that he had had an affair with her sister.

I found her less jumpy. She had slept part of the afternoon, she had not been bored alone for a second, we avoided talking about last night or the past in general, indeed we avoided talking at all, and two quite uneventful hours quickly went by.

The pleasure of being together overcame our respective reasons for fearing the other's company. We lay down in my bed, to sleep.

Sleep did not come.

After an hour we emitted those timeless words cavepeople once probably grunted to one another in one raucous form or another: "Are you asleep?"

"No. I can't get to sleep. What about you?"

"I can't either."

We were lying on our backs, soaked in sweat. I sought Isabel's hand, placed it on my stomach, then placed my own hand on her stomach. My senses, more jangled than blunted by the afternoon's trials, were avid, even more insistent than this afternoon, for further trials that would this time annihilate them beyond recall. The wishes of Aphrodite herself were in full harmony with my own, and the mysteries of existence, of heat, and of the night (it was black as the tomb) hurled us from one in the morning until dawn into the deep-biting snares of very real love and affection.

We awoke at noon.

We repeated yesterday's scenario. Coffee, bread, butter, jam, we drank, masticated, ingurgitated, activities generating considerable amounts of sound and inviting irritating attention if not interrupted, punctuated, adorned, masked by words, but few words were uttered, and those for the most part concerning the endless flight time between Lyon and Sucre. The coup d'état in Bolivia, of which I was miraculously not unaware. The greater frequency of hair washing in summertime. The sun in Lyon.

She washed her hair. She might have been shampooing and massaging a forest of willows, she spent an eternity in the bathroom.

"Your beauty is flawless," I told her when she emerged. "I am sorry that you don't feel more comfortable here. With me. I'm sorry about it. Unhappy."

"I am comfortable with you!" she said in a warm burst of candor. "You know that. I believe I'm very scared of going home." (She forced herself to smile:) "After all, I'm going to build my life all over again."

We drank another coffee.

She would move into her mother's beautiful house at Sucre. A husband, children? Was she thinking along those lines? No, neither a husband nor children, she didn't want them. But she would take up her studies again, medicine, classical violin. She wouldn't travel anymore. Less.

She was tense and excited.

"I feel like taking a short stroll in your city on my own. You won't be angry with me?"

"Of course not. You'll die of the heat."

"I'm used to the heat. I need to move around, I can't stand still."

She was away from 3:00 P.M. to 5:10. I used the time to finish the story of the life of Rainer von Gottardt, his death:

Ana was not there. The miracle had not happened.

I was not displeased to be meeting Hector and Isabel again, those two lunatics. Particularly her.

The moment the concert began I felt very ill.

At last Michel Soler and I were together in this Temple, but side by side and hand in hand. He was holding the hand of the hostile young woman whose soul he was soon to reduce to nothing—and I was holding his hand, and squeezing it, as if this gave me the power to drag my only friend down into death with me!

I gave him my notebook and entrusted him with a message for Ana, whom I had always loved: that I had always loved her.

I knew the cunning devil would try to see her, message or no message. I was afraid for him. But I was henceforth powerless. All I could do was direct him along the path he was preparing to take . . .

"I rejoice in my death. Ah! would I had already found it!" the not incompetent singer was singing.

"Thank you, my friend, thank you for everything," I said to Michel Soler.

"It is I who thank you!"

They were the last words I heard in this world. The moment had come. My weary eyes closed in sweet bliss. I left him alone.

•

The same poor devils were gnawing at the same crusts and drinking the same beer dregs and rolling the same fearful eyes.

It was six o'clock. The Paris plane took off at seven. After Isabel had picked up her tickets, we sat down in the cafeteria to wait.

The waiter brought us I don't remember what.

It was now that Isabel broke the rule of silence we had both been observing about the affair since Léonard Lichem had been hurled into the nocturnal waters of the Spanish sea: "You are going to go on with your investigation?"

"Yes. I don't really see how, but I'll go on."

"Would it help you . . . would it be useful to know who it was . . . who was one of the people who needed Léonard for . . ."

I swallowed a mouthful of I don't remember what.

"Yes," I said simply.

"Do you promise . . . to keep me out of . . . to protect me, to . . . I implore you! Whatever you say, I'm going to tell you, but still, promise me . . . I couldn't have left without speaking to you. I realized it just now in your little red car . . ." (She managed to smile, then put her hand on mine:) "I want to help you. And to have a clear conscience. It's been too dreadful these past two days . . ."

"I promise you," I said, squeezing her hand.

"I believe you. On July 25, at the villa, I received a phone call from a woman who said to me, 'Ana?' I hesitated, then I answered . . . 'yes.' I don't know why. She said in Spanish: 'It's Isabel.'"

I guessed everything that followed. My mad hunch, instantly frisky and well-fed, not to say plump, rushed to center stage, preening its feathers and arrogantly clicking its beak.

"I believe I know who you're talking about," I said quietly. "Your sister and this woman were once very close. Why did you answer yes?"

"I don't know. Out of curiosity. Because my sister's life has always been a mystery to me and I wanted to . . . to say that I was her. Because I didn't feel well, and other reasons, I don't know, because it was . . . easier, you understand?"

"I understand perfectly," I said.

"We went on speaking in Spanish. Since she and Ana had been out of touch for years, I didn't have too much trouble playing the part. Almost at once she asked me if I knew a reliable man I could recommend to her for a job that would be difficult but would pay very well, a small fortune. She would not meet this man. Every precaution had been taken, no one could compromise anyone. It would be best that I myself know nothing, that I serve merely as an intermediary. She needed a man ready to do anything, discreet, efficient, reliable. I thought of Léonard. I said yes again . . . I needed money. And I needed to behave as my sister would have behaved . . . I said yes, she gave me a . . . I'm afraid you will be angry with me, you'll hate me!"

"No," I said. "It's part of the promise. I promise I won't."

"She gave me a phone number to pass on to Léonard, and told me to call her back as soon as I had an answer. I was trembling when I had to ask her for her own phone number, but I managed it all right: such a long time, not sure about the last two numbers, bag left behind in the plane and still not returned to me by the airline . . . I carried it off well. I called Lichem. I outlined the proposition to him. I didn't want to know anything about it, and I wanted half the money. And I never did know anything, do you believe me?"

"I do."

"Léonard called me back. He agreed. He was a man with . . . with good qualities. He did his part, he was discreet, he kept his word in everything. I called Isabel back. She said she would phone me to confirm that everything had gone as planned. That she would be glad to see me again. I told her I was about to leave on a trip, and that I would prefer to call her. And that's about it."

She was still holding my hand. Her face had begun to relax during all that stuff about phone calls.

"You were right to tell me," I said. "You have no more to fear than you ever did. There's nothing that can be held against you. No proofs. Nothing. Put it out of your mind."

A good actress, you had to admit. At Villa Madre de Osdi she had quite cleverly made sure I knew nothing that might harm her. And she had kept her mouth shut. And she hadn't balked too much at not disturbing the local police . . .

I smiled at her.

She rose without releasing my hand, drew me to her, took me in her perfect arms and let herself be comforted like a child after the danger has passed.

"I should have spoken to you right away. I was scared. I couldn't . . . Forgive me!"

"It wouldn't have made any difference," I said. "Not back then either. The other Isabel would have found another Léonard. Forget it. Forget it and enjoy the money."

I walked to the departure gate with her.

"I still want a promise from you," she said. "Be careful. I'm going to be anxious about you. Promise you'll be careful."

"I promise. I have something to tell you too. Yesterday we talked a bit about Rainer von Gottardt the pianist. He recently died. The fact is I met him before he died."

"You knew Rainer von Gottardt."

"Yes. By chance. He knew I was planning to see Ana de Tuermas. Naturally he didn't know why. He asked me to tell her that he had always loved her. That's all, and now I'm telling it to you."

"Is that a declaration?" she asked, elegantly and spiritedly.

"Why not?"

"Then . . . come and see me in Bolivia. It's something I've been thinking about."

"Why not?" I said.

•

No doubt about it, the extreme heat suited my little red car, backfiring with regularity on the short stretch of highway between Satolas and Lyon as I whistled the theme of the last aria of Cantata no. 82, for the Feast of the Purification, and the world got ready to assume its most hideous sneer to match my latest and maddest hunch, born within me and with me at the very hour of my entry into the world! The last, stripped of all mystery: no more visits to Rainer von Gottardt's almost-birth-place on Rue de l'Église in Francheville-le-Haut, no more story of his life to write! No need of a backdrop to see the mysteries of life more clearly, no need, as I had once innocently believed, to ruin my eyes trying to locate the key to the invisible mystery in some corner of the tapestry: now I was going on alone, without help or hindrance from the Maestro, my whole life became a character in the picture, but I plunged right into it and moved inside it with the assurance of a maestro, and found that I myself was tracing the key to the mystery!

I alone knew everything!

Too fast, clumsily, because of the slanting beams of the setting sun, I drove into the long bend linking the highway to Boulevard Laurent Bonnevay, the car screamed off course, a tree loomed terribly close, I pulled up on the parking strip, a few more inches and I would have wrapped myself around that tree like a snake and decorated it with a dozen red spires from its base to its lowest branches.

I roared away.

I speeded up, full of wicked glee. The sun was still right in my face. Ahead, at the very end of the boulevard, above Tête d'Or Park, that setting sun stared at me. Then, filled with my wicked and harrowing glee, I stared back at it, and, good heavens! my eyes did not close, I was able to stare straight at it! I shivered: I swear that for the space of a second the sun paled and all heat ceased. And I swear that it set more swiftly, that between the moment I roared away from that tree and the moment I drove onto the Poincaré Bridge, I saw it visibly sink, more swiftly than other days, hastening the onset of night by just that much!

On the other side of the bridge I turned right onto Rue de Saint-Clair, then immediately turned left into the narrow and winding Chemin de Vassieux, which took me to the heights of Caluire, a district bordering on Rillieux-la-Pape.

I took a road lined with market gardens, went through the Rillieux-la-Pape industrial zone (site of the Dioblaníz Pharmaceutical Laboratories, DPL) and reached the old section of Rillieux clustered around its ancient church. From there Route de Lyon wound off into the countryside.

I passed fewer houses.

Number 43. The Dioblaníz residence was an old farmhouse restored to pristine condition, a cluster of buildings arranged in a rectangle around an inner courtyard you could see from the road through the bars of a grille. This rectangle was further enclosed inside a much larger rectangle of high walls.

Probably because I knew the Dioblanízes and knew they were Bolivians and surrounded by Bolivians, this very Lyonesque farm on the city's outskirts seemed to me in the failing light to be a piece of somewhere else grafted on to Lyon's soil.

I went past 43, stopped a hundred yards beyond, the car pulled in tight against the boundary wall. I climbed onto the roof of the car. I stood on tiptoe. I looked. Nobody. Fruit trees, tall grass. On the right, the dark mass of one wing of the building with few windows.

I drove on to the far end of the property, as far as possible from the house. I climbed onto the car, then onto the wall. Still nobody. I swung by my hands, dropped ten feet or so minus my six feet. I sustained a minor injury to my posterior (after my feet hit the ground I fell back in a squat onto a pointed pebble which almost penetrated my fundament) and to my stomach, a stab down where my wound was.

Léonard Lichem's Lyon weapon was still in the pocket of my jacket, with one round left.

I did not have to use it.

Everything happened with appalling ease. Horror, appalling horror, no longer hid but exposed itself to me.

I headed for the house, hugging the wall, sometimes bent double with my neck at right angles to my torso, sometimes, when a severe crick threatened, with legs bent and thighs spread like a circus clown or freak.

Then I went along the wing of the building that had few windows, only two on the ground floor apparently.

But I had no need to risk getting to a window. I very quickly discovered at my feet a circular basement window, a bull's-eye at ground level divided by a wooden crosspiece into four equal segments. I broke one of these glass panes, the one closest to the window latch, with a stone whose ringing hardness I muffled by rolling it up in my jacket. Very little glass fell inside. Therefore very little noise. The rest of the glass shattered into jagged shapes I carefully lifted out one after the other until I could slip my hand inside and work the latch.

I put my black jacket back on.

I wriggled through. I dropped down into a kind of cellar, full of casks and wicker and metal trunks. I had no trouble opening the door of this cellar. I found myself in a whitewashed corridor with strip lighting and air conditioning, you were hit by a blast of excessive cold. I went forward. The corridor led into another corridor. There were doors every twelve feet or so to right and left of this new corridor. Locked? Yes! A key suddenly turned in the lock of the left-hand door . . .

I fled back into the cellar and glued myself to the wall. A man went by, short, dark-skinned, wearing a white smock. I heard him open the door on the right. Not lock it again, simply slam it.

I waited a few moments, then followed in his footsteps. Gusts of icy air pulsed from grilled apertures overhead. I shivered. I approached the right-hand door, not locked, I was sure.

I opened it softly, but in one movement. Nobody in the large circular room into which I then took a step, Lichem's weapon in my hand.

Three doors opened from it, each with a kind of porthole like those on ships or planes. I went up to the first. I looked through. I saw an operating theater. Nobody inside. An operating theater!

Fluorescent lighting, whiteness, chill. In an unthinking reflex, I came close to zipping up my jacket. An underground clinic . . . My mad hunch was positively jumping with vitality. The second room was merely an annex of the first. The room where the surgeon scrubs up, the room he comes back to after the operation.

Still nobody.

In the third room, comfortable, well equipped, a model hospital room, Madness, Horror, and Aberration were taking their languid ease.

Two children sitting up in identical beds.

Simon de Klef and another child. Jésus Dioblaníz . . .

Pinned to the wall above their beds, a Phil Dreux picture, a crowd of menacing merrymakers made of peelings.

The man in white from the corridor had his back turned to me. He had just finished unrolling a gauze bandage from around Simon's head and eyes.

The bandage came off.

The man then delicately removed the two dressings applied to each of the child's eyes.

The greatest horror of all, which I now witnessed, was slow, silent, gentle. It did not deploy a wealth of unheard of frenzies to seize your attention. No, you had to convince yourself it was actually happening, you had to tell yourself: this is really what I am seeing, this is really what is happening! For this reason, the scream torn from you had all the time in the world to be amplified, expanded, multiplied, distorted by the pitiless operation of thought. But I had to suppress the utterance of that scream, and the resulting mortal injury to the interior of my being would never be healed.

•

Simon de Klef no longer had eyes.

•

The adorable, beautiful, dark child with the smooth hair, the small tormented accomplice of a few strange moments in my life, brother of Michèle de Klef and son of the living corpse Simon de Klef from whose lips no secret would ever be wrested, and, I reminded myself, Liliane Tormes's second adoptive son, no longer had eyes. With the bandage undone, the dressings removed, he turned reddened, vacant sockets upon the world.

He was mechanically turning the handle of a music-box I could not hear. He was wearing smart pajamas like the ones Jésus was wearing. A table was covered with the kinds of cake and sodas children love.

Jésus Dioblaníz, a little boy of the same age, turned eyes that could see upon the world!

Probably just a little bit, badly, only from close up, his gaze — evil! — lighted on me — it did not even occur to me to move back from the porthole — without pausing, without reacting, but his attentive head movements in the direction of his sacrificed companion and of the man in white, the way he lifted one or another of the toys strewn about his bed to his staring, haggard eyes in which unpleasant lights wandered, appearing and disappearing — his gestures, his attitudes were undeniably those of a being who could see!

The man in white raised and lowered Simon's eyelids. Then he patted his cheek.

I moved aside.

Had Perfecto Jinez already been murdered by a Dioblaníz henchman, or did they still need his irreplaceable services? Already murdered, I believed. Shortly after his kidnapping — at Lichem's hands? At someone else's, I believed, in this operation assembled like some labyrinthine piece of machinery in which nobody knew much and everybody followed his own narrow pathway — shortly after being kidnapped, I conjectured, and forced under atrocious pressures to perform the dreadful graft.

Madness, Horror, Aberration!

I left the way I had come.

The heat made me gasp.

I believed I would remain forever a prisoner of the accursed estate, the wall was so high and offered so few hand- and footholds. And this time I really hurt myself. After a strenuous climb, my feet slipped from their inadequate holds, and I was left with my whole weight hanging from my left hand. I felt as if my fingers had been chopped off. Despite the pain, I managed to hoist myself a few inches with my left arm alone and got a grip with my right hand as well.

I crossed over the wall. But I had twisted my left index finger and put a jagged, bleeding cut in it.

I sped off toward Impasse du Jour.

•

It was almost dark.

As she had done the day before, Michèle de Klef put down her book, tossed her cigarette aside, and came to meet me. I did not give her time to question me about my bloody finger nor about my complexion, which wore the grayish hue of a mummy several days after the bandages have been unrolled.

"I'm going to call the police. I've found Simon. Bad news!"

I had told her I would find Simon, I had found him!

I told her everything.

She ran weeping into the house. I followed. I dialed the number of the police on Rue Vauban. Speaking rapidly, I said: "Listen carefully and make a note of what I'm telling you, Simon de Klef, ten years old, has been kidnapped. He is being held at the home of Hector and Isabel Dioblaníz, 43 Route de Lyon, at Rillieux-la-Pape, in a basement converted into a clinic, left wing of the building. Be careful, these people are dangerous lunatics. As soon as you have the child, tell his sister, Michèle de Klef, 812–5347. You may find the ophthalmologist Perfecto Jinez as well."

And I hung up, despite the twelve thousand questions fired at me between the instant I removed the apparatus from my ear and the moment I placed it in its cradle, click-cluck.

And Michèle and I waited for two hours.

I disinfected and bound up my finger. Michèle smoked a pack of cigarettes. Throughout those two hours, the only way I saw her lips was thin, sucked in, whether she was smoking or biting her nails.

The phone rang. She picked up.

The Dioblanízes and several other people had been arrested. Simon had been taken to the hospital in Rillieux. He was sleeping peacefully. There was no bandage on his eyes. His lids were lowered. He was very thin.

He had completely lost his memory. He did not answer questions, or he did so unsatisfactorily, he understood nothing. And he had trouble speaking. From the surgical standpoint, continued the doctor taking care of him, everything was over. Scarification was proceeding normally. As for the rest . . . Simon must immediately be put in the care of a specialized institution, he recommended Evian, it also has residential facilities for you, Miss de Klef, you could live with him, indeed you must—a bracing climate, obviously they would take care of his physical health, but their main concern would be his disastrous psychological condition, using the most modern and the most appropriate techniques. They would evaluate the damage and go on from there. It would take months. An improvement could be expected, but unfortunately was not certain. The process had to begin as soon as possible. Quickly, at once, tomorrow morning. They could set the wheels moving now and the paperwork would be ready by noon.

Simon was sleeping the deep sound sleep of children. His face was at peace. More at peace than ever, I told myself. And Michèle, who was unwilling to wake him, said the same. More at peace and freer than when I had gazed on him at slumber in the house of Liliane, my and his adoptive mother, on Chemin du Regard in my childhood bedroom.

And the face of Michèle herself, unable to take her eyes off him, leaning over him, leaning over his breath, slowly found peace.

She did not want to wake him.

A policeman was waiting for us in the corridor.

·

"Michel Soler, a friend," said Michèle. "He's been with me ever since the . . ."

The superintendent nodded to me and asked us to sit down in his rather pleasant office in the famous headquarters of the Lyon police on the corner of Rue Vauban and Quai du Général Sarrail. He was an elderly man, tall, thin, cursed with a naturally enraged expression, even when he was doing his best to be pleasant his look and his movements seemed full of rage.

The interview did not last long. We had little to say: Simon had been kidnapped late on the day of August 7 on his way from Impasse du Point du Jour to buy drinks at the little Codec grocery store on the same avenue. Very shortly afterward, perhaps even at the same time, a phone call warned Michèle de Klef not to warn the police if she wanted to see her brother alive again. I was the only one she had told. She had a considerable personal fortune, but the days had gone by without a ransom demand. We had waited in terror. We had several times been on the verge of disobeying the criminals' orders, but at the last moment we were paralyzed by fear and said to ourselves: one more day, let's wait one more day.

"It was your prerogative," the superintendent said gently. "But perhaps you should have told us anyway . . ." (Seeking to soothe an itch on his lower right cheek, he landed a slap in that area that almost unhinged his head, then, in the same movement, his hand slammed down on a folder lying on his desk as though he meant to blend it into the wood.)

"I read that your brother was kidnapped once before, along with your father, Colonel de Klef?"

"Yes. I was going to tell you about it," said Michèle. "Obviously it occurred to me that there might be some connection . . . What kind I had no idea. The investigation at the time led nowhere, absolutely nowhere. Basically, I didn't believe in a connection. And this horrible night has proved I was right. Kidnapping Simon for . . . My God!"

Tears came to her eyes. From sheer embarrassment the superintendent passed a hand over his skull with the same energy he might have deployed to pulverize a scorpion.

"We'll see about that," he said. "Now, be patient a little longer, Miss de Klef. You know, we received an anonymous phone call. You have no idea . . ."

He did not finish his sentence.

"About what?" said Michèle, rubbing her eyes.

He straightened, pressing both hands on the edge of his desk, his gaze thunderous, as if he were about to throw us into the street with a volley of oaths.

"Someone in your circle, someone who knew the Dioblanízes as well, who might have had a hand in it and then had remorse — belated remorse, since the harm was already done — or who had turned against the Dioblanízes . . ."

I assumed an expression of bottomless skepticism.

"No," said Michèle. "I'll think about it, but I don't see . . ."

"Very well. And you, sir? Anything to add to Miss de Klef's statement?"

"No," I said. "Nothing."

The Dioblanízes, he informed us, had been under interrogation for the past three hours in another office in the vast police complex. Perfecto Jinez, the winsome ophthalmologist with the roving eye, the fantasist, the musician, had been shot three days earlier through the nape of the neck. Hector and Isabel had admitted everything.

Isabel Dioblaníz's tone had been tranquil, untroubled, without remorse (filled with profound, unassailable, eternal joy, I told myself, that Jésus had been restored to sight). Perfecto Jinez had been expected to tell the ophthalmological conference held in Lyon at the end of July about his discoveries concerning the only factor that, according to him, barred the way to total ocular grafts for those born blind, even grafts of eyes taken from a newly dead body: the instant deterioration, within seconds of death, subtle, practically undetectable deterioration (it had taken him two years of research), of the triparidian nerve, a nerve at the back of the eye that congenitally fails to function in those born blind. Isabel had explained it all to the police with a professional's authority and precision. Ever since Jésus's birth she had been reading journals of ophthalmology, she was abreast of all the latest developments, she had had a chance to discuss the problem with Perfecto Jinez himself (who had twice been invited to the August concerts but had been unable to attend).

She knew that an eye taken from a living person . . .

Who would be the victim? The chosen one . . .

From one of Jésus's friends, a boarder like Simon at Sainte-Croix Academy in Saint-Just, she had heard about Simon de Klef, a child with exceptional eyesight the same age as her Jésus . . . Why not Simon de Klef? The victim, the chosen one, would have exceptional eyesight. So much the better!

She had made inquiries, spied, set others to spy . . .

And she had planned and organized everything, the clinic, the kidnappings, with patience, care, attention to detail. Their planned return to Bolivia had also been part of the scheme. She had at first intended to get rid of Simon as soon as the operation was over, then, seeing he had amnesia, and seized by pity, she had decided to take him with them. Jésus and he would grow up together as very special friends . . . This return was to have been at the beginning of September. She and Hector had been in touch with the members of the new regime since well before the coup d'état.

Reports of their earlier participation in the systematic extermination of a certain number of revolutionaries had indeed been well-founded . . .

Yes, they had admitted everything. Everything, but without compromising or directing suspicion toward anyone at all, not a single accomplice, without uttering the name even of one person who had helped them in their accursed undertaking. And, thought the superintendent, their attitude was unlikely to change. Moreover, the husband, a victim of nerves, had said nothing. He merely rocked his head up and down when Isabel consented to answer and wagged it from left to right whenever she refused to speak. And he was afflicted with an exasperating, even irritating, nervousness. A very very nervous man, they had hesitated to strap him to his chair. A man they had had to prevent from slipping between the metal radiator and the wall. Or from forcing his way into the neck of the bottle of water his wife had requested, and from ingurgitating the two police caps he had snatched with lightning swiftness from the heads of their owners, which had only been removed with the greatest difficulty from the entrance to his esophagus.

Two lunatics, the inspector concluded. Particularly the woman, he believed.

•

Impasse du Point du Jour. I helped Michèle to fill suitcases. We finished at four in the morning. Then we rested stretched out on the couch on the ground floor, a wooden couch made comfortable and uncomfortable at once by a dozen too-small cushions that had to be constantly rearranged.

Michèle smoked. The lights were on.

To my surprise, she fell asleep. She put out a cigarette half smoked, snuggled into my arms, and slept, at peace.

I could not.

I was thinking of Simon.

At 6:00 A.M. she phoned various clinics that might accept her father. A clinic at Oullins agreed. An ambulance would come and collect the invalid (a body, nothing more) at 10:30.

Then we left for the hospital in Rillieux. Michèle wanted to be there when her brother woke up.

He awoke at 7:30. Michèle took his hand and said: "Simon . . . it's me, Michèle."

He smiled.

"It's me, Michèle, your sister! Simon, do you remember me?"

He did not answer. He smiled. Not a foolish smile. A quiet smile, pretty and delicate, not frightening at all.

"I'm hungry," he said, speaking with difficulty.

He too was beginning to speak horse.

A nurse brought in a nice breakfast which he ate hungrily. Michèle spread butter and jam on his bread, put the slices in his hand, helped him dunk them in his café au lait and lift them to his mouth.

As for me, I did not move an eyelash. The urge to weep that had been weighing on me for hours had made me mute and immobile. I gazed at the scene, I looked at Simon, his sister Michèle (Michèle and I had not spoken to one another for hours, or if we had it was to say nothing), I gazed at them united and reconciled.

At last some mysterious knot came undone within me and I was able to approach the bed.

The child did not react to the sound of my steps.

I came to the bed. I knelt down. I put a knee on the ground, I took Simon's limp hand and I kissed it.

"Hello, old buddy," I said, throat pricking, chest filling, eyes burning, "hello, my good old buddy." (I said again:) "My good old buddy. It's Michel, remember me? Same name as your sister. We played a trick on her. We shook that car that was tailing us on the way to Liliane's, remember? Remember the wooden toys?"

I waited.

He shook my hand.

A few large tears flowed from under his closed lids. But his face did not change. A few large tears flowed. No other sign of sorrow. They flowed down cheeks grown thin. Yet he did not look unwell. I dried those large tears with the sheet. I kissed him on his cheeks, on his neck, I pushed his hair back so I could kiss his forehead, I even brushed his lids with my lips.

"Then you remember?"

He still did not answer this question. He let my hand go. He was no longer weeping, he was smiling, the way he had been a moment ago.

I straightened and turned to face Michèle.

I had forgotten my index finger. It started to hurt.

Smiling and weeping at once, Michèle looked at me.

"You'll come and see us at Evian?" she said.

All need to weep had left me. A most fortunate drying up of the spring, otherwise whoever had opened the door of that room in the ensuing minutes would have been swept away and consumed by a flood of tears hot as molten lava. But all need to weep had left me.

I felt a painful stabbing in my index finger.

"Why not?" I said.

Her expression changed.

"You're not sure? You're not sure you'll come?"

"No, I'm not sure," I said, affecting to put on a brave little smile.

But the smile that went with these words could not have been a brave one, it must have been a desperate unbearable grimace, I saw it in Michèle's eyes, and I myself looking at Michèle found it unbearable, and was made desperate by it, and I at once added in a tone that was meant to be one of self-mockery, a pastiche of unrequited love: "I thought you didn't want to see me anymore?"

"Forgive me, it's my fault, it's all my fault!"

"You know that's not so."

Simon, motionless, head up, seemed not to hear us.

"Please come! Not at once, but when you feel like it. I wasn't thinking of what I was saying. Don't condemn me to . . . to die. I would give my life for you too. I love you, I want to see you!"

Boundless powers of seduction! My boundless powers of seduction had shattered all bounds! I looked at the young woman in the little black dress standing in front of me, all trust and supplication. She was a rather pretty young woman, without any particular grace, whose very imperfections were delightful. I recalled having felt a most lively carnal joy with her. With no thought for procreation or conception. And now? Would we someday together give Simon a kind of brother? I did not know.

It was written in the great book of Destiny that Michèle de Klef was destined for me, but the author had not specified for how long. No, it was not a matter of time. This great book teeming with vagueness and unexplained points was in everlasting need of modification. It was not a matter of time. I still loved Michèle, but it was another person I loved, a person who condemned me to more death and to more solitude than the person with whom I had one day fallen in love, suddenly, mysteriously, endlessly, I was suddenly afraid and I answered her in an outburst that passed for an outburst of the same love I had shown her until that moment: "Me too! I want to see you too!"

•

At 10:20, the well-built Annie arrived at Impasse du Point du Jour in a dirty yellow Innocenti borrowed from a friend. We told her what had happened. She left us a little later, begging us to call on her no matter when for no matter what, she would always be ready. Michèle thanked her. They fell into each other's arms.

Then Annie said good-bye to me, kissing me on the cheeks, eyebrows raised in surprise.

At the end of the Impasse her Austin passed the ambulance from Oullins. Two sullen male nurses jumped in unison, or almost, from the ambulance. A quarter-hour later, they drove away again with the total quadriplegic, two suitcases, and a sheaf of medical papers on board.

Michèle watched them leave. She had spoken to her father, loving words, until it was time to leave she kept kissing his forehead.

Then we loaded the trunk of the Lancia with suitcases.

I followed Michèle in the Dauphine.

•

I walked down the corridors of the hospital. I was carrying Simon in my arms. Every two steps I murmured to him: old buddy. Michèle walked by my side, her arm around my waist. She was pale, calm.

•

We had fixed up the Lancia's back seat as a bed. I settled the smiling Simon on it and embraced him one last time. "I'll see you soon, old buddy."

And I took my leave of Michèle de Klef.

She smiled at me. She had a pretty smile, sensual lips. Eyes dark and pale at the same time. Strange tangled hair, neither long nor short, a kind of helmet around her pale face.

"Wait a few days and . . . and then come see us," she said.

"OK," I said. "It'll be soon."

Our lips joined.

"Till then."

"Till then."

She drove away. She drove well. I did some housecleaning (scorning my vacuum cleaner and rapidly wearing myself out with the brush and dustpan, on all fours like an animal), listened many times to Anne's composition, thought about nothing in particular.

That night, before going to bed, I laid out on my table the splendid electric typewriter from Carrefour-Vénissieux, the manuscript on the left of the machine and a ream of blank paper on the right.

I slept deeply.

•

The following day, August 20, and every day until August 31, I typed the whole manuscript, twelve chapters, one chapter a day.

On the evening of the twentieth, Michèle called me from Evian. She told me her father had died on arrival at the clinic. Her morale was at a low ebb. She had asked the Geneva members of her family to come to Lyon and take care of everything. She would make a quick trip to Geneva for the funeral.

Simon de Klef was buried in Geneva.

On August 22 I called Patrice Pierre. We talked about Simon, he had read about it in the papers. It was terrible. I concurred: terrible. I told him I was engaged in an exciting and absorbing musical undertaking. He was pleased for me. He himself, tired of the depressing hospital, was going to start his own practice in September: I was pleased for him. Extraction of that bullet? In September, I told him. And when would we have the pleasure . . . ? In September.

Léonard Lichem's Lyon weapon, loaded with its last cartridge, still lay in the bottom drawer among so many vestiges of my life.

On August 24 I received a phone call from the Hollywood attorney Mark Hirschwald. He informed me that Rainer von Gottardt had named me heir of the few belongings he possessed, in particular his house in Francheville-le-Haut and the profits from future sales of his records. I would be receiving further confirmation. I thanked Mr. Hirschwald.

And I added the following to the last chapter of the manuscript:

> I asked Michel Soler to stop at a post office and mail a letter for me. It was addressed to Mark Hirschwald, my attorney. In this letter I altered the terms of my poor will and bequeathed my few possessions to my only friend.

Also on August 24, Torbjörn Skaldaspilli, the giant who had knelt by my deathbed, had taken my hand and nearly kissed it,

Torbjörn Skaldaspilli explained to me in a second postcard from Kristiansand, carefully handwritten but almost indecipherable, nevertheless I managed, that he had suddenly realized how bad inactivity was for him. He intended to take up some job or other as soon as he returned. Tickled pink by his realization and by his decision, he had felt the need to communicate them to me. And he was counting the days till us and our reunion.

The telephone constituted almost my only link with the world. Michèle de Klef, Anne Miller, and Isabel de Tuermas called me. Michèle had decided against the Granados recording. Later, perhaps. She was relieved relieved. The Dioblanízes, she said, were maintaining a stubborn silence. They would be given life imprisonment. Probably the mystery would never be satisfactorily cleared up. But it no longer mattered much.

Jésus Dioblaníz could see.

Simon, the child on whom grace had fallen so cruelly, remained in his peaceful life-in-death condition. No change, no improvement. As for her, she was fighting off despair and awaiting the blessed moment when she would see me again. Soon? Soon, I told her.

I heard her smoking, blowing the smoke into the phone.

Isabel was happy to be back in her native land, and would be even happier the day I visited her. Was I thinking about it? I was thinking about it, I told her.

Anne was getting over her trying time. She was composing a new piece for the violin. The idea of having me listen to it thrilled her. In September? In September, I told her.

One day, I found that a simple sheet of paper in the refrigerator door made it easy to open and close.

I went once to Liliane's grave, twice to Carrefour-Vénissieux to buy provisions, and three times for a Coke in the fiery glowing red Bar des Archers amid the bedlam of the jukebox and its paso dobles and its simple and despairing love songs, all covering the bedlam of the brother of the owner, the replacement, a ghost abandoned by his spouse, the wretch had decided to seek fresh medical counsel in September. Perhaps, he confided to me one evening, he had surrendered too readily to infirmity.

•

I lived as a recluse. I typed all day long (considerably delaying the healing of my left index finger) without any picture interposing itself between my gaze and the paper.

•

September drew near. Soon the crowds would be back, packed trains, ships, planes, cars. Six people hanging desperately onto one bicycle. Six dogs on the same leash. Multitudinous baskets in the same egg, I remembered when . . .

The burgeoning coolness of autumn.

My multiple projects. What would become of them. I was going to see Anne, Michèle, Isabel again. I was going to inherit property, move, have Lichem's bullet extracted, send my book, my books, the present and the past, to Smikel and Keyelgod, earn thousands and hundreds, start a true pianist's career. Master of the world, thanks to the happenings of this month of August!

And yet what had been, and what had to be having been, and living reclusively in my typewritten intimacy with Rainer von Gottardt, I feared suddenly that my life, more than ever a character in a tapestry — to reiterate the image behind which I had hidden in refusing the Maestro's offer to share his home, and behind which I was still pusillanimously hiding — I feared that this life of mine, entirely the central character, might suddenly become entirely imperceptible backdrop into which I would entirely merge before a single one of the aforementioned projects was inscribed on it.

I would not die, I had known it the day of my death. But, on the evening of August 31, with the book finished and placed in the bottom drawer of the chest stained walnut by the person who had been my companion, no longer was my companion, and never again would be my companion, on the evening of August 31, standing sweating on my semblance of a balcony, my left index finger smarting worse than ever and far from healing, I found myself alone in deserted Lyon.

Because this August 31 was a Saturday and the crowds would not return until tomorrow, Sunday? Perhaps.

Perhaps too September would never come. The sun, cunning devil, victor and vanquished, seemed to have fallen asleep at the height of its ardor. And a threat always present within me and outside me, but henceforth without content, seemed to dry up the flow of time.

Yes, perhaps life would flee, and tomorrow never come. And this past month of August, what I had lived through, would fall into the retribution of oblivion, somewhere, nowhere, like a letter written and never sent.

Master of all I surveyed, I found myself alone in my deserted city.

I did not know.